Val McDermid is a number one bestseller whose novels have been translated into more than thirty languages, and have sold over fifteen million copies. She has won many awards internationally, including the CWA Gold Dagger for best crime novel of the year and the *LA Times* Book of the Year Award. She was inducted into the ITV3 Crime Thriller Awards Hall of Fame in 2009, was the recipient of the CWA Cartier Diamond Dagger in 2010 and received the Lambda Literary Foundation Pioneer Award in 2011. In 2016, Val received the Outstanding Contribution to Crime Fiction Award at the Theakstons Old Peculier Crime Writing Festival and was elected a Fellow of the Royal Society of Literature. In 2017, she received the DIVA Literary Prize for Crime. She writes full time and divides her time between Edinburgh and East Neuk of Fife.

By Val McDermid

A Place of Execution
Killing the Shadows
The Grave Tattoo
Trick of the Dark
The Vanishing Point

TONY HILL/CAROL JORDAN NOVELS

The Mermaids Singing
The Wire in the Blood
The Last Temptation
The Torment of Others
Beneath the Bleeding
Fever of the Bone
The Retribution
Cross and Burn
Splinter the Silence
Insidious Intent

KAREN PIRIE NOVELS

The Distant Echo
A Darker Domain
The Skeleton Road
Out of Bounds
Broken Ground

LINDSAY GORDON NOVELS

Report for Murder
Common Murder
Final Edition
Union Jack
Booked for Murder
Hostage to Murder

KATE BRANNIGAN NOVELS

Dead Beat
Kick Back
Crack Down
Clean Break
Blue Genes
Star Struck

SHORT STORY COLLECTIONS

The Writing on the Wall
Stranded
Christmas is Murder (ebook only)
Gunpowder Plots (ebook only)

NON-FICTION

A Suitable Job for a Woman
Forensics
My Scotland

Val
McDermid

HOW THE DEAD SPEAK

Little, Brown

LITTLE, BROWN

First published in Great Britain in 2019 by Little, Brown

1 3 5 7 9 10 8 6 4 2

All characters and events in this publication, other than those clearly in the public domain, are fictitious and any resemblance to real persons, living or dead, is purely coincidental.

A CIP catalogue record for this book is available from the British Library.

Hardback ISBN 978-1-4087-1225-2
Trade Paperback ISBN 978-1-4087-1226-9

Typeset in Meridien by M Rules
Printed and bound in Great Britain by
Clays Ltd, Elcograf S.p.A.

Papers used by Little, Brown are from well-managed forests and other responsible sources.

Little, Brown
An imprint of
Little, Brown Book Group
Carmelite House
50 Victoria Embankment
London EC4Y 0DZ

An Hachette UK Company
www.hachette.co.uk

www.littlebrown.co.uk

To our friends in the East Neuk

Prologue

We are all creatures of habit. Even murderers. When things work out for us, we fix on some talisman to credit for the success. Lucky pants; not shaving; performing the same actions in the correct sequence; having the identical breakfast; walking on the right side of the street. When murderers reveal their talismans to us, we call it a signature.

From *Reading Crimes* by DR TONY HILL

Eight years previously

Murder had been far from Mark Conway's mind that Saturday afternoon. Although he liked to consider himself an expert on the subject, he was also capable of compartmentalising the different elements of his life. And today, he was all about football. He stood in front of the glass wall of Bradfield Victoria's boardroom, absently swirling the red wine in its generous goblet, gazing down at the crowds pouring into the stadium.

He knew what they were feeling. Conway had been one of the rank and file himself once. Match day meant superstitious rituals. Since the afternoon twenty years ago when the Vics had won the League Cup, he'd always worn the same pair of black socks with Snoopy dancing on each ankle. He still did, though these days he hid the inappropriate graphic beneath thin black silk. Multi-millionaire businessmen didn't wear novelty socks.

Match day also meant a low thrum of anticipation in the chest and the stomach. Even for games that had no bearing on league position or the next round of the cup, the excitement fizzed inside him, electric in his blood. Who would be picked for the team? Who would referee the game? What would the weather hold? Would the end of the afternoon bring rapture or stinging disappointment?

That was what it meant to be a fan. And although Mark Conway was now a member of the board of the club he'd followed from boyhood, he remained just that – a fan. He'd shouted himself hoarse as they climbed up – and memorably once, tumbled down – through the divisions to their current position in sixth place in the Premier League. There was only one thing that thrilled him more than a Vics' victory.

'Fancy our chances today?'

The voice at his shoulder made Conway turn away from the view. The club's commercial director had come up behind him. Conway knew the motive; the man was already trying to confirm pitchside advertising for next season and he'd want to get Conway's name on a contract and his money in the bank sooner rather than later. 'Spurs are a tough side to beat these days,' Conway said. 'But Hazinedar is on great form. Four goals in the last three games. We've got to be in with a shout.'

The commercial director began an exhaustive analysis of both teams. He had no gift for small talk and within a couple of sentences, Conway's attention had drifted, his gaze moving round the room. When he caught sight of Jezza Martinu, his lips twitched in the ghost of a smile. Now there was a man who could have served as the avatar of fandom. Jezza was his cousin; their mothers were sisters. Family legend had it that 'Vics' was the first word Jezza had uttered.

'Excuse me, would you?' Conway drained his drink and stepped past the commercial director. He crossed to the bar, where the young woman serving the drinks abruptly ignored everyone else who was waiting and poured him a fresh glass of wine, delivering it with a quick tight smile. He moved through the thronged boardroom towards his cousin. Jezza was clearly excited, rabbiting away to the poor bloke he'd cornered over by the buffet table. Bradfield Victoria was his obsession. If there had been a church where Jezza could worship the club, he'd have been its archbishop.

When Mark Conway had told his cousin he'd been invited to join the board, he'd thought Jezza was going to faint. The colour had drained from his face and he'd staggered momentarily. 'You can join me in the directors' box,' Conway went on to say. Tears sprang up in his cousin's eyes.

'Really?' he'd gasped. 'You mean it? The directors' box?'

'And the boardroom before and after the game. You'll meet the players.'

'I can't believe this is happening. It's everything I've ever dreamed of.' He pulled Conway into a hug, not noticing the other man flinch. 'You could have chosen anybody,' Jezza added. 'Somebody you wanted to impress. Somebody from work you wanted to reward. But you chose me.' He squeezed again, then let go.

'I knew what it would mean to you.' Which was perfectly true.

'I can never repay you for this.' Jezza roughly wiped his eyes. 'God, Mark, I love you, man.'

This was the moment he'd planned for. It had taken a significant investment and a lot of smarming up to people he despised to get that coveted seat on the board. But he knew that once he'd handed Jezza Martinu the golden ticket, his cousin would do anything to keep it. The final element in his insurance policy in case his ambitious plans didn't pan out. Conway smiled. It looked sincere because it was. 'I'll think of something,' he said.

But he already had.

1

When a small group of FBI agents came up with the idea of offender profiling, the one thing they knew for sure was that they didn't know enough about the minds of those who kept on killing. And so they went looking in the one place where they could be sure of finding experts – behind bars.

From *Reading Crimes* by DR TONY HILL

It was the smell that hammered home his whereabouts as soon as he woke. There was no prospect of drifting out of sleep with that momentary sense of dislocation, that half-awake wondering, Where am I? Home? Hotel? Somebody's guest room? These days, as soon as consciousness arrived, so did the miasma that reminded Dr Tony Hill that he was in jail.

Years of talking to patients in secure mental hospitals and prisons meant he was no stranger to the unpleasant cocktail. Stale sweat, stale smoke, stale bodies, stale cooking, stale farts. The sourness of clothes that had taken too long to dry. The faintly vanilla musk of too much testosterone. And under it all, the harsh tang of cheap cleaning chemicals. In the past, he'd always been glad to escape from the smell of incarceration and back into the outside world. These days, there was no escape.

He'd thought he'd get used to it. That after a while, he'd be inured to it. But six months into his four-year sentence he was still brutally aware of it every single day. Because he was a clinical psychologist, he couldn't help wondering whether there was some deep-seated reason for what had begun to feel like hyper-awareness. Or maybe he simply had a particularly acute sense of smell.

Whatever the reason, he had grown to resent it. Not for him those half-asleep moments where he could imagine himself waking in his bunk on the narrowboat that had become his base, or in the guest suite in Carol Jordan's renovated barn where he'd spent time enough to consider it a second home. Those dreamy fantasies were denied him. He never doubted where he was. All he had to do was breathe.

At least now he had a cell to himself. When he'd been on remand for weary months, he'd had a succession of cellmates whose personal habits had been a particularly arduous punishment in themselves. Dazza, with his tireless commitment to wanking. Ricky, with his phlegm-choked smoker's cough and perpetual hawking into the steel toilet. Marco, with his night terrors, screams that woke half the landing and provoked even more screaming and swearing from their neighbours. Tony had tried to talk to Marco about the bad dreams. But the aggressive little Liverpudlian had leapt up and gone nose to nose with him, denying via most of the swear words Tony had ever encountered that he had ever had a bastarding nightmare.

Worst of all, Maniac Mick, awaiting trial for chopping off the hand of a rival drug dealer. When Mick discovered that Tony had worked with the police, his first response was to grab the front of his shirt and smack him up against the wall. Spittle had flown as he explained to Tony why they called him Maniac and what he was going to do to any fucking fucker who was in the pocket of the fucking feds. His fist – the one tattooed across the knuckles with C-U-N-T – was drawn back, ready for the strike that Tony knew would break something in his face. He closed his eyes.

Nothing happened. He opened one eye and saw a middle-aged black man with his hand between Mick and Tony. Its presence was like an improbable forcefield. 'He's not what you think, Mick.' His voice was soft, almost intimate.

'He's filth,' Mick spat. 'What do you care if he gets what's fucking coming to him?' His mouth was a sneer but his eyes were less certain.

'He's got nothing to do with the likes of us. He doesn't give the steam off his shit for robbers or drug lords or lying scheming bastards like you and me. This man' – the apparent saviour jerked his thumb towards Tony – 'this man put away scum. The animals that kill and torture for the pleasure of it. Not for gain, not for revenge, not to prove how big their dick is. But just for fun. And the people they kill? They're randoms. Could be your missus, could be my kid, could be anybody that's got a face that fits. Just some poor sod that crosses the wrong monster's path. This man is no danger to proper criminals like you and me.' He turned so Mick could see his face, an amiable smile creasing his cheeks.

'Mick, we should be pissed off that he's in here. Because the people we love are safer with him doing his thing on the outside. Believe me, Mick, this man only puts away the kind of animals that never see the inside of a jail because they're doing their multiple life sentences in the nut house. Leave him be, Mick.' He used the man's name like a caress. But Tony sensed threat behind it.

Mick moved his arm sideways, as if it were an intentional action, a planned stretch of his muscles. Then he lowered it to his side. 'I'm gonna take your word for it, Druse.' He stepped back. 'But I'm going to be asking around. And if it's not like you say . . . ' He drew a finger across his throat. The smile that accompanied the gesture made Tony's stomach clench. Maniac Mick swaggered away down the wing, a couple of his sidekicks falling into stride behind him.

Tony let out a long breath. 'Thank you,' he croaked.

Druse held out a hand. It was the first handshake Tony had been offered in the fourteen months he'd been inside. 'I'm Druse. I know who you are.'

Tony shook his hand. It was dry and firm and Tony was ashamed of the sweat he was leaving on it. He smiled with one side of his mouth. 'And yet you saved me.'

'I come from Worcester,' Druse said. 'My sister was in the same English class as Jennifer Maidment.'

The name triggered a series of images. Teenage victims, heart-breaking crimes, a motivation as twisted as a DNA helix. At the time, he'd been struggling himself with the sort of revelation that turned lives inside out. Unravelling his own past as he'd so often done with offenders had nearly driven him to walk away from everything. But this man Druse, whoever he was, would have known nothing of that. Maybe nothing much beyond the headlines. Tony nodded. 'I remember Jennifer Maidment.'

'And I remember what you did. Now, don't be under any

illusions about me, Tony Hill. I'm a very bad man. But even bad men can sometimes do good things. As long as you're in here, nobody's going to bother you.' Then he'd touched one finger to the imaginary brim of an imaginary cap and walked away.

Tony hadn't yet grasped how information moved through a prison. He'd suspected Druse of promising a lot more than he could deliver. But he'd been delighted to be proved wrong. The perpetual undertow of fear that pervaded the remand wing gradually subsided but never dissipated completely. However, Tony was careful not to let his wariness slip; he remained constantly aware of the anarchy that fizzled close to the surface. And anarchy was no respecter of reputation.

Even more surprisingly, somehow Druse's protection had followed him to the Category C prison he'd been assigned to after sentencing. The last thing he'd expected from incarceration was that he'd be protected by organised crime.

Druse had turned into a buffer on one side; Tony's past as a criminal profiler had earned him a similar bulwark on the other. If anyone had ever asked him, he'd have reckoned he'd made more enemies than friends in high places over the years he'd been working with the police and the Home Office. But it turned out he'd been wrong about that too. He'd made a request early in his spell on remand for a laptop. Neither he nor his lawyer had expected it to be granted.

Wrong again. A week later, a battered old machine had turned up. Obviously, it had no internet capability. The only software on board was a primitive word-processing program. While he was sharing his cell, he'd persuaded the officer in charge of the library to let him keep it there.

Otherwise it would have been smashed, stolen or used as an offensive weapon by one of his cell mates. It limited the time Tony could spend with the machine, but that had forced him to be more focused when he did have access. And so, the only person who had reason to be cheerful about Tony's prison term was his publisher, who had come to despair of *Reading Crimes* ever being finished, never mind published.

All of this had left Tony with uncomfortably tangled feelings. Engrossing himself in his writing made it possible to let go the fear that had run like an electric current through his veins from the moment he'd entered custody. That had been relief beyond words. There was no doubt about that. Losing all awareness of his surroundings while he sat at the keyboard and tried to marshal his knowledge and experience into a coherent narrative was a blessing. What tempered these comforts was guilt.

He'd taken a life. That had broken the most fundamental taboo of his profession. The fact that he'd done it to prevent the woman he loved from having to do it herself was no excuse. Nor was their conviction that taking that one life had saved others. The man Tony had killed would have murdered again and again, and who knew whether there would ever have been a shred of significant evidence against him? But that didn't diminish the enormity of what Tony had done.

So he deserved to be suffering. There should be a component of pain and retribution in his days. But truly, all the grief he knew was that he missed Carol. And if he'd been willing to, he could have seen her every time he was granted a visiting order. Refusing to allow her the opportunity to sit with him was a choice he told himself he was making for her sake. Maybe that was his form of atonement. If it was, it was probably a lower price than everybody else he was banged up with was paying.

When he considered what his fellow inmates had lost, he couldn't deny that he felt lucky. All around him, he saw lost livelihoods, lost homes, lost families, lost hopes. He'd escaped all that, but it felt wrong nevertheless. His escape came with a constant scouring of guilt.

And so he'd decided he needed to find a more constructive way to repay what people glibly called the debt to society. He'd use his talents for empathy and communication to try to make a difference in the lives of the men who shared his current address. Starting today.

But before he could get ready for that, he had something far worse to prepare himself for.

His mother was coming to visit. He'd initially refused her request. Vanessa Hill was monstrous. That was a word whose weight he understood and he did not use it lightly. She had blighted his childhood, stolen his chances of knowing his father, attempted to steal his inheritance from him. The last time he'd seen her, he'd hoped it would be *the* last time.

But Vanessa was not so easily thwarted. She'd sent a message via his lawyer. 'I've always known we were the same, you and me. Now you know it too. You owe me, and you know that too.' She still knew how to push his buttons. He'd fallen for it in spite of himself.

Hook, line and sinker.

2

There's a kind of mythology that's sprung up around psychological profiling, not least because some of its early proponents were tremendous self-promoters. They wrote books, delivered lectures, gave interviews where they seemed almost godlike in their ability to read the minds of criminals. The truth is that profilers are only as good as the team they work with.

From *Reading Crimes* by Dr Tony Hill

The great conurbations of the north of England insist on their individuality. But they have one undeniable feature in common: none of them is far from achingly beautiful countryside. Those who work out that sort of thing assert that the Peak District National Park is within an hour's drive of a quarter of the population of England. In normal circumstances, Detective Inspector Paula McIntyre would have relished a day in the woodland of the foothills of the Dark Peak, following twisting paths through what still felt close to a wilderness. Certainly on the high bleak moors above, it was easy to feel that civilisation was a lot further away than the far side of the next ridge.

But these were not normal circumstances. Paula struggled to pull her foot free from the grip of a boggy puddle. It emerged with a disgusting squelch. 'Dear God, look at the state of that,' she complained, glaring at her mud-covered walking boot.

Detective Constable Stacey Chen, who had managed to avoid the puddle thanks to Paula's mishap, screwed up her face in disgust. 'Has it gone inside your boot?'

Paula wiggled her toes. 'I don't think so.' She set off again down the faint trail they'd been following. 'Bloody fucking team-building exercises.'

'At least you already had the gear for it. I've spent a fortune getting kitted out for this. Who knew going for a walk in the woods could cost so much?' Stacey plodded after Paula, tired and glum.

Paula chuckled. 'Most of us don't splash out on a top-of-the-range outdoor wardrobe in a oner. Look at you.' She half-turned and waved a hand at Stacey, clad from head to toe in technical wear. 'Queen of merino and Gore-Tex.'

'You can have it all after we get through today. I never want to wear it again.' The trail ended in a T-junction with a wider path. 'Which way do we go now?'

Paula pulled the map out of her pocket and traced their route with a finger. 'We're going north.'

'That doesn't help me.'

'Look at the trees.'

'They're big tall wooden things. With needles. Which, unlike compass needles, are not helpfully magnetic.'

Paula shook her head in mock-despair. 'Check out the moss. It grows more heavily on the north side of the trunk.'

She moved closer to one of the Scotch pines that grew in a clump by the junction. 'Look. You can see the difference.' She pointed to the left. 'We go this way.'

'How do you know this stuff?'

'Same way you know all the intricacies of the Web. Need to know, plus experience. I probably started hillwalking around the time you got your first computer.' Paula checked her watch. 'We should get to the rendezvous with a bit to spare. You did well to end up with me, we'll get brownie points for making good time.'

'This is a crazy way to spend a day. All we hear is, there's a budget crisis. Whole categories of crime aren't being investigated at all because we don't have the resources. And we're wasting a day yomping through the woods instead of trying to solve crimes. I truly don't see the point of this,' Stacey complained as they set off again at what Paula clearly considered a reasonable pace. As far as Stacey was concerned, it was a route march.

'Me neither. But we're not in Kansas any more.'

'I don't think DCI Rutherford and Carol Jordan even went to the same police college. Carol would never have done this to us. We didn't need to play at team building, we *were* a team.'

There was no arguing with that. ReMIT – the Regional Major Incident Team that DCI Carol Jordan had assembled – had been hand-picked for their skills and their individual approaches to the job. But more than that, they understood how to play nicely with others. As long as the others were inside the tent. But Carol was gone, and ReMIT had only now been resurrected after months of dormancy. According to the ugly sisters, Rumour and Gossip, there had been more than a little uncertainty about the value of a unit that straddled several diverse forces. Those who had originally been in favour had had their fingers burned, while those who had been more cautious were now, paradoxically, more enthusiastic. If there were going to be operational disasters, they thought, better to divert the blame.

So while they'd hummed and hawed, Paula had been transferred back to Bradfield, her home force. She'd been seconded to a long-running investigation into people trafficking and sexual exploitation, an operation that had been emotionally tougher than anything she'd previously encountered. The call back to ReMIT had felt like salvation.

Stacey had been sent on attachment to the Met to work on financial crimes. The hardest aspect of the job had been remembering not to show how much she could do. Working with Carol Jordan, first in Bradfield and then in ReMIT, had given Stacey absolute freedom to go where she wanted online and do whatever they needed her to do. She had become adept at the *post hoc* validation of things she really shouldn't have been poking around in. As long as the end result looked clean, Carol had left her to it.

It had taken her three days to understand that doing things the straight way left her frustrated. Worse, it bored her. It had forced her to recognise that, in spite of her apparent adherence to convention, she was actually more in tune with the renegades than the hunters. 'The only good thing about it is that I've got so much free headspace, I've developed a lovely little app for working out the calorific value of your keystrokes at the computer,' she'd confided to Paula over a Chinese takeaway back in Bradfield.

'Why would anybody want to know that?' Bemused, Paula frowned at the wonton she'd just speared with a chopstick.

'Exercise and diet freaks want to know *everything*. Trust

me, they've elevated narcissism to a whole new level. Got to keep the business moving forward, Paula. It's shark to the max out there. If you stop moving forward, you die.' It was a stealthy reminder that Stacey's police salary was only a fraction of her income. She'd developed her first commercial program when she was an undergraduate and had grown her business quietly and successfully ever since. It was the reason she could afford to be the best-dressed police officer in the North of England. Merino and Gore-tex was a flea bite on her bank account.

She fell into step alongside Paula. 'I'm going to have to be extra careful with the company now,' she said.

'You worried about Rutherford finding out?'

'It's not exactly a secret. But he's so by-the-book, I don't see him turning a blind eye.'

'You do the business in your own time, though. It's not a conflict.'

Stacey shrugged. 'There's an argument that I'm applying knowledge and understanding I acquire from the job.'

'I'd have thought the knowledge transfer went the other way. But it wouldn't be the end of the world if you had to quit, would it?'

'I wouldn't be bored, that's for sure. There's plenty of challenges out there to keep me engaged. But I'd really miss the job.' She cast a sideways glance at her friend. 'I've never said this before to anyone. But I love that being a cop legitimises poking into other people's lives. I know I go above and beyond all the time, and theoretically I could carry on doing that if I wasn't in the job any more. I've still got all the back doors open. But I'd have no justification for it.' She scoffed. 'That sounds crazy, but it's the way I was brought up, I guess. Traditional Chinese values. Or something.'

'Makes sense to me. So let's just tread warily till we have a better sense of the DCI. We both know there's often a disconnect between what the brass say and what they do. Once we're in the thick of it, he might turn as much of a blind eye as Carol.'

'You heard from her lately?' Stacey rummaged in one of her pockets and produced a bar of artisanal chocolate. She broke off a couple of strips and handed one to Paula.

'Mmm, ginger.' Paula approved. 'I try to get out there every couple of weeks. Just to see how she's doing. I feel like the diplomatic mission between North and South Korea. I visit Tony in jail, then I visit Carol in a different kind of prison.'

'He's still refusing to see her?'

'He's convinced she's got PTSD. Which, frankly, is a no-brainer. He's told her, no Visiting Order till she gets treatment for it.'

'And is she? Getting treatment?'

Paula laughed. 'Can you imagine asking Carol Jordan that? "So, boss, how's the PTSD? Are you in therapy yet?" That'd go well.'

'Reading between the lines, though. Do you think she's making any progress?'

'She's not drinking. Which is amazing, all things considered. But as far as the rest is concerned—'

Whatever Paula was about to say was cut off by a short sharp scream from the woodland to the west. 'What the fuck?' she exclaimed.

A wordless cry came next, abruptly cut off. Then the sound of feet crashing through the undergrowth. And Paula was off, dodging through the trees in what she thought was the right direction. Stacey, less practised in direct action, hesitated briefly then set her mouth in a grim line and plunged after her.

Paula pushed on, stopping momentarily to check she was still heading for what sounded like a noisy pursuit. She shifted her orientation and carried on. When the noise stopped abruptly, Paula stopped too, holding up a hand to stop Stacey in her tracks. Then she moved forward as stealthily as possible. In less than a minute, she found herself on the edge of a clearing.

A few metres away, a young woman in running gear was pinned against a tree by a bulky man in jeans and a hoodie. In his right hand he held a knife, it was pressed against her throat.

3

None of us is immune to trauma. Some people seem to shrug off the terrible things life throws in their way; that's an illusion, one whose roots lie deep in their past in the shape of unresolved horrors. When she was working at Broadmoor secure mental hospital, Dr Gwen Adshead used to say, 'Our people come to us as disaster victims. But these people are the disasters in their own lives.' Even the actions of psychopaths are shaped by their own personal traumas . . .

From *Reading Crimes* by DR TONY HILL

Despite having programmed it into her satnav, Carol Jordan had struggled to find Melissa Rintoul's address. She'd only been to Edinburgh a couple of times previously and she held a vague memory of the New Town as a place of wide streets, tall grey Georgian buildings and private gardens enclosed by the kind of iron railings designed to impale trespassers. But behind those severe façades there were apparently mazes of back alleys and narrow mews whose coach houses were now bijou apartments. Or small businesses like the one Carol was looking for.

She'd found a remarkably expensive parking slot for her Land Rover a few streets away and spent the half hour before her appointment prowling round the area. These days, she liked to familiarise herself with the potential escape routes. She never wanted to be cornered again.

Melissa Rintoul operated out of a two-storey cottage in a pretty cobbled lane that cut a narrow slice between tenement blocks. Pots of lavender, rosemary and hydrangea lined the narrow pavement, forcing pedestrians to walk with one foot in the gutter. Carol almost missed the discreet plaque that identified the Recovery Centre, sandwiched between a podiatrist and a boutique selling lamps made from reconfigured industrial machinery.

It wasn't too late. She didn't have to do this. She could carry on shouldering her own burdens. She was surviving, after all. But the voice in her head, the voice she knew as well as her own, wasn't having that. 'Surviving isn't enough.' The last time she'd spoken to Tony Hill in the flesh, he'd said just that. And followed it up with, 'The people who care about you want you to live your life to the full. Surviving shouldn't satisfy you.' The words echoed in her head, trumping her misgivings.

So Carol took a deep breath and pushed open the door. A woman in her twenties dressed in what looked like yoga clothes sat at a small table in one corner of a tiny reception area. Opposite her were two comfortable-looking armchairs. She looked up from her laptop screen with a smile. 'Hi, welcome to the Recovery Centre,' she said. 'How can I help?'

Carol fought the urge to run. 'I have an appointment with Melissa Rintoul.'

Another smile. 'You must be Carol?'

'Yes. I must be.' She gave a tired smile. 'I don't have a choice.'

A flick of the eyebrows. The woman rose in one fluid movement and tapped on a door near the table. She opened it a few inches. 'Carol is here,' she said. The reply was muffled, but she opened the door widely and smiled even more widely. 'Melissa's ready for you.'

The room Carol entered was painted a pale sage green, the floor covered with a carpet a couple of shades darker. Two generous armchairs faced each other in front of a minimalist gas fire whose flames flickered in a low line behind smoked glass. The woman who rose from the upholstered window seat had an air of comfortable calm. Carol, who had trained herself to itemise people as if she would be called on later to provide a police bulletin, found herself struggling for detail. Melissa Rintoul's defining feature was a shoulder-length mop of corkscrew copper curls, but her facial features were somehow harder to pin down. The overall impression was of placidity. But there was nothing bovine or dull about her. She crossed the room and wrapped both hands round Carol's right. 'Come and sit down,' she said. Her voice was deep and warm, her accent faintly Scottish.

The two women sat opposite each other. Melissa met Carol's gaze unwaveringly. 'Can I ask how you found out about us?'

Carol rummaged in her canvas satchel and produced a dog-eared flyer. 'I picked this up in my osteopath's waiting room. I thought it was worth a try.'

'Can I ask what you're hoping for here?'

Carol breathed heavily through her nose. 'Recovery,'

she said. A long pause, which Melissa showed no signs of breaching. 'I believe I'm suffering from PTSD.'

'I see. Have you had a formal diagnosis of post-traumatic stress disorder?'

'It's complicated.' Another pause. Carol knew there was nothing for it but to explain herself but that inevitability didn't make it any easier. 'I'm a former police officer. I led a major incident team. My closest colleague from those days is a clinical psychologist. He was also probably my closest friend. He worked with us for years as an offender profiler. We dealt with the most serious offences you can imagine.' She sighed and stopped.

'You're doing well,' Melissa said. 'I'm not seeking the details of what your work was like. All I'd like to know is what led you here.'

Carol knew she should tell Melissa more about the catastrophic day that had ended with Tony in jail and her in disgrace. But her shame silenced her. She wasn't ready to expose herself so completely. Instead, she said, 'He said he thought I had PTSD. I didn't want to acknowledge it at the time, but I've come to accept it. I had a problem with alcohol. An addiction. He helped me get clear of it. I'm not drinking any more.' Every sentence was like pushing against a closing door.

'How long have you been clean?'

'Coming up for sixteen months.' Carol gave a wry smile. 'I could tell you exactly to the day and week, but that would sound a bit desperate.'

Melissa smiled. 'You're the only one judging you in this room. I'm glad for you that you're doing so well with something that is always difficult. Apart from the addiction issue, did he give any other reasons for his conclusion?'

Carol looked past Melissa to the window beyond her. A thin blind obscured the details, but she had the impression of a tree, leaves gently trembling in the wind. At least, that's what she wanted to imagine. She closed her eyes momentarily then said, 'Risk taking. Recklessness. Aggressiveness. I was putting myself and others in danger.'

'So what did you do to deal with these behaviours?'

Carol raked her fingers through her thick blonde hair. 'Nothing. At first, I did nothing. And then everything went to shit. I . . . I did something that had terrible consequences.' It was as close as she could manage to confession.

'Is that why you're no longer a police officer?'

'I was told to resign before they had to fire me. So I did. And still I did nothing.' Carol wasn't quite sure how Melissa did it, but she seemed to radiate a kind of supportive sympathy. Slowly, it was becoming easier to talk. The tightness in her jaw and neck was less noticeable now.

'But something changed that position?'

Carol felt her throat closing, as if she were about to cry. She felt outraged. She hadn't been able to cry about Tony's absence from her life; it had been a constant pain, a physical ache in her chest for months. But five minutes in this stranger's office and the dam behind her emotions threatened to burst. She cleared her throat noisily and said, 'He's refused to see me until I get help. He told me he loved me and then he refused to see me.' It wasn't what she'd planned to say. It wasn't at all what she'd planned to say.

Melissa nodded. 'I can see how that might provoke you into seeking help. Are we your first port of call? I ask because ours is not the conventional route to recovery, and we generally find people come to us when the more traditional methods haven't worked for them.'

Carol shook her head, still off balance from her moment of revelation. 'I did go to see a therapist.' An image of Jacob Gold sprang into her mind. He'd been the person Tony had turned to over the years when he needed professional support. Jacob had clearly been good at his job but he was entirely wrong for her. She didn't want him inside her head. 'More than one, actually. But I'm naturally quite a private person,' she continued. 'And I've spent years in a job where confidentiality goes with the territory. I've never had the habit of getting things off my chest, and I just couldn't do the talking cure. And besides—' She checked herself.

'Besides?'

Carol shook her head. 'Nothing.'

'Besides, you were smarter?'

Her eyes widened in surprise. 'I didn't say that.'

'No. I made an assumption and you confirmed it.'

Carol almost laughed. 'I used to have a sergeant like you. Best interviewer I ever worked with.'

Melissa nodded. 'Thank you. Carol, I'm not going to ask you about the particular circumstances that led you to our door. I don't need to know that. What we do here is not about words. We have a treatment regime that's about bodywork. Would you like me to explain it to you? And then you can decide whether you think this is for you.'

Carol felt as safe as she had for a very long time. It was a feeling she'd been afraid she'd never know again. 'Yes. Please.'

'Do you know what the fascia are?'

Carol shook her head. 'Apart from the dashboard of a car, I've no idea. But I guess that's not what you're talking about here.'

'No. Fascia are the body's connective tissues. They run in bands and sheaths through the whole body. They link and protect muscle groups and internal organs. It's like a spider web that keeps everything working together. When you're stressed or traumatised, when the adrenaline response of fight or flight kicks in, we're supposed to drop back down to the resting state once the danger or fear is over. Think of it like electricity being grounded so it's safe. But sometimes we overload on the fight or flight reaction and we shift further up the scale into freezing and dissociation. The reaction is so intense that the electricity doesn't get grounded and we don't drop back all the way down to the resting state of relaxed awareness. Are you with me so far?'

'I understand what you're saying, yes.'

Melissa smiled. 'Good. We have, in effect, got two brains. The conscious brain that controls our thoughts and actions. It's aware of the past and the future, it's always busy sending neurological messages back and forth that we're mostly not even aware of. But beneath that is our unconscious brain. It's the leftover from our reptilian days and it's all about survival. It's plugged into the five senses but it only understands the immediate moment. It lives in the present tense. It knows when the adrenaline cycle is complete. But if that doesn't happen, if we're holding on to that stress and trauma, then the survival brain thinks it's continuing. It becomes a loop, constantly re-running. Do you get flashbacks, Carol?'

She nodded, not trusting herself to speak.

'Traditional talking therapy can use those flashbacks as access points to the trauma state, and for some people, that helps. But for others, telling the story can leave you in a dysfunctional state at the survival brain level. So what we need to do is to persuade the fascia to release the stress they're holding on to so the electricity can ground itself.'

'You make it sound very simple. If it's that straightforward, why isn't everyone doing it?'

Melissa's smile remained warm. 'I understand your resistance. You're caught in the loop and deep down you're afraid things will only get worse. The main reason why not everyone is doing it is that there's always opposition to alternative forms of treatment. The medical establishment has a great deal invested in the way they've always done things. All I can tell you by way of reassurance is that ours is a technique backed up by extensive research and approved by the likes of the World Health Organisation. I've been doing this for five years now and I've had a success rate with patients of between seventy-five and eighty per cent. It doesn't work for everyone, though. I'm not going to pretend it does.'

'So how does it work? Is this some sort of massage technique? Are you going to massage my stress away?' Carol could hear the challenge in her voice. *Must be my reptile brain.*

'No. I believe that just as our body heals from physical trauma, so our mind can heal from psychological trauma. I'm going to give you a set of exercises to practise on your own. We're going to start with tiny eye movements that you can work on up to a hundred times a day. Telling your brain it's safe to look. It's called EMDR – Eye Movement Desensitisation and Reprocessing. I won't bore you with the theory. There's plenty of material on the internet. The principle behind it is that it will help you to reprogramme your reaction to the events that have traumatised you. You'll find a way to reframe what's happened to you in terms that no longer trap you in the feedback loop of trauma.'

Melissa demonstrated what she meant. It looked easy

till Carol tried to do it repetitively. After a dozen eye flicks, she felt uneasy. 'It gets more comfortable, I promise,' Melissa said.

The therapist ran through a few more exercises. Pushing slowly and forcefully outwards with the arms, like a sort of breaststroke against imaginary resistance. Kicking the ground as hard as possible for short bursts. Sitting with her feet on the floor and going through the motions of running. Carol copied her, accepting corrections and adjustments. After less than a quarter of an hour, her heart was racing and she felt slightly sick.

'You've done well,' Melissa said. 'I want you to do these exercises every day. Small groups of repetitions as many times as you are comfortable with. It should get easier and you should be able to do more as the days go by. I recommend a course of eight sessions so we can work through the changes. I'd like to see you again in two weeks. Will that be possible?'

Carol stood up. 'I'll be here. I want to get rid of feeling this way.'

'And I imagine you would like to re-establish contact with your friend. That's a goal worth having.'

'I can't even think about that yet.'

'Are you heading back to Bradfield now?'

Carol nodded.

'Driving?'

'Yes, I'm parked a few streets away.'

'Don't get behind the wheel right away. There's a lovely little café at the far end of the lane. Sit down and have a cup of tea and a scone. Breathe. It's possible you might have a powerful emotional reaction to what we've done, so be kind to yourself.' Melissa stood and put a hand on Carol's arm.

'Well done for coming here today. This was not an easy step to take. Go well.'

'Thank you.'

Feeling slightly dazed, Carol stepped out into the lane. While she'd been inside, the day had changed. A broad slice of sunshine lit up her path to the end of the street. Her spirits rose at the sight. 'Oh, for fuck's sake,' she chided herself as she walked toward the café. 'It's just a trick of the weather.'

And yet, she couldn't ignore a flicker of hope. Maybe she really had taken the first step on the road back to herself.

4

We have no difficulty treating extreme repetitious violence as a symptom of mental illness. It's not such a great leap to the notion that most violent crime is a kind of illness. If we change our behaviour, perhaps we can change our outcomes.

From *Reading Crimes* by Dr Tony Hill

Tony found that putting Vanessa out of his mind was easier in theory than in practice. A low hum of anxiety ran beneath his thoughts, making him edgy when he needed to be in command of himself. What he was about to attempt could set the climate of the rest of his prison term. Druse's influence had dialled down the element of fear; but Tony wanted to amplify the element of respect. The only problem was figuring out how.

The answer had arrived a couple of days after he'd been moved to HMP Doniston, the Category C prison where he'd probably serve out the rest of his sentence. The atmosphere was less toxic than on the remand wing, but there was no mistaking the kind of institution he was in.

Nobody who had ever watched a prison drama would have been surprised by Doniston's landings. Two sets of cells faced each other, separated by a corridor along each side of the wing and a void in the middle where stairs rose linking the floors. At ground level, the space contained a couple of pool tables and a table tennis table. The walls were brick, covered in several coats of institutional grey paint, the recessed doorways just deep enough for a man to squeeze into and remain invisible to someone walking down the wing. A perfect recipe for terror was to wait till the target grew level then leap out in front of them with a snarl and a grimace. No assault necessary; the shock and fear were enough to provoke the required response.

Tony's cell was identical to every other he'd glanced into as he'd walked nervously down the wing, his arms occupied with bedding, spare clothes, a box of books and his precious laptop. He'd been the most interesting thing happening that morning. His fellow inmates leaned in doorways, shouting questions and incomprehensible catcalls as he passed.

It had been a relief to walk into his own cell. At first glance, it seemed to be in decent condition, the off-white paintwork only a little scuffed and scarred. A narrow bed, a corner cupboard with three narrow shelves, a tiny table screwed to the floor, and a plastic chair. A radio speaker bolted to the wall above the bed. By the door, a stainless steel toilet and basin separated from the rest of the room by a painted brick wall. 'You can stick stuff up with Blu Tack. Cheer the place up. You can buy it from the shop,' the officer escorting him had said. It would, Tony thought, take more than a few photographs to cheer up this spartan cell. The window, divided into a dozen thick bricks of clear material, had a view of a bit of roof and a ploughed field beyond the perimeter wall. Enough of the outside world to remind him what he'd lost.

Left alone, he'd turned on the inbuilt speaker out of curiosity. He soon understood he was listening to a prisoner interviewing a poet who was running a workshop in the prison library that afternoon. It didn't take long to discover he was listening to Razor Wireless, a radio station run by prisoners. Apparently, Wednesday was Wide Awake Day, when the theme was creativity and educational opportunities. It was clear that although official resources were limited, the inmates had drawn on their own skills to extend their opportunities, from plumbing to cookery. As Tony listened, he started to feel a faint thrill of possibility.

He knew better than to rock up at the radio station without anyone to vouch for him. It had taken him a few days of asking around among the least hostile faces in the canteen and the library, but at last he'd managed to track down Kieran, a twenty-seven-year-old serving three years for, in his words, 'a shitload of burglaries'.

How had he got involved, Tony wondered. 'I liked listening to Razor, but I thought the show they were doing about fitness was way too specialised. I like to stay in shape, but all they were talking about was using the equipment in the gym. Now, the kit they've got in here isn't that brilliant to start with, but the big problem is there's just not enough to go round. Plus a lot of guys, they're not in shape to start with and they're not all that keen on trying to work out beside the gym bunnies,' Kieran explained. 'And then you've got the top dogs and their bitches thinking the gym belongs to them.'

It was more than Tony needed to know, but he understood better than most the value of letting people talk. 'I know what you mean. I'd feel like a complete wuss beside half the lads in here.'

'That's 'cos you are. So I came up with this fitness routine that you can follow in your cell. Dead straightforward stretches and resistance exercises, plenty of reps to build a bit of muscle. Make you a bit more buff.' He reached out and gripped Tony's bicep. 'You could do with a bit of that, Tony.' He chuckled and rolled his shoulders, showing off his own shape.

'I'll check it out. So you just went along and asked to put on a programme?'

Keiran nodded. 'The guys got me to do a run-through for them, made a few suggestions, then they gave me a weekly ten-minute slot. People liked it, so now I do fifteen minutes three times a week. I had to learn all the other stuff as well – how to do the technical shit like sound engineers do on the BBC and all that. Why are you so interested? You want to tell us all about the serial killers you've put away? Give us the inside track? Mind of a murderer, kind of thing?'

'All that's ancient history for me now. There's no way I'll ever get near a murder investigation again.'

Keiran sniggered. 'Not now you've been on the other end of it. But I'll bet you've got some cracking stories to tell.'

'I'm thinking about something a bit different. You want to get people fit. I want to help them change their lives in other ways. So, can you get me an introduction?'

'Sure. Come along with me on Wednesday morning when I'm doing my show. That's the best day, there's a bunch of us in then to plan out the rest of the week.'

Wednesday arrived and he found himself standing

against the wall in a crowded little room filled with radio equipment and half a dozen men who looked like a random selection from the Grayson Street stand at a Bradfield Victoria game. And not just because they were all white, in startling contrast to the general prison population. A couple were shaven-headed, tattoos decorating their arms and creeping up their necks. One looked like a science teacher, glasses slipping down his nose, fiddling with a screwdriver and a connector of some sort. Another – thirties, neat haircut, watchful eyes, big shoulders and the beginnings of a paunch – would have fitted in perfectly in Bradfield Metropolitan Police canteen. Kieran introduced Tony to the man who clearly ran the room.

'Spoony, this is Tony. He's—'

'Yeah, I know. The shrink. We got no couches in here, Doc. And we're already shrunk down to nothing by the system. So what d'you want with us?' Spoony cocked his head, making the tendons in his neck stand out. He was tall and lean, the arms sticking out of his T-shirt resembling an anatomical drawing – here a muscle, there a tendon, here a vein. His face reminded Tony of a tropical bird; all big eyes and hooked nose over a small mouth and a receding chin.

'I want to make a programme.'

Spoony scoffed. The two shaven heads folded their arms across their bellies and laughed. Tweedledum and Tweedledummer. 'Just like that? You think you're something special, just because you made a bit of a name for yourself on the outside?' Spoony turned away and pretended to be engaged with something on one of the monitors. The others took their cue from him and busied themselves with clipboards and screens.

'There's no point in me pretending I've got no skills,' Tony said. 'That would be really stupid, trying to make out I'm just another one of the lads. I've been listening to Razor, and it's equally clear to me that you're not stupid either. I don't want to be arsey about this, but I can give you a programme that could make a difference to people's lives. Maybe help them not to come back here.'

Spoony froze. 'You really think so? You've been in here, what? Five minutes? And you know how to fix us? Think you're fucking Coldplay, do you?'

'I don't even know what that means,' Tony said. 'All I do know is I've got some ideas that I think are worth trying.' He pulled a small notebook from his pocket. Another gift from people in the justice system who knew that he knew where some of the bodies were buried. 'I've drafted out ten minutes. Just to give you a flavour.'

Spoony turned, bending sideways from the waist so he could see past Tony and go eye to eye with Kieran. 'You did right, bringing him along. We're pitifully short on comedy.'

The geek with the screwdriver looked up. 'Wouldn't hurt to give the man a chance.' Judging by the looks of surprise on the others' faces, he wasn't given to expressing opinions.

Spoony blew out a noisy breath. 'Come on then.' He nodded towards a chair with a foam-covered mic in front of it. 'Sit your arse down and lay it on us.'

Tony obeyed, squeezing past the Tweedle twins to get to the chair. He cleared his throat. 'I am prisoner number BV8573. I'm also a clinical psychologist called Tony Hill. I've spent the last twenty-five years working with people like you and me, trying to figure out the reasons why things went wrong for us.' He looked up from his notes. Spoony was leaning back in his chair, fingers locked behind his head, staring at the ceiling.

'I don't believe people are born evil. I think we end up on the wrong side of the law for a variety of reasons and most of them are not our fault. I've said it before and I will probably say it again: Societies get the crimes they deserve. Build a society based on greed, for example, and robbery will become your default crime. Turn sex into a commodity and bingo, sex crimes spawn like tadpoles. So if that's the underlying cause of crime, logically the remedy must lie in our own hands. If we change the script people live by, then surely we should be able to alter our outcomes? I want to talk to you about ways we can change our scripts. And the first thing we have to talk about is fear. Because in here, we're all afraid.'

Abruptly, Spoony jumped up. 'Right, that'll do. You've got balls, I'll say that for you, Doc. Coming in here and making out we're all fucking bricking it.'

Tony sighed and stood up. 'OK. I get the message. I'll just fuck off back to my cell and forget I ever wanted to be the Zoe Ball of HMP Doniston.'

'What are you on about?' Spoony demanded, head thrust forward, all brittle aggression. He snatched the clipboard from Tweedledum. He ran his finger down the page. 'Yeah. Let's cut the Catholics down to half an hour on Friday. You've got fifteen minutes a week for the next month, Doc. If you can cut it, the slot's yours. Now fuck off, we've got programmes to make.'

Tony was halfway out of the door when he heard Spoony's valediction. 'You don't want to disappoint me, Doc. Druse don't cut no ice with the people I know.'

Just like that, the fear ratcheted up the dial again. *No such thing as a place of safety here.*

5

> Every crime scene has its retinue of specialists. Police officers, medics, photographers, forensic specialists, profilers. Just as we all read the same book differently, taking different messages from it and finding different echoes in its pages, so it is with crime scenes. Every specialist reads the scene in their own way. When we put our heads together, it's like a symposium on the dead person.
>
> From *Reading Crimes* by Dr Tony Hill

Paula took a cautious step forward. 'Time to put the knife down,' she said conversationally. 'There's better ways to sort this out.'

The man started, casting a quick glance over his shoulder. But his grip on the woman didn't slacken, nor did he move the knife.

'Let her go. You can walk away from this.' Paula kept her voice level and her body still. 'It's the only way out.'

'Why don't *you* fucking walk away? This is none of your business.' His voice was less assured than his words. The woman squirmed, and he turned away from Paula to push harder against her.

Paula dredged her experience for the right thing to say. 'If you don't stop now, it's your life that ends here,' she said gently. 'There's no going back from this. I don't believe you want that. What's your name? I'm Paula.'

Now his head whipped back to face her. 'What's it to you? Who the fuck do you think you are?'

'I'm just somebody that hates to see a man throwing away his life chances.'

'You sound like a fucking cop,' he exclaimed, outrage in his voice. 'Only a fucking cop talks like that.' And all at once he let the woman go and sprinted across the clearing towards Paula, the knife held out in front of him. The woman ran stumbling in the opposite direction.

'Stacey, get her,' Paula shouted, never taking her eyes off the man. He drew his knife hand back as he came near, preparing to strike. She waited till the last possible moment then stepped smartly to one side, lashing out sideways with her foot.

She'd been hoping for his knee and the scream as he crashed to the ground told her she'd hit lucky. Paula pivoted on one foot, stamped on his knife hand then dropped like a stone on to his back. He was shouting incoherently in pain but she paid no attention. Paula grabbed his right arm and twisted it up his back, then dug with her free hand into her jacket pocket for the plastic cuffs she always carried. It took less than a minute to cuff the man and then to caution him. She pulled him up, using the cuffs for leverage, and he yelped as his knee took his weight. 'Not your day, is it?' she panted, only then searching the trees for any sign of Stacey and the woman.

'You're fucking mental,' the man exploded. 'I'm a bloody copper.'

Paula laughed. 'That's the best one I've heard for a long time.'

Then from behind, she heard a chuckle. 'He's not lying.'

Paula had only been working for Detective Chief Inspector Ian Rutherford for three days. But already she recognised his soft Borders accent. Slowly she turned to face him. 'Sir?' It was a question whose answer she already knew.

'Today isn't just about team building, Inspector McIntyre. It's also about me finding out how you operate under pressure.'

'Is somebody going to get me out of these cuffs? She needs to learn about not making restraints too bloody tight. Not to mention my knee feels fucked.' The man sounded as pissed off as he had every right to be, Paula thought. She didn't imagine he'd expected to be done over by a woman at least ten years older than him.

'Meet DC Thwaite from South Yorkshire. Drafted in for today's little operation. You can release him now.'

As he spoke, the 'victim' pushed her way through a thicket and back into the clearing, closely followed by Stacey, who had lost her hat and gathered a random crop of leaves and twigs in its place. One leg of her trousers was streaked with dark mud. She looked furious. 'And this is DC Vaughn from Manchester,' she said, her mouth tight, her voice clipped. 'Who very kindly helped me out of a ditch.'

'She'd already caught up with me by then, in fairness,' DC Vaughn said with a grin.

Releasing Thwaite, Paula could feel the adrenaline draining from her. DCI Rutherford looked very bloody pleased with himself. He was, she thought, a man who liked to feel pleased with himself. He clearly worked at keeping himself in shape and wore clothes that made sure nobody could miss that. His hair was always beautifully groomed – cut close at the sides to reveal the beginning of silvering, longer on top to prove he still had plenty of it. He could look stern or friendly; his jaw was as square as Clark Kent's. He came with the reputation of doing things by the book, which was also, she thought, all about keeping up appearances. What this episode had shown her was that he was as capable of being devious as Carol Jordan.

To hell with Rutherford and his games. Paula turned to face Stacey and made a point of consulting her watch. 'We've got a rendezvous to make, DC Chen. We'll need to get a move on.' And she retraced her steps towards the track, not needing to check whether Stacey was at her back.

Later, the real team-building exercise happened after they'd all shaken off Rutherford and gone to the pub. Paula and Stacey were joined by their long-standing colleague DS Alvin Ambrose and Steve Nisbet, a new recruit to their team. Nisbet was a recently promoted DS from West Yorkshire police. The grapevine said he was quick on the uptake and a good team player. That didn't necessarily mean he'd be at home with this bunch of misfits, Paula thought.

Alvin and Steve had faced a test too, within fifteen minutes of setting off on their orienteering assignment. They'd rounded a bend and stumbled on a man dragging a woman out of the woods towards a van parked on the track. She was wearing a low-cut short dress, her hands were tied behind her back and she was snarling and shouting in what sounded like Polish. She had one shoe on, its spike heel hanging loose. 'This is the last time you'll fucking run out on me, you fucking whore,' the man yelled.

They were a couple of hundred yards away. But they didn't need to say a word. Whether it was people trafficking or a woman who'd failed to escape an abuser, the only thing that mattered was putting a stop to it. Both men took off at top speed. Steve Nisbet had the wiry build of a runner, but although Alvin was burly, he was fit too and kept pace as they raced down the track together.

There was nothing subtle in their approach and before he could get the woman in the van, the man saw them coming. He moved faster, wrenching the door open and forcing her inside. He slammed the door and made for the driver's side just as the two cops reached the van. 'The girl,' Alvin grunted, cutting to the side to go for the man, already half-inside. Steve opened the door but before he could grab the woman she'd kicked out at him with her bare foot, catching him a glancing blow on the jaw.

'I'm a bloody cop,' he yelled. She recoiled, scrabbling further into the cramped cubicle and screeching incomprehensibly. He tried to climb after her, but she was kicking out like a madwoman.

Meanwhile, Alvin reached the man before he could shut the door. Alvin grabbed it and hauled it open as the driver jammed the key in the ignition and started the engine. Alvin didn't pause for a moment. He leaned in and thrust his arm round the man's neck in a headlock and unceremoniously hauled him out of the van. The man tried to fight free, but Alvin was far too strong.

That was when Rutherford emerged from the trees behind them and called out, 'Take it easy, everybody. We don't want any injuries.'

'He just stood there grinning like an idiot,' Alvin said over his first pint, his voice thick with disgust. 'Telling me what a good job I'd done except for being a bit heavy-handed getting the suspect out of the van.'

'And apparently I was too bloody slow getting to the victim. I should have had her out of there by the time the engine started,' Nisbet complained. 'I'd like to see him do any better with a mad Polish traffic officer from Burnley trying to take his head off. I don't think I've ever spent a more pointless bloody day in eight years on the job.'

'Where's the other two?' Stacey asked. She pushed her chair back, preparing to get another round in, checking whether she should wait for the last two ReMIT members.

'Getting debriefed,' Alvin said. 'Karim said their route took them across a car park and they spotted a lad trying to break into a car. Karim was all for getting stuck in but Sophie wanted to phone for backup. She got her phone out and told him to wait, but he ignored her and came up behind the lad. And just when he got there, a second lad jumped up from behind the car and the pair of them wrestled Karim to the ground. Sophie was still trying to give her location to the control room.'

There was a moment's silence. Looks were exchanged, the three who knew each other well reluctant to speak till they knew which way the wind was blowing with Steve. He shrugged. 'I'm guessing eight years in retail management didn't give Detective Inspector Valente much experience at the sharp end.'

'You can't beat working your way up from the street,'

Alvin said. 'Even Stacey played a blinder today and she hardly ever gets out from behind a desk these days.'

'Carol would never have brought someone in off the direct entry programme,' Paula said. 'We're supposed to be an elite squad, not a babysitting service.' Too late, she caught Alvin's warning shake of the head.

Sophie Valente rounded the wooden partition that had provided the ReMIT team with some privacy. She smiled sweetly at Paula. 'Good to know who's not going to have my back,' she said. 'Anybody ready for another drink?'

6

As the poet Philip Larkin famously said, 'They fuck you up, your mum and dad.' Sometimes, it only takes one of them.

From *Reading Crimes* by DR TONY HILL

The years had been inexplicably kind to Vanessa, Tony thought as he was escorted across the visiting room to where she sat on the far side of a small table. He wondered whether she'd had work done to smooth some of the traces of time and malice from her face. Maybe a discreet lift behind the ears to get rid of any suggestion of a turkey neck? Her hair was the best a salon could provide, an ashy blonde with lowlights and highlights that looked as natural as a teenager's. And as always, she was impeccably turned out. Linen jacket, silk scarf artfully draped. She was close to seventy, but she could have passed for early fifties. She looked like nobody else in the place, and he was aware of the frank curiosity of his fellow inmates and their visitors. He knew he'd be grilled relentlessly at that evening's free association. There was always somebody looking for an angle and that was exactly what Vanessa was.

Focusing on her appearance spared him having to consider what lay beneath. This was the woman whose narcissism and casual cruelty had made his early years a place of fear, insecurity and humiliation. A life deprived of love and respect could so easily have set him on the same road as the people he'd hunted and treated over the years. But he'd been lucky. One woman had spotted his pain and vulnerability and taken him under her wing just in time to show him a different possibility. But despite that, being raised by Vanessa had left him vulnerable to the cruelty of strangers. It was Vanessa, he believed, who lay at the root of the sexual and emotional impotence that had marked his adult life.

And yet here he was, crossing the floor to face her again. He'd promised himself he was done with her. But deep down, he knew there would always be unfinished business between them till the day they put her in the ground. A ceremony he'd promised himself he would not attend. Once upon a time, he could have counted on Carol to hold him to that.

Vanessa gave him a long cool stare as he sat down opposite her. Not a trace of a smile. 'We are not the same,' he said. 'Not by any stretch of the imagination.'

She seemed genuinely amused. 'We both killed a man. We both used a knife. Up close and personal. And we were both set up. Most people would say, like mother, like son.'

'What do you mean, "we were both set up"?' He understood very well the equivalence she was claiming, but he wasn't prepared to let it pass without challenge. She'd come out on top against a determined killer, but Tony knew that hadn't been the first time she'd resorted to a sharp knife to resolve her difficulties. Another reason he hated their undeniable connection.

'That night, you didn't warn me there might be a homicidal maniac turning up on my doorstep. You set me up to be killed. But I outsmarted you, Tony. And you? You were set up by Carol Jordan.' He tried to speak but she steamrollered straight over him and childhood habit made him give way. 'I don't suppose either of you would admit that. But I think she set out that day to commit murder in the sure and certain knowledge that you would do whatever it took to prevent that happening. And here you are: the living proof.'

'You never did let the facts get in the way of a good story.'

She smiled. 'Self-defence, Tony. The way you set me up, you gave me that get-out. That's why I'm on this side of the table and you're on that one. Poor judgement. All those years and you hadn't learned to cover your back.'

Why had he agreed to this? She knew how to push his buttons. She didn't excoriate him the way it had when he was a boy, but still she could sting. 'Did you just come here to gloat? I was under the impression that you wanted something. You usually do.'

Vanessa's face had resumed its usual repose. 'I've been robbed.'

'And why has that got anything to do with me?'

'Because I need Carol Jordan to deal with it.'

He couldn't stop the bark of laughter that spilled from his mouth. 'Are you suffering from dementia? For one thing, Carol isn't a cop any more. And for another thing, she'd crawl across the Pennines on broken glass before she'd lift a finger for you.'

'I know both of those details. For one thing,' she echoed

sarcastically. 'I don't want a cop. And for another thing, what she won't do for me, she'll do for you.'

They glared at each other, neither bothering to disguise their feelings. 'If you've been robbed, the police are the ones to help.'

Vanessa shook her head impatiently. She leaned back and crossed her elegant legs. 'The police are not going to get my money back. If they're very lucky, they'll arrest the bastard and stick him in here with you. But I'll never see a penny of my money again. Carol, on the other hand . . . Well, from what I hear, she's got her own way of doing things.'

'You're going to need to explain what has happened.'

To his surprise, Vanessa looked away, focusing on the vending machine on the far side of the visiting room. 'About three years ago, a colleague recommended a financial adviser to me. Harrison Gardner. He'd been producing consistently good results for her investments, she said. Not spectacular or sensational. Nothing suspicious. Just a point or two above the market, which isn't so different from what some of the bespoke funds manage. She introduced us at a business conference and I thought he was impressive. He didn't make ridiculous boasts or inflated promises. He said he'd worked for one of the big city firms and gave me the business card of someone I could check him out with.'

'Which you duly did.'

'Of course I did. I realise now it was part of the set-up, but it sounded kosher. The number took me to a woman who claimed to be the referee's secretary and she put me through. I got a glowing recommendation. So I thought I'd give him a try. I put in twenty K to start with. Just a taster to see what he could do.' Her mouth twisted in a bitter smile.

Tony almost felt a stab of sympathy before he remembered

who he was listening to. 'It's hard for me to feel much sympathy for someone who thinks twenty thousand pounds is a taster.'

Vanessa's eyes narrowed and she swung back to face him. 'I've worked all my life, you little shit. Worked to keep a roof over your head, I might point out. Unlike some of us, unlike you, nobody left me a wedge of cash I'd done nothing to earn. I deserved what I had.' She swallowed and composed herself again. 'I gave him six months. The interest payments were good. Better than average but nothing sensational. There was even one month when there was a dip. Market fluctuation, he said. But I was still coming out well ahead. So after six months, I trusted him enough to put most of my funds in his hands. Everything was going fine till three weeks ago. My monthly cheque was late. And two days later, some twerp from the Serious Fraud Office rolled up at my door and told me Harrison Gardner had been running a Ponzi scheme.' She slapped her hands down on the table, provoking the nearest officer to move closer to them.

'It's OK,' Tony said, smiling at the officer. 'She's my mother, it upsets her seeing me in here.' The guard nodded and moved back against the wall.

'You know what a Ponzi scheme is?' Vanessa demanded.

'A fake investment fund. They work on the principle of greed. They offer better rates than everybody else and they use the money from new investors to pay off the earlier backers. It usually falls apart if it stops growing.'

'Or if the bastard behind it rakes in enough money to give him the offshore life of Riley,' Vanessa said savagely.

'How much?'

'Five and a quarter million.' Now she looked her age,

disgust revealing the harsh lines round her mouth. 'I sold the company.'

Tony whistled softly. 'And that's everything? Gone?'

'Gone. My pension, my bucket list.'

'A bucket list?' He gave a laugh that was more like a cough. 'You were planning on spending it so I wouldn't get a penny, am I right?'

She recovered herself. 'Why would I leave it to someone who set me up to be murdered? Of course I was going to bloody spend it.'

'Looks like your friend Harrison saved you the bother.'

'I want it back. And I want Carol to sort it for me.'

Tony shook his head in genuine bewilderment. He'd thought he was beyond surprise where Vanessa's self-obsession was concerned, but this time she had bested him. 'Why would Carol lift a finger for you? She despises you.'

Vanessa rolled her eyes. 'She thinks she's hard as me, but she's not. Where you're concerned, she's as hard as a marshmallow. So you're going to ask her for me.'

He grinned. 'You really have lost it, Vanessa.'

'Don't mock me, Tony. It's not too late for me to give an exclusive interview to one of the tabloids. How my son conspired with the police to deliberately stake me out like a sacrificial lamb to tempt a serial killer out of hiding.'

She would do it in a heartbeat too, he thought. 'Why do you think that would bother me? I'm already a pariah in the only professional world I know. You can't damage a reputation that's already destroyed.'

And then came the treacherous smile that still made his guts clench. The smile that signalled she had the fourth ace up her sleeve. 'I hear you're writing a book,' she said. 'I doubt your publishers think all publicity is good publicity.'

Dismay curdled his brief moment of satisfaction. How did she do it? How did she always find his Achilles heel? The one hope he was clinging to, the one key that might unlock some sort of future, and somehow she'd winkled it out.

Vanessa read him as she always had. 'I know you can't write a nice little note here. So when we're done, you can sort out a phone call and leave a message on my voicemail that I can play back to Carol.' She got to her feet. 'Otherwise I'll make the call. And it won't just be you I'll trash. It'll be her too.'

7

One of the less obvious effects of austerity has been the increase in the numbers of the visible vulnerable. For predators, it's been a gift-wrapped opportunity to expand their choice of victims.

From *Reading Crimes* by Dr Tony Hill

Even after midnight on a week night, the Temple Fields district of Bradfield was buzzing. The compact warren of streets attached to the city centre like a carbuncle was the opposite of a chameleon; every time the mainstream caught up with its edginess and innovation, it refused to blend in and adopted the next set of transgressions. Not many years before, it had been the red-light district, dingy streets lit by occasional neons, a poor man's film noir. It was the place to go for sleaze, and jazz clubs that survived because of the cheap rents.

There had been a couple of gay bars on the fringes. Then when it dawned on entrepreneurs that the pink pound was a thing, over the space of a few years the main drag sprouted a rash of gay bars and clubs so achingly cool that they were eventually colonised by everybody else. Now, in more gender-fluid times, no matter where someone sat on the spectrum, they could find somewhere to hang out where they'd be unexceptional. Mark Conway thought that must really piss off some of them.

It amused him to think that he wasn't unique either. He wasn't the first person to trawl the shoals of Temple Fields in search of someone special. Of course, he was looking for recruits, not victims. Not like those others he vaguely remembered. There had been one weirdo who had killed a string of men and dumped their bodies in the area. And another one who was responsible for torturing and killing hookers. The cases had had a lot of lurid publicity because the cops had been working with a psychological profiler. A strange little guy who always looked a bit distracted when you saw him in TV interviews until you noticed how sharp his eyes were when they flickered across the screen.

Turned out the shrink had the same kind of killer inside as the murderers he'd helped to put away. He was safely behind bars himself now. Mark had been aware of him for a long time; he'd almost had one eye on an imaginary rear-view mirror to see if the profiler was on his tail. Now he could afford to relax a bit. He didn't think the cops would be so quick to hire another profiler in case the next one went rogue too.

But one less foe to worry about didn't mean he could relax his vigilance. Thus far, he'd covered his tracks so well that nobody had even noticed what he was doing. What that said to Conway was that he was indeed doing the right thing. He was offering salvation to the hopeless. Not everyone was capable of redemption in this life. Growing up under the strictures of the religious brotherhood, he'd absorbed that message loud and clear. What he was doing was the obvious extension of that. The relief he felt after he'd saved another soul from degradation and despair was all the proof he needed.

As usual, he walked into Temple Fields from the car park off Bellwether Square. He cut down an alley, a shortcut for anyone who didn't mind the smell from the waste bins behind the burger bar and the gastropub, and took a baseball cap from his pocket. He pulled the brim down low on his forehead and swiftly turned his reversible rain jacket inside out, transforming dark red into black. By the time he re-emerged from the CCTV blind spot, respectable Mark Conway had disappeared.

The nights he spent quartering the streets of Temple Fields were a form of talent-spotting. He refused to believe that the one and only person he'd ever recruited from among the junkies and rough sleepers was a once-in-a-lifetime lottery win that would never happen again. Because Gareth had turned out to be a star. So much of a star that he'd been head-hunted two years into what was supposed to be a stellar career under Mark's wing. Now the ungrateful little shit was based in Singapore, teetering on the upper rungs of corporate life. And Mark had yet to find a replacement.

He was looking for legacy. That was what all the top businessmen wanted, he'd realised early on in his career. It wasn't enough to be a success. Legendary status didn't come to men who'd simply made it to the top. What Mark wanted – no, what he craved – was a dynastic succession. But not the usual sort of dynasty. You didn't have to be a psychologist to see the pattern that dogged business titans and their children. The kids never replicated the drive of their parents. They pissed it all away, secure in the knowledge of the safety net that extreme wealth provided.

No, Mark's dynasty would be a very different thing. He'd find another Gareth. Correction. He'd find more than one Gareth. He'd pluck them from their deprived lives, lives like the one he'd endured before he dragged himself up from the gutter. And he'd help them to be the next generation of stars who would take his legacy and build higher and further and stronger.

He'd found people in the system who could do the job. That hadn't been the problem. What he hadn't found was another gem he could mine from the rough and transform into a glittering diamond. He wanted to show people he had something special that spotted talent and transformed lives. Something that journalists would write about, that people would respect. That would make people sit up straight in front of their granola, mouths open, wondering, could that really be Mark Conway talking on the breakfast show couch? Mark Conway who sat behind me in Year Eight Maths? Mark Conway who only ever scored one goal in ten years of football, and that only because the ball hit his arse when he was standing next to the goal? Mark Conway, whose blazer sleeves were always too short, his shoes coming apart along the welts? *That* Mark Conway?

To be *that* Mark Conway, he had to be more than just another businessman. He had to be the one who plucked young men from the jaws of despair and disaster and turned their lives around. Their saviour. It wasn't an easy job but he knew it could be done. He'd done it for himself; he could pass on what he'd learned and make it work for someone else. It was just a case of finding the right one. And then the next one.

It had to be men. He had no time for women in business. They were too flaky. Hormones and babies. No focus, no single-mindedness. Of course, you couldn't say anything like that these days. Not even among friends. There was nobody to whom he could explain why it was men he was looking for. Every time.

So he made his way through Temple Fields, baseball cap low over his eyes, glasses with clear lenses perched on his nose. Tonight he wore black jeans, black trainers. They looked nondescript, but to a young man on the streets, on the make, they said, designer. They said, money. They said, pay attention.

Conway didn't slow his pace when he saw he'd snagged someone's interest. Not on the first pass. He simply registered the moment and walked on. Then he'd circle back and find a vantage point where he could watch. Was this really someone close to hitting bottom or a tourist who had a back door out of street life? Was he hustling with an edge of creativity or repeating a monotonous mantra? Was he fucked up completely by the incomprehensible street drugs that looped through endless changes of formulae till nobody knew any more whether the next hit was going to fry their brains or just smooth out the darkness of the day? Or was he salvageable?

He'd watch for as long as he could, standing among the smokers outside a bar, then sitting in the window of a coffee shop making a flat white last for an hour. He'd watch transactions on the street, coins tossed in coffee cups, little huddles of exchange and mart. Then he'd take a second pass, to see if his target had enough about him for a second moment of recognition. Did he brighten up, dismiss him, or just look blank? Conway flared his nostrils as he passed, to catch a whiff of his smell. Too thick and dark and he'd keep moving, never go back. But if it was tolerable, he'd walk to the end of the street then turn. If the young man was still flicking glances his way, he'd saunter back and stop. Offer a cigarette. Or a beer. Or a coffee.

First time, that would be all that was on offer. He'd take it easy. Let the mark come to him. Show what he wanted out of the arrangement. Too often, what they thought he wanted was sex. They were even affronted sometimes when he knocked them back. He didn't want sex, not from them. He wanted to transform them. He wanted to give them something much more meaningful than sex.

If they passed his exacting standards, he'd take them back to his place. Leave temptation in their path. Easy pickings. Wallet on the kitchen worktop. Drink and drugs there for the asking. Gareth had ignored all that, made it clear that what he wanted from Mark was exactly what he had to give.

Of course, disappointment was the price he had to pay for his ambition. Sometimes, like tonight, it was clear none of them had a spark he could fan to a flame, so he'd go home empty-handed. Not everyone could make the grade. And once he'd let them glimpse the possibilities, then face the crushing realisation that his world was never going to be theirs, there was no letting them down gently. Really, what he was doing was a kindness.

8

Although narcissists can appear charismatic, that charm is always and only exercised in the service of their own greater glory. They disregard the feelings and the interests of others and are often skilled at manipulating them into providing what the narcissist wants right here, right now.

From *Reading Crimes* by DR TONY HILL

Renovating the traditional stone barn where she lived had awakened something unexpected in Carol Jordan. To her surprise, she'd discovered she not only enjoyed working with her hands, but she was also good at it. The previous couple of years had taught her, in part thanks to Tony's guidance, that the way for her to stay on anything approaching an even keel was to be busy. So once there was no detail left to complete on the barn, she had taken up carpentry. Now she was on the final stages of her first project: a bedside table with turned legs and a drawer. 'YouTube saved my life,' she remarked to Flash, her Border collie. The dog, as usual, was leaning into her leg. 'I'd never have worked out what I was doing wrong with the mortice and tenon by myself.'

She put down the fine-grained sandpaper and stood up, rolling the tightness out of her shoulders. Time to do the exercises Melissa Rintoul had schooled her in. It was early days, and so far Carol couldn't honestly say she'd noticed any difference. She still felt like an alien in her own skin, the woman she had been a distant and implausible memory. But Melissa hadn't suggested this would be a quick fix. And if there was one thing that remained of who Carol had been, it was her persistence.

She was halfway through her arm exercises when Flash scrambled to her feet and ran to the door, belly close to the flagged floor as if she was herding a recalcitrant tup. Carol paused, then she heard what Flash had picked up ahead of her. A car turning off the road and into her parking area. Four in the afternoon on a weekday? Not Paula, who always texted first. Maybe George Nicholas, her nearest neighbour, stopping by on his way home to the big house on the other side of the hill, bearing one of his regular gifts. A brace of pheasants; a box of duck eggs; or an 'interesting' cheese he'd found in some farm shop. He was nicer by far than she deserved.

She wasn't always pleased to see George. But even on her worst days, she'd have been a hell of a lot more pleased to see him than the person on her doorstep, fingers poised over the brass bell pull. Instinctively, she dropped one hand and buried it in Flash's ruff. 'Really? You?' It was as sarcastic as she could make it.

Vanessa's smile could have cut coal. 'I'd always thought you'd been brought up to be polite.'

'I was. But for you, I'll always make an exception. What are you doing here?'

In reply, Vanessa held up her mobile phone and pressed PLAY on her voicemail screen.

The voice was unmistakable despite the poor quality of the reproduction. It was a jolt to the heart, literally. Carol felt her chest constrict and her stomach flip in that moment of recognition. 'Carol? I'm really sorry about this.' A pause, a sigh. 'Look, I told Vanessa I wouldn't ask you to help her, just to listen to what she has to say.' Another sigh. 'I really hope you're doing well.'

Vanessa dropped the phone back into her coat pocket. 'Now do I get to come in? I don't know why you have to live out in the middle of nowhere, there's a bloody gale coming off that moor top.'

Carol wanted to tell her to fuck off. But if she did that, she wouldn't have the chance to listen to Tony's message again. She'd ached to hear his voice every day since he'd banished her. She could hardly bear the bitter irony that she had Vanessa to thank for this moment. What, she wondered, had the woman used as a pressure point to force him into that recording? He wouldn't have done it voluntarily. She stepped back, holding the door ajar, pulling Flash to one side.

Vanessa swept in, scrutinising the interior with all the acumen of an estate agent. 'Nice job,' she drawled. 'No one would ever guess it was a crime scene. I'm amazed you can live under the same roof where—'

'That's my business.' Carol understood that Vanessa's cruelty was calculated to soften her up for whatever was coming. But her defences had risen the moment she'd opened the door, and not even the sound of Tony's voice had weakened her enough to let Vanessa breach them. 'So, what is it that you have to say?'

Vanessa settled herself into an armchair, crossing her legs and casually laying her hands in her lap. 'I need you to find someone for me. And when you've found him, I need you to "persuade" him to return what he stole from me.'

'I'm not a police officer.' Carol leaned against the wall, arms folded across her chest, Flash at her feet. 'I couldn't care less about you being robbed.'

Vanessa sighed. 'I'm astonished that both you and my son think I'm stupid. I know both of those things. But I also know that what you won't do for me, you'll do for him. I'll cut to the chase, Carol. Think about how I could spin the way you two set me up to confront a killer. If you don't help, I'll use the press and social media to make sure that what remains of his reputation is destroyed. You would just be collateral damage. I'm not asking much. For a detective of your calibre, it should be child's play.' She smiled. It was more unnerving than a snarl. 'Or you could refuse. And sit back and watch while I trash Tony's life.'

The coercion came as no surprise to Carol, given what she'd made it her business to find out about Vanessa's past. What kind of a woman tried to kill her fiancé for the insurance money? What kind of mother tried to cheat her son out of his father's legacy? What was frustrating was that what she knew didn't give her enough leverage for a comeback. 'For Tony's sake, I'll listen,' she said. 'But that's all I'm promising.'

Vanessa made short work of repeating what she'd told Tony. 'You can see why I want you on this and not the police,' she concluded. 'I want what's mine. And although you really don't want to help me there's a bit of you that relishes the thought of giving that dirty crook the come-uppance he deserves. Be honest, Carol. You love nailing predators. And it's not like you've got anything else to do right now.' She glanced across the room to where Carol had been working on her carpentry and her lip twisted in a sneer.

Carol hated that Vanessa read her so well. Maybe Tony's gift of empathy had an element of heredity, she thought wryly. 'If the police haven't found him, it can't be that straightforward,' she said, hedging on a commitment.

'They don't know what I know,' Vanessa said. 'I didn't tell them everything. Because I knew you'd be doing my legwork. Harrison Gardner has a ready-made bolthole. And it's not in some distant tax haven without an extradition treaty. It's right here in the UK.'

'Why would he stay in the UK when the police are looking for him? That makes no sense.'

'Because they won't find any tracks when they investigate flight manifests or passport controls. He's not the sort of criminal who knows people who can fit him up with a fake ID. He'll have to bide his time before he can make his exit . . .'

In spite of herself, Carol was intrigued. 'So how has he done it? And how do you know so much about it?'

'We were having a little drink one evening and he was talking about tax shelters. He told me he'd set up a trust in the name of his son when the boy was just a baby. He deliberately failed to mention its existence to the boy or his mother, just salted money away whenever he had any to spare. He used some of it to buy a cottage in Northumberland in the name of the trust, he told me. One of those picture postcard coastal villages that's been hollowed out by holiday homes, where there aren't enough locals left to pay much attention to who comes and goes. He told me he'd go there on his own every few weeks for a night or two. Shouldn't be too hard to find for someone with your talents. A holiday cottage that never has any holiday lets.'

It wasn't much to go on. 'And that's it? That's the crucial information you held back from the Serious Fraud Office? It's a lot of maybes.' Carol repaid Vanessa's sneer with one of her own.

'Are you going to do it?'

The one thing Carol wanted in her life right now was a bridge back to Tony. He'd said he wasn't asking her to help Vanessa, but if that was going to protect him from the dark side of the media and the internet trolls who loved to hate, surely he'd have to accept she'd done the right thing? That she'd made the first down-payment on the debt she owed him? 'There's not much chance of success, based on what you've given me. But I'll take a look.'

'Good girl. There's more. I just didn't want to give you enough for you to go after the cash on your own account.'

Carol shook her head scornfully 'You are a piece of work. I don't want your money. I don't want anything you have to sell.'

Vanessa raised one shoulder in a tiny shrug. 'Everybody wants more than they have. Why should you be any different? The son is seventeen now. So you know roughly when the trust bought the property. He told me it had a view of Holy Island, so that narrows it down.' She stood up and pulled a file of papers from her bag. 'I made copies of all the statements and correspondence. I don't see anything of any use there. But you might. Call me when you've got some news.' She dropped the folder on a side table as she passed. 'Make it soon, though. I'm not a patient woman. But you probably worked that out for yourself.'

9

Most murders are spontaneous. They usually involve drink or drugs and they're solved by the first police officer on the scene. The most challenging homicides are the ones that have been planned in advance. It's not the killing itself that is the hard part, at least not in practical terms. There are many relatively easy ways to kill another human being. The hard part is disposing successfully of the body so that it doesn't turn up like Banquo's ghost, pointing an accusing finger at the killer.

From *Reading Crimes* by DR TONY HILL

For once, Paula and her partner had sat down to breakfast with Torin, their teenage ward. Between the irregular demands of Elinor's job as an A&E consultant, Paula's unpredictable hours and Torin's weekend lie-ins, they seldom managed a communal breakfast more than once a week. Paula celebrated by making scrambled eggs and mushrooms for everyone. Torin manned the toaster, producing a pile of perfectly browned granary slices dripping in butter. In the background, the radio muttered and Elinor quizzed Torin about the progress of his A level studies in Politics, History and Philosophy.

'We're doing free will just now,' Torin said, dumping a plate of toast on the table. 'It doesn't actually exist, really.'

'What do you mean? Of course it exists,' Elinor protested.

'Well, does it? Why do you make the choices you do?'

'Because they seem best to me in the circumstances.'

'Exactly. So you've not got free will, because you make your choices according to the situation and according to who you—'

'Ssh, quiet a minute, please,' Paula cut in. 'Let me listen to this.'

'... at a former girls' home in Bradesden, on the outskirts of Bradfield,' the slightly breathless radio reporter announced. 'According to police sources, there could be as many as thirty sets of human remains in unmarked graves. The home, run by a Catholic order of nuns, was closed down just over five years ago. The convent and the grounds were sold to a property development company whose workers made the gruesome discovery yesterday when they began to clear the grounds. More on our main bulletin in half an hour.'

'Crikey,' Elinor said.

'Wow. Killer nuns,' Torin mumbled through a mouthful of toast. 'I thought that only happened in crap horror movies. Will you get sent out on that, Paula?'

She shrugged. 'Shouldn't think so.' She poured a cup of tea. 'It's not really the kind of thing ReMIT is supposed to do.'

'Sounds like a major incident to me,' Elinor said.

'Yes, but it's more of a cold case thing. Endless picking through bones and running tests. It'll keep the forensic anthropologists going for weeks.'

'But eventually they'll have to figure out who did it,' Torin said. 'Somebody'll have to be charged, surely? They don't just get a free pass for being nuns.'

Elinor poked him in the arm. 'But if there's no such thing as free will, then they had no choice. So what right do we have to punish them?'

Paula groaned. 'You two make my head hurt. It's too early for this.'

Torin grinned. 'Can I take a packet of biscuits with me? For the boat?' He had become the default caretaker of Tony's narrowboat on its permanent mooring in Minster Basin. He went there after school two or three times a week to turn over the engine and check everything was secure. Lately he'd taken to staying for an hour or two, reading where there were no distractions.

'As long as you don't stuff yourself with the whole packet before you come home for dinner,' Elinor said. 'Exercise your free will and resist.'

'Resistance is futile, El.' He shovelled the last of his eggs and toast into his mouth and, still chewing, headed for the hall, grabbing his backpack of school books on the way. 'Laters, ladies.'

'He's very sparky just now,' Paula said.

'Moving to sixth-form college has made all the difference. Nobody knows that his mother was murdered three years ago and nobody knows about that stupid nonsense last year. He's got the break he deserved.' Elinor gathered dirty plates, mugs and cutlery and loaded the dishwasher.

'Next lesson, clearing up after himself,' Paula sighed.

'I'll put you both down for that course.'

Paula leaned across the open dishwasher and kissed Elinor's forehead. 'I need to run, sorry. See you tonight.'

'Good luck with Rutherford.'

Paula groaned. 'Oh, how I miss Carol Jordan.'

Although the ReMIT team occupied the same offices as they had under Carol's command, there were several key differences. Most important, in Paula's opinion, was the disappearance of the state-of-the-art bean-to-cup coffee machine. Its replacement by a kettle and a jar of instant felt like a studied insult to the past. Another difference was that Stacey had been turfed out of her cloistered enclosure and shifted to a corner of the main office. She was still more or less walled off by her array of half a dozen monitors, but Paula knew her friend interpreted the move as an indication of mistrust, and that stung.

'I always delivered,' Stacey had complained. 'I don't need people looking over my shoulder while I'm doing it.' She had a point. It wasn't always helpful to know how she got her results. And she always had a beautifully constructed explanation, so everything looked kosher. Paula thought in these days of fake news and data manipulation on an industrial scale, they needed Stacey's black arts more than ever. What they didn't need was to make her feel like she was under suspicious scrutiny.

The main office now sported whiteboards and crime scene boards all round the walls. No chance now of staring into the middle distance once a major investigation got under way, Paula thought.

Rutherford had safeguarded his own personal space, moving into Carol Jordan's old domain, adding a whole new row of filing cabinets. That morning, however, the office was empty, the monitor on the desk grey and dead. Everyone else was at their desk, doing whatever they thought made them look busy. In Carol's day, when ReMIT didn't have a live case, they'd sometimes taken a look at unsolved cases, often ones that Tony had reckoned might yield fresh results. It kept them occupied and it felt worthwhile even though the cases didn't always make much progress. But Rutherford hadn't yet laid down any guidelines for how they should occupy themselves when there was no major incident on their desks.

Karim was hunched over his desk, checking out the overnight reports, obviously looking for something that might have the potential to fall their way. He'd joined Carol Jordan's ReMIT full of enthusiasm for the job, amazed at what he saw as his luck. Twenty-six, three years out of university with the law degree his family had pushed him into, he'd admitted to Paula that joining the crack unit had more than made up for the disappointment his parents gave regular voice to. 'I always wanted to be a cop,' he'd said. 'It's not like it was ever a secret. "You're too little," my mum used to say. "You're too skinny," my brother still tells me. It's tough, taking all the crap whenever the aunties and uncles come round. But it's my life.'

He'd been shy at first, but his keenness had been obvious from the beginning. He was good with women witnesses; big brown eyes and lovely skin, they all wanted to snog him or mother him. Now he'd grown in confidence and Paula reckoned it wouldn't be long before he got his sergeant's stripes. He moved his chair to the side so he could see Paula across their back-to-back desks. His voice was soft, pitched so only she would hear. 'What do you think the point of yesterday was?'

Paula raised her eyebrows. 'Team building, DC Hussain.' Heavy on the irony. 'Which bits of you still hurt?'

'Mostly my ribs. The guy that brought me down fell on me like a tree. I wasn't feeling a lot of solidarity with my partner right then.'

'Not enough weeks on the street. Be interesting to see how Rutherford plays that one in the debrief.'

Before Karim could reply, DCI Rutherford strode in. 'Morning briefing, everyone,' he announced cheerily, striding across to take up position in front of one of the whiteboards. Everyone turned to face him. 'Useful though yesterday was, it's time for us to get down to some proper police work.' From his hearty tone, he made police work sound on a par with a box of assorted doughnuts. 'One of the things I expect all my officers to do is to keep an ear on the local radio news. It's a great way to take the temperature of your patch. That being so, I'm sure some of you at least heard the interesting news this morning.' He looked round expectantly.

Paula exchanged glances with Alvin Ambrose. It felt like being back at primary school. Who was going to make a bid for teacher's pet? Predictably, Sophie Valente bent her arm at the elbow in a half-raise.

Rutherford smiled. 'Sophie? Care to share?'

'The human remains in the convent grounds,' she said confidently.

Uneasy now, Paula deliberately stared at the floor, not risking meeting anyone else's dubious eyes. As she'd explained to Torin, this didn't feel like the sort of case ReMIT had been created for.

Rutherford beamed at his favourite pupil, her failures of the previous day clearly filed under 'not wanted on voyage'. 'Exactly. You might be a newcomer to Bradfield like me,

Sophie, but it's good to see you're paying attention. For those of you who missed it, a property company sent the bulldozers in to a former convent and girls' home that they acquired after it closed down five years ago. The convent of the Order of the Blessed Pearl at Bradesden. The home was called the St Margaret Clitherow Refuge and School.' He paused and looked around. 'Feel free to make notes.' Karim and Steve fumbled with pens and pads. The others didn't even fidget. 'When the diggers started work, they turned up human remains. Bones, to be precise. Not a bonny sight. It's hard to be sure at this stage how many bodies we're looking at but it's likely to be more than thirty. Maybe a lot more. And our job is to find out who those skeletons belonged to and who put them there. And whether we're looking at suspicious deaths. Which, if you ask me, is a no-brainer, given the scale of the thing.' He paused for dramatic effect.

'Do we have any indications of how long they've been in the ground?' Paula asked.

Rutherford's smile tightened at the corners. 'Well, I think it's safe to assume they've been there at least five years, given when the nuns departed and the school closed down. But how recent they are? Well, we'll have to wait for the forensics on that one. Carbon dating, and all that. Alvin, I want you to liaise with the lab on that one. They won't want to spend their budget on it, but push them. Play the emotional blackmail card if you have to. "All those wee lassies belonged to somebody."'

'Do we know they're all female?'

'It's a reasonable assumption, given that it was a convent and a home for girls. Alvin, lean on the labs for that too.' Alvin looked glum. He'd never been drawn to the scientific end of investigations.

Rutherford's paternal condescension was clearly going to be an issue, Paula thought. 'But don't be jealous of Alvin having all the fun. There's plenty of work to go round on this one. DC Chen, I want you to go through all the records pertaining to the home. The Catholic Church must have details, even if they're not on the census or anything official. I want to know who lived there and when and for how long.'

Stacey visibly perked up. Paula knew there was nothing she liked better than mission impossible. 'I'm on it,' she said, turning her attention back to her screens, her fingers whispering over the keyboard.

'DI McIntyre, I want you to liaise with DC Chen on tracking down these nuns and any former residents of the home. We need to interview as many of them as quickly as we can. Karim can give you a hand with that. So get those leads coming, Chen, and get those interviews ticked off, Inspector. Sophie, I want you down at the crime scene to talk to DCI Fielding and see what's what, and when you've got a handle on what it's like down there, you can set yourself up back here as the clearing house for all the information as it comes through.'

It was, Paula thought, a big job for someone who didn't have much experience of major incident rooms. Sure, Sophie seemed to have the organisational skills. Hell, you had to be organised to be so well-groomed this early in the day. The kind of make-up that looked effortless but actually took more time than slapping it on with a trowel; glossy chestnut hair in an immaculate French pleat; clothes that matched, barely a crease in sight. And that was how she looked every morning. She wasn't easily flustered either. It would be interesting to see how she negotiated the complicated no man's land between Rutherford and Fielding. Not a job Paula envied her.

Rutherford noticed Steve fidgeting. 'Steve. There must have been men who worked there. A priest. Maybe a handyman. Or a driver. The local education authority must have been involved too. Even if the kids were schooled in the convent, there would have had to be inspections and such. A GP. They must have had a GP practice registration. Check all that out. Alvin can double up with you once he's rattled the cages down at the labs.'

It wasn't the most coherent allocation of tasks Paula had ever heard. She wasn't unhappy with her lot; she knew her skills lay in interviewing witnesses and teasing out key information from suspects. But the rest of it seemed a bit hit and miss. She'd also noticed the way he addressed them. She and Stacey were always rank and surname. Stacey didn't even get rank always. Everybody else was on first-name terms. The guys, obviously, because policing was all about man-to-man bonding. And Sophie presumably because she was one of the DCI's chosen few. She wondered if Rutherford even knew he was doing it. She'd try not to let it bug her too much. And in the meantime, she'd show Rutherford she wasn't there to make up the numbers. 'There'll be a Mother House for the Order of the Blessed Pearl,' she said. 'I'll see what I can find out online while I'm waiting for Stacey to come up with something I can chase down.'

'As good a place to start as any.' Rutherford sounded unimpressed. He squared his shoulders and fastened the middle button of his suit jacket. 'Let's get on with it. I want answers and I want them to start arriving soon.'

10

Some people kill because they want to do things with a body that they can't do with a living person. Some kill because they take pleasure in the process of stripping someone else's life away. And some kill because they believe it's the only solution to the position they find themselves in. They're the ones who take the most elaborate route to hiding the body because they don't want it hanging around reminding them of who they really are.

From *Reading Crimes* by Dr Tony Hill

The woman still formally known as Sister Mary Patrick sat with her face pointing towards the window. She might as well have been blind for all she registered beyond the glass. Her fingers moved below the desktop, slipping from one amber bead to the next as she methodically told the rosary. It was a habit so ingrained it had become unconscious, just the thing she did with her hands when they weren't otherwise occupied. Atonement was a long road, one she'd barely started down. Or so she was told with monotonous regularity. Easy for them to say.

She managed to listen to the BBC radio news every morning, despite not living in the UK any longer. To her amazement, there was Wi-Fi in the house where she'd been put. When she'd walked into the town and bought herself a smartphone, she hadn't been struck down by a thunderbolt, nor had anyone seemed to take any interest in her acquisition. And so she could listen covertly to the radio on her earphones in the privacy of her cell. Well, it was a room, really, but the monastic habit of thought had stayed with her and she thought of it as a cell. Particularly since she was enduring a sort of imprisonment.

She'd always known that one day she'd hear a headline that brought the past right into the present. Other people seemed to have been convinced that their history was dead and buried along with the bodies in the linen winding sheets, but she'd known the truth. She'd read her Faulkner. 'The past is never dead. It's not even past.' She carried that past with her everywhere she went, every night when she laid her head down on the hard pillow, every morning when she opened her eyes after an apparently blameless sleep. The past didn't keep her awake; instead it haunted her consciousness like a stalker.

She'd learned to live with the easy rush to judgement of others, the ones whose world hadn't collided with the kind of girls the sisters had had to deal with. It wasn't the nice girls who ended up at St Margaret Clitherow. Not the well-brought-up lasses who never answered back and stuck in at school. No, what she was landed with were the ones nobody else wanted. The ones who ran wild, the ones who made a vulgar jibe out of the home's very name, the ones with the eating disorders, the ones who were already in love with drink and drugs before they even made it into their teens. The self-righteous who were so ready to condemn her wouldn't have lasted five minutes in the convent of the Order of the Blessed Pearl.

She'd always known there would be consequences. And she'd rather they came in this world. Better that than prejudicing her chances in the next one. All the same, if she could keep things neatly boxed off in the confessional and the manageable penance of Hail Marys and decades of the rosary, so much the better.

That morning, in the measured tones of the news reader, laden with middle-class *sang froid*, she'd felt the weight of her personal impending disaster come hurtling towards her. It had taken its time to build up momentum, but now it was barrelling down the road in a straight line. The Church had done all it could to keep its dirty linen walled up in a dark hiding place.

But now the stone had been rolled away by the unlikely angel of the BBC.

11

The pressure to find someone to blame when investigators are faced with the darkest of crimes is almost overwhelming. Senior officers, the media, the family and friends of the victim – they all demand answers. As if answers were as easy to come by as the common cold.

From *Reading Crimes* by Dr Tony Hill

Her encounter with Vanessa had left Carol agitated and angry. She reached for her usual calming solution – boots, outdoor jacket, hat, Buff and gloves – and strode up the rough slope behind the barn, Flash running elaborate figures of eight around her. There was a chill wind sweeping down from the moor top, bringing tears to her eyes. She told herself it was just the wind, but when she turned into the lee of the ridge, the tears took a little longer to dry than her excuse could justify.

Bloody Vanessa. The woman didn't care how low she sank to find the leverage she needed to have her way.

Whatever gun she'd held to Tony's head, it had worked. It didn't matter that Tony had said he wasn't asking Carol to do what Vanessa asked; they both knew she wouldn't refuse. She was past caring about herself or the tatters of her reputation. But Tony was a different matter.

She'd once reached a point where she'd thought she could walk away from her feelings towards him. Leave behind all the complicated emotional baggage and rebuild her life without him at the heart of it. That hadn't lasted beyond the first threat to his future. That time, it had been Paula who had drawn them back together. Carol had never imagined that this time it would be Vanessa. 'It's not like you've got anything better to do,' she'd said, her scorn for Carol's handiwork palpable.

In that moment, Carol experienced an unexpected flash of insight. The first case she'd worked with Tony, more years ago than she cared to count, they'd been tracking a killer who had made beautifully crafted medieval torture engines to harrow his victims. Had she unconsciously been building a weird link to their past with that choice to work in wood? Or was she just reaching for any connection to their joint history?

Carol breathed deeply and ran through a couple of her exercises. 'Put it out of your mind,' she muttered. What she had to concentrate on now was figuring out how to track down the fraudster who had been reckless enough to cross Vanessa. There wasn't much to go on. A name, the suggestion of a trust, a vague hint at location. At least Harrison Gardner was an uncommon name. Thankfully, these days, records of births, marriages and deaths were accessible online. No more traipsing down to London and poring over registers till your eyes burned and the skin on your fingers grew dry from turning pages. She could glean that information in a matter of minutes. Probably.

But what then? Carol knew that it was possible to search the Land Registry by name to discover what properties were owned by that individual. She also knew from past experience that this was an index available under strictly limited criteria. Doing Vanessa's dirty work didn't remotely fit any of those criteria. In one previous investigation, Carol's Major Incident Team had had to get a warrant from a judge before they were allowed to interrogate that list. But now she was no longer a police officer, she had no conceivable standing to apply for such a warrant.

On the other hand, when legal options were unavailable, there were sometimes other possible approaches. And Carol was no stranger to unorthodox methods. She hated asking favours on her own account, but she could swallow her pride and ask on Tony's behalf. Especially since the person she'd be making demands of would understand very well what was at stake.

Satisfied that she'd figured out the first couple of steps, Carol turned to head back home. There was no defined path for the first part of her descent, so all her attention was on her feet as she moved swiftly across the rough grasses dotted with clumps of bilberry and heather. On days like this – the larks filling the air with streams of song, the breeze stirring the gorse bushes and not another building in sight – it was hard to believe the urban sprawl of Bradfield was only forty minutes' drive away. When she finally met the narrow track that led to the converted barn she'd turned into an enviable home, she was able to look around again, to appreciate the long vista across the moorland to the rise of the next range of hills. But her scrutiny was rudely interrupted as her gaze travelled over the slates of her roof.

A sleek black car sat on her driveway alongside Carol's Land Rover. She didn't recognise the car and she wasn't expecting visitors. Two unheralded callers in one day was unheard of. She felt a familiar tension build in her chest, the precursor to a choking sense of panic. Instead of giving in to it, she remembered the exercises she'd learned in Edinburgh and slowly stretched her arms out, pushing against an imaginary weight, sweeping them round to the sides as if thrusting something away from her. Again and again, she repeated the exercise and gradually, the anxiety receded a little.

Carol crouched low to the ground and breathed deeply. She practised the tiny eye flicks Melissa Rintoul had shown her, fleeting glances to either side. Ten, fifteen, twenty-five, till at last she felt her heart rate slow to something approaching normal. Now it was safe to look. Now she could think rationally about what to do.

There was nothing to see. Just a stranger's car parked outside her home. Nobody got out to ring her doorbell. Presumably they'd already done that while she was concentrating on Vanessa's problem or on her fancy footwork coming down the hill. Her first instinct was to stay put. They'd leave eventually. Bound to, she thought. If her visitor was an urban dweller, they might not think to look up the hill to see whether she was there. So she could wait them out and return to the security of her four stone walls.

But they might have already spotted her. If it had been Carol or one of her well-drilled team, they'd have rung the bell then, when there was no reply, scanned the hillside to see whether she was anywhere to be seen. If they'd been acute enough to do that, they'd know she was out on the hill. They'd know they could stay in the warmth and comfort of their car while it got cold and dark on the exposed hillside. That she'd have to come down eventually.

And there was no guarantee that they weren't watching her right now. Carol wasn't wearing bright clothes, but that didn't mean she was camouflaged against the mixed yellows, greys and greens of the moor. Even though Flash was belly-down beside her, the dog's black-and-white coat stood out like a waving flag among the vegetation.

Carol stood up and started moving down the hill at a steady pace, gaze shifting constantly between the uneven path and her destination. She knew Melissa wouldn't approve. It would come under the heading of reckless behaviour, no doubt. But on balance, this wasn't a Mexican stand-off she could win. Better to get it over and done with and confront whoever was in the black car while she had the energy to seize the upper hand.

As she neared the level ground behind the barn, the driver's door opened. So she'd been right. Her visitor knew exactly where she was and had been keeping her under surveillance. Carol signalled Flash to come to heel and moved steadily forward, hands loose at her side, ready for whatever challenge lay ahead. She was going to feel really stupid if this was her neighbour George Nicholas come to show off a new car.

But it wasn't George who began to emerge. Not unless he had taken to wearing black stockings and stilettos. A swagger of camel cashmere covering a tailored charcoal suit followed the legs. A flourish of shoulder-length hair whose fifty shades of dark blonde bore testament to an expensive hairdresser's talents. A skilful make-up job that banished the years as surely as Vanessa Hill's. A juddering moment of recognition pitched Carol into the physical and emotional reaction she now recognised as PTSD. For years, this woman had been her adversary. But the last time she'd seen her had been at Tony's trial, the defence solicitor constantly on the shoulder of his barrister.

Now Bronwen Scott had come calling. And Carol's heart raced when she considered why that might be.

12

It's the job of police officers to investigate the backgrounds of suspects. They have access to all sorts of information that's not readily available to anyone else. The product of those inquiries is the invaluable raw material for any psychologist who is advising them on angles of approach in an interview.

From *Reading Crimes* by DR TONY HILL

One of the secrets of Paula's success as an interviewer was to suck up as much background information about her subject as possible. So much so that Stacey had once referred to them as Paula's 'victims'. She'd said it was a slip of the tongue, but none of the others in the squad had pulled her up on it. So while Stacey was data-mining for individuals they could pursue, Paula set about a different kind of digging. Stacey might be all over the dark side of the information highway, but Paula knew how to google.

When the Blessed Pearl had closed down five years before, it hadn't made much of a stir online. The closure of a convent and its associated children's home wasn't of much interest, not even in nearby Bradfield. There were no allegations of sexual abuse against the nuns and priests of the Blessed Pearl, and if anybody had been complaining about any other kind of abuse, it hadn't grabbed the interest of the mainstream media or the citizen journalists of cyberspace.

So the *Bradfield Evening Sentinel Times* had contented itself with a short news feature about the closure of an institution that had existed almost unnoticed on the edge of the satellite village of Bradesden for more than seventy years. They had a quote from the Mother Superior, a woman weirdly called Sister Mary Patrick: 'It's very sad to see the end of a community that has educated and raised hundreds of children and led them to productive lives in society. But there are fewer women entering the Order of the Blessed Pearl and we can no longer sustain the level of involvement and training required to care for girls who are often very disturbed and have complex emotional needs. St Margaret Clitherow Refuge and School has been an anchor for those children but now it's time to pass the baton to others.'

The archdiocese had chipped in too. 'The sisters of the Order of the Blessed Pearl have given remarkable service to generations of young people. We salute their hard work and sacrifice. Young people will always find a home in the Catholic Church, but in less formal arrangements than before.'

Interestingly, in the light of what the bulldozers had uncovered, there were no quotes from any of the former residents of the St Margaret Clitherow Refuge and School. Paula knew journalists could be lazy, letting themselves be spoon-fed easy answers. But not to have sought out any of the children who'd been raised by the sisters seemed wilfully negligent, given the level of allegations of sexual abuse that had risen like a polluted tide around the Catholic Church in recent years.

Perhaps the answer was even more mundane than over-worked or under-curious hacks. Perhaps the answer was that the dead of St Margaret Clitherow were the victims of a different kind of abuse. It was certainly worth considering.

Towards the end of the article, the fate of the nuns from Bradesden was reported. According to the Mother Superior, they were to be redistributed among the other establishments run by the order. Paula wondered if that was the whole story. If she was running an order of nuns and it looked like at least some of them had been engaged in questionable behaviour, she'd want to farm them out to another sisterhood altogether. Somewhere nobody would come looking. The Little Sisters of Perpetual Hypocrisy, or something.

Paula carried on googling, looking for any hints of impropriety surrounding the wider Order of the Blessed Pearl. It was named for St Margaret Clitherow, a Catholic martyr in Elizabethan England, she discovered. She'd been known locally as the Blessed Pearl of York. The order honouring her had been established in 1930, a year after Margaret had been beatified by Pope Pius XI. Paula read about Margaret's sixteenth-century martyrdom with the same sickening disgust that years of working serial homicide had provoked. Her executioners had stripped her naked and laid her flat on the ground, a sharp stone pressing into her spine. Then they'd laid a heavy door on top of her and piled it with rocks till her spine was broken and her chest crushed so she could no longer breathe. Her crime? Hiding Catholic priests from the post-Reformation Protestant zealots. Paula wondered what Tony would make of them, and the Virgin Queen who had been head of their church. Though it turned out Elizabeth had written to the populace of York expressing her unhappiness at the execution. Not at the method, but the fact that Margaret, as a woman, shouldn't have been executed. Tony was big on rehabilitation and redemption but Paula had a hunch Elizabeth's letter wouldn't have cut it.

Margaret had acquired the status of a local hero, a rallying point for Catholics hiding their faith. Then, when it became possible openly to espouse that faith, she became the focus of a campaign for sainthood, led by the sisters of the Order of the Blessed Pearl, who got their reward in 1970 when Margaret was canonised by Pope Paul VI.

According to Wikipedia, the Blessed Pearl had never been one of the major orders of nuns. The Mother House was in York, less than a mile away from the house in the Shambles where Margaret had lived with her butcher husband and three children. And, apparently, assorted hidden priests. The chapel of the Mother House held the order's most sacred relic, the embalmed heart of the saint. Again, Paula felt that shudder of revulsion. It seemed fundamentally primitive to her to revere the body parts of the long dead, however spiritual they might be considered.

Apart from the Bradesden establishment, there were also convent houses in Liverpool, Galway and another in rural Norfolk. None of them had schools attached, though the Norfolk nuns had run a children's home until 1982. There appeared to be no whiff of scandal associated with any of them. Lives of quiet piety seemed to be their speciality. They didn't even go in for the obvious good works of teaching or caring for the sick and elderly in the wider community. Really, Paula thought, what was the point of them?

She'd got this far in her deliberations when Stacey dropped a sheaf of papers on her desk. 'I've sent you digital copies, but I know you like to work with paper,' she said.

'What's this?' Paula glanced at the top sheet, a list of names.

'Electoral rolls. Nuns vote. Who knew? And they have to register under their real names, not their aliases, so it makes it easier to track them from place to place.' Stacey picked up the first group. 'These are the nuns who were at Bradesden when it closed down. Or at least they were there when the electoral roll was compiled the previous year. I've got twenty-three of them at that address.' She gave a quick glance round the room and dropped her voice.

'I matched them against the 2011 census, and they all showed up – all except one. That gave me details on age, and that in turn let me in to birth records. So I've got them all down with d.o.b. and the address of where their family was living when they were born. Not hugely helpful, but it might come in useful.'

'Nice one,' Paula said. 'Can you search the current electoral register for these other locations?' She pointed at the list of convents on her screen. 'Supposedly the nuns from Bradesden were shared out among the other houses of the Blessed Pearl. Let's find out who's where, and if anybody's unaccounted for. Oh, and while you're at it, can you go back further and get me a list of the nuns who were at Bradesden five and ten years before the closure? I've got a feeling the women we're really going to be interested in are the ones who were there for a long time.'

Stacey folded her hands in the namaste gesture and dipped her head in a bow. 'Your mouth to my ear.'

Paula snorted and cut a knowing glance towards Sophie. 'Just make sure you cover your back.'

'Don't worry. I'll fill in the trench as I go. You won't get anything that doesn't have the patina of legitimacy.'

Which, Paula thought, would slow things up no end. 'I'm not even sure why Rutherford thinks we should be investigating this. All we've got is a collection of bones. OK, when there are that many, chances are something very wrong has gone on. But unless they've been shot through the head or hit with knives or machetes so hard there are notches on the bones, we've got no way of establishing suspicious death, let alone murder. At best, all we're going to be able to do is charge a bunch of probably elderly nuns with illegal disposal of bodies. Which is not what this unit was set up to do.'

Stacey nodded. 'It might not even be illegal disposal. I've been looking at the crime scene photos and there's a whole graveyard round the other side of the convent. Headstones and marble chips and everything. Nuns and priests, that's who got the grave marker treatment. So they probably had all the licences and permits necessary for burials.' She shrugged. 'Let's just hope there's not some proper major incident going unnoticed out there.'

13

Not everyone involved in law enforcement is comfortable with the idea that psychology is a legitimate science. They prefer the more quantifiable hard sciences where samples can be analysed using replicable and reliable methods. In an ideal world all cases would provide that sort of evidence. In reality? Dream on.

From *Reading Crimes* by DR TONY HILL

The intricacies of forensic science had never been Alvin Ambrose's comfort zone. He hadn't even got a single science GCSE. He wondered whether the new guv'nor was deliberately trying to wrongfoot him or just didn't know enough about the skill sets of his team members yet. Either way, it wasn't the perfect strategy for getting the best out of him. Or out of the crime scene techs and the lab team.

Just as five police forces had banded together to form ReMIT, so they had collaborated with a private company in setting up a joint forensic science service. The days when crime scene evidence was analysed by a national forensic service paid for by taxpayers were long gone. Now the jobs went to the lowest bidder. And the collective lab somehow always seemed to end up in that slot.

The labs were physically situated on an industrial estate just off the M62, theoretically equidistant from each of the five contributors. In reality, traffic density meant it took longer from Bradfield than from any of the other four HQs. By the time he reached the labs, Alvin was already grumpy from spending most of his morning in nearly stationary traffic. He almost wished he'd listened to his wife, who regularly told him, in the same patient tones she used with the kids, that he should start listening to talking books. 'You're always complaining that between the job and the kids, you don't get time to read any more. So use all that hanging around time to listen to one.'

He'd tried to explain that most of his hanging around time involved being watchful and alert, not absorbed in whatever Harry Bosch was up to. She'd harrumphed at him and muttered, 'Excuses, excuses. That's all I ever hear from you and the kids. Either do what I'm telling you or stop complaining, Alvin, you big baby.'

He navigated his way past the reception desk, mostly by flashing his ID and using his most intimidating frown. Even in a law enforcement establishment, his size and the colour of his skin tended to provoke anxiety and induce compliance. He followed the receptionist's meek directions to the room where the scientists talked to investigating officers. It had a glass wall that looked into a lab that was satisfyingly similar to the sort of scenes he'd seen on TV. People in white coats and nitrile gloves with masks and protective goggles fiddling with equipment and looking down microscopes or deep in conversation over some glassware on a bench. All very reassuring.

The woman who was waiting for him looked like someone who had served her time at the rock face. Brown hair threaded with silver pulled back in one of those buns that resembled a Danish pastry. He couldn't for the life of him figure out how they worked. Outsize glasses with black frames that reminded him of Brains in the *Thunderbirds* movie that his kids had once been obsessed with for about six weeks. Lines round her eyes that he could have mistaken for laughter lines if he hadn't also clocked the pursed lines round her lips. But she smiled warmly enough when she extended a hand. 'Sergeant Ambrose? I'm Dr O'Farrelly. Chrissie O'Farrelly. I'm the associate director here, I generally handle the police liaison. Take a seat.'

A small conference table with half a dozen chairs. Alvin chose one facing the lab and Dr O'Farrelly sat opposite him. 'You're here about the remains found in the grounds of the Blessed Pearl convent, am I right?' The phrasing betrayed the faintest trace of an Irish accent.

'That's right. I know it's early doors, but anything you can give us at this stage ... Well, it'd maybe get us moving.'

She nodded and opened the folder she'd been carrying. 'You'll appreciate this is a large and complex inquiry. We're estimating somewhere in the region of forty individuals, all of them children. So far, there are no fleshed remains, just bones and some clumps of hair. Our first job is the jigsaw puzzle of what belongs to whom. We might be able to get DNA from some of the skeletal remains but it'll take time, and unless you've got relatives to compare it against, it's probably not going to help much with positive identification.'

'Given the kind of backgrounds some of the kids probably came from, we might well find familial matches on the database. You never know. Can you tell how long the bodies have been there for?'

She shook her head. 'It's not easy to say. Once the soft tissue is gone, it's pretty much a guessing game.'

'Can't you do carbon dating?' He parroted Rutherford's words as if he had the faintest idea what they meant.

'I could tell you whether they were three hundred years old or three thousand. But even with the atmospheric changes following the nuclear tests of the 1950s, which altered the balance of radioactive isotopes globally, it's still only a macro.'

Alvin tried not to show he was lost already. 'That'd be a no, then?'

A quick smile. 'I'm afraid so. But there is a little ray of hope. We've got some strands of fabric among the bones. From our preliminary examinations, it looks like the bodies were wrapped in shrouds, probably linen or a linen mix. And underneath those shrouds, they were wearing underclothes. The natural fabrics have rotted, but a significant number of the labels are synthetic fibres. That tells us two things. Firstly, these are relatively modern bodies. Woven labels really only started appearing in the early twentieth century and synthetic ones didn't become commonplace until the 1960s. What we're seeing are quite badly stained, but we should be able to read them.'

'How will that help us?' Alvin was afraid the question made him sound stupid, but that was a price he was prepared to pay if it carried them forward.

Again the twitch of a swift smile. 'Well, apart from the washing instructions ... Some will have the name of the shop they came from. They'll have sizes, which helps us with the inexact science of ageing the remains. They might have elements that allow us to date them more precisely. When you take your pants off tonight, have a look at the label. It'll probably have a code on it that corresponds to the retailer's database. It's possible they'd still have records for those codes. Again, not very accurate for somewhere like a children's home, where clothes might well be handed down. But at least it gives you an end point.'

Alvin nodded, glum. 'It's not much to go on, is it?'

She silently tapped her fingers on the edge of the table, as if she were playing a piano. 'Not at this point. But it is early days.' She glanced back at the folder, flicking over the top sheet of paper. 'One of my colleagues who is at the site is fairly confident that the graves were dug with a mechanical digger.'

'You can tell that by looking?'

'The bucket of the backhoe compresses the soil as it cuts through. Even after it's been filled, it's sometimes possible to see where the bucket has sliced through. I'm sorry we've not got more for you yet. However, sometimes when we examine the soil around the remains more closely, we find external evidence of dating. A dropped coin. A piece of jewellery with engraving. Sometimes even a credit card, though obviously with children, that's a pretty remote possibility.'

'Sounds like we're really up against it.' Alvin rubbed the back of his shaved head, a familiar gesture of frustration. 'I suppose it's too early to say how they died?'

Dr O'Farrelly gave him the sort of look his mother handed out when he'd done something particularly inane. 'We might never know. So far, from the very superficial look I've had at some of the remains, there's nothing obvious like bullet holes or smashed skulls. This one is going to run and run, Sergeant Ambrose. There's going to be a lot of powerful people demanding answers. And just as many determined to keep those answers under wraps.'

Alvin hated to admit it, but he had a dread feeling she might be right.

14

Every offender who commits acts of sexual homicide has an individual initiating stressor – what the lay person would call a 'hot button'. I examine every aspect of the commission of a crime that I can access and I try to draw inferences from that information that can lead me back to identifying stressors, thereby creating a picture of the offender's psychological state but also of the circumstances of their history. Figuring out hot buttons can be just as useful when it comes to setting up an effective interview. And not just where killers are concerned.

From *Reading Crimes* by DR TONY HILL

The shock of recognition made Carol stumble slightly. She caught herself then walked slowly towards Bronwen Scott. No time for social niceties. 'Has something happened to Tony?' Carol demanded, halting a few feet away.

Bronwen smiled. Carol thought it was probably meant to

be reassuring. If so, it hadn't scored a pass mark. 'I'm not here because of Tony. I'm here to see you, Carol.'

Her words achieved what her smile hadn't. Carol could feel the physical release in her chest. But the second part made no sense. As far as Carol was aware, her sheet had been wiped clean when she'd left the job. It had been one of the conditions both sides had been happy to agree on. There were things in her past that reflected just as badly on her employers as they did on her. She didn't need a defence lawyer.

The only thing she could think of was that Bronwen wanted to use something in her past as leverage in the defence of one of her clients. In which case, she'd had a wasted journey. 'I'm not going into the witness box for you,' she said, moving past the car and heading for the front door.

'That's not what this is about,' Bronwen said, catching her up as she put her key in the lock. 'Carol, all I'm asking is a few minutes of your time. If you have something else lined up' – she couldn't quite control the quirk of her lips, suggesting incredulity – 'I can come back another time.'

Carol paused, head down, breathing deeply, staring at the key in the lock. 'The life I lead now – you've no place in that, Bronwen. I know you did a terrific job for Tony and that tips the scales back to somewhere around even. But that was then and this is now.'

'Please, Carol.'

She turned her head, wondering. She'd never heard Bronwen plead, and that had definitely been a plea. In spite of herself, Carol was intrigued. 'Five minutes,' she said, unlocking the door and walking inside without a backward glance. She took off her jacket and boots and carried on into the main room of the barn.

'Wow,' Bronwen said, close on her heels. 'You did all this restoration yourself, didn't you?'

Carol felt the mixture of pride and regret that the barn provoked whenever she stopped to think about it as more than just a machine for living. 'Yes. I had to learn a lot of unfamiliar skills. Turns out you can teach an old dog new tricks.' She turned to face Bronwen, Flash taking up her station between them, her ears pricked. 'You're wasting your minutes, though.'

'Fine. Here's the pitch. Everybody talks about what a great cop you were, meaning a great detective. I don't disagree with that, but the one thing I admired about you more than any other aspect of your police work was your absolute commitment to justice. I spotted that early on as the thing that drove you.'

Now she had Carol's full attention. Because Bronwen had alighted on the element of her personality that Tony had valued too. Had he briefed her? Was he behind this second unexpected approach too?

'You might not think so, given my track record of defending people you consider to be guilty, but I share your commitment to justice. The law is what fails us, Carol. As a lawyer, it's my job to exploit the flaws and loopholes to do the best I can for my clients. I know you probably don't believe me, but I would actually prefer it if that was a harder ask. And I do acknowledge that some of the people I get off should not be back on the streets.' She bit her lip. 'This is the bit I know you're going to struggle with.' She pushed her hair back from her face and met Carol's eyes straight on.

'I need some kind of balance in my professional life. I suppose you could call it atonement.'

Carol couldn't help the derisive grin spreading across her face. 'You could just stop defending the scumbags.'

Bronwen dipped her head, conceding. 'Everybody's entitled to a defence, Carol. And if it wasn't me, it would be somebody else. And they'd do it less well, so there would be even more work for the Appeal Court.' She matched Carol's grin with her own, proclaiming chutzpah. 'I'm not here to make you approve of me. I know that's probably never going to happen. I'm here to put a proposition to you. And since I've only got five minutes, here it is.'

Deep breath. 'Innocent people end up in jail. Usually because of incompetence. Cops, lawyers, expert witnesses. We're all guilty of failures, bad faith sometimes, occasionally downright crookedness. Sometimes it's because the evidence at the time of conviction wasn't capable of particular forensic analysis. Whatever the reason, people end up behind bars who shouldn't be there. You agree?'

Carol nodded. 'It happens. You're the one who mentioned the Appeal Court. That's what it's there for. That and the Criminal Cases Review Commission.'

'The mechanism's there, but the resources to produce the evidence to convince aren't. There's no provision for Legal Aid to pursue speculative investigations. And some of us think that's unacceptable. So we've formed an informal group of professionals to look into cases where we think there's been a serious miscarriage of justice. We're in the process of taking our first case through the CCRC and we're feeling confident about the court overturning a life sentence for arson.'

'Good for you.' Carol folded her arms across her chest. She knew where this was going and she didn't want to go there.

'We want you to join us.'

'I'm not interested. I'm done with that part of my life.'

Bronwen looked round, her eyes snagging on Carol's half-finished carpentry. 'Given it up for woodworking, have you? You think Tony's going to join you making dovetailed joints when he gets out of prison?' Her tone was light but the intent was not.

'I'm so far beyond the point where I can be taunted into things. I'm not interested in putting myself back in the front line of investigation.'

'It's hardly the front line, Carol. It's digging through old files and trying to find a loose end to tug on. Maybe the occasional conversation with a witness.'

Carol really didn't want to engage, but there was one question she had to ask. 'So who else have you talked into this?'

Bronwen was smart enough to show no hint of triumph. 'Two other lawyers – Cora Bryant, the QC, and Hector Marsh. He used to be with the CPS but he's given up prosecuting and joined my firm. Morna Thorsson, who's a law professor at Bradfield University, Dr Claire Morgan, who teaches forensic science there.' She paused for effect. 'And Grisha Shatalov.'

That startled Carol. She'd worked closely with Dr Grisha Shatalov over several years. The Canadian had been the Home Office pathologist based in Bradfield for as long as Carol had worked there and she admired his attitude. He was thorough, respectful and willing to go beyond observation to offer theories as to how injuries might have happened. But as well as acknowledging his professionalism, she also liked him. He had a considerate manner and a quiet but sometimes lacerating sense of humour. She'd eaten supper round his table with his wife and family more than once. If he'd nailed his colours to the mast of Bronwen's project, it wasn't so easy to dismiss as a waste of time.

And the lawyer was right. It had always been Carol's sense of justice that had fired her up as a detective. So often, there was a gap between the law and justice. What charges could be brought, what the courts handed down, what the limits on sentencing were – so often, the victims, their families and the witnesses were left feeling bewildered and cheated. Not just them – Carol had sat gloomily in pubs with her team while they unpicked the many ways in which the system had failed to deliver yet again. There had been nothing in her professional life that angered and disappointed her more than that. She'd even had to admit to herself earlier that day that a small part of why she'd let herself be pushed into investigating Vanessa's conman was the potential pleasure of seeing him pay the price, both literal and metaphorical.

'I know you know Grisha,' Bronwen said after a long moment. 'He was the one who suggested inviting you on board. I wanted him to come and talk to you himself.' Another quick flash of a smile. 'I reckoned he'd have more chance of persuading you than I have. But he refused. He said you'd feel you'd been tricked if he talked you into joining us then discovered I was running the show.' She spread her arms wide. 'So that's why I'm here instead of him. Carol, you are a brilliant detective. You are the smartest cop I ever butted heads with. You can't just sit here whittling bits of wood and wasting that investigative talent.' She dropped her hands to her side and shook her head. 'I say this not out of emotional blackmail—'

'Which means that's exactly what you're about to commit,' Carol interrupted, chin up, eyes defiant. 'I'd put money on you saying something along the lines of how disappointed Tony would be that I'm not using my skills and experience to serve justice.'

'I'll let you do the job for me,' Bronwen said. She reached inside the extravagant swagger of her coat and opened a soft leather satchel slung across her body beneath its folds. She took out a slim brown A4 envelope and held it out towards Carol. 'This is the case where I think you'd make a difference.'

Carol made no move to accept it. 'Not interested,' she repeated.

Bronwen carried on regardless. It was, Carol thought, a performance not many would have the nerve to give. 'Saul Neilson. He was only twenty-eight when he was sentenced to life three years ago for murder. It's particularly interesting because it's a no body case. He didn't do it, Carol.' Bronwen tossed the envelope on to a nearby chair. 'Here's another bet for you. You'll have opened that envelope before my tail lights are out of sight.'

She turned and walked out of the door, Flash following close on her heels as if to make sure she was really going. The latch snicked into place. The car door shut with a heavy thunk. The rich grunt of a well-tuned engine starting, then its diminuendo as it headed back down the road. Then silence as thick as the darkness outside.

Carol picked up the envelope and carried it through to the kitchen, where she dropped it in the waste paper recycling box. Whatever was on TV that evening, it would be better than opening Bronwen Scott's envelope. She stabbed the button on the Sonos system and Alison Moyet's glorious voice filled the room. But even that couldn't block out Tony's voice in her head, repeating 'Come on, Carol. You know you want to.'

15

This type of murder is the end of a process that can take anything from minutes to years. The first step is the identification of possible prey. The second step is not to throw caution to the wind.

From *Reading Crimes* by DR TONY HILL

Mark Conway liked to take his time. His mother's words echoed in his brain: 'More haste, less speed.' She'd had an unerring ability to find the perfect cliché. He couldn't remember her ever expressing an original thought. As a child, he'd had no appreciation of how hackneyed her speech was, or how closely that mapped on to her thoughts. It had taken years for him to realise it was like living with a particularly well-trained parrot. It had taken even more years for him to retrain his own speech habits. He'd made the change a conscious choice because he wanted to free his own thoughts and plans from the preordained channels and patterns he'd absorbed from her and the Christian Brothers.

He liked to think he'd ended up with a nimble mind, with an agile grasp of possibilities, and flexible mental reactions. He'd built his business from the ground up in record time because he was quick to respond to changing circumstances. He employed people whose minds didn't run in tramlines and he was always on the lookout for fresh talent. And because he'd had to break into business the hard way, he was willing to look in places as unconventional as his own starting point to find the next game-changer.

Urgent though that search was, he was going to have to put it on hold. That morning's news had hit him with the force of a hand squeezing his heart. He'd actually felt physically stricken by the newsreader's words. He'd staggered to a chair and fallen into it like a sack of sand till he'd processed the words. Human remains uncovered at the convent of the Blessed Pearl was his worst nightmare.

But as the ringing in his head subsided, he understood that this was nothing to do with him. The skeletal remains of children? That was down to the nuns.

All the same ... why had Jezza not warned him? What the actual fuck was that about? He must have known the bulldozers were about to move in. Was he really too stupid to understand how this news would have sounded to his cousin?

A wave of nausea swept through him and he stumbled to the sink, barely making it before his orange juice and granola pebble-dashed the stainless steel. He gasped and retched till there was nothing more to come. Panting, he rinsed his mouth under the tap. Thank God Jezza hadn't seen that. If they were going to make it through this, they'd do it because Conway was strong and smart and always one step ahead of the opposition.

He sat down again. He needed to think this through. Jezza had been adamant that he'd done nothing that would put Conway at risk of discovery. The narrow strip of land that held the raised beds and the vegetable patches had been let to Jezza on a fifty-year lease when the convent had closed down. Although there was no actual fence or wall, they weren't part of the land that the developers had bought. Jezza had always been clear on that point. And he swore that none of the graves the nuns had instructed him to dig were anywhere near where he'd deposited Conway's failed recruitments. Plus, he'd promised, they were buried much deeper. And even if they were unearthed? Well, he wasn't the one the fingers would point to.

So really, there was no reason to panic. And clearly, for all his stupidity, Jezza wasn't panicking either. Otherwise he'd have been ringing Conway's phone off the hook. He'd see Jezza at the football. There was a game in a couple of days, Manchester City at the Etihad. They'd drive down together, as usual. Spend the evening at the game. Act normally. He'd find out what was going on and make sure Jezza was primed to give nothing away.

He just needed to stay away from the Blessed Pearl till everything died down.

More importantly, he had to curb his enthusiasm. No more trawling Temple Fields in search of the special boy he could mould into someone fit to follow his example, the successor who would cement his legacy. But it would be a pause, not a full stop. If Jezza was no longer the answer to his failures, he'd find another solution.

His was the nimble mind, after all.

16

When I trained as a clinical psychologist, I envisaged a life working in some therapeutic institution, helping people come to terms with what had afflicted their lives. I had no notion of where this career would take me, which is probably just as well.

From *Reading Crimes* by DR TONY HILL

On the principle of setting a thief to catch a thief, running a man like Mark Conway to ground would take another nimble mind. Once upon a time that would have been a task laid at Tony's door, Carol looking over his shoulder, eager for any insights that would help her team to make progress.

But now, he didn't even know Mark Conway existed nor how many victims he'd persuaded himself he'd saved from a worse fate. Tony's world had shrunk to his immediate surroundings, his only imperative to stay out of trouble he wouldn't know how to handle. Keeping his head down, quietly getting on with writing his book, occupying a niche with the prison radio station – that was all he should focus on right now. Anything else was a distraction. There would be time enough to figure out what kind of life he might have in future. Time enough to explore whether he and Carol might find a way back to each other.

Groggy from a restless night on his comfortless mattress, he ground through his morning routine on automatic pilot. Shave in lukewarm water, dress in jeans and T-shirt, everything a day or two past where he'd have worn it on the outside. The small degradations that all made it impossible to forget he was being punished. Then down to a breakfast of flabby sweating sausages and potato hash, half an eye on what was going on around him in case it might kick off in a fashion that could drag him into somebody else's war. All clear, he headed back to his cell. Someone further down the wing was screaming about some perceived injustice. There was something wrong with the heating and in his brief absence, his cell had warmed up to an uncomfortable degree, amplifying the familiar smells. Still, he'd be able to carve out an hour for writing before he had to report for his shift.

Two days ago, he'd been assigned to work three shifts a week in the prison laundry. This would be his second day of wheeling baskets through the wings, collecting dirty clothes and bedding and carting it down to the laundry where vast industrial machines grunted and churned. It was, he was told with some resentment, a cushy number.

On the second day, the man he had learned was top dog on his landing stopped him on the way from breakfast. 'Laundry boy,' he'd begun, his voice loaded with disdain. 'You know what your name is now?'

'Maybe you could tell me?' Tony tried for a conciliatory smile, knowing even as he did that it was an epic fail.

'Postman Pat.'

It wasn't what he'd expected. 'First-class mail?'

The man grinned sourly. 'I'm the cunt who makes the jokes round here. You'll be delivering packages for me on your rounds. Is that clear?'

Heart sinking, Tony had agreed that yes, he'd be the new delivery boy. He suspected the prison officers knew perfectly well what was going on but it was easier to let it slide than put a stop to it and have to figure out what had replaced it.

That morning, before he could write more than a couple of sentences, a skinny prisoner with elaborate tattoos of serpents and naked women sidled into his cell. Tony had no recollection of seeing him before and was instantly wary. The man had a gaunt face and cropped dark hair with glints of silver at the temples. 'You the shrink guy?' he demanded. His accent was some sort of East European.

It wasn't the time to get into the shades of difference between psychologists, psychiatrists and psychotherapists. 'I guess,' Tony said. 'Dr Tony Hill, that's me.'

'I am Matis Kalvaitis. You are an educated man.' He took a couple of steps further inside the cell. He folded his arms across his chest, the ropes of muscle making his tattoos move in a sinister dance.

'Most people would say so.' Tony felt the familiar tightening of fear in his chest. What did this man want?

'I need you.' He let his arms drop to his side and pulled a folded piece of paper from his pocket. 'I need you to write this for me.' He thrust it at Tony, who studied it as he unfolded it. It was a printout from a website explaining the grounds for appealing against deportation following a criminal conviction.

'They want to deport you?'

'Back to Lithuania. That's no good for me.'

'You think you've got grounds for appealing?'

Kalvaitis nodded vigorously. 'Fucking right. I have been in UK for eleven years. I work in garage, I am mechanic. I have English wife since eight years. I have two boys. Six and four years.' He shrugged. 'I got in stupid fight.' He clapped himself on the chest. 'I am good fighter. Too good for stupid bastard who started it. They say I am dangerous man but I just want to stay with my family. You will write letter.' It wasn't really a question.

'You've got the paperwork? Your marriage certificate, work records, the birth certificates for your lads?' Tony stalled.

'Yes, yes, my wife keeps stupid papers, never throws anything away. You write letter, she will do rest.'

'Why can't she write the letter?'

He snorted. 'Because she is not an educated woman. We have no money for lawyer and we don't have pitiful story for people to tweet about. You write letter and I will be your friend. Everybody needs friends in prison.'

In Tony's view, it wasn't so much that you needed friends, more that you needed to avoid making enemies. The last thing he wanted was to make an enemy of a good fighter. 'Leave it with me,' he said. 'I'll see what I can do.'

Kalvaitis gave him a long hard stare. 'I'll see what you can do, Dr Hill.' He turned on his heel and slipped out without a backward glance. Tony looked at the paper again. It shouldn't be too difficult to draft an appeal. Kalvaitis' poorly educated wife could fill in the gaps, or get someone else to do that for her.

Tony closed his laptop and turned to a fresh page in his pad. If it kept him even a fraction safer, it would be worth it. Survival, that was the prime directive.

17

At the first seminar I attended as a callow student of psychology, the lecturer began with a glib line designed to make him look smart. 'You have two ears and one mouth. When it comes to practising psychology, try to use them in that proportion.' My prescription would be a bit different. 'You've got four organs of perception and observation – two eyes and two ears – and one for interrogation. You usually learn least by using your mouth.'

From *Reading Crimes* by Dr Tony Hill

Sophie Valente followed her GPS faithfully through the undistinguished village of Bradesden, a development of identical houses jammed together behind a main street of low stone cottages with a village store and an ugly pub. The village was surrounded by rolling fields, broken up by low hedgerows and clumps of trees whose names she was perfectly happy to remain ignorant of. Sophie was a city girl; the countryside held no attractions for her. What did people *do* all day?

The satnav brought her to a narrow lane. The cars parked along the verge indicated she was in the right place. The huddles of men and women leaning on car bonnets, toting shotgun mics and long lenses, confirmed that. They looked up hopefully as she drove past but dismissed her so abruptly she felt insulted.

The police cordon consisted of an officer in a high-vis jacket standing in the middle of the road by a liveried police car. He took a step forward as she approached, holding his clipboard out as if it had the power to repel boarders. *Here we go, today's first dick-wave.* Sophie wound down her window and presented her ID. 'DI Valente from ReMIT.'

He looked unimpressed. 'Car park's full,' he said. 'You'll have to park down the lane and walk back up.'

She could see empty verges beyond his car. 'Thanks, Constable, but I think I'll just park up ahead here in the lane.'

'I'm supposed to keep the roadside clear.'

How they enjoyed the exercise of their petty little fragments of power, she thought. She knew she couldn't afford to back down, not so early in her new role. Everybody seemed to know her background and, given that her own immediate colleagues didn't rate her, she couldn't afford to lose any more face. 'And I'm supposed to be at the crime scene. I'm not asking your permission, I'm telling you to let me through.'

She could imagine his steady stubborn stare wearing down most people. Because most people had limited defences against silence in a face-to-face encounter. But Sophie had worked hard at not being most people. If she'd stayed in retail, she knew she'd have ended up near the top of the tree. But it had bored her. Being a cop seemed a more exciting option once the possibility opened up of not having to grind her way through the ranks to the interesting levels. And she wasn't going to be put off by men who thought she shouldn't be where she was, men who didn't have the faintest idea what transferrable skills were. 'I don't want to waste my time explaining to your boss why I've kept him waiting.'

Slowly he stepped aside, making a show of writing on his clipboard. As she passed, she smiled. Not triumphant, not apologetic. Just a straightforward smile. 'Thanks. I'll mention how helpful you've been.' His head came up and she caught a momentary flash of alarm. It was clear he really didn't want his colleagues thinking he'd gone out of his way to be nice to the rookie inspector.

She drove on, parking behind the first car she came to, reasoning that it would likely be the last in the queue. She had a pair of wellies in the boot and she swapped them for her low-heeled court shoes before she headed up the lane and through a pair of stone pillars whose wrought-iron gates had been opened as wide as they would go. The tiny car park of the convent had probably never seen so much traffic, she thought. Police cars, the mobile forensics lab, the mortuary van, not to mention a canine patrol van. The whole of one side was occupied by the mobile incident room trailer, its generator keeping up a low grumble in the background.

Sophie made for the incident room. She had a name – DCI Alex Fielding – and she planned to use it. She walked in, passing a couple of uniforms who were heading out. Nobody looked up as she walked in; they all had their tasks and that was what they were focused on. She admired that. She stopped at the first desk she came to and cleared her throat.

A grey-faced young man dragged his red-rimmed eyes from the screen. 'Yeah?' he said.

'I'm DI Valente. I'm looking for DCI Fielding.'

'Over in the big blue tent. Where they're sorting out the bones.' He returned to his screen.

The big blue tent was impossible to miss. It stood beyond the car park, obscuring much of a dirty white crenelated building in the Victorian Gothic style. Sophie assumed it was the convent of the Order of the Blessed Pearl. She pulled open the flap and stared into something that she supposed should be horrifying but which struck her as actually quite banal. A dozen or more trestle tables were scattered round the tent, each with its own bundle of bones laid out in approximate skeletons. Figures in the regulation white suits, bootees and nitrile gloves were either intently examining the remains or taking pictures on mobile phones and making notes on clipboards. A tall man was moving from table to table, asking questions and scribbling answers. DCI Fielding, Sophie guessed.

She waited till he approached the end of the tent where she stood then called, 'Excuse me? DCI Fielding? I'm DI Valente from ReMIT.'

He looked startled, then amused. 'You think I'm DCI Fielding? Your investigative skills need a bit of work, love.' He turned and indicated a small figure deep in conversation with someone pointing his way through an array of bones. 'That's DCI Fielding.' He raised his voice. 'Guv?'

Fielding looked round. 'What is it, Skip?'

'Somebody here for you. From ReMIT.'

She rolled her eyes in the unmistakable FFS expression. 'Give me a minute. Let me finish here.' Irritation made her Scottish accent unmistakable. 'And you, from ReMIT? Wait outside.'

Sophie backed out through the tent flap. Fuck. Why had nobody thought to mention that Alex Fielding was a woman? Was it a genuine oversight or had her supposed misjudgement on the team-building exercise made her a target for humiliation? Now she was stuck here, the only officer who manifestly had nothing to do.

Thankfully Fielding didn't keep her waiting long. She was probably the smallest police officer Sophie had ever seen. She'd heard Scottish people were shorter, so maybe their standards for joining the police were literally lower. Fielding sized her up, sharp eyes nested in wrinkles, mouth tight in a sardonic smile. 'Nobody told you I was a woman, did they?' Although she was small, her presence was substantial.

Sophie shook her head. 'No, ma'am. I just presumed . . .' She felt herself blush under the unsparing scrutiny. 'Sorry, ma'am.'

'Paula McIntyre still hasn't learned how to play nice, even though she's finally made DI.' Fielding sighed. 'So, why are you here?'

This was just getting worse. Clearly Rutherford hadn't bothered to tell Fielding he was swiping her case out from under her. Suddenly she wanted urgently to pee. She cleared her throat. 'ReMIT are taking over the lead on the case. I'm here to introduce myself as the case manager. DI Valente. Everything will be going through me.'

'Is this some kind of a joke? This is not a ReMIT case. I've got a team on the ground who actually know what they're doing. As opposed to a shop assistant.' Fielding scowled. 'Yes, DI Valente, your reputation precedes you.'

'DCI Rutherford believes we've got particular skills. He can provide valuable leadership,' Sophie tried.

Fielding's expression shouted scorn more eloquently than

words could have managed. 'So *you* are going to manage the room? And I suppose you'll be expecting me to provide bodies to do the donkey work? Because you haven't got that many bodies, have you? Christ, I've got more bodies in that tent than you've got in your whole team.'

'That is what DCI Rutherford envisages, yes, ma'am. I'm here as a courtesy. I'll be setting up the room back at Skenfrith Street as soon as I've walked the crime scene.' Sophie had no idea where that came from, other than the instinct that the only way to deal with bullies was to pay them back in their own currency.

Fielding waved her arm in a mocking bow. 'Good luck with that,' she said, no possibility of missing the sarcasm in her voice. 'Be my guest. We'll just get on with the grunt work like the good second-class citizens we are. I'll liaise with Rutherford about how we staff up the room. Just remember, though. He's not my boss. He's my equal in rank. Be careful where you walk, DI Valente. Literally and figuratively.'

She turned on her heel and stalked back inside the tent. Sophie's sense of relief was palpable. She walked to the far end of the tent, considering Fielding's parting shot. She took her time to absorb the scene before she messed up by walking through the middle of it.

Now she could see the former convent in its full decaying glory. It was a huge sprawl of a building, with a central castellated tower in the middle, flanked by smaller versions at the four corners of the three-storey building. The stucco that covered it had probably been white originally, but it was flaking off in places. Spreading rust stained the areas round the joins in the drainpipes, moss crawled up unevenly from ground level. In its heyday, it must have been an awe-inspiring sight. Considering the backgrounds of the kids she imagined ending up here, it was more likely to have made them think of horror movies.

The perimeter of the property was marked out by a high stone wall lined with dense shrubbery and mature trees. The open ground to one side of the main frontage was the site of intense activity. A couple of dozen people in white suits were working with trowels and hand spades in a series of holes of different depths, breaking up what had obviously been a lawn. Surrounding the house was more lawn, surprisingly well-tended. It didn't look like the grounds of somewhere abandoned five years before.

She walked to the far corner of the frontage and turned down the side. Once she was a few yards from the corner, the activities in the rest of the grounds were invisible. Just the subdued mumble of generators and the occasional raised voice indicated what was going on out of sight.

Another grassy area, and beyond it, near the shrubbery, neat rows of vegetables. Beyond them, raised beds full of healthy-looking plants. The nuns might have gone but someone was taking care of these grounds. Sophie rounded the next corner and beyond a narrow strip of grass she saw a walled graveyard. Curious, she crossed the lawn and entered via a double wrought-iron gate, wide enough to accommodate a coffin and pall-bearers. There must have been a couple of dozen grey granite crosses, all similarly inscribed. On the top section, IHS. Across the middle, the names of nuns in plain lettering. Sister Mary Catherine, Sister Theresa, Sister Mary Joseph, Sister Margaret Mary, and so on. Dates of birth and death. Then RIP. It reminded her of a small-scale version of the military cemeteries she'd visited on a school trip to the First World War battlefields.

In the furthest corner stood a slightly larger version of the cross. Same lettering, but this time the long arm of the cross read, *Father Joseph Peter Toner, 1912–1975*.

She couldn't have explained why, but Sophie found herself gazing up above the treetops to the sky where thin skeins of cloud straggled across the blue. In spite of her suspicions about what these nuns had presided over, she was strangely moved by the little cemetery. She gave herself a mental shake and returned to the here and now, her eyes sweeping across the last corner of the grounds. To her surprise, through the trees she saw the outline of a cottage. Intrigued, she retraced her steps through the graveyard and headed towards it.

Set behind a low wall surmounted by iron railings, the cottage was a squat stone building, cramped windows flanking a front porch the size of a sentry box, two more dormer windows upstairs that couldn't have let in much light. But it was trim and well-kept. A greenhouse sat in one corner, filled with luxuriant greenery, the occasional red of a tomato showing through. At the foot of the back garden, she glimpsed the wall of the convent grounds.

Sophie opened the gate and walked up the flagstone path. No doorbell, just a heavy brass knocker, polished to a high shine. She raised it and let it fall with a heavy thud. No response. She decided to take a look through the windows, because why not? The living room on the left featured a long leather sofa well past its prime and a couple of armchairs that had seen less use. Opposite the sofa, hanging above the fireplace, was a massive flat-screen TV. A single mug sat on a low coffee table; she was pleased with herself for recognising the logo of Bradfield Victoria FC.

She turned to check out the other ground-floor windows

and nearly screamed. On the path, a few feet from her, a man stood, a hammer dangling from one hand. He wore a Bradfield Vics replica top over his bulky torso. Heavy denim jeans that owed no debt to fashion and a pair of well-worn work boots completed his ensemble. Sophie took all this in as she collected herself and finally checked out his face. Somewhere in his thirties, she estimated. A mop of thick straight dark hair. 'Can I help you?' He looked East European, but he sounded local.

'I'm with the police. Detective Inspector Valente.' She pulled her ID from her pocket. 'And you are ... ?' Trying very hard to sound calm and authoritative while her heart continued its pounding. She hadn't heard him approach, nor sensed his presence. That was what freaked her out.

'Jerome Martinu. Everybody calls me Jezza. I'm the groundsman here.'

'And you live here?'

He sighed. 'Look, I've explained all this already to you guys. I bought the cottage off the church. This is my property. The church pays me to keep the grounds from getting out of hand. End of. Now, if you don't mind, I've got work to do.' He moved towards the cottage.

'What's the hammer for?'

He stopped and shook his head. 'Knocking in nails.' He glanced over his shoulder, probably to see whether she was smiling. She wasn't. 'One of the raised beds needed a bit of attention.' Then he was gone, surprising her with his turn of speed as he rounded the corner and made for the rear of his property.

She hadn't seen him over by the raised beds. But then, she hadn't been paying that much attention. If he'd already been checked out, there was no need for her to repeat someone else's work. Now she had a sense of what things were like out here, it was time to head back and set up the operations room back in the Skenfrith Street police station. The sooner she got that up and running, the sooner she'd be able to impress Rutherford – and the rest of the team. She had ground to make up, so she'd better start running.

18

> **Babies are biologically programmed to smile from birth. It makes them more appealing to adults, who are also programmed to respond. But beyond that, when it comes to forming relationships, we shift into the realms of learned behaviour. And too many people fail to learn what they need to be comfortable in their skins. Mostly because they never encountered anyone to learn from.**
>
> From *Reading Crimes* by DR TONY HILL

Steve Nisbet hadn't imagined his first assignment with the Regional Major Incident Team would be talking to a social worker about a bunch of nuns. He'd applied to join ReMIT when Carol Jordan had first set it up and been bitterly disappointed when he'd failed to make the cut. He'd followed their every step from a distance, longing to be part of what he believed was the absolute pinnacle of modern coppering. His mum was always singing a song by some Irish bloke, Pierce something or other, 'I am the boy to be with'. And for Steve, ReMIT were definitely the boys to be with.

Until the day when the all wheels came careening off so catastrophically. But even then, even as his mates were telling him he'd dodged a bullet, he secretly regretted not being one of the shattered team left licking their wounds and picking up the pieces.

When the news got out that a revamped ReMIT was to be launched, the word in the locker room had been that signing up was most likely to be career suicide. None of his crew could understand why Steve, tipped as 'most likely to succeed', would want to leave a well-set billet for such a precarious berth. But Steve knew this was where he wanted to be. It might no longer be led by the legendary Carol Jordan, but he couldn't believe her DNA wasn't still running through the squad.

His eagerness had taken a bit of a dent on the supposed team-building day. And during the briefing, the old hands – Paula, Stacey, Alvin and Karim – had stuck together, constantly sharing glances, checking each other out before they expressed an opinion, clearly not quite sure which of their new colleagues they could afford to trust yet. He'd hoped his collaboration with Alvin had done enough to break down some of those barriers but he recognised there was a way to go yet. He'd win them over in time, he was sure of that. He was good with people. He never went long between girlfriends.

The big disappointment was Rutherford. Everything he'd heard about Carol Jordan signalled that she was one of a kind. He didn't think Rutherford had that degree of individuality or originality. The briefing that morning hadn't done anything to change that opinion. It had felt sketchy, not thought through. And now here he was, kicking his heels in some social worker's office while she tried to find someone who had actually had any face-to-face dealings with the nuns of the Blessed Pearl.

The woman had been flustered, unwilling at first to cooperate. But Steve had laid it on thick. This could be a murder inquiry, he reminded her. It wouldn't look good if it came out later that the council's social work department hadn't gone out of its way to try to identify some of these child victims. He could see the calculation going on behind her eyes, remembering the way social work bosses had been destroyed in the media over perceived past failings. So off she'd scuttled to track down one of the poor sods whose names were on the files.

Steve was on his third game of online Scrabble when the door opened and a head appeared round the edge. Hair in a neat brown bob, glasses with oversized black frames, an anxious expression and a nervous half-smile. 'Sergeant Nisbet?' The voice was surprisingly confident, warm and cultivated.

Steve sprang to his feet. 'That's me. Come in.'

A different woman entered, plump and self-effacing, a folder clutched to her chest, a plain wedding band tight on a chubby finger. He imagined her married to some *Guardian*-reading couch potato. She gave a nervous smile. 'Sarah said we could use her office.' She looked around for somewhere to sit that wasn't her boss's chair but had to give up. She edged round the desk and perched uneasily on the chair. 'I'm Jackie Johnston. Sarah said you wanted to talk to the social worker who dealt with the children at the St Margaret Clitherow Refuge and School?'

'That's right.'

She nodded. 'That would be me, certainly for the last few years they were up and running.'

'You'll have heard about the discoveries that have been made in the grounds of the convent of the Blessed Pearl?' Unless you've been walking around with your eyes shut and your fingers in your ears.

She closed her eyes momentarily. 'It's appalling. And I know we're going to end up carrying the can for it.'

'It's not my job to dish out blame, Jackie. I'm just trying to get a picture of what the home was like. How it was run. How much you knew about the lives of the children there.'

She made a nervous sound in the back of her throat. 'The answer is, a lot less than you probably expect.' She picked up a pen from the desk and fiddled with it, clicking it on and off continuously.

'You're going to have to explain that to me, Jackie.' Keep using her name, remind her she's here, now.

'We didn't technically have responsibility for most of the girls in the home,' she said in a rush. 'Very few of them were placed there by the local authority. And those were the only ones we actually had any authority for. We had no records of anybody else.'

'What? There was an orphanage full of girls on your patch and you had no idea how many? Or who they were? Or where they came from?' Steve couldn't keep the incredulity from his voice or his face.

Jackie shuffled backwards in the chair. 'The nuns turned evasiveness into a fine art,' she said, a hint of defiance in her tone. They weren't the only ones, Steve thought. 'They'd deny that any of the other girls were permanent residents. They'd say the girls were there for a visit. Or to give their mothers respite after a new baby, a difficult birth. Or to get fresh country air. Or because their parents had split up and the family hadn't made alternative arrangements yet. It was all very plausible, very matter-of-fact. There was no way we could disprove it, not without records. And we had no right to their records.'

'I'm struggling to credit this.' Steve scratched his head furiously. 'So where did these other girls come from?'

'The Mother Superior, Sister Mary Patrick, she said they were mostly there on the recommendation of their parish priests. She said they came from various parts of the country. Some were even from Ireland.' Jackie sighed. 'I tried, I really tried. But it was impossible. It wasn't like they were going to a local school where we might have been able to get access to their names and their records. They were educated in the convent. Perfectly properly, I might say.'

'It sounds like they were prisoners, not residents.'

'Whenever I visited, there was no sign of duress. They all seemed well-behaved and contented.'

'How many did you have responsibility for?'

'St Margaret Clitherow's was on my caseload for four years. I had seven girls there permanently for those four years. Six of them were orphans and the other one, her mother had died and her father wasn't able to take care of her. They were all Catholic girls and the refuge seemed like the best option.'

'How often did you visit?'

Jackie opened her file. 'Every six months.' She looked up swiftly, fearful. 'Look, I know that sounds bad. But like everybody in this department, I don't have a caseload so much as a case overload. I had – I have to deal with domestic violence, drug abuse, alcohol abuse, mental health problems, threats of eviction, allegations of child sex abuse, teenage runaways, issues with benefits. The home was run on proper lines, the girls were divided up into small family-style groups in the care of two or three nuns. The girls we sent to the nuns seemed well nourished, well cared for, well educated. They never had much to say for themselves, they were always quite subdued. It's easy to say with hindsight that they might have been cowed into submission. But I had no reason to suspect there was any kind of issue. To be honest, it felt like a relief to have seven kids on my books that didn't seem to be at risk.' Her lips trembled and she closed her eyes again.

He wanted to put his head in his hands and growl like an angry dog. Instead he bit back his anger and said, 'You didn't see signs of any kind of abuse?'

'If I had, I would have taken action. I'm not completely rubbish at my job.' The piteous expression on her face gave the lie to her words.

'What happened to the girls when the refuge closed?'

A momentary flash of spirit. 'Well, they were all alive and accounted for, if that's what you're getting at.' Again she consulted the folder. 'The one whose dad was still alive? She went to live with him and her stepmum. The other six went into foster care. Two of them are over eighteen now and they've both slipped off the radar. The other four . . .' She looked stricken. 'Two runaways. One fifteen, the other sixteen. Reported to the local police. Not exactly high priority for your lot.'

'In fairness, they don't usually want to be found,' Steve said. 'Bradfield's a big city. It's not hard to fall off the map. That leaves two. Where are they?'

Jackie frowned at the folder again. 'It's not great, really. One committed suicide three years ago. Paracetamol and vodka. The other one is in hospital. Sectioned, actually. Severe anorexia and mental health problems.'

Steve stared at Jackie. 'Not exactly a sparkling set of outcomes for a bunch of girls who were supposedly in a "proper" care home.'

'No,' Jackie said. 'But sadly it's not exceptional for kids who have grown up in the care system.'

'I'm going to need details of all these girls,' he said.

Jackie quickly closed the file and held it to her chest. 'I'm not sure that's allowed.' Her air of anxiety was rising towards panic.

People would try anything to cover their backs. 'We're looking at upwards of thirty dead children here. If you want to make absolutely sure you and your colleagues get the blame for what happened at the Blessed Pearl, just keep on obstructing our inquiries. Now go and get your boss to authorise you handing over all of the files on these seven girls.' He folded his arms. 'I'm going nowhere until you do. Don't make me sit here and get one of my tame media pals to tweet about how all Bradfield Social Services care about is their reputation.'

'You wouldn't dare.'

He gave her a sour smile. 'Why are you still here, Jackie? It's not too late to start to do your job.'

19

For too long, people clung to the idea that criminals were born bad. It let all of us off the hook – what's the point of trying to make society better if those 'born bad' criminals are just going to come along and trash everything? But slowly, we've come to realise that most criminal behaviour is situational and circumstantial. And the idea that it's possible to change people's narratives has recently started to gain serious traction.

From *Reading Crimes* by Dr Tony Hill

Tony lay on his narrow bunk, hands clasped behind his head, staring up at the blank magnolia ceiling of his cell. It was annoyingly free of cracks and blemishes he could translate into a fantasy map or some ancient Babylonian cuneiform. There was nothing to distract him from the low cacophony of the prison. It was impossible to ignore the constant noise; waiting for the next scream or outburst of rage that was bound to come, he felt the perpetual tug of anxiety.

He was trying to work out a script for his next broadcast. It wasn't like delivering a lecture to students or a seminar to peers. There, he'd always known broadly what he was going to say. He might even have managed to organise some PowerPoint slides to keep him on track. He could be pitch-perfect without being word-perfect. But on Razor Wireless, he couldn't afford to put a foot wrong. His audience would be on the lookout for any jarring notes, eager to find a reason to pounce on any potential offence. There were limits to protection, and he was in no hurry to find the provocation that would test them. He always needed to rehearse what he was going to say and he needed to get it right.

It was at times like these that missing Carol was close to a physical pain – a tightening across his temples and a tension in his neck. He knew he had an unusual gift for empathy when it came to figuring out what went on inside the heads of the damaged and the lost. But he also knew that his social skills sometimes didn't measure up. He sometimes said the most interesting thing that came into his head without considering whether it was a helpful conversational gambit. He'd learned over the years to run controversial ideas past Carol before blurting them out to others. She was good at helping him tweak what he wanted to say without losing its meaning or its positive impact. He didn't always manage to figure things out far enough in advance to use her to his best advantage, but he had definitely been getting better at it.

This would have been the perfect opportunity to use her help. And she'd have been happy to give it. But he'd put himself beyond that. He'd pushed her away for all the right reasons. As long as he was there for her, she'd always find reasons not to confront her demons and tackle the PTSD that was making her a danger to herself and to the people around her. He knew she felt it like a punishment. He wasn't sure whether she knew that he did too. What would she say to him now? What would be her advice? Most days since he'd arrived at Doniston, it had taken all his willpower to stick to the decision he'd made to keep his distance.

That morning, for example. It had kicked off at breakfast. He hadn't seen it coming. Out of nowhere, two men were wrestling across the table. Half a dozen others piled in and by the time it was over, there was blood on the table, a jagged white tooth fragment stark against the red.

And so today he wanted to use his broadcast to talk about fear again because fear underpinned every aspect of life in jail. Everyone was always afraid, even the kingpins and hard men. Maybe the kingpins and hard men most of all, because nobody had more to lose than them. He wanted to talk about that fear in a way that wouldn't sound like a challenge or an insult to their manhood. Because helping them to cope with their anxiety was the first step towards changing their future.

'There's one thing we all have in common inside these walls,' he said softly. 'Whether we're a prisoner or a prison officer. We're all living in a permanent state of fear.' He said it again, testing it for potential pitfalls.

'Acknowledging our fear, even if it's only to ourselves, isn't cowardice. It's the opposite of cowardice. It's bravery. Deep down, I think what we fear most is that we've become stuck in a way of life that means we're never going to escape the cycle of prison and its consequences. That it's going to be like the Hotel California. You can check out, but you can never leave.' That wasn't bad. Maybe a bit too formal, too jargon-heavy in the middle. And he should probably take out the reference to prison officers. Neither side of the dividing line would want to be lumped together on this one.

Where to now? 'Before I ended up here, I spent most of my working life trying to help people avoid their future being as much of a car crash as their past. The question outsiders asked me most often was how I could stand to spend my days being drawn into those messy lives, those messy heads. The answer's simple. Sometimes I could help them to rewrite the script. To give themselves a different future.' God, he sounded so bloody worthy. He was going to have to work on that. Make it more conversational, not like he was condescending to them. That would be a one-way ticket to a good kicking.

'Maybe you've lost heart about what lies ahead of you. Maybe you've lost your wife, your lover, your kids, your home already. I do understand what loss feels like, how empty you feel inside. I won't pretend there's an easy way to make those feelings disappear. But there are things you can do to help yourself feel better. To imagine a future that doesn't include coming back here.' And then he'd segue into the meditation script he'd been refining since his first broadcast.

He'd been afraid his fellow inmates would probably think it was a stupid hippy-dippy thing to try. But he'd known there were prisoners here who were a long way from being hopeless cases. A few of them might give meditation a go in the privacy of their own cells once they were banged up for the night. If they could learn how to turn themselves into their own oasis of quiet and calm in the midst of the turmoil, it would be a step towards a different future.

What was the worst that could happen, he'd asked himself. He didn't think he'd provoke anything more than a heavy dose of the verbals from some of the men whose self-image as hard men was more precarious than they'd ever admit. And he had to do something constructive with his time behind bars. It wasn't enough just to play to his own self-interest by writing his book.

It had played out better than he'd hoped. Not many of the men gave him positive feedback, but the jeering and the put-downs had gradually diminished. The hardcore hard cases left him alone these days. And every now and again, someone on the wing would mutter something positive in passing.

For the sake of his own self-respect, he'd had to find a way to use his skills. Otherwise he'd have been no better than the worst of them. And that was a judgement he couldn't face having to make.

20

One of the hardest things we have to do is learn to take responsibility for our own actions. Trying to sidestep actions that deep down we know are shameful is a powerful instinct.

From *Reading Crimes* by Dr Tony Hill

Jezza Martinu didn't look back to check that the woman cop was actually leaving. He thought that might look as if he had a guilty conscience. The cops and the forensic experts were totally occupied right now with excavating the remains and putting the jigsaw skeletons back together, but sooner or later, they were going to start asking different questions. Nobody would believe a bunch of nuns had dug those graves. Especially since most of them were knocking on a bit. Then the finger would point at him. And he'd better have his ducks in a row.

He unlocked the substantial shed at the bottom of his garden and stepped inside. He closed the door and leaned against it, breathing deeply until his heart stopped galloping like a runaway pony. He hung the hammer in its slot on the peg board that held his tools, checking first that it didn't need cleaning. Jezza took pride in his tools, just as he did in the quality of his work. He tried not to think about the examples of his work that the police were busily excavating right now.

Until he'd caught the woman peering in through his living room window, the only cop he'd spoken to had been a young lad in uniform. He looked like he'd have no trouble qualifying to play for the Vics' U21 side. He'd just taken a note of Jezza's name and his mobile number and a few details about his work. 'I mow the grass and keep the place tidy. I've got a long-term lease on the land around the vegetable beds for growing my own produce.' The cop had nodded and scribbled some notes.

But they'd be back.

Meanwhile, he had to keep busy. If he started fretting about what they might ask him and what he might say, he'd start to come apart at the seams. He couldn't afford to do that. He had far too much to lose.

Jezza turned to the large cardboard carton that occupied half the floor space of the shed. It had a certain resemblance to a cardboard coffin. He couldn't suppress a nervous snigger. What would that female cop have thought if she'd seen that?

He took down a craft knife and swiftly slit the adhesive tape that held the box shut. The top folded back to reveal a stack of MDF panels of different sizes. A packet of screws, dowels and hinges was taped to the side, along with a booklet of instructions. Under his expert hands, it would soon resolve itself into a cabinet that would provide the perfect storage for his collection of Bradfield Victoria programmes.

He'd already downloaded a graphic of the club crest and had it made into a pair of stencils for the cabinet door.

Jezza sighed with contentment. Assembling the cabinet then filing his programmes. Here was something to take his mind off the craziness going on beyond his front door.

Everything was going to be fine.

21

It's axiomatic that in order to read a crime scene, you have to know where the crime took place. That might seem insultingly self-evident, but appearances can be deceptive, especially if you're dealing with a killer who can keep a cool head. Seeing beyond that mask is the hardest part.

From *Reading Crimes* by Dr Tony Hill

Interview rooms in lawyers' offices had nothing in common with those in police stations. Carol supposed she'd better get used to that. There was something to be said for her new circumstances – a comfortable chair, a plate of expensive biscuits, a mug of decent coffee, a couple of impressively dramatic paintings of coastal landscapes on the wall . . . Even a box of tissues, just in case. And not a trace of recording equipment anywhere.

She had no nostalgia for her former working environment, however. She just wasn't sure this was somewhere she could comfortably use her skills. She glanced at her phone. Bronwen Scott was late. When Carol had called to say she was willing to have a further discussion, Bronwen had suggested meeting at her office during the lunchtime court recess, but Carol knew it was more than likely that something had cropped up in court that had encroached on the lawyer's time. She'd give her half an hour, then she'd have to leave for her next meeting.

Carol shook her head, smiling at herself. Overnight she'd gone from having nothing but time to being a woman with appointments. In spite of her best intentions, she found she didn't mind. She'd worked through her PTSD exercises before she'd left home and while she couldn't say she felt entirely in command of herself, she thought she could handle a couple of meetings.

On that thought, Bronwen Scott bustled into the room. 'Sorry, Carol. Tiny bit of hand-holding required.' She let herself fall into a chair with an 'oof' of relief. 'Thanks for coming in.'

Carol started to say something but Bronwen held up a hand and steamrollered over her. 'I know you're not committing to anything by being here, but I appreciate your willingness to even consider this.'

A tap on the door and a young man in shirtsleeves came in with a blue cardboard folder. 'The Neilson summary,' he said, handing it to Bronwen. He gave Carol a tight little smile and hustled out.

'That's John. He's a trainee and he's smart enough to know that volunteering on this will earn him a place in my good books.'

It was, Carol thought, precisely the sort of line people expected from Bronwen and she suspected that was the reason for its delivery. She nodded at the folder. 'This is the case?'

'Saul Neilson. Currently serving life for murder. He's thirty-one now, sentenced when he was twenty-eight for a crime he allegedly committed when he was twenty-seven. He was a landscape architect, living in Bradfield but working for a firm based in Leeds.' Bronwen opened the folder and passed it to Carol. The top sheet was a head shot of a scowling mixed-race man, brows drawn down over liquid brown eyes. There was nothing particularly striking about him, apart from his beautiful eyes. 'That's Saul.'

'Looks innocuous,' Carol said, non-committal.

'He is. No previous, never been in trouble with the law, happy at work, no beef of any substance with any of his colleagues. Member of the local squash club, round about the middle of the ranking ladder. Owned a high-end mountain bike, went out at weekends with a couple of mates.'

'Sounds like a model citizen.' Carol flipped to the next page. 'Until he was charged with the murder of Lyle Tate.' She looked up. 'Somebody's parents had a sweet tooth or a poor sense of humour.'

Bronwen scoffed. 'Or they were too thick to notice they were naming their lad after a bag of sugar. But, yes. Until he was charged with Lyle Tate's murder, he'd not put a foot wrong.'

'What's so special about this case?' Carol knew she'd find the answer in the file, but it was always helpful to hear what struck other people as important.

'It's a no body. They nailed him on circumstantial and the interpretation of the forensic evidence. He's always maintained his innocence, his explanation is credible. What we need is to find a loose thread to pull so we can unravel the prosecution case enough to get him in front of the Court of Appeal. And that's where a good investigator comes in.'

Bronwen gave her a cheerful grin. 'That would be you, in case you're in any doubt.'

'I've not said I'm in yet.' Carol could feel the stubborn set of her jaw muscles right up into her temples.

'You will be.' Bronwen stood up. 'You're welcome to stay here and read the file. Or take it away with you, if you prefer to work in your own space. I have to get back to court before the wheels come off. Bloody baby barristers who need propping up every step of the way.' Carol was glad not to be the bloody baby barrister in question. 'Get back to me when you're ready to talk strategy.'

And she was gone. The traits that made her such a formidable and irritating adversary could, Carol saw, make her a powerful and maybe even inspirational ally. She checked the time. She had just long enough to take a quick pass through the file before her next meeting. She could skim the surface, and if she was lucky, she'd stub her toe on something that disrupted its smoothness.

On the second page, she found the secret that had lurked behind Saul Neilson's public face. He was gay. Which was only an issue in the UK at this point in the twenty-first century if your father was a prominent Pentecostal Christian minister. A regular on *Thought for the Day.* Saul didn't want to hurt or disappoint or embarrass his parents – whom he loved and respected – so he hid that part of himself.

Her years as a cop working the twisted side of the street had taught Carol that a life of pretence always created tensions, pressures and fears that had a nasty habit of bursting like a boil, covering the conventional surface of a life with purulent fallout. So it had been for Saul Neilson. He'd avoided gay bars and clubs, but the advent of internet dating apps had allowed him finally to have a sex life, even if it was deeper in the closet than Narnia. But Saul didn't want to risk casual hook-ups that might have consequences; he preferred to keep the transactions businesslike so he used rent boys. Not via agencies, where there would be a record of credit card payments. No, Saul had gradually built up a small discreet stable of young men who would come to his flat for hectic sex, take their payment in cash, and leave. He was paranoid about his privacy, using burner phones to contact them and not going back too often to the same rent boy.

Carol paused for thought. No body cases were notoriously difficult to prove. Juries liked the incontrovertible fact of a corpse. Hell, detectives liked the incontrovertible fact of a corpse. Killers often believed that successfully disposing of a body meant they couldn't be successfully prosecuted. History had proved them wrong, time and time again. But those results gave the prosecution more ammunition to convince a jury that it was perfectly valid to convict on a supposition.

Was that what had happened to Saul Neilson? Based on her first look, Carol thought there was every chance that he was telling the truth. But finding evidence of that would be a long hard road, with no guarantee of success. And this time, she'd be doing it without backup. No Tony to help her make sense of the twists and turns of human behaviour. She wasn't sure whether she was ready for that.

But maybe she was ready to take a small step. Carol trusted her instincts and her skills. She'd give Saul Neilson the courtesy of reading his file with the attention she'd have paid to any case that had crossed her desk when she was running a murder squad. But that was all.

Something she could walk away from. Definitely.

22

I've always found it useful to see the crime scene while the body is in situ. It's a distressing experience but it's invariably more informative than crime scene photos. Once the initial discovery of the victim and the forensic examination of the crime scene have taken place, there's not much practical use for the profiler. Nevertheless, I try to stick around as much as I can, because not all the ideas that are tossed around in the investigation make it past the 'random thought' stage. And you never know which shreds of information will illuminate the profiler's process down the line.

From *Reading Crimes* by DR TONY HILL

Stacey considered she had good reason to feel pleased with herself. From the electoral roll she had the official names of the nuns who had been at the Blessed Pearl when it had closed down. Unofficial access to the last census had given her ages for most of them. Armed with that knowledge, official registers had given her dates of birth for almost all of them. She'd cross-checked with the electoral rolls that covered the other three UK convents and discovered that all but two of the Bradesden nuns had ended up there.

Knowing that her colleague preferred hard copies, she took the printouts across to Paula and laid them out in front of her. 'I think it's reasonable to assume that these two apparently missing nuns' – she tapped two names with her Blackwing pencil – 'have ended up in the order's house in Galway. I managed to get hold of the convent rosters.' She shuffled the papers and put a different one in front of Paula.

'I'm not going to ask.'

'Good move. By the process of elimination, the two nun aliases not accounted for in the English convents are Sister Mary Patrick and Sister Brigid Augustine.'

'Sister Mary Patrick was the Mother Superior,' Paula said, thoughtful. 'Makes you wonder if the church found out what had been going on at Bradesden and decided to close the place down while the going was good.'

'If they knew, then surely they wouldn't have sold the site for development?'

'Good point. Maybe they knew there was abuse going on but didn't realise the extent of it?'

Stacey shrugged. 'That would make more sense. You'd think they might have wondered where all those kids were going, though.'

'Easy enough to cover up. "They've gone back to their family." "They've been adopted." "They left school and went to college somewhere else."'

'Are we at least going to interview the nuns?' Karim demanded from the other side of the desk.

'I'd like to track down some of the girls and talk to them first. We need a pressure point and so far we've not got that from the remains. We've got to nail down at least approximate dates for some of them and we won't have that till forensics come back to us with something concrete. Alvin called to say they think they can make some headway with clothes labels, but that'll take time,' Paula said.

Right on cue, Steve pushed open the door and swaggered in. 'Ask me who managed to get information out of social services?' he called across the room.

'Did you use the thumbscrews?' Paula asked.

'Didn't even have to get out the cattle prod,' Steve said. He produced a bundle of printed sheets with a flourish. 'Ta da.'

Paula almost snatched them from him and quickly glanced through. Her excitement turned to disappointment. 'Is that it? Seven girls?'

'The local authority didn't have responsibility for the others. They came from other places – families who couldn't cope, recommendations from parish priests, whatever. So the social workers didn't know anything about them.'

'What? All those girls and nobody even knew who was there?'

Steve gestured at the records he'd obtained. 'That's all there is, boss. I agree with you, it's totally fucked up, but that's how it is.'

Paula sighed. 'It's not much to go on. We only know where one of them is, and that's a secure unit for teenagers with mental health problems.'

Steve shrugged. 'I know, it's not a sparkling start. But these are outcomes that tell us something about the regime at the Blessed Pearl. These girls definitely didn't come away from that place happy and well-balanced, did they?'

'It doesn't seem that way,' Karim said, leaning across and taking a look at the papers. 'But on the other hand, I have no idea how that compares with outcomes for kids in care generally speaking.'

'Either way, it's not good.'

Stacey picked up the paperwork. 'I'll see if I can track any of them down.' She skimmed the details. 'The one who went back to her dad or the over-eighteens might be our best bet.'

'Nobody really cares about kids that fall off the radar, do they?' Karim sounded disgusted. 'We get all sentimental about kids, but the truth is, soon as they get to be a problem, they're disposable.'

Nobody said anything but they all had a shamefaced air as they set about returning to the investigation. Stacey leaned into Paula and said, 'I'll get to this as soon as I can. I've just got to nip out for a quick meeting.'

Paula nodded. 'No problem. I'll get on to the hospital, see whether there's any point talking to what's-her-name. The one with anorexia.'

Stacey rolled her eyes. 'Call yourself a detective? You not going to ask who I'm meeting?'

'Who are you meeting, Stacey?' Paula asked with artificial brightness.

Stacey was three strides away before she said, 'Carol Jordan.'

Paula's mouth fell open. Stacey and Carol? What was that about? And why was she only hearing about it now? She knew it was a childish reaction, but she was Carol's friend, not Stacey. What was going on? She half-rose from her chair then fell back again. She'd find out soon enough, after all. If Stacey planned on keeping it a secret, she wouldn't have told Paula about their appointment.

Would she?

And then her phone rang and all thoughts of this strange meeting were banished. The voice at the other end of the phone was abrupt and to the point. 'PC Diamond at the front desk, ma'am. I've got a young woman here says she wants to talk to you about the Blessed Pearl.'

23

The psychologist who is brought in to participate in a criminal investigation and to draw up a profile of a killer or a serious sexual offender should apply their skills not only to the victim and the perpetrator but also to the police officers attached to the inquiry. Their predispositions and biases can shape not only the investigation but also the way the case is presented to the psychologist. And that can lead to an unfortunate amount of galumphing up blind alleys. Always consider the mindset of your supposed allies!

From *Reading Crimes* by DR TONY HILL

Carol had chosen the rendezvous with Stacey with some care. Pubs were out. Too many cops escaped there for a swift respite at any time of the day or night, especially pubs within walking distance of their base. Coffee shops, for the same reason. So she'd suggested the City Art Gallery, a mere five minutes' walk from ReMIT's squad room in Skenfrith

Street. It might as well have been on another planet. Carol would have bet hard cash that the overwhelming majority of officers stationed in Skenfrith Street would struggle even to give directions to the imposing Edwardian building. It was the visual equivalent of elevator music.

She had suggested the first-floor gallery housing a couple of large Turner landscapes. She'd always liked Turner, ever since her father had taken her to the National Gallery. Neither of them knew much about art but he'd thought it would be an interesting day out. Carol had fallen in love with *Rain, Steam and Speed* and *The Fighting Temeraire*. She'd had prints of them on her wall all through university, and even now she had a print of *Westminster Sunset* on her bedroom wall. The pair that hung in the Bradfield gallery were not his finest work but she reckoned they knocked spots off almost anything else in the building.

Carol sat on a padded leather bench facing the larger of the two paintings, a view of a Northumberland landscape in a chilly winter light. It reminded her of the moor above her barn on frosty mornings when she and Flash had climbed up to the ridge to catch the sunrise, the only figures in the landscape. Tony seldom joined her at that time of day; it was a safe memory for her, no painful tug at the heart here.

She felt rather than saw Stacey join her. A displacement of the cushion under her, a faint waft of the citrus sharp fragrance she used. 'Afternoon, boss,' Stacey said.

'I'm not your boss any more, Stacey. Call me Carol.' She turned in time to catch Stacey looking appalled.

'I don't think I'd ever be able to do that,' she said. 'It just feels wrong.'

'So does "boss".' Carol hoped her regret didn't show. 'Just say, "hey, you!"'

'Or not.' Stacey gave her a faint smile. 'Nice painting. Excellent choice. It's good to see you. How are you?'

'I'm still standing. Well, I'm working at it. And you? How is it being back in ReMIT?'

'It feels very different. I don't think DCI Rutherford gets us.'

Carol surprised herself by chuckling. 'Let's face it, Stacey, he'd have to be pretty special to do that. He does have a good reputation, though.'

'He's a bit gung-ho.' She cut her eyes at Carol. 'We had a team-building exercise on Monday.'

Her intonation was the prompt her words weren't. Carol obeyed. 'And how was that?'

Permission granted, Stacey told her. Without the sort of bold embellishment Paula would have given the tale, but leaving Carol in no doubt as to the level of effectiveness of the team building. And the quality of their new recruits. 'At least you know a bit more about the newbies now,' Carol said, her tone wry.

'And we walked straight back into a case. The skeletons in the convent?'

'Really? I heard about it on the news.' Carol was surprised but tried not to show it. 'Historic remains? Not a ReMIT kind of thing, I'd have thought.'

'We're not sure how historic. Either way, the DCI can't wait to get stuck in. It's a bit of a dog's breakfast, to be honest. I can't stay out too long. I've got analyses to do for Paula. It's not that I don't want to catch up – I do, of course ...'

It was one of the longer speeches Carol had heard from Stacey. She didn't do overt emotional displays. Not even during her ill-fated relationship with Sam Evans. Though the pair had been close colleagues, she hadn't guessed from

Stacey's demeanour that there was anything more between them. It was only after it was over, when Sam's career had crashed and burned, that Paula had filled Carol in on the relationship and the break-up. Carol didn't like herself for the suspicion, but she couldn't help wondering whether Sam's fall from grace had included a push from his former lover's cyber skills. Not a woman you'd want to cross, she thought.

'I need a favour,' Carol said. 'But then, you'll have worked that out for yourself.'

Stacey shrugged. 'It's OK. The kind of history we've got – favours are part of our DNA.'

Carol acknowledged the truth of that with a dip of her chin. 'Did you ever meet Tony's mother? Vanessa?'

Stacey's immediate impassivity was the equivalent of breathless interest in anyone else. 'I never met her. What I know, I know from Paula. I think that's probably more than enough.'

'Can't disagree with that. Tony says she's a classic narcissist. Me, I think she's just a bitch. But she's a bitch who knows how to manipulate people. And right now, I'm the one she's manipulating.' Carol closed her eyes momentarily and breathed slow and deep. Then she straightened up and told Stacey what she was obliged to do for Vanessa. It got no prettier in the telling.

'I'm sorry to drag you into this,' she said. 'But I don't know anybody else who can find this information for me. I've tracked down Harrison Gardner's son's details. He's called Oliver—' She pulled a folded sheet of paper from her satchel. 'His birth certificate. He's seventeen, which narrows down the window for the setting up of the trust and the purchase of the cottage. I can't access the Land Registry—'

'I can,' Stacey said flatly.

'It's a big ask.'

Stacey grinned. 'No. It's really not. It's mildly tedious to winnow through the results but it's not *difficult*. Northumberland, you say?'

'That's what Vanessa said. On the coast, with a view of Holy Island.'

'I'll leave that bit up to you, if you don't mind. I'll get you a list of properties that changed hands in the time window with owners that might fit what you're looking for, but winnowing them down with an OS map? That's up to you.'

'I wouldn't expect you to do that end of it,' Carol said. 'I'm after a favour, not martyrdom.'

'What are you going to do when you find him?'

Carol breathed in heavily through her nose. 'Speak softly but carry a big stick. He's met Vanessa, after all. That should be enough to persuade him to hand over the readies.'

'From what I've heard, I'd say you're probably right.' Stacey stood up. 'I need to get back. It's been good to see you. I'll be in touch when I have something for you. Maybe we could all meet up for dinner? You and me and Paula?'

'I'd like that,' Carol said, taken aback to find she meant it. 'Good luck with the nuns.'

Stacey drew down the corners of her mouth. 'Now there's an institution that knows how to keep its secrets. You wouldn't believe how much of the Catholic church's records are still on paper. It's like they were behind the door when the digital revolution happened.'

'Let's hope you get a proper ReMIT case before too long.'

Stacey shook her head. 'I'm being very careful what I wish for these days. Take care.' She'd taken two steps when she stopped and turned back. 'Carol. Take care.'

24

Sifting through the evidence, however well-prepared it is, can only take us so far. There comes a point when the profiler has to sit down with witnesses and investigators in an attempt to give amorphous shape to the perpetrator.

From *Reading Crimes* by DR TONY HILL

Paula studied the young woman sitting opposite her in the interview room. She'd have put Louise Brand in her mid- to late-twenties. Her long dark hair was pulled back in a ponytail which did her slightly pudgy face no favours. Her brows had been severely plucked, her mascara so thickly applied it had clumped in places. She'd chewed off most of her pale pink lipstick, revealing chapped skin underneath. A line of silver star-shaped studs ran up the helix of her left ear.

'Thanks for coming in to talk to us, Louise. I understand you spent some time living in the St Margaret Clitherow Refuge? And going to the school there.'

Louise took a deep shuddering breath. 'I don't know if I'm doing the right thing, but I saw about the bodies on the news this morning and it freaked me out.'

'I'm not surprised.' That was all Paula managed before Louise was off again.

'Because I might have known some of them, with me being there for the best part of three years. And some lasses did just vanish. We were told their families had come for them, or they were being adopted, or they'd had an accident and had to go to hospital and when they didn't come back, the nuns just brushed it off, said they'd been moved to another kids' home where they'd fit in better. And now it looks like that were a load of bollocks.' She ran out of steam and looked around her. 'I bet I can't smoke in here, right?'

Paula nodded. 'I'm afraid not.'

'Typical. And then when my dad came back for me, well, it kind of made me believe what the nuns had said. Because that's what did happen to me.'

'I want to take you through this in order,' Paula said patiently. 'But first, I need some details about you.'

Some witnesses needed to be drawn out carefully and thoughtfully. Some drowned their interviewer in a torrent of information, inference, rumour, gossip and speculation. Paula knew already which kind Louise was. Within minutes, she had permission to record their conversation; the woman's full name; a d.o.b. that put her a few years younger than Paula had guessed; the address where she lived with her father and her stepmother, though Louise didn't think of her as the motherly type, not like her own mum who had died, and besides, her dad wasn't married to the new one; the name of the pub where she worked five nights a week, on the books like a proper person, nothing dodgy there; and that she was studying for a Certificate of Higher Education in Children and Families at the Open University. Paula was experienced enough not to show her surprise at that last piece of information and chided herself mentally for being too quick to judge.

'I didn't do well at school. Margaret Clitherow put me right off, and I never really settled after that, but I want to work with children. Maybe be a nursery worker or even a nanny and I saw about the Open University on the telly and I thought, that's not for the likes of you, Lou, but my boss at work, she said I should go for it. So I did,' Louise blurted out. 'It's weird, doing homework at my age, but it turns out I'm quite good at it. Who knew?'

'Good for you. It's never too late. So, can you tell me when you were at St Margaret Clitherow?'

'Maggie Clit, we used to call it.' Louise sniggered. 'I didn't even know what a clit was when I went there. I was nine. And I was there till just before my twelfth birthday. You can do the sums.'

'How did you end up there?'

Louise's spark dimmed. 'My mum got cancer. She was proper poorly, and I was a wild little madam. Then she died, and I went even more wild. Stealing from the local shops, but in a totally crap way, like I didn't care if I was caught or not. Stopping out late, bunking off school, being a right bastard to my dad. He couldn't manage, poor sod. He couldn't deal with his own grief because I was using up all his energy. The parish priest said he could put me into Maggie Clit's till I'd calmed down and got it out of my system, then my dad could bring me home. So I got dumped with that bunch of sadistic cows. I thought it would just be for a couple of weeks, but it ended up being nearly three years. I cried myself to sleep wishing for my dad to come back for bloody months.' For a moment, she had nothing more to say, silenced by the weight of the memory.

'Did your dad not visit?'

A bitter laugh and a knitting of the forehead. 'Twice, he came. At the time, I thought he was getting his own back on me for being such a total shit to him. But after I went home, I fronted him up about it and he said the nuns told him to stay away. That it made the girls unsettled if their families visited. It was all about making their lives easier – those bitches. He'd wanted to see me. He'd even come to the Blessed Pearl a couple of other times and they made excuses. Said I was out on a day trip. Which was bollocks, because we never went out on day trips. It was like being in jail.'

Paula let the silence grow, respecting the other woman's corrosive memories. Then she said softly, 'How did they treat you?'

Louise picked at the skin round her thumbnail. 'It was harsh.' She met Paula's eyes, her own bright with unshed tears. 'There was a lot of talk there about the love of God but not one of them ever showed us a scrap of love. There were rules about everything. When you went to bed. When you got up. How often you had a shower and how long for. What you were allowed to wear. When you had to shut up and when you could talk and what you were allowed to talk about.' She shook her head, uneasy at the memory.

'And what happened if you broke the rules?' Paula probed gently.

'You were punished.' Louise rubbed her eyes with her fingertips, shedding mascara on her cheeks.

'Punished how?'

'Depends what you'd done. They had ... I suppose you'd have to call them punishment cells. Just a tiny bare room with nothing except a bucket to piss and shit in. No mattress, no blanket, no nothing. You'd get locked in there overnight. Or sometimes for two or three nights. No food, just a cup of water twice a day. It was freezing in the winter and roasting in the summer. You wouldn't treat a dog like that, not legally.'

Now Paula could feel the slow burn of anger in her belly. 'You definitely shouldn't treat a child like that. Did that ever happen to you?'

Louise blinked hard. A tiny tear escaped from the corner of one eye. 'Just the once. I refused to eat my dinner. It was liver and onions.' She shuddered. 'I've always hated liver. It's the texture as much as the taste. Yuck. And they cooked it till it was like shoe leather. One of the nuns dragged me away from the table by the hair. Then they grabbed my arms so tight I had bruises and took me to the punishment cell. I was bloody terrified. I thought I was going mad. I tell you, I never refused liver again. But even the smell of it makes me gag to this day.'

'I can imagine. Were there other punishments handed out by the nuns?'

Louise sighed. 'You bet. They stuck to the bible. You know that bit where it says, "spare the rod and spoil the child"? They made bloody sure we weren't going to be spoilt. The lowest level of physical punishment was the ruler. You remember those thin rulers we had in school? Wooden or plastic, about thirty centimetres long? Well, they'd set those against the back of your legs or your hands, bend them back and then let them go. You wouldn't think something so little could cause so much pain, but it was bloody excruciating.

Especially on the backs of your hands. There's no flesh there to protect you.' She grimaced and rubbed the backs of her hands as if she were washing them.

'I bet that stung. One of the boys in my class once did that on the back of my thigh, I was wearing trousers, but I can still remember how it burned.'

'That wasn't enough for Sister Mary Patrick. The Mother Superior. She had a leather belt, a proper heavy-duty one. Girls would get a beating with the belt for what she reckoned were serious crimes. Like being cheeky to a nun or being late for Mass. There was a story went the rounds that sometimes she'd use the buckle end of the belt.'

The thought of what that could do to the fragile body of a growing girl made Paula feel physically sick.

Louise studied Paula's face, as if weighing something in the balance. Her lips tightened, then she said, 'Maybe it was just the older girls trying to frighten the little kids. But there were stories that Sister Mary Patrick didn't always know when to stop.'

25

One of the first serial offenders I profiled was a sadistic rapist who specialised in dumping his victims at sites where other women had previously been murdered. He told his victims the gruesome history of the places as part of his strategy to force their silence. Not so much revisiting the scene of the crime as annexing the horror of someone else's.

From *Reading Crimes* by DR TONY HILL

It was only a slight detour for Alvin to visit the crime scene on his way to the office. He wanted to see the place for himself, to fix it in his mind's eye so that as evidence began to trickle in, he could place it within his own mental map. He was luckier than Sophie; there was space in the car park by the time he arrived.

As he walked towards the mobile incident room, he took in the extent of the convent and its grounds. With the right people in charge, this could have been an amazing place to grow up. Space to run around. Trees to climb, countryside to go for walks. What had happened instead felt like a double whammy.

He checked in at the mobile incident room then headed for the blue tent. He found an extra-large protective suit in the pile by the door and was soon almost anonymous within its folds. Bootees over his shoes, gloves on his hands and a face mask completed his camouflage. It wasn't that he was hiding; he just didn't want to draw attention to himself. He had a feeling the new boss wouldn't be happy at his officers going off piste. Rutherford would find out soon enough that was how ReMIT functioned. But Alvin didn't feel the need to be first out of the gate.

He spotted the diminutive figure of DCI Fielding and headed in the opposite direction. The very protective gear that disguised him made it hard to identify someone he could count on to fill him in on the details of the investigation. Frustrated, he headed out of the far side of the tent to where the excavation work was being carried out. It looked like a deep gash had been ploughed in the earth a couple of metres wide and about fifty metres long, and teams of white-suited figures were working their way along it, trowels and brushes in hand. Cameras on tripods had been set up alongside, flashguns firing at intervals. They would, he knew, provide a record of the excavations being carried out.

He walked past the trench, keeping well away from the edge. Halfway along, an officer was standing with a clipboard. As he drew near, Alvin recognised him as one of the CID aides at Skenfrith Street. He couldn't remember the lad's name, but he could be fairly sure he'd be recognised. Even now there weren't many black detectives in Bradfield, and certainly none as distinctive as him.

Alvin stopped beside the aide and nodded a greeting. 'You registering finds?'

'Yeah. I just make a brief note and send them inside. That's where the real work's being done.' He sounded wistful. Alvin couldn't blame him. Nobody wanted to be a glorified clerk on an investigation like this.

'Tell me what I'm looking at,' he said.

The lad flashed him a quick look of surprise. 'The developers sent the bulldozers in yesterday morning. First off, they sent a ripper down. That's a sort of blade they put on the back of a 'dozer to literally rip the ground up. Behind it goes the actual bulldozer with the big blade that kind of digs the trench. The driver of the second bulldozer was about halfway along when he saw the ripper kicking up what looked like a skull. By the time he'd stopped and shouted to the foreman that there was a problem, the ripper had gone right along to the end. And when they looked closer, they could see what looked like a lot of bones. They were a bit stained from being in the earth, but they could still see they were bones.' He pulled a face. 'Especially the skulls. Little skulls, Sarge. It turns your stomach.'

Alvin had children. He understood the power of finding remains like these. 'I bet,' he said. 'So who's doing the excavations? We don't have enough forensic specialists round here for something on this scale, surely?'

'They contacted Manchester University. They've got a big archaeology department. They sent a whole team out this morning. More to come tomorrow, apparently. There's a squad from the forensic science course at Bradfield Uni in the tent, helping to sort out the bones. It's massive, Sarge.'

'A bit of a nightmare,' Alvin agreed. 'And we don't even know if there's anything criminal gone on.'

This time the aide didn't hide his surprise. 'Well, there's something. I heard DCI Fielding telling her team that they've spoken to the top nun at the Order of the Blessed Pearl and there's been no authorised burials here aside from the nuns round the back. So at the very least, it's illegal disposal of the bodies.'

'I get that. But we don't know yet when that happened. They've been here since 1930. We don't have any professional interest in anything older than seventy years. So it might not be anywhere near our remit.'

His face fell. 'I hadn't thought of that. That'll be why Fielding's in such a bad mood. This'll totally bust her budget. And she might not have owt to show for it.'

She might not have anything to show for it either way, Alvin thought. If there was glory to be had here, he had a hunch DCI Rutherford would be hugging it to his chest like a newborn. 'It's got to be done, though.' Alvin clapped the aide on the shoulder and carried on along the trench. When he reached the end and rounded the corner of the convent building, he noticed the raised beds and neat rows of vegetables arrayed along the far side of the grounds. It wasn't the horticulture that interested him, however.

It was the dog handler moving towards the cultivated area with her golden retriever. What piqued his curiosity was that Alvin happened to know this was no regular police dog partnership. He recognised the woman trotting alongside the handsome dog because he'd encountered her back when he'd still been with West Mercia, before Carol Jordan had recruited him for ReMIT. Sergeant Josy Rivera had brought her dog Paco along to one of the regular training weekends officers had to attend to maintain current knowledge of procedures and forensic developments.

The course had been held in a hotel with a health club and swimming pool. Josy had asked them to meet her in the locker room at the start of the session for a practical demonstration. Even Alvin's human nose could detect a variety of scents – chlorine, sweat, the chemical fragrances of deodorants, hair products and colognes. 'In one of these lockers is a dead rabbit,' Sergeant Rivera had said. 'It's wrapped in clingfilm and double-bagged in sealed plastic bags. One of your colleagues brought it here this morning and decided where to put it. Even I don't know which locker it's in.' She waved a key at them. 'I have the key, but as you can see, there's no number tag attached to it.'

She'd brought Paco in and immediately the dog had reacted with excitement, his tail sweeping to and fro, sniffing the air and casting back and forth. Within two minutes, he'd jumped up on a bench and directed their attention to one locker in particular. When Sergeant Rivera opened it, there was the packaged rabbit, just as she'd described it.

There had been a talk afterwards. Because the demonstration had been so effective, even to this day he could remember bits and pieces of what she'd said. Dogs have a sense of smell that's up to a thousand times more powerful than humans. The man sitting next to Alvin had leaned across to mutter, 'And yet they sniff each other's arses. No accounting for taste.'

It took up to two years to train a cadaver dog, mostly because human bodies produce more than four hundred different volatile chemicals as they go through the five basic stages of decomposition. To help train the dogs, an American chemical company had produced synthetic corpse scents. Among them, Alvin vividly recalled, were 'recently dead' and 'decomposed'. Not the sort of fragrance you'd be spraying on if you were hoping for a romantic evening.

'If you've been to the scene of a death, you'll have experienced some of those smells,' Rivera had said, and the room full of hardened cops had all shifted in their seats. 'Rotting flesh, urine, faeces, something like extreme halitosis. What you're getting is the orchestral equivalent of a triangle. The dog gets the full symphony.'

Long after a body had been buried, those scents carried on telling tales. It made perfect sense to Alvin that Paco and his handler had been called in. Scientists were working on a machine that would be even more sensitive than the dogs, but that was a long way off yet. There were only a handful of cadaver dogs in the whole country; he supposed Paco was based closest to hand. Given the discovery of so many human remains, it would have been negligent not to examine the rest of the convent grounds just in case there were even more.

He thought about going over to say hello, but decided it wouldn't be welcome while dog and handler were working. But he'd move a little closer and watch them for a while. He was intrigued to see the dog quartering the area, nose to the ground then rising to sniff the air, then back to snuffle at the grass and the earth.

Alvin had been watching for less than fifteen minutes when Paco's behaviour altered suddenly. The dog's hindquarters dropped to the ground and he began to growl. Four deep barks, then a pause. Four more barks, and Rivera was at his side, feeding him treats from a pouch on her belt. Alvin broke into a run and reached her as she was radioing through to the incident room.

'The dog's found something,' he heard her say. 'Round the side by the vegetable patch. I need a team here now.'

26

Children who have experienced extreme trauma in childhood often find it difficult to produce appropriate responses to trauma in later life. Sometimes they can't cry. Often they are unable to articulate what they're feeling and fear the consequences if they were to speak. It's one of the reasons why victims of child sex abuse struggle with coming forward afterwards. They come to believe that the sky will fall if they speak the unspeakable.

From *Reading Crimes* by DR TONY HILL

Every interview had a tipping point. On one side, triumph. On the other, car crash. Paula had always had an instinct for that moment. Carol Jordan had spotted her talent for drawing witnesses and suspects into revelations they hadn't intended to make, and over the years, Paula had seized every opportunity to take courses to refine her skills. Elinor had once observed that when it came to the secrets we keep, she had no defences against her partner, but they both knew that was a tease. Somehow, when it came to worming information out of Elinor, and now Torin, Paula never quite succeeded as well as her track record at work might have suggested. Even the best have blind spots.

When it came to the battle of wills in the interview room, however, she felt confident that she could usually find a way to the truth. It was partly an empathetic understanding of what people needed to hear and partly her ability to make even the most defensive and suspicious individual believe she felt sympathy for them. There were occasions when she wished she could scrub the inside of her head after someone had divulged the dark perversions at the root of their lives. But she consoled herself that she was helping to clean the streets.

So she met Louise Brand's frightened blinking with an even gaze. 'You've been carrying this inside for a long time, Louise. It's time to share the weight. I know you want to break your silence, and this is a safe place for you to do that. Nobody here is judging you. What do you mean when you say Sister Mary Patrick didn't always know when to stop?'

Louise picked ferociously at the skin round her thumb. A jagged line of blood oozed out. 'It was just what some girls said. You know what teenage girls are like. They pick up on something and nothing and spin a whole story out of it.'

'It's preyed on your mind all these years, though. There must have been something about what they said that made you think there was truth in it?'

Louise sighed, her eyes pleading. 'Look, I don't have any evidence. There were ... incidents. This girl in my family group – they called us family groups, which was just laughable because so many of the girls came from dysfunctional families and now they'd been shunted into a so-called family that was every bit as fucked-up as what they'd left behind. Anyway, this girl in my family group, Jaya her name was, she got caught stealing food from the kitchen – which was fucked-up in itself because the food was so shit. But we were always on starvation rations, always hungry, so Jaya stole some bread rolls from the kitchen, only she got caught.' She ran out of momentum and stopped.

Paula waited, then prompted her gently, 'What happened to Jaya?'

'Thou shalt not steal. Seventh Commandment. The nuns were shit hot on the Ten Commandments. It's a pity the bible didn't think of including, "Thou shalt not batter the living daylights out of the children in your care."' Bitter anger was creeping into Louise's voice now. 'One of the nuns hit her so hard with a rolling pin she broke her arm.'

Medical records, Paula thought. There had to be medical records. 'Did they take Jaya to hospital?'

Louise made a scornful noise. 'Did they buggery! A couple of the nuns were trained nurses, they dealt with everything in-house. Except a couple of times. One girl had a burst appendix, she'd been complaining of stomach pains for days but they paid no bloody attention. Another one – I don't know exactly what happened but she was asthmatic and she got a bad chest infection. Anyway, both times they weren't there one morning. Supposedly they were off to hospital, but they didn't come back. One of the girls in my family group asked when the asthmatic lass was coming back and Sister Catherine just said they'd sent her to the convent in Ireland because the sea air would do her good.' She looked close to tears. 'But now there's all these skeletons turning up . . . What if they never went to hospital at all?'

'We'll be doing our best to establish the identities of the

people buried in the grounds. Right now, we don't even know how long they've been there. It might be that they were all buried there years before you ever went to St Margaret Clitherow.' Paula's voice was calm and reassuring even though inside she was raging. What sort of interpretation of Christianity was this? It gave a whole new meaning to 'suffer little children'.

'That was always the story we got when girls disappeared: they'd been sent to Ireland for the sea air. Or they'd been sent to York because they'd made unsuitable friendships. Or their parents had turned up and reclaimed them, which I always thought was bollocks until it happened to me, so maybe that story was true. But other times, girls were sent to the punishment cells and we never saw them again.' She looked down at the table and let out a long, shuddering breath. 'I think maybe we wanted to believe what we were told because the alternative was just too grim to take in.'

'I'd have been the same, I'm sure. When you know people, even if they're deeply unpleasant, it's hard to picture them as killers.' A pause. 'The ill-treatment – was it just the Mother Superior, Sister Mary Patrick, who carried it out?'

Louise shook her head. 'No. It was standard treatment. The old nuns were the worst, they treated us like dirt. Talk about taking the sins of the parents out on the children – it was what they lived by. Because we'd ended up there, we were automatically sinners. It felt like they were determined to beat the sin out of us. There were three or four of the younger sisters who still had a bit of kindness about them, but only when the old bitches weren't looking.'

'Did you or any of your friends ever consider complaining?'

There was naked despair in Louise's face. 'Complain? Who could we complain to? The priest didn't want to know. If you talked to him, he'd grass you up to Sister Mary Patrick. Same if you wrote to your family or spoke out of turn to anybody visiting the perfect bloody Maggie Clit school. Sister Mary Patrick just turned on the charm and reminded them that these girls were here because nobody else could manage them, lying came to them as easily as breathing. And God help you when she got her hands on you afterwards.' She scoffed. 'What am I saying? God help you? He never helped us.'

'After you went back to live with your father, did you ever tell him what went on inside the convent?'

Louise chewed her bottom lip. 'No. Sister Mary Patrick said that if I ever spoke a word against her or any of the nuns, she would destroy any chance I had of making my way in the world. She'd tell everyone what a lying, scheming, thieving little bitch I was.' Tears pricked her eyes. 'You're not Catholic, are you?'

Paula shook her head. 'I'm nothing.'

'The Church still has massive power over people's lives. Even though you know in your heart you should be able to stand up to what they threaten you with, it's hard to defy them. There are a lot of good people in the Church, don't get me wrong. But we're just beginning to find out now how many evil people did terrible things to children and hid behind the Church to get away with it.' A single tear trickled down her cheek. 'Even now, today, I feel like a traitor. I bet hardly anybody's come forward out of all the girls who went through Maggie Clit's.'

'You're the only one so far.' Paula owed her that. 'You're the bravest, no question.'

Louise shook her head. 'I'm not brave. I'm bloody terrified. My dad and his wife, they go to Mass. If this comes out, if I have to go to court and talk about this, it'll blow a hole in their lives. But all those dead kids – somebody has to speak for them, right?'

Before Paula could answer, there was a soft tap at the door and Karim poked his head into the room. He flashed a smile at Louise, then said, 'I'm sorry to interrupt, guv, but you're needed upstairs. Now.'

'Thanks, Karim.' He withdrew and Paula turned back to face Louise. 'I think you've maybe had enough of an ordeal for today anyway. I will be back in touch with you, and in the meantime it would be very helpful if you could make a list for me of all the girls you can remember. And all the nuns too.'

Louise nodded, gathering herself together and sniffing hard. 'You've been really lovely, thank you for believing me.'

Paula knew they would go over every detail of Louise's story but she had no doubt it would check out. Sometimes, you just knew. She showed Louise out of the station and headed back upstairs. Karim was hovering outside the squad room. 'What's going on?' Paula demanded. 'That was a key interview. Lucky for you we were at a good place to break.'

'They've found more bodies out at the Blessed Pearl,' he said. 'Only these ones are different.'

27

It's always easier to do the same thing than to reinvent the wheel. But sometimes we need to examine our way of going about things to see whether we might be able to do it more effectively. We need to be willing to integrate new elements into our process if we're to avoid becoming stale and inflexible.

From *Reading Crimes* by Dr Tony Hill

Given that meditation was supposed to produce a sense of calm and well-being, an observer would have to conclude that Tony Hill hadn't quite got the hang of it. At the end of his first fifteen-minute broadcast, he'd looked more like a man who'd just been for a run. Uphill and into a strong wind. His face had been red, his body perspiring and his hands clenched into fists. He'd hoped his listeners had achieved a greater level of inner harmony. Otherwise he'd probably not have a second chance behind the mic.

He'd peeled the headphones off as Razor Wireless segued into a pre-recorded preview of the weekend's football. He'd leaned back in the chair and exhaled, rolling his head and feeling the crepitation in his neck. Then he'd jumped to his feet, trying to look like a man on top of his game and given a thumbs-up to Spoony on the other side of the glass. Spoony's face had been impassive and he'd turned away to fiddle with the faders on his deck. Nervous, Tony had emerged from the booth and grinned at Tweedledum and Tweedledummer. 'All right?' he'd said.

Spoony had glanced across at him. 'Never heard anything like it. Quite fucking remarkable.' No clue in his tone as to whether that was a good or a bad thing.

'I suppose it's hard to tell, when you're working in here rather than listening to it in your cell. I guess I'll just have to wait for feedback from the listeners, eh?' Tony had known he was gabbling but he couldn't stop himself.

Spoony's mouth had twisted in a one-sided grin. 'You'll get feedback, all right. Same time next week, then? Unless we get overwhelmed with negative criticism, obviously.'

Tony could still remember how embarrassed he'd been at the level of relief he felt. He hadn't been that desperate for approval since he'd been trying to impress his PhD supervisor with the innovative brilliance of his thinking.

'Load of bollocks, mind,' Tweedledum had muttered as Tony left to walk back down the block to his cell.

He had a feeling he was going to hear that again before the day was out. But he made it back to his wing that first time without encountering anyone eager to share their response. Or maybe they just didn't know who he was. He'd almost reached the sanctuary of his cell when Kieran came bounding up to him. 'That was all right,' he said, giving Tony a friendly punch to the shoulder. 'Never done nothing like that before and I got no idea if I was doing it right, and I did feel a bit of a divvie, but I can see there might be something in it.'

'Thanks. I felt a bit like I was walking out on a high wire. I hope everybody's as chilled about it as you are.'

'I doubt it, mate. You'll probably get the piss taken out of you something chronic, but I don't think anybody's going to deck you over it.'

That had been months ago. Now Tony arrived at his cell to find Kieran leaning against the door jamb. From his back pocket, he pulled a tightly folded newspaper. He'd somehow acquired a friendly prison officer who passed him a paper every couple of days. It was never that morning's edition, and it was only ever a tabloid, but it was a slender line of connection to the outside world. Kieran tossed it over to him. Caught by surprise, Tony nearly fumbled it but managed a comedy save. Since he'd joined the Razor Wireless community, Tony had earned the right to share this bounty.

'Page four,' Kieran said. 'Right up your street, I would have thought.'

He waited while Tony found the page and read the story of human remains found in the grounds of a convent on the outskirts of Bradfield. He vaguely remembered Bradesden. Part of the canal network ran across the edge of the village and he'd cruised down there one summer's afternoon in *Steeler* with Paula, Elinor and Torin. They'd had a picnic in a charming little basin a mile or so further down then returned to his mooring in Minster Basin. In his mind's eye, he summoned up a straggle of low cottages and a square church tower. Nothing that resembled a convent, though.

Up to forty sets of bones, apparently. They'd literally start with a head count, he thought. Skulls were unmistakable; everybody had one and only one. He imagined they'd turn out to be historic, the relics of some Victorian outbreak of cholera or typhoid. There would be a fuss for a few days then it would all be consigned to the dustbin of history. No grieving relatives to put pressure on for a full investigation.

It was the kind of thing Carol would have taken a quick sideways look at then passed along to a regular CID unit. Look away now, nothing to see here.

'What about them nuns, then?' Kieran could contain himself no longer. 'You think they were all at it, or was it just one mad serial killer nun? Stalking the convent like a homicidal penguin?'

'I think it's more likely that it was something like Spanish flu. The article suggests the bodies were children, and if I remember right, it was the young who were most susceptible to that.'

'Flu? What, like my nan gets a jab for every winter?'

'It killed somewhere around a hundred million people right after the First World War. So if this place was a children's home then, it'd make sense.'

'Aw,' Kieran groaned. 'There was me thinking we could have a juicy little programme on the Razor, you doing your very own *Mind of a Murderer* about the killer nun of Bradesden.' He put on a spooky voice. 'Death stalked the aisles of a Northern nunnery, not caring where he struck with his scythe. The instrument of death? A bride of Christ who turned into the Bride of Frankenstein.'

Tony couldn't help laughing. 'Is that what you think I used to do on the outside?'

Kieran grinned. 'It probably wasn't as much fun as that, am I right?'

'It was never what you'd call fun. But it was rewarding when we got it right. Because it usually meant stopping someone before they took more lives.' He let himself remember that sense of satisfaction. One he'd probably have no opportunity to know again.

'So will you go back to that when you get out of here?'

Tony shook his head. 'No chance. Can you imagine what the likes of this' – he slapped his hand against the paper – 'would make of it? Fox in the henhouse would have nothing on me.'

Kieran shrugged. 'Yeah, but you could argue, set a thief to catch a thief. I bet you could have your own TV show. A podcast at least. You're writing a book about all them killers you helped put away, right? People are going to be all over that. And most people can't be arsed reading a whole book, so they're going to want to watch it or listen to it. Mate, you'll have it made. You'll be the People's Profiler.'

It was, Tony thought, a horrifying prospect. The worst of it was, Kieran was probably right. And after all, what else was he good for?

28

People sometimes mistakenly believe that profiling serial offenders is about making assumptions. The reality is that it's based on probability. When I look at a case file, I'm always consciously looking for similarities. The key to our present behaviour lies in our past. And the key to understanding present crimes is often through the lens of the past.

From *Reading Crimes* by Dr Tony Hill

Rutherford was sitting on a desk at the far end of the room, arms folded across his chest. He didn't look happy. The rest of the team were scattered around, except for Alvin, who was still at the crime scene. 'Right, then,' he said. 'We've found a second deposition site, thanks to the cadaver dog I organised.' He stood up and pointed to a plan of the site. Using a laser pointer, he circled the area where the skeletons had been uncovered. 'First indications are that there are the remains of around forty young people in this area.' He moved the red dot to the side of the convent building.

'Round here, close to the perimeter, there's a kitchen garden and half a dozen raised beds for growing herbs and vegetables. The dog showed initial interest in this raised bed here—' He indicated the first oblong on the drawing. 'And subsequently . . . ' The red dot landed a further six times.

'By happy chance, Alvin was on site.' Rutherford didn't sound in the least happy. 'There was some debate with the forensics team and the university archaeologists about the best way to proceed, but DCI Fielding decided that time was of the essence so they dismantled the timbers around the raised bed to make excavation easier. Once they'd cleared the plants away and started scraping the soil layers down, they found a body-shaped mass wrapped in black bin bags. The body appears to be the size of a young adult. It's being removed to the mortuary where it'll be unwrapped and autopsied.

'So we're looking at something very different here. Different disposal, different victim profile, different wrapping.' He shook his head and sighed heavily. 'If the dog's right, it looks like we've got two separate sets of serial murders in the same place. What are the chances of that?'

'Maybe it's the same killer. Or killers,' Sophie volunteered. 'For whatever reason, they changed their methodology.'

'There's no point in speculating till we hear from the pathologist and the forensics team. And the body-recovery crews,' Rutherford said repressively. 'Alvin is on site with a watching brief for us. Meanwhile we forge ahead with the initial inquiry. We need to make as much progress on that as we can so we're able to take the lead on what looks like a second investigation. Sophie, what's coming out of that so far?'

Sophie consulted her tablet. She was clearly in her comfort zone here. She listed the different actions being taken on the ground and in the lab. 'DC Chen is working on identifying the nuns based at the convent and the girls who lived and were schooled there. Once we have a list, we'll allocate interviews to officers.'

'Chen, where are you up to?'

'I know where the nuns were dispersed to. And DS Nisbet has some leads on a few girls via the local authority. I'll have a much fuller picture by tomorrow.'

'Good work, Steve. Chen, pass on what you have to Sophie's incident room team, and pull all the stops out to find out what you can ASAP. Legitimately, DC Chen.' There was a clear warning in his voice.

They'd be here till Christmas if Stacey heeded him, Paula thought. 'Sir?'

'DI McIntyre? Something to report?'

'I've just conducted an interview with a former resident of St Margaret Clitherow Refuge. And if what she's telling us is the truth – and I've no reason to doubt that – then we're going to be looking at live cases to pursue, not historic ones we can draw a line under. According to her, the nuns dished out brutal punishments. And they kept difficult girls in solitary confinement, sometimes without food.'

'Why am I only hearing about this now? You need to keep me abreast of developments, Inspector.' Rutherford's accent became noticeably broader when he was irritated. That would be a useful indicator for future engagements, Paula thought.

'She walked in off the street. I came straight from interviewing her to this briefing.'

Rutherford considered for a moment then, mollified, said, 'And she's the only one who's come forward?'

'So far. There might be more, obviously, but now I've heard her story, I wouldn't be surprised if we struggle to get walk-ins on this one. Those nuns apparently ran a rule of terror and intimidation. And because of the grip the Church still has, those girls feel under threat even now.'

'Or else they're so messed up by what happened in that convent that they're not going to be very reliable witnesses,' Steve added gloomily.

'Well, we'll just have to get past those obstacles. We need strong witness statements, we need strong forensic evidence. Steve, go and talk to the neighbours. Somebody must have seen something. There must have been gossip in the local pub.'

Sophie cleared her throat. 'We should probably talk to the groundsman,' she said. 'That's his vegetable patch.'

There was a moment of stunned silence. 'There's a groundsman?' Rutherford stuttered.

'Yes. He lives in a cottage at the back of the convent. He told me it's his own place, he bought it from the church. And he leases the land to grow vegetables.'

'He told you? You mean, you've spoken to him?'

'Yes, only briefly, though.'

Rutherford spoke low and slow, emphasising every word. 'You spoke to the groundsman of a site where forty skeletons have been found and you didn't think to bring him in for formal questioning?'

Sophie flushed. 'I was told DCI Fielding's people had already spoken to him.'

'And have you found a statement from him in your incident room files?'

'I haven't seen anything.' Her voice was barely above a whisper.

'Jesus Christ,' Rutherford exploded. 'Paula, get your arse over there right away and take a witness statement from this—what's his name?'

Sophie looked at her tablet. 'Jerome Martinu.'

'And if you think he needs bringing in, bring him in.' Rutherford shook his head. 'We're supposed to be the elite,' he said bitterly. 'DCI Fielding's going to have a field day with this.'

'With all due respect, sir, shouldn't her team have interviewed this Martinu guy? And if they have and it's not in the system, it's not Sophie's fault.' Paula's attempt at conciliation didn't get her very far.

'When you get out there, check with Fielding if there's already an interview. And if there is, where the fuck is it? Then do your own, because I don't want to rely on Fielding's shower for such a crucial interview. Got it?'

Paula gave him a level stare. 'Sir.'

'Did you record your interview with this woman? What's her name, by the way?' He grabbed a marker pen and stood poised at the whiteboard.

'Louise Brand. I recorded the interview and pinged the recording across to the incident room for transcription.' *Because I am not a fuckwit.*

'Good. Have we got a name for the resident priest at the convent yet?'

'I've just filed it with the incident room. He's currently a parish priest in Sheffield,' Stacey said. All this and a meeting with Carol Jordan? Her friend had been working like a woman possessed, Paula thought.

'Nice work, Chen. Karim, off you go to Sheffield. DI McIntyre, why are you still here?'

Really? Was this how it was going to be? Rutherford had been watching too many ancient TV cop shows, Paula decided. Sooner rather than later, she'd be injecting a bit of *Prime Suspect* into the mix. But in the meantime, she needed to forge an alliance.

29

Years ago, I had a conversation with an actor who maintained, 'Once you can fake sincerity, you can achieve anything.' Even when I had no respect for the people I was dealing with, it was important to behave as if I did.

From *Reading Crimes* by Dr Tony Hill

Imran Hussein had a favourite line whenever he was introducing his policeman brother. 'This is Karim. You have to hope he's a more observant copper than he is a Muslim.' The rest of his family tutted at Imran, but Karim was pretty sure that deep down they agreed with him and that it grieved his father in particular. But he didn't believe in the performance of faith for its own sake. His beliefs were his own business, no matter what cajoling, bribery or bullying his father tried in order to get him to Friday prayers.

So when it came to interviewing a priest, he wasn't going to be in awe of the man's position or his devoutness. This was the twenty-first century, after all. Father Michael

Keenan would be just another witness. At least he wasn't one of those nuns that Karim feared would be like a massed phalanx of aunties judging him.

But the woman who opened the door of the priest's grey stone house made Karim feel like he'd stepped back a hundred years. She could have been any age between fifty and seventy. Her greying hair was pulled back in a tight bun, her severe glasses made her eyes shrink to black buttons and her mouth was an unsympathetic line. She wore a floral tabard over a nondescript black dress, the fingers of a pair of rubber gloves poking out of the pouch pocket on the front. She frowned. 'Yes?' It was as if her words were rationed and she wasn't going to waste them on him.

'I'd like to see Father Keenan,' Karim said. 'Father Michael Keenan.' She remained impassive. He took out his ID and held it out. 'I'm DC Karim Hussein. From the Regional Major Incident Team.'

'He's busy.' She went to close the door. 'You'll have to make an appointment.'

Karim put a hand on the door. 'That's not how it works. I'd appreciate it if you'd tell Father Keenan I'm here and that I would like to see him now.'

'He's a very busy man.'

Karim smiled. 'So am I. And I've come all the way from Bradfield to talk to him, so I'd be grateful if you'd go and fetch him.'

At 'Bradfield', her face had changed. Karim couldn't say how or why, just that he'd seen a fleeting shift in her tight features. 'Wait here,' she said. 'I need to close the door to keep the heat in.'

He dropped his hand and stood staring at the highly polished brass knocker. A couple of minutes went by. He listened to the cars and buses passing in the road behind him. He wondered whether the encounter would have gone quite so badly if it had been Steve Nisbet on the step.

Karim was on the point of ringing the bell again when the door opened. A thin man in what he thought of as a priest's uniform of dog collar, cassock and crucifix on a chain peered at him through gold-rimmed granny glasses, a shock of black hair falling across his forehead. Hollow cheeks, a bony jaw and a sharp nose reminded him of a friend of his father's, Zahid, who believed he was fated to live an ascetic life because that was the meaning of his given name. 'You're a policeman, Mrs Grimes tells me.'

'Father Keenan?'

'Well, of course, who else would it be in Father Keenan's house dressed like this?' His voice was a light tenor, his tone sarcastic, his accent faintly Irish.

Karim introduced himself again and proffered his ID.

'What does the Regional whatsit want with me? I'm just an ordinary parish priest.' Keenan frowned, three deep parallel lines between his eyebrows.

'I'd like to talk to you about your time as resident chaplain at the Order of the Blessed Pearl in Bradesden. I'm sure you've seen the news coverage today?'

Keenan cocked his head to one side, like a puzzled hen. 'What news coverage? I've got better things to do with my time than watch TV.'

'If I could come in?' Karim took a step forward. 'This isn't something we should discuss on the pavement, Mr Keenan.'

'It's Father Keenan, son.' He sighed and stepped back. 'You can come in, but keep it brief. I've got parishioners to visit, letters to write.' He led the way down a hall whose parquet flooring smelled of lavender polish, into a small room. A sofa and a pair of upright chairs sat around a low table. The walls were painted a soft green. A crucifix hung over a simple wooden fireplace with a fake coal gas fire. A pair of faded reproductions of Italian Renaissance paintings were the only other decoration. Karim had no idea what they represented, except that one of the figures had wings and so was presumably an angel.

The priest sat on one of the chairs and primly crossed one leg over the other, gesturing to Karim that he should be seated. 'So now presumably you can tell me what this visit is in aid of?'

'I'd like to establish some background information before I go into the details,' Karim said, phone at the ready. 'I'd prefer to record our conversation, it's more reliable than notes. And it's always better to be accurate.' He produced his most winning smile. He'd spent long enough with Paula to have picked up one or two of her tricks. He pressed the red record button as inconspicuously as he could.

'What kind of background information?' Keenan wasn't making this easy.

'How long were you the resident chaplain at the convent in Bradesden?'

He gave a long-suffering sigh, a man used to tedium. 'I was there for five years and seven months. Right up until the closure of the convent and the refuge.'

'And were you also responsible for the spiritual well-being of the girls in the St Margaret Clitherow Refuge?' Karim wasn't sure if that was the right expression but he'd heard it in TV dramas and films.

'I was.'

'What did that consist of, exactly?'

Keenan rolled his eyes. 'The usual duties of a priest. But

I suppose you know nothing of that, Constable. I took services in the chapel, I heard confession, I engaged in spiritual discussion with the Mother Superior. Where the girls were concerned, I also prepared them for their first communion. And I gave them religious instruction within a school context. I can assure you there was nothing untoward in my interactions at the Blessed Pearl.' His voice was haughty, but now he was confident in his superiority, his posture relaxed a little.

'As you rightly say, I don't know how things work in the priesthood. How did you come to be the priest at the Blessed Pearl? Did you apply for the job?'

Keenan screwed up his face in disdain. 'The priesthood is a vocation, not a job. We go where we are sent. My bishop sent me to the Blessed Pearl and so it was my duty to work with the community there.'

'Had you worked with nuns before? Was that why you were chosen?'

'I was a priest in an inner-city group practice in Glasgow, then I was chaplain for a couple of years at Deeside University in Aberdeen. So I had experience of chaplaincy but not within a convent.'

'Did you enjoy it?'

He seemed offended by the question. 'I didn't become a priest to enjoy myself. I found it fulfilling to work in that community. It was a unique opportunity for a practical ministry as well as the contemplative life.'

'Not much time for contemplation as a parish priest, I imagine.'

'Indeed.' Keenan was apparently determined to keep his own counsel. 'I think it's about time you told me why you are here. Has someone made allegations about my conduct?'

'Would it surprise you if they had?'

'It would astonish me. Because any such claims would be utterly baseless. But we in the church have become easy targets in recent years for unscrupulous people seeking to make money from lies and false allegations.' He held a hand up to stop an interruption Karim had no intention of making. 'I'm not denying there have been appalling cases of child sex abuse committed by priests. But the scale is of it is wildly exaggerated. And I've never laid an inappropriate hand on a child.'

The very vehemence of the denial made Karim wonder whether Keenan had even more to hide than he'd first thought. 'Are you aware that the convent and its grounds were sold to developers?'

The change of tack startled Keenan. 'Of course. We all knew that. It happened very shortly after it was decided to close the convent.'

'Why was that decision made?' *Keep moving around, don't let them settle.* Karim could hear Paula's voice in his head.

'Not for any sinister reason, I assure you. The numbers entering holy orders have been falling lately. We'd reached a point where very soon there would no longer be enough nuns to run the school and the home. And so the Mother House decided it was better to close the establishment altogether and divide the remaining sisters among the order's other convents.' His hand crept up to his crucifix, his long slender fingers caressing the heavy silver.

'It's taken a while for the developers to raise the capital and sort out the planning permission but they started work this week. And they've discovered human remains in the grounds.'

Keenan showed no surprise. 'Of course they have. There was a graveyard for the nuns and their previous priests.'

'That's not what I'm talking about. I'm talking about the bodies of up to forty children who are buried under the front lawn of the convent.'

The priest's fingers stopped stroking his crucifix. He sat stock-still. Not a muscle quivered.

'What can you tell me about that?' Karim asked. 'You were living there. You can't have failed to notice what was going on.'

Keenan cleared his throat. He uncrossed his legs and attempted a more casual pose. 'Children die, Constable. It's very sad, but it happens. The children at St Margaret Clitherow were there because they had no one else. Better to bury them in the grounds of the convent than hand them over to the local authority for a pauper's grave. I don't know what the custom is in your culture, Constable, but we believe in proper burial in consecrated ground.'

'In my culture, we don't dump our children in an unmarked hole in the ground,' Karim said, trying to hold his anger in check. 'Not even in times of war. Not even in refugee camps. We treat them with dignity.'

'On what basis do you suggest the nuns of the Blessed Pearl didn't do just that?'

'There are no grave markers. No coffins. No indication that this is anything other than a front lawn. The kind of place children would run around and play on, not be buried under. And you knew about this?'

For the first time, Keenan looked uncertain. 'I was aware of the practice, yes. As I said, children die. They fall ill. They have accidents. Many of them arrived undernourished and vulnerable to disease. The nuns arranged the burials in the grounds to keep them close to where they had been cared for. In some cases, the only place they had ever been cared for.'

'Did you take part in those burials?'

'I did not. I held a short formal service in the chapel before they were buried, but that was the extent of my involvement.'

'Did you give these dying children the last rites?'

He looked up at the crucifix above the fireplace. 'On occasion, yes.'

'How many occasions?'

'I really couldn't say. It was a long time ago.'

'Forty times?'

'Don't be ridiculous.' Keenan flared up, two spots of colour on his cheeks. 'The convent had been there since 1930. That's more than eighty years of girls who came through those doors. One death every two years, that's hardly surprising.'

'You think?' Karim couldn't keep his shock and outrage hidden now. 'I went through thirteen years of school and three years of university and I was never in the same class as a kid who died. And you're trying to tell me that the death rate at the Blessed Pearl was *normal*?'

Keenen flushed but it was clearly from anger rather than shame. 'You have no idea what you're talking about.' He shook his head. 'The condition some of these girls were in when they came to the convent, you wouldn't believe. They'd been undernourished since the day they were born. They were frail. They had tapeworms. Diseases of deprivation like TB. They were susceptible to the kind of illnesses that you or I would shake off. It's amazing the nuns kept so many of them alive.'

Chastened, Karim paused for a moment before continuing.

'Nevertheless. We've been told that the nuns ran a brutal regime in recent years. That harsh beatings and physical punishments were routine. That girls were punished with solitary confinement.' Karim had moved well and truly into bad cop now, his voice steely, his gaze uncompromising. 'You must have been aware of that?'

'I knew nothing of that. I saw nothing of the sort. Sister Mary Patrick provided the only proper stable home most of those girls had known. None of them ever made any complaint to me.' Keenan met implacable with implacable.

'I find that hard to credit. You were living under the same roof where girls were being brutalised and imprisoned, you had a pastoral role in their lives and yet you knew nothing about it?'

Keenan got to his feet. His mouth twisted in a dark smile. 'We have a saying in the church: "That's where your faith comes in." We're done here, Constable. I'd be obliged if you'd leave and take your shabby insinuations with you.'

'Just one more thing—' Karim's intention to raise the question of the other bodies was thwarted as the priest swept from the room, leaving him stranded. He didn't know what to do. He had no grounds for chasing the man through his own home. You couldn't drag a man of the cloth down to a police station just because he gave you the creeps. He stood up, undecided.

The housekeeper appeared in the doorway as silently as if she'd traversed the hall on a cushion of air. 'I'll see you out,' she said disdainfully. As he preceded her down the hall, she said, 'You've some cheek, coming here with your accusations. Father Keenan is a good man. Not like you lot.'

Karim turned swiftly to face her. 'What do you mean, my lot?'

She gave a tight smile of triumph. 'Coppers. What did you think I meant?' She reached past him to open the door. 'Off you go and bother some other poor innocent. God forbid you should actually catch some criminals.'

The door closed behind him with a sharp snap. Karim let out a long breath. On a scale of one to shit, that had come in somewhere around eleven. He had a sneaking feeling that where Father Michael Keenan was concerned, ReMIT had only just begun.

30

We talk about 'gut instinct' or 'feminine intuition' and often dismiss them. We say they're unscientific, they're not something you can take into the witness box and make a case out of. But more often than not, these hunches are reliable indicators. They're conclusions we draw based on experience, readings of human behaviour we trust because we've seen them before. Of course prejudice can creep in and skew our responses, but we shouldn't ignore those moments when our hackles rise or our spines shiver. They're just as valuable as those moments of instant attraction that so often lead us into love affairs ...

From *Reading Crimes* by DR TONY HILL

Paula waited till she was in her car before she rang Sophie Valente's number. With luck, her colleague would be back in the incident room, well away from Rutherford's ears.

Sophie sounded wary when she answered. 'Paula? What can I do for you?'

'I'm on my way to interview Martinu. I can't believe nobody from Fielding's team has spoken to him. I wouldn't put it past her to be arsey about uploading everything, just because she's narked that we've snatched her case out from under her.'

A moment's silence, then Sophie said, 'I take your point. Did you want to see my notes?'

'That would be great, if you've had time to write them up. But I'd like to see Fielding's officer's notes too. First interview, and all that. Can you have a word with her and ask her to make them available to the incident room?' Paula hoped Sophie's obvious ambition would temper her apparent lack of collegiality, pulled out into the clotted city centre traffic, trying to work out which was the least congested route to Bradesden.

'Is there a reason why you can't ask her yourself when you get there?'

Paula rolled her eyes, hope extinguished. Was this Sophie's revenge for her casual slight in the pub after the team-building fiasco? 'Yes, Sophie, there is a reason. Fielding hates me. I was seconded to her team before ReMIT was set up and it wasn't what you'd call a success. If I ask for the file, we'll both be collecting our pensions before it shows up.'

'She'd sabotage the investigation just to get back at you?' Sophie sounded curious rather than incredulous.

'She wants to come out on top here, Sophie. And if she can make me look rubbish along the way, that's a bonus. She's more likely to help you out because, frankly, you're the darling of the top brass because . . .' Paula paused, groping for the right words ' . . . you've arrived with a fanfare of trumpets. And if she does right by you, you might put in a good word for her when the kudos gets handed out.'

'She didn't exactly roll out the red carpet for me earlier.'

'I need a break, Sophie. You scratch my back . . . ' Please let her have the sense to play nice, Paula thought.

'Sure. ReMIT isn't going to work unless we pull together. I'll call Fielding and as soon as the interview file hits the system, I'll ping it across to you. Talk later.'

And she was gone. Not exactly best mates, but self-interest had at least given it a start. Maybe Paula should have paired up with Sophie on the team-building day, but she'd put friendship first. She knew Stacey would struggle out in the depths of the countryside so she'd gone for standing by her pal rather than forging links with the new girl. Really, there had been nothing about that disastrous day that had been worthwhile.

It took the best part of an hour for the initial interview notes to arrive in Paula's inbox. She'd passed the time with a coffee in the village pub in Bradesden, a former working men's drinking den that had been transformed into a bijou gastropub. A handful of hardbitten hacks were wolfing down assorted gourmet pies with truffle mash and roast vegetables, none of them paying her any attention as they vied loudly to share the most scurrilous piece of gossip about colleagues and rivals.

The initial interview had been conducted by a DC whose name she didn't recognise. It seemed pretty cursory, but then it had only been a preliminary chat, done before anyone had had a sense of the scale of what they were dealing with. All the basic details were there – Jerome 'Jezza' Martinu, native of Bradfield, thirty-seven. Started work at the Blessed Pearl twenty years ago as assistant to the groundsman and handyman, took over when the old man retired sixteen years ago. Bought his cottage and garden when the convent was being closed, leased another strip of land for his vegetables. Yes, he'd dug graves at the behest of the nuns, thought nothing of it. The girls were orphans, nobody claimed their bodies. Nothing suspicious about that.

The officer had concluded Jezza was a bit simple. Paula had had enough dealings with killers to wonder who the simple one really was.

The single truly useful piece of information from the interview was that Martinu's property had a back gate into the lane behind the convent. If she approached from the opposite direction, she would miss the press pack that she was sure would be all but blocking the lane. More to the point, she'd bypass Fielding and her team.

The last mile from the main road was a narrow lane that twisted between towering hedgerows, the verges overgrown and unkempt. In the distance, Paula could see the dark line of the high moors rising against a bruised sky full of the rain that was falling on Bradesden too. On a fine day, it must convince the village dwellers that they really had made the escape to the country.

As she'd expected, there was a uniformed constable in a high-vis jacket stationed at the double wooden doors in the wall, looking miserable in the thin drizzle that had set in. Paula pulled up on the verge in front of the liveried police car and collected the cardboard cup of mocha that she'd brought from the pub. She identified herself and explained why she was there.

'I'm not supposed to let anyone in this way,' the PC said, sounding as bored and mutinous as she looked.

'I'm with ReMIT,' Paula said. 'Not the *Daily Mirror*. I'm here to conduct an interview, that's all. I'm trying to avoid the circus out front.' She grinned. 'I have a bribe.' She proffered the cup. 'Mocha. Nice and hot.'

At once, the PC thawed. She took the cup and stepped aside. 'Be my guest, Inspector.' Then she frowned. 'You OK on your own? He's a big bloke.'

Paula hesitated for a moment. 'I'll be fine.' She patted her pocket. 'I've got my Airwave handy if he turns out to be a bit of a handful. Plenty of support at hand.'

The gate gave on to a short rutted track through the tall hedge that lined the grounds then opened out into a neat back garden with a fruit cage along one border and a substantial shed opposite. The cottage itself was squat and unprepossessing but well-maintained. Paula walked down the gravel path and knocked on the back door. She heard footsteps approaching. Boots on flagstones, by the sound of it.

The man who opened the door looked like he'd have no trouble toting bodies around the parkland. He was stocky, muscle rather than fat revealed by a snug Bradfield Vics replica top. His thick dark hair, clean and glossy, showed the remains of a decent haircut. A couple of days' stubble blurred his strong jaw and heavy brows formed a ledge above his broad face. He frowned. 'Are you another cop?'

Paula flashed her ID. 'Detective Inspector McIntyre,' she said. 'Can I come in?'

'I've already spoken to two of you. How many more times do I have to go over the same ground?' He spoke mildly, without aggression, his Bradfield accent obvious.

'Not quite the same ground,' Paula said. 'The more we dig up, the more we need to ask you about.'

Wariness crept over his face. 'What's that supposed to mean?'

'Why don't I come inside and we can talk out of the rain?'

He gave a quick, sly grin. 'I'm not in the rain.'

'If I'd been digging graves for little girls, I'd be going out of my way to be nice to police officers.' Paula smiled.

'Look, I already told you people. I've no idea what went on inside the convent. I did what the Reverend Mother told me to do. Mow the lawns. Grow the vegetables. Drains and gutters. And when one of the girls died, make sure they had a proper grave. I've got nothing else to say.' He folded his arms across his chest.

'You've not been out this afternoon, then?'

'No. Because I can't get any work done with you people crawling all over the grounds. Why? What am I supposed to have done?' Now he looked defiant. It was, Paula knew, the ugly twin of fear. Something she could capitalise on.

'Are you going to let me in? Or are we going to have to have this conversation at a police station?' She leaned in. 'What's it to be, Jezza? Because you can bet your last pay cheque I'll be driving past the press posse if I've got you in the back of a police car.'

He shook his head, blowing air into his cheeks in an unconvincing display of exasperation. 'Come in, then. I've got nothing to hide. There's no cause to drag me down the nick.'

She followed him into a stone-flagged kitchen, neat and clean. The dish drainer held a bowl and plate, a kitchen knife, spoon and fork in the cutlery section. Four chairs were tucked under a spotless pine table; the kettle and toaster gleamed on the work surface. On the stove, a battered pressure cooker squatted, out of place in the overly tidy room. He pulled out a chair and sat down, big hands clasped on the table in front of him.

Paula chose a chair at right angles to him. If she wasn't happy with his responses there would be plenty of opportunity for the head-on confrontational position. For now, she wanted to get a sense of what was going on behind Martinu's front. Because it was a front, she was sure of that. Not for the first time, she wished Tony was part of the team. She was good at interviews, but it was always helpful to have somebody else involved who had a different style. 'We've found the other bodies,' she said.

He frowned. 'What other bodies?'

Paula chuckled. 'You're going to have to do better than that, Jezza, You know what other bodies. You're the man who digs the graves round here.'

'You mean the ones in the cemetery? The nuns?' Eyes innocent, the way every amateur had learned from bad Hollywood movies.

Paula shook her head. 'The time for playing dumb is over. What you missed this afternoon is the cadaver dog earning its keep. You know what a cadaver dog is? It's a specially trained dog that can nose out dead bodies. Even when they've been buried for a long time. Even when they've been buried good and deep. I'm not talking about the cemetery, Jezza, I'm talking about the bodies at the bottom of your raised beds. Oh, and the couple of other ones underneath your vegetable patch.'

His eyes glazed over. He stared straight ahead, unblinking. Then a flurry of fast eye movements, flicking from side to side and his eyelids fluttered like the wings of a moth. 'It's nothing to do with me.' It sounded as if he couldn't even convince himself.

'You're the gravedigger around here, Jezza. Do you seriously expect me to believe there were two of you at it? And that the other one just happened to choose burial sites under the very places you were growing your vegetables? I bet you win first prize at the village show every year, with all that fertiliser feeding your soil.'

He pushed back from the table, the chair legs screaming against the stone. 'I just did what I was told. It's my job.'

Time to press harder. She sensed he was close to cracking. 'Are you saying the nuns asked you to dig a whole other set of graves? Because we already know these aren't girls from the children's home. Are you trying to tell me you had a bunch of homicidal nuns here? Or was it just one serial killer nun?'

'You've got it all wrong,' he shouted. He crossed his arms, clutching his shoulders in a tight embrace.

'So it wasn't the nuns? Was it you, then, Jezza? Are you the serial killer?'

He stood up, backing away. 'I never killed anybody. I just did my job, I swear. You're not going to pin this on me.'

Paula got to her feet. She hadn't expected this to go so far so fast. 'Give me one good reason why I should believe you, Jezza.'

31

The greatest handicap in profiling is the same as it is for any investigator – we need full disclosure of the evidence, however insignificant a particular element might seem.

From *Reading Crimes* by Dr Tony Hill

Before the day was out, Carol was reminded of Bronwen Scott's perennial refusal to take no for an answer. Her phone had rung while she was working her way through the background reading on Saul Neilson. As soon as Carol had answered, Bronwen had launched straight into her pitch. 'I thought it would be good for you to meet some of the other people involved in the project, so I invited a couple of the girls around for this evening. We've got a little office at the university, courtesy of our DNA expert, Kit Salvesen, but I thought it would be good to meet more informally. So, my place, half past seven. I'll text you the details. You can park in one of the guest spaces under the building.'

'I can't make it tonight, I've got something else on.'

'You can't postpone it?' Bronwen sounded astonished. 'Email me your availability, then, we'll sort out another time.'

'I'm not sure I—' But it was too late. The line was dead. Bloody woman. But in spite of her irritation with Bronwen, now she'd had the chance to drill down into the file Carol had to acknowledge she was intrigued by the slenderness of the case against Saul Neilson. According to Lyle Tate's phone records and the text messages on the phone the police had recovered from Neilson's flat, Sugar Lyle – as he was known – had been summoned there eight times in the six months leading up to his disappearance and presumed death. That was the first brick in the shaky wall.

One evening, he'd told his flatmate he was going to see a regular who liked it 'full on'. A bit rough, though he paid well. Sugar Lyle never returned to his flat. Second brick.

The flatmate, a fellow sex worker, reported him missing two days later. The investigation had been fairly desultory at first. Lyle was an adult, he lived on the margins, he had no real ties to the flat or the area. It wasn't hard to make the case that someone might have made him an offer he couldn't refuse. For all the police knew, Sugar Lyle was sunning himself in Ibiza with a sugar daddy. They'd found a notebook in his bedroom that listed the names and addresses of his clients along with the dates he'd been with them. That eventually took them to Saul Neilson, who was clearly freaked out by their visit. At first he denied ever having met Lyle Tate or having heard of him, but faced with the evidence of Tate's list, he capitulated. A palpable lie always added an extra course of bricks to the wall of evidence.

One of the officers found the twitchiness of his reaction suspicious. She knew nothing of Neilson's closeted state; she assumed his panic was to do with what had happened with Lyle Tate rather than fear of his parents finding out he'd been paying for sex with a male prostitute. So she'd asked to use the bathroom and had a good look around while she was in there. And behind the pedestal of the sink, she spotted what looked like a streak of blood.

She said nothing at the time but as soon as they'd left, she was on to her DCI, suggesting they should get a warrant for Saul Neilson's flat. It was the last place Lyle Tate was known to have been, Neilson had lied about him, and there was blood in the bathroom. It was thin, but cops always knew which magistrates to go to when they wanted a warrant based on thin.

The forensic techs did their thing with different coloured lights and found a substantial amount of blood spatter traces that had been cleaned up in the bathroom. There was evidence of a spray of blood on the laminate wood floor of the living room too. Because Lyle Tate was no stranger to selling sex and buying drugs, his DNA was on the database. It was a match with the smear of blood behind the sink pedestal.

And Lyle Tate was still missing. Nobody had seen him since he'd gone to Saul Neilson's for sex. A more thorough search of his room revealed that he'd left his passport, his driving licence, three wraps of cocaine and £735 in cash in the zipped pocket of the backpack in the bottom of his clothes cupboard. So he obviously hadn't been planning to go anywhere other than his next job. He was a potential threat to Saul Neilson's lovely life. And his blood was all over the flat. Well, in the bathroom and the living room. You'd have to stand on tiptoe to see over the wall now, even if it was highly circumstantial.

Neilson's version of events was that they'd been wrestling

on the living room floor. Foreplay masquerading as horseplay. Or vice versa, depending on how you looked at it. Either way, it wasn't Carol's idea of a good time. But then, it had been so long since she'd had any sort of a good time, who was she to judge?

Neilson had accidentally whacked Tate with his elbow. Blood sprayed out from his nose, landing on the wood floor. Neilson had helped him through to the bathroom and it had taken a few minutes to stop the bleeding. They'd taken cocaine together earlier in the evening, so Tate's blood pressure would have been elevated and the flow more aggressive. He'd freaked out, according to Neilson. He'd kept shaking his head, so there were drops of blood everywhere. Finally the bleeding had stopped and Neilson had put an ice pack on Tate's swollen nose. They hadn't felt like sex after that drama, so they'd just had a couple of beers and watched some TV. Then Neilson had paid Tate as usual and he'd left.

It was plausible, Carol thought. It was also the kind of plausible a smart man could concoct to cover something much more sinister. It was highly circumstantial, but the blood spatter expert had testified that the blood was surprisingly widely distributed for a simple nosebleed. In her opinion, it corresponded to a much more serious injury.

And there was the inconvenient fact that nobody had seen Lyle Tate since.

After two days of deliberation the jury had decided by a majority of ten against two that Saul Neilson was guilty of manslaughter. Carol thought it was a borderline decision, based on the evidence alone. When you added Saul Neilson's background to the scales, she'd have expected him to walk. Never in trouble with the police, strong family background, good job. What had happened in the courtroom to tip the balance against him? Why had the jury condemned Mr Respectable?

Carol sighed. Bronwen had reeled her in like a rookie. Only a face-to-face interview with Saul Neilson would help her understand what had gone wrong. Still she tried to convince herself she wasn't committing herself. An exploratory meeting, that's what it would be. Walking away from the paperwork, she told Flash, 'I don't owe Bronwen Scott a damn thing.'

The dog wagged her tail. At least one of them was convinced.

32

> We often have very fixed ideas about the identity of the interviewer in relation to the person we're seeking information from. 'Send a woman to interview a man who likes to think of himself as powerful because he'll believe he can dominate her.' Or 'Don't send a young male officer to interview a young woman or she'll try to flirt with him.' These are the kind of judgements that don't take account of the particular skills of individual interviewers. I advise senior officers to look at the available talent in their team and go with the person most likely to get results, regardless of age, gender or attractiveness.
>
> From *Reading Crimes* by Dr Tony Hill

Rutherford considered his options. He'd done management courses that supposedly revealed how to run a team in a major operation. And the ideas were sound, in an ideal world where there were no fast-moving changes of circumstance. The problem was that in the real world, events conspired to prevent him making the best use of his resources. Take now, for example. Somebody needed to go to York to the Mother House of the Order of the Blessed Pearl to interview the nuns who had been stationed – was that the word, 'stationed'? – at Bradesden in an attempt to understand what had gone on there and who was responsible. His choice would have been to send Paula, who was said to be the best on the squad when it came to persuading the reluctant to talk.

But Paula had just called to say she was bringing in the groundsman from the convent to interview him under caution. He couldn't argue with that – obviously, the discovery of the second group of bodies in the man's personal area of the grounds begged too many questions to ignore. Either he was a serial killer – Rutherford cringed inside at the term, guaranteed as it was to whip up public hysteria and a media-feeding frenzy – or he knew who was.

Rutherford supposed there was a third possibility – that somebody else, presumably under cover of darkness – had been digging up the man's vegetable beds, planting bodies then restoring them to their original state without the owner noticing. He supposed it was just about possible. If the killer waited till the right moment, when the crop had been harvested and the ground dug over in preparation for the next sowing, they might manage it. But it would be hard to know exactly when that would happen; surely no killer would allow their urges to be governed by somebody else's gardening practices? No, that was a nonsense. It would be a desperate defence counsel who'd try to lead them up that particular garden path.

He was happy that they were making progress of a sort, but it was annoying that it meant his best interviewer was tied up. It could possibly wait till the morning, when Paula might have moved things along far enough to leave them on the back burner while she pursued the nuns. But that was a risky endeavour, and the longer he let things lie, the better prepared the nuns would be. Rutherford, a well-brought-up Scottish Presbyterian, had no doubt they'd have established a common line, even if it ran counter to what they believed had really happened. After all, if you could swallow the virgin birth and the resurrection and the turning of bread and wine into flesh and blood, you'd had plenty of practice in putting your fingers in your ears and going, 'La la la la la la.'

This was supposed to be a big step up for him. On paper, it had sounded impressive. But the truth was, his options weren't brilliant. To keep some sort of control over the whole operation he'd had to put Sophie Valente in charge of the incident room, which, in fairness, she seemed to be handling well. Her background in management and organisational skills meant she knew how to run the information flow. To take her off that would disrupt both sides of the inquiry. The only other woman on the squad was Stacey Chen. The idea of sending her to interrogate a bunch of nuns brought a grim smile to his lips. Chen was the mistress of machines, not people.

But maybe a woman wasn't the best person for the job anyway. Rutherford's hazy knowledge of the hierarchies of Catholic life made him suspect that although the Mother Superior was always perceived and portrayed as ruling her nuns with a rod of iron, she herself was answerable to the convent's resident priest. Ultimately, women were pretty powerless in the church. They couldn't even be priests, not like in his Church, where they had no pope or bishops telling them what to do. The Church of Scotland had even had women Moderators, which was the nearest they got to having someone in charge. But if you'd always been subject to the authority of men, maybe it would make more sense to have a man asking the questions.

He sighed. This was the downside of having a small hand-picked team. When you were in a live investigation, you were always stretched. And it was never a good move to pull in local officers for the truly crucial interviews. Everybody might theoretically be after the same result – answers, a conviction, an appropriate sentence – but too often office politics got in the way. He wasn't anywhere near sure enough of DCI Alex Fielding to entrust the vital interviews to members of her team he knew even less well than his own players.

Karim was keen but too inexperienced. And besides, although Rutherford daren't say it aloud these days, he had a suspicion that culturally he might be inclined to defer to older women. Steve was persistent, a grafter who'd dig and dig and dig, but the big question mark for his boss was whether he had the finesse to handle this. And besides, Paula had asked for him to sit in with her on the interview with Martinu.

Alvin Ambrose might not be the first name in the frame when it came to finesse either, but Rutherford liked what he'd seen of him so far. In spite of an intimidating physical presence, he could put people at their ease. 'Gentle giant' was a cliché but it was credible enough for people to buy into. And there was a popular misconception that if you looked like a heavyweight boxer on his day off, you weren't going to be too bright. Maybe Ambrose could lull the nuns into a false sense of security.

*

And so Alvin found himself on the outskirts of York, driving through an estate of modern brick boxes. He thought he'd lost his way; it didn't look like convent country to him, despite the twin towers of York Minster peeping over distant rooftops. But at the end of what he feared was a cul-de-sac he arrived at a wide gateway in a high stone wall. A discreet sign on the right-hand gatepost announced that he had reached the Mother House Convent of the Order of the Blessed Pearl. At the end of the short driveway sat an elegant Georgian house. Perfectly symmetrical around a pillared porch with a circular window above it, three storeys of windows divided into small panes, eight windows to a side. It was hard to tell how far back it extended but Alvin had a hunch it was a lot more than one room deep. How did these nuns end up with such grand accommodation? Last he'd heard, they were supposed to be all about poverty, chastity and obedience. Still, as Meatloaf pointed out, two out of three ain't bad.

As he grew closer, he could see his first impression wasn't quite borne out close-up. It reminded him of a soap star he'd once met in the course of an inquiry. The distance of the camera lent her a perfection that across an interview room table felt more like a clever disguise. Up close, the flaws and the passage of time were perceptible. So it was with the convent. The paint on the window frames had gone one winter beyond its prime; the masonry showed signs of wear round edges and corners that were no longer precise; and he could just make out something surprisingly sturdy growing out of the huddle of chimney pots that adorned one gable.

He parked on the tarmacked area in front of the building. His was the only car there, but a narrow drive ran round one side of the building, a sign saying PRIVATE leaning at a slightly drunken angle beside it. Alvin got out, shaking each leg like a dog that's been confined for too long. He took his time walking up to the door. More Western gunslinger pace than Tactical Support Group raid. He knew he was looking smart enough for the encounter. His wife Esme wouldn't let him out of the house unless he looked enough like the good guys not to be mistaken for a villain. So, dark grey suit, pale blue shirt, peacock blue tie. Because a man had to have a splash of colour, right? Otherwise he'd be just like anyone else. When he'd first said this to Esme years before, she'd hooted with laughter. 'Alvin, you couldn't be less like anyone else,' she'd said, reaching up to pinch his cheek.

As he often did, he remembered reading the opening of Raymond Chandler's *The Big Sleep*, where Philip Marlowe itemises his smartest outfit then observes, 'I was neat, clean, shaved and sober, and I didn't care who knew it. I was everything the well-dressed private detective ought to be. I was calling on four million dollars.' OK, Alvin was a cop, not a PI. And he'd yet to call on four million dollars. But the principle was the same. You respect yourself, it makes it harder for others to disrespect you.

He pulled a brass knob and heard an old-fashioned brass bell echoing inside. There was a long pause. Alvin bent down and pushed open the brass letter box. A black-and-white tiled marble floor was all he could see beneath the internal flap. He stood up and rang the bell again. This time there was a scurry of soft footfalls and the door swung open. A woman of indeterminate age in a grey skirt and cardigan, her hair covered with the sort of headgear he was more used to seeing worn at hen nights or fancy-dress parties. A heavy silver crucifix hung on a bosom like a solid shelf. 'We are at prayer,' she said severely. 'Psalm one hundred and nineteen. "Seven times a day I have given praise to thee."'

'I'm sorry,' Alvin said. He held up his ID. She peered at it through gold-rimmed glasses. 'I was hoping to talk to the Mother Superior.'

The woman tutted. 'This is the Mother House. You mean the Superior General. Mother Benedict.'

Oh boy. Talk about being outside his comfort zone. He gave what he hoped was an apologetic grimace. 'You have to forgive me, I'm not familiar with how you run things here.'

Her lips pursed in what might have been a tart little smile. 'You're right, I do have to forgive you. Come in, Sergeant Ambrose. Vespers will be over shortly and Mother Benedict will see you then.'

He stepped inside, the hard heels of his shoes loud on the tiles.

She walked away, looking over her shoulder as if to encourage him to follow her. 'We've been expecting you.'

33

I've read a lot of theories about how to tell when someone is lying. They fidget. They keep preternaturally still. Their eyes go up to the top left corner of the room. They sweat. They keep touching their face. The truth is, there is no standard tell.

From *Reading Crimes* by DR TONY HILL

The last shreds of Jezza Martinu's composure had vanished by the time he reached a police interview room. Skenfrith Street station had been extensively renovated in recent years but a decision had been taken to maintain the studied lack of amenity in the interview rooms. Nobody wanted to spend money on the comfort of the accused. Tony had once tried to make the case for providing a more welcoming environment. Carol had scoffed, 'What? You think we should get the recording equipment in pastel colours, with matching décor? That would make it less unsettling, you think?' Ever since that exchange, Paula couldn't help picturing the whole of Skenfrith Street in the palette of *The Truman Show*. That was far more disturbing than the reality.

In truth, she didn't think it would matter whether the interview suite was decked out like a five-star hotel, complete with fruit basket. Once that door closed and the recording equipment beeped, everybody knew what they were there for. Even those who had nothing to be guilty about felt the creep of anxiety in the hairs on the back of their neck. Even, she sometimes thought, the ones who had no hair on the back of their neck.

Before they went in, Paula led Steve Nisbet into the observation room. Martinu was constantly shifting in his seat. 'There's a man who doesn't like being cooped up,' Steve said. 'Stands to reason, doing what he does. Out in the open in all weathers. He's going to get more and more uncomfortable the longer we keep him here.'

'Not necessarily,' Paula said. 'Some people settle down once they realise there's nothing they can do to make it go away. It's like they sink into a sort of zen interview state. But I think you're probably right about Jezza. There's something eating him and we've got to get him to give it up.'

'How are we playing this, then?' He was eager, no doubt about that. Jacket off, tie loosened, he had the air of a man ready for a long night. Even his neat little quiff looked more buoyant. He pointed at Paula. 'Good cop?' Then at himself. 'Bad cop?'

Paula wondered fleetingly whether working with Steve was such a good idea. 'No,' she said. She laid a palm on her chest. 'Good cop.' Then nodded at him. 'Silent cop. Taking notes cop. Interesting facial expressions cop. You can look as menacing as you like, but I don't want you buggering up the tempo of my questions.'

His face turned surly. 'But what if I want to ask something you've missed?'

'Don't assume I've missed it. I might be circling round to it from a different direction. If you think there's something significant I've not picked up on, you can tell me when we break and I'll hit him with it when we go back in.'

'I'm not used to—'

'It'll be fine, Steve. Trust me, I'm good at this.' Hand on the door handle. 'Let's do it.'

Whoever Martinu had used his one phone call on had sorted him out with a solicitor. Not one of the low-paid duties, who dressed like drones in an insurance office and always looked in need of a visit to the hairdresser. This young man was wearing a perfectly lovely dark grey tweed suit with a tasteful burgundy silk tie and Paula was not in the least surprised when the business card he prodded towards her revealed that he worked for Bronwen Scott's firm. What did surprise her was that Jezza Martinu could afford Richard Cohen.

They moved swiftly through the routine of beginning the recording and identifying those present. Thanks to TV, the accused knew the drill as well as the cops and the lawyers. 'Thanks for coming in, Mr Martinu,' Paula said.

'You didn't give me much choice,' he grumbled, expression surly, shoulders rounded.

'My client is not under arrest and is free to leave at any time,' Cohen clarified.

'Indeed. Though of course, that could change, depending on what he has to tell us.' Paula smiled, and not just because of the consternation on Martinu's face.

'Can we get to the point, Inspector?' Cohen affected an air of boredom. Paula looked forward to blowing it to smithereens.

'Mr Martinu, you are the groundsman at the convent of the Order of the Blessed Pearl?'

'You know all this,' Martinu said. 'I told you already. All three of you that came round to hassle me.'

'How long have you worked there?'

'Do I have to go over all this again?' Plaintive, looking at his lawyer.

'For the tape,' Paula said.

Cohen nodded. 'It's irritating, but it's fine. I'll tell you when it's not fine.'

'Twenty years. When they shut down the convent, they kept me on a retainer to look after the grounds. So it wouldn't look like it had gone to seed. I bought my cottage off them and I lease the land where I grow my fruit and veg.'

'What did your job entail, Mr Martinu?'

'Mowing the grass. I've got a ride-on mower, you need it for a place that size. I supplied some of the fruit and veg for the convent and the school. Not all of it. I mean, obviously. It's not a farm, just a bit of a market garden sort of thing. I looked after the odd jobs around the building – checking the guttering, bits of joinery, repairs, the occasional bit of plumbing or electrics. Nothing major. They got contractors in for stuff like painting and decorating and fixing the roof.'

'Sounds like they'd have been lost without you,' Paula said. 'You had another job too, didn't you?'

He glanced at his lawyer, who leaned forward. 'Where are we going with this, Inspector?'

'Mr Martinu's already explained his role in the discoveries that have been made in the convent grounds. I'm referring initially to the extensive human remains that have been uncovered under the lawn in front of the main convent building. Jezza, tell me about those graves.'

He looked helplessly at his lawyer. 'I didn't do anything wrong. I just did what I was told.'

'You didn't question what they were asking you to do?' Paula persisted.

He frowned, uncomprehending. 'It was my job. I'm a good Catholic. They're nuns, they're in charge. Doing God's work. It's not for me to question them.'

Steve shifted in his chair. Paula hoped he'd stay quiet. 'Was it the Reverend Mother who gave you those orders?'

'Not always. Sometimes it was Sister Mary Aquinas. She was kind of Sister Mary Patrick's deputy. You could see it wasn't easy for them, when a girl died. But they wanted to do the best they could by them. Those girls, they had nobody. No visitors, no family, no nothing except St Margaret Clitherow's. Sister Mary Aquinas said it could be a blessing, when you thought how their lives might end up. "Easier to be with God," she'd say, so's I wouldn't feel too bad about it.'

It was chilling to hear the matter of fact way Martinu wrote off the dead girls. She couldn't quite work out whether this was the detached attitude of the psychopath or the profound lack of imagination of someone who simply wasn't very bright. 'And so, what? You'd dig a grave?'

He nodded, with another uneasy glance at his lawyer. Paula was mildly surprised at the lack of intervention from the brief.

'Did nobody ever stop and ask you what you were doing? None of the other girls?'

Martinu frowned. 'I did it after dark. The dormitories were round the back, so they wouldn't see the lights. The nuns didn't want to upset the other girls, see? So I'd dig the grave, then the nuns would do the funeral service and I'd fill it in again.'

'Just the nuns? Not the priest?'

A long moment of silence. Martinu stared at the table, brow furrowed, apparently deep in thought. 'No,' he said at last, meeting her eye. 'Never the priest.'

'And you didn't think that was odd? A funeral without a priest?' Paula didn't know much about Catholic doctrine but she was pretty sure there was supposed to be a priest. Particularly in a church that paid so little regard to any woman who wasn't the Virgin Mary.

'Look, I did what I was told. Reverend Mother, she said it was OK, she said they'd had the proper service in the chapel, this was only the burial.' His strong hands bunched into fists. 'I didn't do anything wrong. I just did my job.'

'As my client says. What exactly do you imagine you're going to charge him with?' At last, an intervention from the lawyer.

'This is a witness interview, Mr Cohen. Any charges arising? That's above my pay grade.' Paula smiled. 'Has this been going on all the time you were working for the nuns, Jezza? The whole twenty years?'

He frowned. She could see the wheels going round. Was it memory or scheming? Hard to tell. At last, he said, 'I'd been there about four or five years before the Reverend Mother asked me to do it.'

'Sister Mary Patrick?'

'No, it was before her time. Sister Bernadette, it was back then.'

'How many girls have you buried over the years, Jezza?'

Another sideways glance at the lawyer. 'I didn't keep count,' he said. 'It's not like it happened every week, or anything. Maybe once or twice a year at the most.'

Shaken by the numbers as well as his casual demeanour,

Paula struggled to maintain her composure. 'Once or twice a year? For, what, fifteen? Sixteen years? That's a helluva lot of dead girls not to be asking about, Jezza.'

'Look, if you think something dodgy went on with them, you need to be talking to the nuns. All I did was put them in the ground, like I was told to.' He scowled at her, daring her to take issue with him.

'And we will be talking to the nuns, Jezza. But right now, we need to talk about the other bodies.'

Now the solicitor sat up straight in his seat. 'Other bodies?'

'Did your client not mention them when he briefed you? I guess they haven't made the headlines yet. We've discovered a second group of human remains. Not in the lawn. It's early days yet. We don't have much detail but they don't appear to be young girls. And they're buried in your market garden, Jezza. At the bottom of your raised beds and under your vegetable plots.' Paula sat back, watching the impact of her words. Martinu seemed to shrink into himself, shoulders hunched, hands clasped between his knees.

Not even his years of training and experience could keep Cohen from looking startled. His eyes widened and his pen stopped mid-word on his pad. 'I need a word with my client,' he gabbled.

They went through the rigmarole of turning off the recording, then Paula and Steve left the room. 'You think I didn't push him hard enough, don't you?' Paula leaned against the wall, longing for a cigarette. This was when the old cravings hit hardest. Mostly she didn't miss smoking, though she could tell anyone who was interested when it was she'd smoked her last cigarette, down to the day and the hour. But in an interview, when she was trying to get the better of someone who didn't want to give something up, that was when she longed for the business of lighting up, drawing hard and deep and feeling that glorious buzz.

'I'd have gone in harder,' Steve said.

'We can't afford to be that bothered about the nuns, even though they were clearly a bunch of sadistic heartless bitches. We'll never get a cause of death on those kids. We'll be lucky to get assault charges on what happened to those poor bloody girls. I don't see the CPS pursuing conspiracy to prevent a lawful and decent burial. It's not something they'd relish taking through the courts. It's complicated and difficult and you can bet the nuns will all be hiding behind each other. It's not like these girls have got families screaming for justice. But the bodies in the raised beds? That's a different story. Sophie texted me earlier to say the victims have got plastic bags taped over their heads. That's murder right there. And that's what we're going to hit him with as soon as the suit calls us back in.'

'I still think—'

But whatever Steve thought was lost as the lawyer's head appeared at the door. 'We're ready, Inspector.'

Act Two got under way without delay. 'Not little girls, these bodies,' Paula said. Jezza glared at her, his face immobile. 'As I said, early days yet. We don't know much about them. What we do know is that they were murdered.'

Jezza jerked involuntarily.

'What do you say to that, Jezza?' Paula leaned in, forearms on the table, eyes not leaving his.

'No comment.' His voice was cracked and dry.

'They had plastic bags taped round their heads, Jezza. I don't think the nuns did that, do you?'

'No comment.'

'Plastic holds fingerprints really well. So does adhesive

tape. You'd be amazed how many people leave prints on the sticky side of the tape. Usually from the last time they used it before they taped up some part of someone's body. Are we going to find your prints, Jezza? Your DNA?'

'No comment.' It was almost a howl. Cohen put a hand on his client's arm, but Martinu flinched away from him. 'I never killed anybody,' he shouted.

Paula shook her head, apparently more in sorrow than in anger. 'You see, that's not how it looks, Jezza. Your vegetable garden. Raised beds that you built. You've got the shed full of tools. You've got the digger. You've been burying bodies for the nuns for years. You can see why I'm thinking we don't have to look any further for our killer.'

'You're badgering my client, Inspector. This is purely circumstantial. You have no evidence.' He pushed his chair back. 'Come on, Mr Martinu. We're leaving now.'

Martinu looked confused, but he stumbled to his feet.

Paula stood. 'Not so fast, Mr Cohen.' She jerked her head towards the door and Steve moved to cut off the exit. 'Jerome Martinu, I am arresting you on suspicion of murder—'

'It wasn't me,' Martinu shouted, lunging towards her. 'It was that fucking priest.'

34

As we become a more secular society, you'd imagine the numbers of killers claiming religious reasons for their crimes would diminish. I don't have statistics on this, but anecdotally, if anything it's on the increase . . .

From *Reading Crimes* by Dr Tony Hill

Alvin was left in a small anteroom off the tiled hallway. It resembled a police interview room in layout, but no police interview room ever boasted a burnished table with the kind of curly legs he'd only ever seen in antique shops. On one side stood a carved wooden seat with broad arms; on the other, a pair of severe and sturdy chairs. He stayed on his feet, studying the prints on the wall. They looked like the kind of old paintings you got on Christmas cards from people who wanted you to think they were more cultured than you.

The door opened behind him and he turned to see a tall nun in the doorway. The fabric of her habit was so perfectly black it made her look like negative space. On her head was a complicated starched confection that reminded Alvin of the TV adaptation of *The Handmaid's Tale*, if Offred's headgear had been folded back in a kind of go-faster spoiler. With the light behind her, her face looked austere and unlined. She could have been any age between thirty and sixty. 'Sergeant Ambrose? I am the Superior General of the Order of the Blessed Pearl.' As she spoke she moved to the ornate chair and gestured that he should sit opposite. 'You may call me Mother Benedict.'

'Thanks for seeing me.' Alvin sat down on one of the least comfortable chairs he'd ever experienced.

'We are aware of the outside world, Sergeant. We saw the news about the Bradesden house. We anticipated a visit from the police.' Now the light was falling on her face, he could see there were fine lines around her eyes and on her forehead. Nearer fifty than thirty, then. Delicate features, dark eyes under surprisingly heavy brows.

'I understand some of the nuns from Bradesden are living here now?'

She inclined her head. 'Can I ask exactly what you think you have discovered in the grounds of Bradesden?'

That was how it was going to be, then. 'We know we have discovered the remains of up to forty children and adolescents. We know the approximate number based on the skulls that have been recovered so far. As far as we can ascertain, there are no records of any formal burials at the convent apart from those of nuns and priests in the official graveyard.'

'And you think this has something to do with the members of the order?'

'It seems likely,' Alvin said. He stretched his legs in front of him and crossed them at the ankles. 'Being as how the skeletons have been there longer than the five years since the convent closed. And early forensic evidence indicates that at least some of them definitely went in the ground while the convent was up and running.'

Her hand went to the mother of pearl-encrusted crucifix that hung on her chest. 'God rest their souls. But how can you place responsibility for this at the door of our sisters?'

He didn't think she was stupid, but if she wanted to play that game, he'd indulge her. 'Well, they were responsible for the girls in the refuge and the school.'

'But you don't know for certain that these remains are of any of our girls.'

'I don't think there's much likelihood of them *not* being your girls. But wherever they came from, they ended up under your front lawn, Mother. And that means I need to talk to the sisters who came to you from Bradesden.'

She gave a small sharp sigh. 'I'm not sure that will be of much use to you.'

'Why not? They must have seen something. You don't have your front lawn dug up forty times and not notice.'

Another sigh. 'Nuns are not like other people, Sergeant. Even in a working order such as ours, we strive to focus on the interior life. Worldly concerns often don't penetrate our consciousness.'

Did she really expect him to fall for this? 'Nuns are human beings, though. And curiosity afflicts all of us to some extent. I will need to talk to the sisters.'

'Women become nuns for all sorts of reasons. Some have a very clear religious vocation, an irresistible desire to offer up their lives to the service of God. Some come to us because they see this life as an escape from the modern world and all its temptations and troubles, only to find that their troubles accompany them and must still be faced. Some come seeking the contemplative life, a devotion to the beauty of our daily offices. One thing we all have in common in the Order of the Blessed Pearl is a repudiation of the outside world. And of course, the vow of obedience. If they were told to ask no questions and put something from their mind, they will have done so.'

Alvin stared at her in disbelief. 'You're saying the Mother Superior could do whatever she liked, with total immunity? Just tell the nuns to forget anything dodgy, and bingo! It's forgotten?'

'Reverend Mothers are not prone to what you call "dodgy" behaviour. But in essence, what you are saying is correct. The nuns under her supervision are obliged to put aside their God-given free will and accept the need to obey in all things.' Her expression was placid, as if this were a matter of no account.

'So, they could have been turning a blind eye to all sorts of things? And if they talked about it, they'd be in trouble?'

'If a nun is privy to something that troubles her conscience, she can bring it to her priest.'

Alvin scoffed. 'And that's covered by the seal of the confessional, right?'

'Yes.'

He shook his head. 'You make the mafia look like chatterboxes.'

'I'm not being deliberately obstructive, Sergeant. But this is the rule we've lived by for centuries.'

'It protects the guilty.'

A faint smile. 'It would be our contention that we are not "the guilty". That when we do fall short, we confess our failings and we are shriven. The nuns who came here from Bradesden will not be able to further your inquiries. Their Reverend Mother, possibly. But she is not among us.'

'I'm struggling with this, Mother Benedict. We're talking about the bodies of forty young girls, girls who were almost certainly in the care of your order. And you're hiding behind an outdated set of rules.' He shifted his position, elbows on his knees, his big head thrust forward. 'There will be a coroner's inquest at the very least. Your nuns will be under oath. They'll have to answer then. They might as well answer now.'

Her hand moved to her crucifix again. 'And the answer will be the same. They know nothing. The sisters who came to us from Bradesden are the most elderly members of the community. Two of them are suffering from dementia, so you must rule them out immediately. I can assure you that the others know nothing about these matters. If you insist, you may interview them. But their answers will be the same.'

Three hours and eight nuns later, Alvin learned she was telling no less than the truth. The six who did not have dementia had as much to say on the subject of dead children as those who barely knew their own names. Whatever they might have known, they'd consigned to a place in their heads behind a heavy door with more bolts and padlocks than he could unfasten. Three simply stared at him in bewilderment so perfect he began to doubt himself. One couldn't stop talking about the wonderful life of the convent and the blessing of being given the care of such promising girls and the joy of being in the service of a nun like Mother Mary Patrick. A fifth refused to meet his eyes, staring into her lap for the duration of the interview and barely responding in monosyllables. The wrong monosyllables, in Alvin's opinion. The sixth admonished him to judge not lest he be judged and refused to comment further except to say, 'Whatever happened at Bradesden, it happened under the watchful eye of Our Lady and St Margaret Clitherow. They would not tolerate any occasion of sin under their roof.'

Through it all, Mother Benedict sat unsmiling, her fingers moving continuously over the glowing amber beads of a rosary. As the last nun left the room, she rose to her feet. 'I'm sorry you've wasted so much of your time, Sergeant. You really should have taken my word for what the sisters would be able to tell you.' She finally gave a full smile, her eyes crinkling at the corners. 'Poverty, chastity and obedience, Sergeant. And the greatest of these is obedience. Nuns don't lie. We simply train ourselves to forget that which we are not supposed to know.'

35

When we see Freudian analysis portrayed in films and TV, they often make a thing out of the fact that the psychoanalyst seldom speaks. There's a rationale in that approach. Silence is the interviewer's friend. Most of us struggle with the overwhelming urge to fill it.

From *Reading Crimes* by Dr Tony Hill

Paula rested her head on the steering wheel of her car and breathed deeply. She was hungry, tired and late for the evening arrangement she'd been looking forward to. But Martinu's sudden accusation provoked one of those sudden flurries of activity that descended on major investigations whenever there came an unexpected change of direction.

Paula and Steve had of course promptly steered Martinu and his lawyer back to the table to continue the interview. Initially, Martinu had sat hunched over, his head in his hands, rocking to and fro on his chair. But Paula caught a glimpse of him flicking a glance at her through his fingers and found herself less than convinced by his apparent come-apart.

'Come on, Jezza,' she said gently, not letting her doubt show. 'I know this is hard, but you will feel like a weight's come off your shoulders when you tell us what you know. You're not betraying Father Keenan, you're doing the right thing.'

He looked up, his features squeezed tight in an expression of pain. 'He was my priest. He said I wouldn't understand what he was involved in, but it was God's work.' He spread his hands, palms upwards. 'What was I supposed to do?'

'He had no right to involve you in any of this,' Paula said. 'But we need to get to the bottom of it, and you can help us here, Jezza. And you can help yourself too. Things look pretty bad for you right now, I won't lie. But if you tell us the whole story, explain to us how you got drawn into it, it'll make a difference for you.'

He rubbed his eyes then looked at his lawyer. 'I'm going to tell them,' he said.

Cohen patted his arm. 'That's your choice, Mr Martinu. But I will intervene if I think you're potentially making things worse for yourself.'

Martinu shook his head. 'She's right. I've been carrying this weight around and I'm tired of it.'

'What did you do?'

Martinu looked away, twisting his fingers round each other. 'Same as I did for the nuns. I dug holes when I was asked to. But I never filled them in for the priest. He did that himself.'

'Talk me through it,' Paula said.

He was shifting in his seat, uneasy and struggling. His manner was completely different from when he'd told them about digging the graves for the nuns. She reckoned he'd known all along it was wrong but he hadn't known how to make it right, how to stand up to a priest. 'He came to me ... it must have been seven or eight years ago. He said he'd been doing a lot of work with the homeless in Bradfield.' He gave her an imploring look. 'It's the kind of thing a priest's supposed to do, right? Help people down the bottom of the pile?'

And God knew there were enough of those in Bradfield, Paula thought. The back streets around Temple Fields and behind Bellwether Square crawled with the flotsam and jetsam of the city. Spice, the drug of choice among the destitute, had hollowed out lives, leaving human husks to stumble around in a haze. People complained the police were failing in their job to keep the streets safe, but what were they supposed to do? There was nowhere for them to take the street people where they could start climbing out of the pit they'd collapsed into. 'Go on,' Paula said, when Martinu slowed to a halt.

'So he said that sometimes people died on the streets and there was nobody to claim them. Nobody to give them a decent burial. He said they just got cremated and their ashes scattered like they were rubbish. He said he wanted something better for them. And since the convent was sacred ground, he wanted to bury them here. Only, he'd be breaking the law, taking their bodies away without telling the police or the social services.' He gnawed at the skin on the side of his thumbnail, his eyes flicking back and forth like a frightened animal.

'He asked you for help?'

Martinu nodded. 'He said it wouldn't happen often. But it does happen, you must know that, in your job. People just die on the streets, and half the time nobody even knows their real name or where they come from. He said when he heard about it happening, there might be times when he'd want to bring them here, so they could have a proper resting place.'

Steve couldn't contain himself any longer. He leaned forward, getting in Martinu's space. 'And you didn't think there was anything weird about that? Anything *wrong*?'

Martinu grimaced, as if he was fighting tears. But his eyes were dry, Paula noticed. 'He was a fucking priest. Don't you get it? You grow up a Catholic, it's ingrained from birth. The priest can do no wrong. Even when he's wrong, he's right. It wasn't my place to go questioning him. He said it was a kind of blessing, laying them to rest. And all he was asking me to do was dig a hole.'

'How did it work?' Paula spoke quietly, taking the heat out of the room. 'Did Father Keenan just turn up with a body?'

A slow shake of the head. 'He'd speak to me earlier in the day. Say he'd heard from one of his contacts about a death, that they'd be protecting the body till he could get there. I'd make a grave somewhere in the vegetable garden. There was always somewhere needing cleared out. Then he'd turn up in the evening at my back gate. After dark. He'd drive in, usually with some deadbeat in the passenger seat. I've got an old roadworks lantern, the light just comes out in one direction. I used to put that by the grave so they could see it coming from my place but you couldn't really see it from the convent side.' He paused again. It was an effort to gather himself.

Paula waited. Silence could often be the best tool, especially once the accused had broken the seal of their own secret. It was like opening a bag of Maltesers, she thought.

Once you'd started, you might kid yourself that you were going to stop. But you couldn't. 'I left them to it,' he said. 'I never saw the bodies. I suppose they must have been in the boot. Father Keenan would knock on the back door when they'd finished and just say, "That's us done. God bless you, Jezza."'

And so they leaned on him for another hour. Stop, start. Eight bodies, Martinu admitted, though he wasn't certain about the total. The last one about seven months before. For even though the priest had moved away, he maintained his work with the destitute of Bradfield. No, he couldn't remember exact dates. He'd given a harsh bark of incredulous laughter at that point. How would he remember the dates?

Paula had pointed out his obsession with Bradfield Vics; maybe he remembered one of the burials because it was just before or just after a big game?

At the mention of the club, he'd become agitated. There was, he insisted, no way he paid attention to the dates. He put them out of his mind as soon as they were done with because they made him uneasy. Even though the priest said it was OK, it still made him uncomfortable.

When they'd started going round in circles, Paula had brought it to a close, leaving Martinu to talk to his lawyer before he was bedded down in a cell for the night. Rutherford had been preening himself all round the incident room, making it clear whose team had scored the breakthrough. Paula was tasked with bringing Father Keenan in for interview first thing.

Remembering Karim been assigned to interviewing the priest, she went looking for him. He was nowhere to be seen and his interview hadn't been posted to the incident room. She tried calling him, but his phone went straight to voicemail. No reason to be worried, she told herself. He could have had to hang around waiting for the priest to become available. And worked late enough to feel justified in knocking off for the day. There was no overtime in ReMIT, after all.

Really, no reason to be worried.

Paula lifted her head off the steering wheel and drove to the family-run Italian restaurant that was close enough to home to be a regular haven for her and Elinor. That night, they'd arranged to meet a third person for dinner. Paula was almost an hour late, but she knew there would be no recriminations. Elinor and Carol Jordan both understood jobs that required a response to ever-changing circumstances. No overtime for a hospital consultant either.

During the years when Paula had carried a faintly flickering torch for Carol, it had never crossed her mind to hug her boss. Now that flame was dead, now there was no longer rank between them, whenever they met, it began with a hug. Hugging Carol was a bit like hugging a tree – a slender silver birch, not the thick trunk of an oak, but stiff and unyielding nonetheless – but it was a validation of a friendship. So they embraced, then Paula kissed Elinor on the corner of her mouth and sat down, feeling some of the day fall away from her shoulders.

'We've had antipasti,' Elinor said. 'And I ordered a family-sized bowl of spaghetti alla nonna to be cooked the moment you walked in.' She turned and gave the thumbs up to Donatella.

'It's on its way,' she called back.

'Thank you.' Paula let out a long breath and reached for the bottle of Primitivo. Only one glass gone so far, and the remains of that in front of Elinor. Out of the corner of her eye, she noticed the bottle of San Pellegrino next to Carol. Always a relief.

'You'll have had quite a day,' Carol said. 'Elinor said you were working the bones at the convent. I was surprised, I didn't think it would be ReMIT territory.'

'It wouldn't be, normally. Not without evidence of suspicious death, which we all know wouldn't come till the anthros have had their way with the bones. But Rutherford wanted it and he trampled over Alex Fielding to get it.'

Carol winced. 'He may live to regret that.'

'Annoyingly, it's just as well he did. We've not gone public with it yet but there's another set of remains that are quite distinct from the original discovery.' Paula reached for the last couple of olives in the bowl.

'That's weird,' Elinor said. 'Do you think they're connected? Like, someone who knew about the first bodies deciding that was a good place to hide their victim?'

'Victims, plural.' Paula shrugged. 'We don't know yet.'

'It would be an extraordinary coincidence if not. And—' Carol gave a wry grin as she and Paula chorused, 'We don't like coincidence.'

'It's a strange one,' Paula said. 'And here comes heaven,' she added as Donatella arrived with a steaming bowl of pasta. The aroma made Paula's mouth fill with saliva.

The three women took it in turn to exclaim and serve themselves. Carol spooned grated pecorino over her food and said, almost casually, 'You must miss Tony at a time like this.'

'Not just at a time like this. I'm due to see him soon, I'll see if he has any interesting insights to point us in the right direction.' Everyone had their eyes on their plates in a rare moment when discretion trumped curiosity.

Eating consumed them for a few minutes, then Carol said, 'Bronwen Scott turned up at my place the other day.'

Paula raised her eyebrows, a forkful of pasta halfway to her mouth. 'What on earth did she want?'

'She's part of an informal group of professionals running their own small-scale version of the Innocence Project. Working on miscarriages of justice. They call themselves After Proven Guilty. As in—'

'Yeah, I get it,' Paula chipped in with a wry smile. 'Innocent until proven guilty,' she added for Elinor's benefit.

'In one.' Carol sipped her water. 'She wants me on board.'

'That's a no-brainer,' Elinor said. 'That's right up your street, isn't it?'

Carol gave a one-shoulder shrug. 'I don't know. I always said you're only as good as your team. I've no idea whether I can cut it as a solo player.'

'I wouldn't worry about that. Has she dangled something in front of you?'

'Oh yes.' And between mouthfuls, she told them about Saul Neilson and Lyle Tate.

'No body and circumstantial,' Paula said. 'Getting a conviction must have been tricky.'

Elinor put down her fork. 'I guess that makes overturning it so much harder.'

Carol gave her a considering look. 'Is that the sound of a gauntlet being slapped down?'

Paula groaned. 'What have you done, Doc? Carol Jordan and Bronwen Scott? The last time you two worked together you nearly destroyed Bradfield Metropolitan Police.'

Carol grinned. 'Better run for the hills, Paula.'

*

Half a bottle of Primitivo and a complimentary grappa meant leaving the car outside the restaurant. Carol offered to drive them home but their polite excuses tumbled over each other – 'It's out of your way,' 'It's no distance,' 'I need the fresh air.' And so Elinor and Paula walked companionably back through deserted streets, still holding hands after all those years, swapping the inconsequential conversational exchanges of two people who know what the other is thinking and feeling about most things.

'It's good to see Carol doing what she's best at,' Elinor said.

'I suppose. I was hoping she'd maybe find something else to be good at. I don't like to think of her hankering after the life she can't have any more.'

'She's lost so much, Paula. She needs something to anchor her to her old self while she works out what her new one is. She's clearly trying to sort herself out so she can find a way back to Tony. Before you arrived, she admitted she's seeing a therapist who specialises in treating PTSD.'

Paula squeezed Elinor's hand. 'That's good news. Let's hope it helps.'

'I thought she seemed a bit more relaxed this evening. And she's not drinking.'

'Unlike me.' Paula gave a wry laugh. 'A day like today, a decent glass of wine feels like a lifeline to normality. I was looking at those crime scene pics and thinking if Torin hadn't pitched up with us, he could have ended up like one of those kids. Stuck in some abusive institution or living on the streets. Doesn't bear thinking about.'

'I know.' Elinor sighed. 'I see them all the time in A&E. Young kids, wrecked from drugs and street life. The older ones who're pretty much derelict from drink and homelessness. Some of them come in just for a place to sit and be warm in the middle of the night. Some of them are having mental health episodes. And some of them are too far gone for us to be of any use. Did you know that homeless people have a life expectancy that's thirty years less than the rest of us? If we'd been homeless for the last ten years, Paula, we'd be at death's door.'

Before Paula could reply, her ringtone cut through the background city hum. She let go Elinor's hand to dig it out of her pocket. Glancing at the screen, she said, 'Sorry, I've got to . . .'

Elinor walked on a few steps, and as Paula raised the phone to her ear, she felt an unexpected jolt of love as she took in her partner, long black hair gleaming under the street light, the familiar planes and angles of her lovely face as striking as when she'd first seen them. She turned away as Karim's voice spoke. 'Boss? I just got your message.'

'Where are you? What happened with the priest? Why haven't you been in touch? Or filed a report?' She rattled the questions at him without giving him a chance to reply.

'I came home, boss. It was late, there was nothing to say.'

'What? You didn't see the priest?'

'Yeah, I saw him. But he had nothing useful to say. He knew about the graves but as far as he was concerned, the deaths were all natural and he didn't take any part in the actual burials. He denied all knowledge of any abuse by the nuns. Boss, he totally had nothing helpful to say.'

'It doesn't matter, Karim. You should have filed your report. What did he say when you asked him about the second group of remains?' A moment's silence. Paula felt the tension released by the wine reassert itself in her neck. 'Karim? What did he say?'

'I didn't get the chance to ask him.' He sounded sheepish.

'What do you mean, you didn't get the chance? You were interviewing him, Karim.'

'He chucked me out. He got pissed off with the questions, he didn't like the implication that bad things had been happening and he'd been part of them. He told me it was over and he just walked out of the room.'

'And you let him?' Paula's voice rose almost to a yelp.

'What was I supposed to do? I couldn't go chasing him through his own house. He's just a witness, boss. I didn't have any power to detain him.'

'He's not just a witness, Karim. He's a person of interest. The groundsman, Martinu? He gave up Father bloody Keenan when we interviewed him earlier. If you'd phoned in like you should have, you'd be sitting outside his house right now, making sure he doesn't do a runner.'

'Oh shit,' Karim whispered.

'Oh, shit is right, Karim. So you're going back there first thing in the morning with me and we are going to bring him in. I want you outside my house at six a.m. With a decent cup of coffee and a bacon roll. And meanwhile, get your fucking report filed with the incident room and start praying Rutherford doesn't find out how comprehensively you've bollocksed this up.'

36

Some people discover they have a talent for music or painting. Pursuing it gives them a mission in life. Unfortunately, some people discover they have a talent for violence and their mission brings misery to everyone around them. Part of the problem is that we all like to have a sense of purpose; it's hard to turn your back on something you're good at.

From *Reading Crimes* by DR TONY HILL

It turned out that Matis Kalvaitis wasn't just a good fighter. He was also a good publicist. Writing the draft appeal against his deportation had occupied Tony for a couple of days. He'd done some research in the prison library. It had an interesting if random collection of law books, which the prisoner on library duty had described as 'the DIY section'. He'd found what he needed to put together a letter that he thought covered the bases, attaching a note that made it clear what additional information was needed and where it should go. He'd handed it over at the first opportunity and let it slide from the front of his mind, which was by then occupied with writing a chapter on misogyny.

The next morning, when he'd returned from breakfast, three prisoners were hanging around on the landing outside his cell. He felt the sudden fizz of adrenaline. Had he pissed someone off? Was this a punishment crew? Before he could turn and walk away, one of them called to him. 'Don't freak out, Doc. It's not what you think. Well, not yet, anyway.'

It turned out that Kalvaitis had been so impressed with what Tony had done that he'd told all his mates. Who had told all their mates. Not only did the shrink write good English, he had nice handwriting too. The kind of writing that would impress a woman, or cheer up a kid or make you look like you weren't a complete loser.

Three inmates, three demands. A letter to a landlord demanding that he fix the troublesome toilet in the flat where the man's girlfriend and three kids were living; a birthday message to a mother; and a bedtime story for a three-year-old daughter. 'It doesn't have to be long, or fancy. Just a little bit of a story that her mum can read to her.'

Tony was nonplussed. He hadn't written a story since his third year at high school. 'I don't know,' he said, dubious. 'Why can't you read her a story down the phone?'

The man's hands had clenched into fists. 'If I could . . .' He cleared his throat. 'It's fucking impossible to get on the phone at the right time, you know what it's like. No point in a bedtime story at three o'clock, is there?'

And Tony understood. It wasn't the story that was the issue, it was the reading. He couldn't write a story because he couldn't write. He couldn't read to his daughter because he couldn't read. 'I'll try,' he said. 'What does she like?'

'Princesses and space rockets,' the man muttered. 'I'll pay you in phone cards.'

Which would be fine, Tony thought, if he had anyone to phone. He wasn't without friends. Paula and Elinor had become close in recent years. He and Torin were mates, going to Bradfield Vics and hanging out on his narrowboat together. And then there was Carol ... But he'd always struggled with talking on the phone. He felt at a disadvantage when he couldn't see people's body language, gauge the changing messages of their faces. Besides, what could he talk about? 'Thanks,' he said. At least phone cards were currency. He'd find something he wanted to trade them for.

But the encounter made him think. He suspected these wouldn't be the last things he'd be asked to write. As he pushed his laundry basket round the wing, he mulled it over. And remembered hearing about a scheme to combat violent crime he'd read about in a psychology journal. One of the key points where changes in behaviour could be effected, the article said, was when violent men became fathers. They longed to be proper fathers but they didn't know how; either their fathers had been absent or they'd been abusive in a terrifying range of ways.

The researchers had uncovered the fact that there was a high rate of limited literacy among their target group. In the face of resistance from men who didn't want to be seen reading 'kid stuff', they'd worked on teaching them enough basic reading skills to be able to read their young children a bedtime story. It didn't sound much, but the reported effects had been significant. Building bonds with their children had put a brake on criminal activity that punishment had failed to manage. It wasn't an overnight transformation but it was clear that something had shifted for some of these men.

Tony considered how he could use this nugget of information. He supposed he could make an appointment with one of the assistant governors and suggest setting up a basic literacy course for the inmates. He suspected that would get him precisely nowhere. Ever since he'd arrived in custody, all he'd heard was that the budgets were stretched to breaking point. Prisoners were supposed to have access to education but programmes were limited and waiting lists long. Going down the official route was almost certainly a waste of time.

But he'd quickly learned that there were unofficial routes to everything in a prison. The library had space; they ran a couple of book groups already. Maybe he could get something going. He'd have to think carefully what to call it. Admitting you couldn't read or write was one of the handful of things that was still shaming. Because it was something that anybody could do, wasn't it? Kids could do it. Fuckwits could do it. Screws could do it. And in prison, no one ever chose to look vulnerable.

It had to be something with no challenge in it. He couldn't call it 'How to be a dad' because that would suggest they didn't know how to be dads, which was tantamount to saying they didn't know how to be men. 'Reading with your kids'? Or maybe, 'Books to share with your kids'? That was more like it. Suggestions rather than instructions.

Tony didn't know much about teaching people to read. But he did have some experience of teaching. And if they started with basic alphabet books, how hard could it be? The prison library probably didn't have anything like that. But he had a publisher. And he had a phone card.

And now he had a purpose.

37

In crime fiction, the culprit is generally the least likely person. In real life, the opposite holds true. Usually, it's the most obvious person.

From *Reading Crimes* by DR TONY HILL

Because half past five would come round far too soon. Elinor had opted for the spare room, so Paula was able to privilege speed over stealth. Hand slapped on the phone to turn off the alarm, quick burst of a shower, towel dry and into today's maroon polo neck under the grey suit from Hobbs' sale. She was downstairs and ready to roll twenty minutes later, staring out of the window at the street, orange juice in hand, wishing she hadn't given up smoking. Oh, for that first hit of the day, the blessed nicotine hitting the bloodstream and snapping the synapses to attention.

Right on cue, a black BMW nosed into sight and Karim double-parked outside her front door. Paula was down the path and in the passenger seat inside a minute. A bacon roll in a paper bag sat on the dashboard, a halo of condensation around it on the windscreen. A carton of coffee in the cupholder, a wisp of steam escaping from the slit in the lid. 'Full marks for obeying one set of instructions,' she said, reaching for the sandwich and checking for brown sauce. 'But you're not out of my personal doghouse yet. I was nearly worried about you.'

'Worried?' He pulled away.

'Well, it turns out you'd been interviewing someone accused of a series of murders. And you were off the radar.' She bit into the roll. 'Mmm. That's magnificent. You should have got one for yourself.'

He rolled his eyes. 'Yeah, the classic muzza breakfast. What, you thought he'd topped me?'

Chew. Swallow. 'Not really. On reflection, I thought you were probably being a lazy git who wanted to get back to his sexy new girlfriend before she went off the boil.'

Karim scowled. 'I don't have a girlfriend right now.'

'No excuse, then.'

'So what did the lawnmower say?'

'The lawnmower?' For a moment, Paula was lost. Then the penny dropped with a clatter. 'The groundsman.' Between sips of coffee and mouthfuls of bread and crispy bacon, she ran through the interview with Jezza Martinu.

'You believe him?' Karim asked when she'd done.

'I definitely believe it wasn't Martinu who killed them. But I'm not a hundred per cent that he's giving us the whole story. What's he like, this priest?'

'Irish. Looks like he hasn't had a square meal in months. A bit full of himself. Not used to being questioned. Got really snippy when I suggested it was hard to believe he didn't know what was going on with the nuns. And then he decided he'd had enough and he just walked out.' He gave a sharp sigh. 'What would you have done, boss?'

What would she have done? It wouldn't help to say she wouldn't have let it get to that point in the first place. 'It's a tough call but I'd probably have waited him out. He'd have to come back eventually.'

'You'd just have sat there?'

'Yes. Because my mindset is that it isn't over till I say it's over.'

They drove in glum silence for a few minutes. Then Karim said, 'I've got a lot to learn, right?'

'Yeah. But knowing that is half the battle.'

There was no sign of activity in the priest's house. Upstairs and downstairs, in one room apiece, curtains were drawn. 'Nice gaff,' Paula said. 'They do all right in spite of the theoretical poverty.'

She rang the bell, stepped back and waited. Nothing. Not even a twitch of the curtain. Another ring, more nothing. She nodded at Karim and indicated the knocker. He grinned and banged it as hard as he could three times. 'I hope he hasn't done one,' Karim muttered, hammering the knocker again.

This time, the door opened on the chain. One bleary eye and a section of unshaven chin appeared in the gap. 'What are you doing here at this time of the morning?' Pissed off, rather than worried, Paula thought. She stepped forward. 'And who are you?'

'I am Detective Inspector McIntyre of the Regional Major Incident Team. Open the door, please, sir.'

'Why should I? I said all I had to say to your ... your colleague yesterday. This is outrageous. I was in bed, asleep. And you come banging on the door—'

Paula talked right over him. 'There are two ways to do this. You open the door and let us in. Or I call in the local tactical support group and they arrive with sirens and flashing lights and break your door down. It's your choice, but you have to make it in the next thirty seconds. You should take it as read that I am not bluffing. I got up very early to be here now and I am not going away without what I came for.'

His mouth hung open. Paula doubted anyone had spoken to him like that in years. He pushed the door almost closed; the chain rattled as fingers clumsy with sleep or fear fumbled it out of its track. Then the door edged open. Father Keenan stood in his rumpled state, skinny legs covered in thick black hair sticking out of the bottom of a woollen dressing gown over a white T-shirt. He backed up enough to let them in and Karim closed the door behind him.

'You are Father Michael Keenan?' Paula asked.

'I am he.' Imperious tone, the shock ebbing out of him.

We'll see about that. 'Michael Keenan, I am arresting you on suspicion of murder. You do not have to say anything. But, it may harm your defence if you do not mention when questioned something which you later rely on in court. Anything you do say may be given in evidence.'

He took a step back, horrified incredulity on his face. He raised his hands, palms out, as if fending off a blow. 'This is crazy,' he protested. 'I had nothing to do with those girls. Nothing.' He pointed at Karim. 'He said nothing about murder.'

'It's not the girls we're here about,' Paula said. 'It's the other bodies.'

He blinked rapidly, aghast. 'What are you talking about? What other bodies?'

'Father Keenan, I'm going to have to ask you to get

dressed and come with us to Bradfield, where you will be formally interviewed. DC Hussein will accompany you upstairs to get dressed.'

'This is madness. I'm not going anywhere with you. You can't just march in here with your nonsense.' Karim moved towards him but he shied away. 'I want a lawyer before I set one foot out of here.'

'You can consult with a lawyer at the police station. But right now, you are under arrest and you are coming to Bradfield with us. If you don't want to get dressed, I'm quite happy to handcuff you and frogmarch you out to our car for all your neighbours to see. How do you think that'll go down with your parishioners? With your bishop?' Paula sighed. 'Karim?'

He grabbed Keenan's arm and with his other hand pulled a set of plastic cuffs from his pocket.

'All right,' the priest shouted. 'May God forgive you for this outrage. I'll get dressed.' Karim let him go and followed him upstairs.

Paula let out a long breath. Was that the reaction of an innocent man? Or one cunning enough to have carried out these crimes in the first place? Too soon to know. But she'd get there. One way or another.

38

However bizarre the sequence of actions undertaken by a serial murderer, they will all have meaning for the killer. No two sequences are ever identical. And there is no limit to how grotesque they can seem.

From *Reading Crimes* by Dr Tony Hill

Rutherford had called just as Alvin was finishing breakfast. Whenever he could manage it, he sat down to eat with Esme and the kids. He'd been brought up in the belief that eating together had a value that went far beyond the calorific. That morning, he'd been first downstairs, beating eggs in a bowl and scrambling them with a handful of cheese, spring onions and a scatter of chilli flakes. Thick slices of crusty white toast slathered with butter on the side. 'Breakfast of champions,' he announced as they sat down together. Esme rolled her eyes, her response as predictable as his words. The kids said nothing, too busy eating.

When his phone rang, Alvin automatically got up from

the table and closed the door behind him as he headed into the hall. Rutherford launched straight in. 'Sergeant, don't bother coming in for the early briefing. I want you to go straight to the lab and see what they have to tell us about the second set of remains. I realise it's early days, but I want them to know we're staying right on top of this. Whatever they've got at this point, I want it. Clear on that?'

It was hard to imagine what could be unclear about Rutherford's instructions. Alvin wondered if the man was unconsciously racist or whether he treated everyone as if they were a bit on the slow side. He'd have to check that with Paula. 'Clear, sir,' was all he said. 'I'm on my way.'

He checked the time. If he dropped the kids at school, it would only take him a few minutes out of his road. A few minutes that nobody would notice. And it would mean starting his day with a better taste in his mouth than Rutherford's patronising words.

He'd called ahead to let Chrissie O'Farrelly know he was coming and she was waiting for him at the reception desk. As they made their way up to the room with the view of the lab, she brought him up to speed on the second group of remains. 'They've gone in the first instance to the mortuary so the pathologists can make their primary findings. Some of the bodies are partially fleshed, so there may be indications of what happened to them before they went into the ground,' she said, leading the way and sitting down.

'So you can't tell me much about where we're up to right now?' Alvin was disappointed. He still clung to the idea that forensics experts could work magic, and almost instantly. If pushed, he'd have had to admit to watching too much *CSI*.

She took off her glasses and polished them on the sleeve

of her lab coat. Her face was transformed into something far less intimidating. 'We have a real-time link with the pathology suite these days,' she said, replacing her glasses and re-establishing the hierarchy. 'We hear their findings as they make them. It's very useful to have such a joined-up process.'

'And?' He looked expectant.

'So far we have discovered eight sets of remains and we're in the process of recovering them. It's not quite as straightforward as the bones because, as I said, some of them are partially fleshed because of the conditions of the burials. That means we have to take rather more time in removing them, and the surrounding soil. It's not pretty,' she added, a faint curl of the lip for emphasis.

'It sounds like these are definitely in a different category from the human remains in the front lawn?' This was one assertion he felt fairly confident about making. Particularly in the light of what he'd heard of Martinu's revelations.

A fleeting smile. 'You know we hate to leap to conclusions here, Sergeant. But first impressions are that these body disposals are different in every way. For starters, the wrappings are entirely different. As I told you, the girls' bodies were enclosed in shrouds made from a linen and cotton mixture. The second group have been wrapped in bed sheets – a polyester cotton mix, so what we've got are bits of dyed polyester, elastic from the corners of fitted sheets and fragments of relatively intact material. The sheets were sealed with packing tape, which hasn't decayed, so some of the original fabric was sandwiched between bits of tape.'

'And labels? Sheets have labels, right?'

Dr O'Farrelly smiled. 'You're a fast learner, Sergeant. I've no doubt we'll find some labels in the environment of the bodies. Now, most of these bodies are practically skeletonised, so they've clearly been in the ground for a while. Years, probably, in most cases. We've do have quite a few bits of clothing, though. Man-made fabrics of one sort or another. Polyester, lycra, the plastic of trainers, metal eyelets from lace-holes, rivets and zips from jeans. Elastic from jogging bottoms. Other stuff. A couple of replica football shirts, for example. Still surprisingly identifiable. One Arsenal, one Bradfield Victoria.' She paused, her line of sight drifting up to the corner of the ceiling, as if she was searching for the right words.

'These are without doubt homicide victims.' She spoke flatly, without inflection.

Alvin sat to attention. 'You can be sure about that? Already?'

Dr O'Farrelly looked out at the lab where her team were squirrelling away at their several tasks. She sighed. 'They had plastic bags taped over their heads. They will have asphyxiated.'

'All of them?' He imagined the struggle for breath and felt sick.

She nodded. 'All of them. The older bodies have decomposed, so what happens over time is that the bodies decay as they normally would. The neck eventually decomposes sufficiently to allow the environments inside and outside the bag to become continuous. Eventually, there'll be no discernible difference in the state of the head and the rest of the body. Except that there'll be a taped-up plastic bag over the skull to tell the tale of how they died.'

'Bloody hell,' Alvin said.

'Well, not bloody, actually, as homicide goes. There is one body, however, that is slightly different. My soil scientist colleague put her head together with an anthropologist who specialises in rates of decay, and between them they estimate it's only been in the ground for a matter of months. Somewhere between six and eight months. There's reasonably advanced decomposition of the body, so there has been some access via the neck to the head. Inside the bag . . . well, let me just say there are some things I am very grateful to see on a screen rather than in reality.'

Alvin took a deep breath. 'I don't want to hear this but you're going to have to tell me.'

'The flesh is mushy. The whole head is sitting in what looks like a puddle of slimy vomit. Murky milky pools inside the bag. The skin's slipped off, taking the hair with it. One of my colleagues referred to it as "hairy soup with bits of skin like torn up lasagne floating in it". The smell will have been hideous.'

Alvin could feel his stomach folding in on itself. He fought the urge to run from the room and find the nearest toilet. Swallowed hard. Wiped a sheen of sweat from his top lip.

She fetched a bottle of water from a cabinet in the corner and handed it to him. 'Drink,' she commanded. Alvin did as he was told. He felt the water run down his gullet, its cold passage taking his mind off the nausea.

Dr O'Farrelly waited till he'd composed himself then said, 'Nothing glamorous in this line of work, we both know that. But there is a marginal upside, which is that we should be able to give you DNA on your man fairly quickly.'

'"Your man"?'

She nodded. 'So far, three bodies have been examined in some detail and the pathologists can say with a high degree of certainty that these are the bodies of young men. Definitely not little girls from the convent.'

'That's something.'

'It's about all I have for you right now. It all takes time, and we never have enough technicians to do the work. And every time you turn around, there's something new coming at you down the turnpike. I was at a meeting last week where they were telling us that you can find DNA even after the bloodstain's been washed out of clothing. The chromophores disappear but the DNA remains. Great, I'm thinking. As if we didn't have enough of a backlog. Now we're looking for the invisible man.' She shook her head.

'Believe me, I know what that feels like. Is there any possibility of getting the killer's DNA or prints from the adhesive tape?'

'Hard to say at this stage. But obviously we'll be looking for that. The bags themselves don't offer any clues. Three different supermarkets, two sports stores and three blanks. Our best chance might be the inside of the plastic bags.'

Alvin nodded. 'When you stick your hand inside a plastic bag to get it to open up. I get you.'

'I wouldn't hold out too much hope, though. The action of the fluids inside those plastic bags . . .'

'There's got to be something that nails this bastard,' Alvin growled.

'You'd think so, wouldn't you? But it doesn't always work out that way.'

39

The art of profiling depends on our ability to see beyond the obvious to the overlooked.

From *Reading Crimes* by DR TONY HILL

Even in the relatively short time that Carol had been out of the police force, the regulations about what was permissible for anyone visiting prison in an official capacity had become yet more draconian. When they'd met for Carol to pick up her letter of accreditation, Bronwen had explained. 'Every prison is a bit of a law unto itself, but Strangeways is the worst of the lot. They change the rules from week to week, just to get under our skin.'

'You can still take a bag in?'

'You can, but it's not worth it. The only things allowed in it are a pen, papers and glasses, if you need them. If there are any paperclips on your files, they have to be removed. Last time I went to Strangeways, they even made me take the elastic bands and the barrister's ribbon off the brief because they were potential weapons.'

'Death by elastic band?' Carol was incredulous.

'Could be a thing, apparently.' Bronwen looked scornful. 'But really, it's all about power and control. So, the basics are: no train tickets or timetables, no food or drink, no smart watches or anything with the capability of accessing the big bad internet. Absolutely no phones. Strangeways won't let you wear a watch or any kind of fitness tracker, which is a shame because sometimes you end up walking a long way to the interview room.' She grinned. 'Just take the minimum with you and leave everything in the locker except for your files, your legal pad and your pen. Make sure it's a nice new pen because they'll probably only let you take one in and if it runs out, tough.' She handed over a letter identifying Carol as a paralegal investigator for her firm.

'Go with the flow, Carol,' she added. 'I know it'll kill you but be meek and accommodating. It's tempting, but don't pick a fight. The most important person in this is the client. Getting yourself kicked out before you've had your sit-down with him defeats the object.'

Carol raised her eyebrows. 'I'm not a novice.'

Bronwen shrugged. 'You are on this side of the fence. You're used to being in the driving seat. The defence team don't even get to sit in the car.'

So Carol had played the game, swallowing the contempt of the swaggering officers who had painstakingly inspected her passport and the letter from Bronwen, then reluctantly pointed her to the locker where she'd deposited everything except the essentials. She'd been patient and pleasant in the face of their arrogance and her reward was now to walk through the metal detector at HMP Manchester.

The prison had been renamed in an attempt to scrub it of its notoriety, but everyone on both sides of the law continued to refer to it by its old name – Strangeways, notorious for its tough regime and even tougher inmates. Carol followed a wide-hipped male officer down a hallway that smelled of aggressive cleaning chemicals, through a sally port and a series of locked gates. Eventually, she was led into a tiny interview room with barely enough space for two chairs and a table that was wide enough to make any hand contact difficult. The officer left her alone to stare at the wall for more than ten minutes before Saul Neilson was led in through a door in the wall opposite the one Carol had entered by.

Prison did nobody any favours and Saul was no exception. He'd lost weight and there was a dullness in his eyes that she suspected was recent. When Carol introduced herself, he barely stirred. 'I'm here because we think your conviction is unsafe,' she said.

He snorted. 'Of course it's "unsafe". I was found guilty of something I didn't do. It doesn't get more unsafe than that. I've never been in trouble with the law. Not even stopped and searched which, you know, is kind of unusual for a black lad who drives a nice car. But the jury? They thought a gay black man had to be guilty of something and it might as well be murder.'

Carol nodded. 'You're probably right that racist attitudes played a part in your conviction. But there's no way to prove it, and proof is what we need to change this story.'

'How are you going to do that, then?' His chin came up in a challenge.

'I'm going to start with the genuine presumption that you're innocent. Please don't take this the wrong way, but I was a cop for the best part of twenty years. For most of that time, I was a detective. I ended up running a Major Incident Team.'

He scowled. 'Like that's going to make me trust you. Who do you think put me in here?'

'You can trust that I know what I'm doing. And that I know how cops put cases together. For example, there's usually a period of time between someone being arrested and actually being interviewed on tape. Sometimes police officers claim a suspect said things on the way to the police station and then refused to repeat them in the interview.'

He sighed. 'Being verballed is what they call it in here. But that didn't happen with me. No fabricated evidence claiming I'd said things I hadn't.'

'It cuts both ways,' Carol said. 'Sometimes a suspect says something in that unrecorded window that's totally unhelpful to the prosecution case. The officers conveniently forget about it when it comes to the sit-down interview and don't allude to it. So it doesn't appear on the record. In the shock and panic of being arrested and questioned and charged, it's easy to forget about it. If people remember it at all, it's sometimes not until they get to court, when it's too late for the defence to do anything about it. In English courtrooms, it doesn't happen like an American crime drama, where a crucial piece of evidence lands at the last minute and turns everything on its head. Can you remember anything like that?'

He frowned, concentration knitting his brows and drawing down the corners of his mouth. 'I don't think so,' he said at last, shaking his head. 'Like you said, it was all shock and panic. Not just because of the kind of crime they were talking about, but because ... well, because I was such a sad fucking closet case and I realised that the life I'd had was over. Whatever happened about Lyle, I was going to lose my family.'

'Because of your sexuality.'

His eyes glistened with emotion. 'Yes. And I was right. My father hasn't spoken to me since the day I was arrested. Neither of my parents visited me when I was on remand or since I was convicted. My sister writes to me, but she doesn't visit either. I lost everything, and all over something I didn't do.'

His pain was obvious. She knew that feeling, loss and anger and nowhere to put it. Carol knew better than to rush to judgement, but what she thought she recognised in Saul Neilson was an innocent man. 'Maybe we can fix at least some of that.'

'I don't see how. Unless some new evidence fell out of the sky.'

'Not yet.' She opened the file of papers she'd brought in with her. 'I've been reading the files relating to your case. And I've been reading them in a particular way. What we call "walking back the cat".'

'I don't know what that even means.'

'It means tracing something back to its dubious origins and figuring out the steps along the way. In this instance, it's about looking for what's not there.'

He scratched his jaw. 'How do you look for what's not there? And if it's not there, how do you know you've found it?'

It was a good question. What was that poem Tony always quoted at them? 'Yesterday, upon the stair, I met a man who wasn't there. He wasn't there again today. Oh, how I wish he'd go away.' But the only way to make him disappear was to shine a light on him. 'Experience. You're a landscape architect, right?'

'You know that, why ask?'

She gave a rueful smile. 'Force of habit. Always check. I imagine when you look at a project, you know instinctively what would complete it? It's the same for me. I read a court file and I think, What would I have asked that these detectives didn't ask? I was lucky – I used to work with a detective who had an extraordinary talent for interviewing and I learned a lot from watching her. So I bring a lot of experience to the table.'

He was alert now, head cocked, assessing her. 'And what did your experience show you was missing in my file?'

'I've not dug deep into all of it yet,' she admitted. 'But there's one thing I would have asked in that first interview that isn't there. And I can't see the answer to it anywhere in the case papers.'

'So what's this big question the Bradfield cops didn't manage to ask me?' There was a challenge in his expression now, an engagement that hadn't been there earlier.

'It's not a big question. But it might have a big answer. Did Lyle Tate say anything about where he was going after he left you?'

40

A profile only has investigative value. Not probative. It's guidance, not evidence. But for detectives attempting to accumulate evidence, it can often point them in directions they hadn't fully considered.

From *Reading Crimes* by DR TONY HILL

Steve Nisbet was dangerously close to too close to Paula. 'Why's Karim doing the interview with you?' he demanded. 'It was our interview that put Keenan in the frame, not his. I've seen his report. He didn't even *ask* the priest about the other bodies.'

Paula gave him her hardest stare, refusing to speak till he backed away a half-step. 'When it comes to the conduct of interviews, you do not question my decisions, Sergeant.' She placed the emphasis on his rank.

He glared back at her, breathing heavily through his nose. 'Fine.' He turned on his heel and stalked off.

From over her shoulder, Karim spoke quietly. 'I don't mind if you'd rather use Steve.'

'Don't you start questioning me, Karim. Shouting or whispering, it comes down to the same thing. Come on, Keenan's had long enough with his lawyer. It's time to get this show on the road.' Paula headed out of the squad room towards the interview room.

'How do we play this?' he asked, hot on her heels.

'I'll take the lead. You make a show of writing down some of the things he says. It doesn't much matter which things, it's all about unsettling him. Making him think we know more than we do.'

At the door to the interview room, Paula paused, fingertips on the door handle. She took a deep breath, allowed herself to consider what she knew and what she believed about Father Michael Keenan, then walked in, barely sparing him a glance. She didn't recognise the lawyer, a worn-looking woman in her forties in a jacket that was too tight in the shoulders and upper arms. Paula had a sneaking suspicion she didn't give a flying fuck about it.

Karim pressed the buttons and everyone recited their name for the tape. Before Paula could ask the first question, Keenan was right in there. 'I want to make an official protest about the way I've been treated. I am an ordained priest of the Catholic Church. If you had asked me to come here to be interviewed, I would have done so. To drag me out of my home at the break of day is offensive to me.'

Paula adopted an air of boredom as he spoke. 'Are you finished?'

'Did you hear what I said?' His cheeks were flushed with annoyance.

'It's on the tape. I'd like to remind you that you are under arrest on suspicion of murder and this is an interview under caution.'

'Precisely whom is my client supposed to have murdered?' The lawyer's accent was about three levels further up the social scale than Paula's. She sounded like the lady of the manor meeting the peasants at the annual opening of the garden to the public. It was completely at odds with her appearance.

'Person or persons unknown, at various points over the past ten years. Approximately.'

The woman's eyebrows rose. 'Could you be any more vague, Inspector?'

'The bodies we have recovered are not readily identifiable, but we are confident that forensics will yield some positive IDs as we move on. We do have the remains of eight bodies so far—'

'He said forty yesterday,' Keenan interrupted, pointing dramatically at Karim. 'Which is it? Forty or eight? There's a bit of a difference.'

'That does seem extraordinary,' the lawyer chipped in before Paula had a chance to reply.

'Bizarre though it may sound, we're looking at two separate groups of human remains. My colleague interviewed your client yesterday about the discovery of approximately forty skeletons of girls discovered in the convent grounds. At this point, we're not considering charging your client in respect of those remains. The focus of this interview is a second set of partially skeletonised bodies found in a different part of the grounds. They came to light as the result of a search using a cadaver dog. So far, we've found eight bodies. Initial forensic examination indicates they are homicide victims.' Paula delivered the information in her calmest tones.

'It certainly does sound bizarre,' the lawyer said. 'And why do you think this is anything to do with my client?'

'We have a witness statement that implicates your client.'

'That's nonsense,' Keenan protested. 'It's madness to suggest I have anything to do with this. I couldn't kill someone if my life depended on it. They must be more girls from the convent, you need to be asking the nuns these questions, not me.'

'These are not girls from the convent,' Paula said. 'They're young men.'

Keenan reared back in his seat, apparently thunderstruck. 'That's impossible,' he gasped.

'I have some questions I'd like to put to your client,' Paula said.

'I have advised him not to answer anything—'

'I have nothing to hide,' Keenan shouted over his lawyer. 'I know nothing about this. This is an outrage. You're going to be very, very sorry for what you've done today.'

'Your pastoral care when you were at the Bradesden house of the Order of the Blessed Pearl – did that extend beyond the convent at all?'

Clearly, it wasn't what he expected. 'No, my ministry was to the nuns and the girls in their charge.' Then he turned on Karim. 'What are you writing down? You've got this on tape, why do you keep writing stuff down?'

Paula answered for him. 'The tape doesn't always indicate demeanour, Father Keenan. We like our record to be as complete as possible. Did you do any work with the homeless in Bradfield?'

'The homeless?' He couldn't have sounded more surprised if she'd asked about his ministry to the royal family. Doubt stirred in Paula's mind for the first time. She'd encountered premier league liars over the years, however. A priest was someone accustomed to presenting a façade to the world. She wanted to see his reaction to more pressure than this before she seriously considered whether his protestations might be for real. 'Why would you think that?'

She shrugged. 'I'd have thought they're a group who need all the support they can muster. I'm no expert, but I'm sure you've heard the line before – if Jesus came back among us, he wouldn't be hanging out with the priests and bishops, he'd be down among the drunks and the junkies and the homeless.'

Keenan looked as if he wanted to hit her. He clenched his fists then, realising what he'd done, he swiftly moved his hands under the table. He leaned forward. 'Of course the church has an active ministry among the weakest members of our society. But I am not part of that team.'

'That's odd. We've been told that you took a very active role within that community.'

He flushed. 'Oh, is that what this is? Dead young men and a priest in the vicinity. Nothing like a sitting duck, is there? Not all priests are abusive. Not all of us are hiding terrible secrets. I am not homosexual. I am not a paedophile. I am no kind of predator, I am a dedicated priest. Whoever these poor souls buried in the convent grounds are, they are nothing to do with me.' His rage ran out of steam and he hung his head, breathing heavily. 'Nothing. To do. With me.'

Paula waited a few seconds then continued. 'Our witness says you brought these bodies to the convent for burial. That you said they were young men who had been living on the streets when they died. Young men who had nobody to give them a Christian burial.'

Keenan gave his lawyer a desperate look. 'This is

madness,' he protested. 'How am I supposed to have brought these dead bodies to the convent? On the number forty-seven bus?'

'In your car,' Paula said.

'I don't have a car,' he said, enunciating every word distinctly. 'I don't even have a driving licence. You can check with the authorities here and back in Ireland. I have never had so much as a driving lesson. So how exactly am I supposed to be driving around Bradfield with a boot full of bodies?'

It was, thought Paula, something of a killer punch. 'According to our witness, you turned up with another man. It must have been his car.'

'And who is this mystery man?' The lawyer finally interrupted the flow. 'Do we have a name? A description? A make and model of the car? A registration number? If I saw a pair of men regularly dumping bodies, I'm pretty sure I would have jotted down a few details.' She paused. 'No? Nothing?'

Paula ignored the lawyer and said, 'How did you get around when you were based at the convent, without a car?'

'It's not like I went running around all over the place,' he said. 'Mostly, I stayed put. The convent had a couple of cars and if I needed to go somewhere, one of the nuns would run me up to the main road to catch the bus. Or they'd give me a lift.'

'So you had access to a car?'

'Theoretically, I suppose. But I can't drive. So what use would it be to me?' Keenan ran a hand through his hair. 'This so-called witness of yours? Is it Jezza Martinu?'

Paula said nothing, staring him out.

'It is, isn't it? He's the only one who could possibly have

witnessed anything like what you've accused me of. Why are you believing him, not me? He's the one who dug all the graves for the nuns. If anybody was burying bodies at the Blessed Pearl, it must have been him. Him or somebody he owed a favour to. And I'll tell you one thing for nothing. I'm the last man walking that Jezza Martinu would do a favour for.'

41

Examining the contradictions between witness statements often tells us where we need to look to find what we need to learn . . .

From *Reading Crimes* by Dr Tony Hill

Rutherford pounced as soon as Paula and Karim left the interview room. 'I was observing you,' he said. 'Nicely done. I've told Sophie to set up a ReMIT briefing straight away so we can decide how to progress this new information. Squad room—' He glanced at his smart watch and tapped the face. 'Ten minutes.' He walked briskly away.

'Barely time for a pee and a coffee, never mind digesting what we've just heard,' Paula grumbled, heading in the opposite direction. Karim hesitated for a moment, then made his way to the squad room. By the time Paula arrived, he was tapping frenziedly at his keyboard. Clearly he wasn't going to be caught napping with his reports a second time.

By the time Rutherford returned, they were all there. Alvin had scarcely had time to take his jacket off, but the

DCI turned to him first, asking for an update from the forensics lab. Alvin flicked through the pages of his notebook, passing on what Chrissie O'Farrelly had said. He spared them no details and was gratified to see a couple of them looked as green around the gills as he'd felt when he got to the bit about the contents of the plastic bag. 'They're confident they'll get DNA for some of the victims,' he concluded. 'But that may not in itself lead us to an ID if they're not on the database.'

'Which is a pity,' Paula said. 'As Tony Hill always says, the more you learn about the victims, the more you know about their killer.'

Rutherford gave her an unfathomable glance. 'Well, theory is all very well, but we're dealing in hard facts here, DI McIntyre. Which brings us to DC Chen. What have you got for us?'

Stacey glanced over from behind her barricade of screens. 'I've tracked down all of the nuns from the Bradesden convent. Alvin has already spoken to the ones in York. The Mother Superior was sent to Galway in the first instance and although she doesn't show up in the convent roster now, she's on the electoral register and I have an address for her that appears to be very close to the convent. There are four other women registered at that same address, but none of them corresponds to the names on the electoral roll for Bradesden.'

Rutherford nodded. 'We're going to have to talk to her sooner rather than later. I'll task that later today when I have a better sense of who's doing what. Anything on the second group of victims?'

'I've compiled a list of misper males who fit the rough age guidelines and the timeline we've got so far,' Stacey said.

'But I don't have to tell you how partial that's likely to be when it comes to street people. They're where they are for all sorts of reasons and a sizeable tranche of them will not have been reported missing. To make it to the list, you have to have come from a place where somebody cares enough to mind that you're not around.'

A moment's silence as they all digested that. 'Pass that list to Sophie,' Rutherford said. 'Sophie, spread that out among DCI Fielding's team. Let's get as much background running as we can.'

Good luck with that. Paula was relieved she hadn't been landed with that particular piece of baton-passing. But her turn was coming.

Rutherford took a long swig from his brushed steel water bottle. 'DI McIntyre. Today's star turn so far. Time to share your interview product.'

Paula led them through their interview with Father Keenan, step by step, giving her opinion on his demeanour throughout. She gave Karim regular questioning glances, checking that her recollection chimed with his. 'His denials were, as I've said, vehement and apparently sincere. We'll have to check his assertions about access to a vehicle and lack of driving experience and the absence of a licence, or indeed a driving test. Where it gets interesting, I think, is when he puts two and two together and works out that Martinu is our key witness against him.'

She leaned forward in her chair, elbows on knees, hands clasped. 'He claims Martinu has made accusations against him because he bears a grudge. Once he'd calmed down a bit, Keenan made a serious allegation against Martinu. He says he caught Martinu spying on the older girls' dormitory. Quite a detailed claim – Martinu had drilled a spyhole in the ceiling of the room. The priest discovered it because Martinu had to pass his rooms to get to the loft above the dormitory. He wondered why the handyman was going up to the loft so often at odd times – first thing in the morning, late in the evening. So next time he passed, he followed him and caught him in the act. Keenan claims he thought Martinu was going to attack him but thought better of it. Keenan reported the matter to the Mother Superior, Mother Mary Patrick. Martinu was abjectly contrite, offered to do whatever penance they thought was appropriate, begged to keep his job.'

'Should have reported the sleazebag to us,' Steve muttered.

'You're probably right, Steve,' Rutherford said. 'But when you preach the forgiveness of sins all the time, you have to put the theory into practice every now and then.'

'And it meant his employer had power over him,' Paula said. 'Anyway, by that time, Martinu had bought his cottage from the church. Mother Mary Patrick and Keenan both knew the convent closure was on the cards. The last thing they wanted was a stain on their reputation as they continued their careers in the church. So it suited everybody to keep quiet. The key part of this sordid tale is that Martinu isn't interested in boys. He's very interested in teenage girls.'

'That's borne out by the internet porn he accesses most frequently,' Stacey chipped in. 'He's not been looking at guy-on-guy action at all. It's all straight, a bit rapey, but nothing that would indicate any homosexual tendencies.'

'Yeah, but you don't have to be gay to kill men,' Steve offered. 'It might be that his victims were gay? They might have come on to him and he was so disgusted that he decided they didn't deserve to live.'

Paula pulled a face. 'Once or twice, maybe. But eight times? He's not that hench. I can't see him regularly sending out the kind of signals that would draw enough attention from gay men to provoke a murderous response. I'm not saying this lets Keenan off the hook, but it does speak to Martinu having a reason for dropping him in the shit.'

'We need to check out his assertions about cars and driving licences. DC Chen, get on that right away. Alvin, you spoke to the nuns in York. Get back on to them and ask whether Keenan ever drove them around.' Rutherford turned back to Paula. 'But you're not finished, are you?' His smile was conspiratorial. A man happy to take credit for the successes of his team.

'He harped on about Martinu being the gravedigger. He had the equipment and the expertise and nobody would question whatever he was doing in the grounds. He said if it wasn't Martinu doing the killings, it must be somebody he knew. One of his friends, or some other kind of contact. When I pressed him for more detail, the only name he could come up with was Martinu's cousin. Martinu's big obsession is Bradfield Victoria, and his cousin shares that. The cousin regularly comes round to Martinu's cottage to watch football on his big fuck-off TV. But it's Martinu who owes his cousin big time, because the cousin is on the board of Bradfield Vics and they go together to games, home and away. Martinu goes to the board rooms with him, watches the games from the directors' box, gets to meet the players.'

'We know this how?' Alvin asked.

'Keenan says Martinu would get autographed photos of the players for the girls sometimes.'

'So who is this mysterious cousin who's important enough to be on the board of a top-flight football club?' Rutherford butted in. He knew the answer; he'd been observing the interview. But he clearly enjoyed a grandstand moment.

'He's a businessman called Mark Conway. He owns the MARC sportswear chain. And a couple of smaller, more exclusive outdoor stores. He's—'

'Mark Conway?' It was Sophie, startled into looking up from her tablet. 'You're kidding, right?'

'No, why would I be kidding?' Paula was bemused.

Sophie shook her head, bewilderment on her face. 'I used to work for Mark Conway.'

42

By its nature, therapeutic practice is a lonely business. You are hedged in on every side by patient confidentiality and you can't readily bounce your ideas off anyone. Working as a profiler is the diametric opposite of that.

From *Reading Crimes* by Dr Tony Hill

Just as the briefing was coming to an end, Paula felt the vibration of a phone alert against her leg. She slipped her phone out of her pocket and gave the screen a quick nonchalant glance. A flash of panic seized her and her heart raced. She'd completely forgotten that she'd booked a couple of hours out that afternoon. The office diary said 'hospital appointment' but that was not her destination.

Rutherford finished handing out assignments, charging her with interviewing Martinu again. She waited till the others had filed out then spoke to him. 'I've got a hospital appointment,' she said. 'It's a scan. It might be serious. I'll only be gone a couple of hours and then I'll get straight back to Martinu. In the meantime, Karim can build some background?'

He looked outraged. 'Can it not wait?'

'I've been waiting. It's women's stuff, you know? It's hard to concentrate, worrying all the time.'

He shook his head and sighed, the perennial put-upon man. 'I thought your partner was a senior consultant? Can she not pull some strings, rearrange the appointment?'

'She's already pulled strings, that's how I got this slot.'

With ill grace, he turned away. 'Get back as soon as you can.'

Sometimes it worried Paula, how convincingly she could lie. By teatime, half the squad would be convinced she was facing terminal cancer. She didn't enjoy being duplicitous but she knew there was no chance of keeping her appointment if she'd told the truth.

The traffic was relatively light and she got out of town on to the motorway sooner than she'd anticipated. The journey passed quickly; Sophie's revelation had given her food for thought. At first, they'd all expected her to be able to give them an inside track on Mark Conway. But it was soon clear that although Sophie had climbed the managerial ranks, she hadn't got high enough up the greasy pole to make it to a level where she'd learned anything beyond the superficial. At least, that was all she was admitting to, and Paula had no reason to doubt her.

Paula parked the car and walked up to the entrance of HMP Doniston. She mingled with the other visitors then, when her name was called, presented her VO, gritted her teeth through the humiliating procedures and finally followed the flow into the dispiriting visiting room. Serried rows of tables, uncomfortable chairs facing each other. It looked like speed-dating for the dysfunctional.

She could have used the fact of her job to make a police visit. But that would have been a flashing light in the system that a routine visit was not. So she endured the waiting and the humiliation for half an hour with one of her best friends.

Tony was third through the door, his face lighting up at the sight of her. He dropped into his chair and grinned. 'It's great to see you.' His face looked puffy and pale, but that was the only real change in his appearance. His body remained wiry and lean, his eyes as sharp and lively as ever. He sniffed noisily. 'You use Evian skin cream, and sometimes you wear L'Air du Temps ... but not today.'

She snorted with laughter, recognising the quote. 'And how are you doing, Dr Lecter?'

'I think I'm slowly getting the hang of this place. How to keep busy, how to stay out of trouble. How to be useful.' His smile was tinged with sadness. 'I've always liked to be useful.'

'Still teaching them how to meditate?'

He smiled 'It's a better way of helping people stay calm than the sea of drugs that washes up in here.'

'No blowback from twats who think you're taking the piss?'

He shook his head. 'They probably think I'm too insignificant to bother with. I'm no threat to their little fiefdoms and smacking me around would just give me credibility. The other thing I'm trying to get off the ground is basic literacy classes. I'm dressing it up as a way to be a better dad. Learn to read to your kids, give them the childhood you never had.' His hands were moving constantly, fingers fidgeting, touching the table, touching his thighs. There was a nervous energy to him that was unfamiliar to her.

'That's an interesting approach. How are you going to

manage that? I don't imagine you've got many kids' books in the prison library.'

Tony tapped the side of his nose. 'I called my publisher, who is very happy with me because I'm writing the book they contracted years ago. I told him we needed a big box of children's books ASAP, and he's promised to sort it out.'

'Result. And how is the book going?'

'Well, I've got no excuse not to be writing, have I? Five hundred words a day – I should have the first draft by the end of the year. The only problem is not having access to my notes or to the internet. I'm having to rely on memory, so there'll be a lot of fact-checking and filling in the blanks afterwards.'

'Is there anything we can send you? Books, or copies of your notes? Torin's down at *Steeler* two or three times a week, he likes the peace and quiet down there. It'd be easy enough for him to dig out what you need.'

Tony smiled. 'You're such a good friend, Paula. I'm not asking any more of you guys than you're already doing for me. How is Torin? And Elinor?'

She gave him a quick update, then added, 'We had dinner with Carol last night.'

The fidgeting stopped. 'How is she?'

'She told Elinor she's seeing someone about her PTSD. An alternative therapy, apparently. I don't really understand it, but it's all about bodywork?'

He closed his eyes momentarily, then gave a pained smile. 'I've heard about it. With a degree of scepticism, I have to admit. But if it's helping her . . . that's the best news I've had in a while.'

'She seems less wound up, that's for sure. She's not drinking. And she's doing some investigative work.'

He looked suddenly wary. 'What do you mean?'

'There's a group of professionals who have got together to form a sort of Innocence Project. They call it After Proven Guilty. They work on it in their own time, they take on cases where they think there's been a miscarriage of justice and they reinvestigate. It's Bronwen Scott's baby, so that should give you a flavour of how seriously it's being run. Anyway, Bronwen showed up at the barn and pitched Carol. She's a bit tentative about it but I think she's definitely hooked. And that can only be a good thing, right? Using the skills she's got?'

Tony ruminated for a moment. 'Probably. What happened to the carpentry thing? Is she still doing that?'

Paula spread her hands. 'As far as I know. She was the last time I was out there. She learned so many new things when she was gutting the barn and rebuilding it, I think she's really come to enjoy working with her hands. But it's good for her to be using her head too, I reckon.'

'And that's the only investigative work she's doing?'

It was, she thought, an odd question. 'It's all she told us about. Unless you know different?' And how would he, given he hadn't been in touch with Carol since he'd begun his prison sentence. Unless . . . ?

'I know nothing,' he said, channelling Manuel from *Fawlty Towers*. 'I just wondered if she'd got the taste for it again. But what about you? What are you working on?'

And so she told him. A breakneck run-through of the past few days, a key-point breakdown of what they were looking at. As she spoke, she saw the old Tony surfacing. The frown of concentration, the flicker of the eyes as he scanned his memory banks, the tilt of the head as if he was listening to an interior voice. 'Clearly separate cases,' he said when she finished her account of the interview with Keenan. 'Do you like the priest for it?'

Paula gave a sardonic chuckle. 'I did until I interviewed him properly. Now? I'm not so sure.'

'He's an easy scapegoat. These days, Catholic priests have got a target painted on their backs, and for good reason. If I was looking for somebody to frame for a crime like this and I had a priest handy, that'd be my first port of call. Do you think the groundsman is smart enough to have worked that out?'

'I'm not sure. He's hard to read. He's scared of something, but we both know that might just be the product of being arrested and locked up. And he's admitted to digging the graves. He knows that means he's more than likely going to jail. Which is also a scary prospect.'

'Tell me about it. He could just have kept his mouth shut. But he chose to go for the priest. He's trying to divert attention from someone he's worried about betraying. Is it because he's scared of that person? Or is it because he can't bring himself to betray someone he owes a debt to?'

'You're thinking about the cousin,' Paula said. 'Mark Conway. Sophie was adamant that it couldn't be him. She had a senior job in one of his retail companies before she joined the police, she had direct dealings with him. She says he was all about getting people to be the best they could be with a carrot, not a stick. Doesn't sound like a serial killer of homeless lads to me.'

'Is he married? Does he have kids?'

'I don't know. Why are you asking?' There had to be a reason. Tony never went in for idle questions.

'I'm curious. To build an empire like he has, a person has to have real drive. And the one thing they always want once they've succeeded is legacy. They want to pass on the torch, to know the empire will continue to thrive. To grow, even. I just wonder where Mark Conway is looking for his legacy. You need to find out more about his background.'

'Don't worry, we will be. But what should we be looking for?'

'No obvious heirs. No sons, sisters' sons. I'd be interested in his own jumping-off point too. What was his childhood like? How did he get started in business? Does it map on to the victims in any way?'

Paula stared at Tony. Not for the first time, his lateral approach caught her on the hop. 'But why would he kill kids with the same sort of background he had? Surely he'd be looking to find a way to help them reach their potential? That's what Sophie says he's like.'

'What if you made your selection and they weren't up to the mark? What if they weren't a mini-me? Worse, what if they were complete no-hopers? How would you feel then? What a judgement that would be on your acumen.'

The words hung in the air between them. It was an angle, Paula thought. More than that, it was a motive. Over the years, Tony had persuaded her to the belief that nobody does anything without a reason. They might not be able clearly to articulate that reason. Or it might be a reason that made sense to them and no other living soul. She might think a failure of judgement an insufficient reason for murder. But Mark Conway might not. She sighed.

'Something to think about, at least,' Tony said. 'But since I have no access to the files, maybe not something to grace with a lot of weight.'

'You're always worth listening to. And not just

professionally. We miss you, mate. But I'm really glad to hear you're doing positive things now. You and Carol – you're both healing, aren't you? In your different ways?'

He dipped his head. 'I hope so, Paula. I needed to make changes. The work was eating into me.' He gave a little laugh. 'I wish I'd found a slightly less disruptive way of going about it.'

She shook her head. 'You know that was never going to happen. Doing things by half measures isn't your style.'

'No. I sometimes wonder if that's the one useful thing I inherited from Vanessa.'

'There has to be something, I suppose.' She checked the wall clock behind Tony's head. 'I'm going to have to run. I told a little white lie to get out of the office and it's got a limited shelf life.'

'OK. I'll see you in a week or two?'

'Yes, send me a VO. And maybe at some point, you could send one for Torin? I know he'd like to see you.'

Sadness filled his eyes. 'Do you think that's a good idea? I'm not much of a role model in here.'

'You're the best man in his life, Tony. By a long way. Let him back in.'

43

It's a rare criminal who doesn't resort in the first instance to denial. But the form and shape of that denial can be very telling.

From *Reading Crimes* by Dr Tony Hill

Paula managed to slip back into the squad room without encountering Rutherford. Not glancing up from his screen, Karim said, 'He's been off for the last hour having a meeting with DCI Fielding. You're in the clear.'

'OK. Got anything interesting on Mark Conway?'

'Are you OK, guv?' Karim's eyes were worried. 'Like, with you being at the hospital.'

'No secrets in a nick,' Paula said ruefully. 'Just some tests, Karim. It's something and nothing. Women's stuff.'

He didn't look reassured. 'Yeah, but I got a mum and sisters and aunties. I know "women's stuff" covers all the ground between something and nothing.'

'Don't fret, I promise there's no need. Mark Conway?' She pulled up a chair and sat at the end of his desk.

Karim brought up a page of notes on his screen. 'No criminal record. Clean driving licence. Drives a Porsche Cayenne. You know, the big SUV.'

Paula grinned. 'You know Phill Jupitus? The stand-up? I once heard him do this brilliant routine about a "Porsche four-by-what's-it-for". So we do know fairly definitively that Conway's a bit of a wanker.'

'A self-made wanker, though.' Karim clicked to a magazine profile of Mark Conway. He looked crisp and clean-cut in the photos. Conway in hill-walking gear with somewhere in the White Peak in the background; Conway in shorts and T-shirt (sensibly not lycra) on a bike trail in a wood; Conway in a sharp suit and open-necked shirt on the pitch at Bradfield Vics. 'He had a pretty rough upbringing. Never knew his father, then his mother died when he was eleven. He was taken into care, spent the next five years in children's homes.' He highlighted a section of text.

I hated every minute of it. It was a training ground for bullies and abusers. The so-called carers turned a blind eye. It was too much trouble to try to police what was going on. As soon as I turned sixteen, I got a job on a market stall selling fake branded trainers. That was me done with the home. For the first six weeks, I slept under the stall, till I got enough money together to rent a bedsit.

'Interesting,' Paula said.

'Yeah. He's had a taste of life on the streets. Just like the victims, apparently.'

Paula shook her head. 'It's too early to jump to conclusions, Karim. We've not got IDs yet. We don't know if these victims really were homeless. We've only got Martinu's word for that, and he might be spinning us a pack of lies. And even if they do turn out to have been living on the streets . . . I think if Tony was around, he'd be cautioning us against mapping one thing directly on to another.'

'What do you mean?'

'We shouldn't leap to the conclusion that Conway's tough teenage years give him some connection to victims who've had similar experiences. A connection isn't necessarily a consequential relationship.'

As she spoke, Sophie walked past Karim. She glanced at the screen and stopped in her tracks. 'You're not still on about Mark Conway? I'm telling you, Paula, you are so wasting your time looking at him.'

'Gotta follow where the breadcrumbs lead us,' Paula said. 'You're probably right, but it's not just in Agatha Christie novels that the least likely person turns out to be the one with the darkest secret.'

Sophie tutted. 'You should be looking at Martinu's other contacts. Going through his phone and his email.'

'We are,' Paula said. 'His computer's an open book, according to Stacey. If we don't get anywhere with Conway, we'll dig deeper. Don't worry, we're not obsessing with one single line of inquiry. What have you got going on in the incident room? Anything coming out of interest?'

Sophie shook her head. 'The cupboard is bare. Fielding's champing at the bit to interview nuns. She wasn't happy to hear Sergeant Ambrose had already been to York. She's pitching to do Norfolk, Liverpool and Galway, but the boss is holding his ground. He said his way might take longer but it would be consistent.'

Paula smiled. 'Good to hear.' She stood up. 'Right. We're off to talk to Martinu again. See what he has to say about the non-driving priest.'

She watched Sophie continue on her way, but before she

could drill Karim on the forthcoming interview, Stacey slipped out from behind her screens. 'I don't know if it helps, but I checked out Martinu's cottage. There's no mortgage registered on it, but there's a charge on the property.'

'What's that?' Karim asked.

'One day, when you're old enough to buy a house, chances are you'll have to borrow the cash,' Paula teased. 'Whoever you borrow your money from registers a charge on the property. When it's sold, whoever holds the charge on the property has to be paid off before you get anything. So come on, Stacey, I know you're dying to tell me. Who owns the charge on Martinu's cottage? Is it the Order of the Blessed Pearl?'

'Oh no, it's much more interesting than that.'

'We've got a bit of a problem here, Jezza,' Paula said, forearms on the table, hands clasped. 'You told us the priest brought the bodies to the convent to bury them in the holes you'd previously dug?'

'That's right, Inspector,' Karim said, referring to his notebook.

Martinu looked at his lawyer for guidance. Cohen nodded. He was equally immaculate today, his suit a dark blue with the faintest of pearl grey pinstripes, his tie a rich purple shot silk. 'You've answered this before.'

'Yeah,' Martinu grunted.

'Constable, what exactly did Jezza say?' Paula kept her eyes fixed on Martinu.

Karim flicked the pages till he came to the line he'd lifted from the recording. '"He'd drive in, usually with some deadbeat in the passenger seat."'

'You're sure about that, are you? He'd bring a passenger with him?'

He nodded. 'Mostly. Not every time.'

'You see, that's what I'm having trouble with. Father Keenan doesn't have a car. He didn't have a car then. In fact, he's never had a car.'

Martinu's eyes widened as he saw the chasm open at his feet. 'He must have hired one, then. Or borrowed one. They all hang together, these priests.' He spoke quickly, his eyes flicking to his lawyer.

'He couldn't have hired one, Jezza. Because he's never had a driving licence. Not here. Not in Ireland.' Paula tipped her head towards Karim. 'Constable Hussein checked it out. He's very thorough, is Constable Hussein. Michael Keenan can't drive. He's never even had a provisional licence. Never had driving lessons. He was too busy studying to be a priest.'

A long silence. Martinu swallowed hard. Cohen cleared his throat. 'My client may have been mistaken in his recollection. Mr Martinu, perhaps, thinking back, you might have misremembered?'

Martinu clutched at the straw. 'Maybe I did. It was dark when they came. I might not have seen exactly who was where.' It sounded weak, unconvincing.

'I don't think so,' Paula said gently. 'I think the priest was just a handy scapegoat. Not a very clever move, to try to frame someone who knows your own little secrets.'

Martinu flushed a dark red. 'He's a liar.'

'You don't even know what I'm going to say.'

'It doesn't matter, it'll be a lie. He's trying to smear me, to make out like I'm the guilty one, the liar.'

'To be honest, Jezza, we don't need Father Keenan's testimony to work out that you're a liar. And besides, the material on your computer reinforces what he told us. You lied about who delivered those bodies.'

'Is there a question in there, Inspector?' Cohen was

trying belligerence now, but his manner was too languid to be entirely convincing.

'No, but there is one coming. You leave us with two options, Jezza. Either you committed these murders yourself—'

'I never,' he shouted. 'I'm not a killer.' He slammed his hands down on the table. 'I never killed anybody.'

'Either you committed these murders yourself or you're shielding the person who did,' Paula continued, apparently unperturbed. 'Which is it?'

Martinu looked at the table. 'I did not kill those people.'

'Then who are you covering for? Whoever it is, they clearly don't give a damn about you. They're happy to let you sit here, hour after hour, carrying the can. You let yourself be used when you dug those graves, and you're letting yourself be used again now.'

Cohen leaned over and murmured something in Martinu's ear. He nodded and straightened up. 'No comment.'

'A bit late for that, Jezza. You're already condemned out of your own mouth. Illegal burials. Aiding and abetting a murderer. You're going to jail, Jezza. For a long time. Maybe a life sentence. Say goodbye to fresh air and fresh vegetables and the boardroom at Bradfield Vic and spying on teenage girls in their underwear. And for what? For somebody who'll stay in the shadows and watch you twist in the wind.'

He clenched his fists tight and glared at Paula. 'No comment,' he ground out, his lips tight over his teeth.

Paula let the silence grow. She could almost feel a crackle in the air from the electricity between them. Then she glanced casually at Cohen. 'Is it the same person who's paying for your expensive lawyer and his expensive suit? Because I don't usually see Mr Cohen in here defending working-class lads like you. He doesn't usually get out of bed for anyone who lives in a house worth less than a cool million. Who are you shielding, Jezza?'

He blinked furiously, as if on the point of tears he'd die before shedding. 'No fucking comment.'

'Is it Mark? Your generous cousin Mark who takes you to the boardroom at Victoria Park? Your helpful cousin Mark, who lent you the money to buy your little slice of paradise, complete with its unorthodox fertiliser?'

Martinu stiffened, gripping the edge of the table white-knuckled.

Paula waited. Then said, 'Not got a "No comment" for me this time?'

'This. Is. Nothing. To do. With Mark.' He spat the words out.

'I don't believe you, Jezza. I'm not seeing anybody else in your life that you'd protect like this. I'm giving you a chance now to save a bit of your skin. I can't keep you out of prison, but if you help us now, we can find a way to keep your jail time as low as possible.'

Again, Cohen leaned into his client's ear. He put a hand on Martinu's arm and gave it a squeeze. Martinu looked away, and this time when he met Paula's eye, there was something like a plea there. He sighed. 'No comment.'

'You leave me no choice, Jezza.' Paula's voice was a caress. She stood up and casually said to Karim, 'Charge him,' before walking out of the room.

She made it to the women's toilet before she started shaking from the release of tension. Every time she came up against the moment in an interview when she knew she'd found the answer, it was the same old story. The cold sweat running down her body, the racing of the pulse and the clenching in her guts. She'd seen colleagues come out of the interview room punching the air and doing little victory dances. She'd seen Carol Jordan walking away as if she'd done nothing more momentous than the weekly shop. But for Paula, every time was a starburst of debilitating relief that she could still knock an interview out of the park. She leaned her forehead against the wall, breathing as rapidly as if she'd run up too many flights of stairs and wondered how many more times she could do this before she ended up as damaged as Carol Jordan.

44

It's always tempting to wait for more information when you're preparing a profile. But criminal investigations proceed piecemeal and it's very rare that you get all the pieces for your particular jigsaw. Sometimes you have to work with what little you have.

From *Reading Crimes* by Dr Tony Hill

The rising sun was a dim red ball behind a bank of cloud. A thin north wind brushed the surface of the sea into stiff waves. Carol savoured the salty air as she walked along a narrow path behind low sand dunes. Not another living soul in sight, not even an early morning dog walker. The peace and the view were scant compensation for being the tool of Vanessa's vengeance.

She'd arrived in the tiny Northumberland coastal village under cover of darkness and scoped out the address Stacey Chen had pulled out of the Land Registry records. Carol wasn't sure how she'd narrowed down the dozens of seaside properties that must have changed hands around the right time, but there it was on the record. Cove Cottage, owned by OTG Holdings. OTG – the initials of Oliver Tapsell Gardner.

I can't find anything on OTG Holdings, Stacey's covering email had said. *That would lean towards it being a private trust rather than any kind of company. It fits with the info you gave me. They bought Cove Cottage eleven months after Oliver Gardner was born and it's not listed as a holiday rental with any of the online agencies. The council tax is paid by OTG Holdings from a bank account in the Isle of Man. No chance of getting any more information out of them. Not even I can manage that. Balmouth is blink-and-you'd-miss-it. The winter population is three hundred and forty, which climbs to around six hundred when the holiday cottages fill up. There's not much there – a general store and a pub that only opens at lunchtimes. It's got a rather lovely white sandy beach but there isn't a lot of it – cliffs at one end and it's cut off by the estuary of the River Balm at the other end. There are a lot of bigger beaches with more amenities dotted up and down the coast, so it's mostly a haven for locals trying to escape the crowds.*

As she had many times before, Carol marvelled at what Stacey could dig up in what must have been a short break from the Bradesden convent inquiries. Now she'd have to play a waiting game. She'd parked her car at the far end of the village and set off along the path, which was separated from the seafront cottages by a narrow strip of scrubby marram grass and a single-lane tarmacked road. Cove Cottage was marked clearly on the Land Registry plan and Carol was trying to identify it as she walked. Second cottage past the pub, she thought, slowing slightly. She could see a name etched in a curly script on a piece of slate but it was too small to read at this distance.

As yet there had been no sign of anything with a pulse in

Balmouth. So she took a chance and strolled across the grass towards the cottage. As she drew near, she felt a moment's satisfaction as she read COVE COTTAGE. There was a narrow passage that ran down the side of the cottage and she turned down as if it had been her destination all along.

The cottage looked well-maintained. The render was painted sky blue, with the windowsills and the front door a contrasting darker shade. Two windows on either side of the front door, three windows on the first floor. She took all this in as she passed, as well as the fact that the curtains were drawn in the downstairs rooms and one upstairs window. No lights were showing yet, but it was early. And drawn curtains weren't incontrovertible evidence that there was anyone home.

Cove Cottage was clearly a single room deep, with a boxy extension on the back that looked like a kitchen with a bathroom above. A low wall surrounded a paved back yard, just big enough for an uncomfortable-looking wrought-iron table and two chairs, and beyond them, a trio of wheelie bins. No plants; nothing that demanded attention. Beyond it, a single-storey building shielded it from whatever lay on the other side.

Carol emerged from the alleyway on to another single-lane roadway, lined with a similar group of cottages. A couple of them had cars parked in what had clearly been part of their original front gardens, but the road was too narrow to allow roadside parking. Nowhere to sit unobtrusively in a car. No café with a convenient window table for a stake-out. No handy woodland to lurk in. Harrison Gardner – if this was indeed his bolthole – had chosen well.

Carol ambled along the road, still the only visible living thing. She wished she had Flash at her side, for companionship as much as camouflage. But she'd had no idea what the day might bring, so she'd left her with her neighbour. She had brought a pair of binoculars, thinking she might be able to pose as a birdwatcher. A website she'd checked had informed her that this part of the coast was famous for its seabirds. 'Particularly migratory birds,' it had said. Not that she would have recognised one of those if it had landed on the bonnet of her car. The only drawback was that any self-respecting twitcher would be looking out to sea, not focusing on one of the cottages in the middle of the village.

She came to the end of the cottages and turned back towards the waterfront. She gazed up at the cliff and wondered if she could find a vantage point there that would allow her to look down at the cottage. Only one way to find out.

Quarter of an hour later, Carol was perched on a flat rock close to the edge of the cliff, her binoculars trained on the front of Cove Cottage, grateful for the level of fitness she'd gained from walking the moors a couple of times a day with Flash. It turned out that the dog had bestowed more than companionship on her. She'd scrambled easily up the precipitous track that twisted up from the dunes, almost losing her footing only once when a shard of loose sandstone had slipped from under her boot.

She'd come equipped for a long wait. She took a folding sit-mat from her day pack and opened it on the rock. Carol was trying to avoid thinking about Vanessa. The only way she could get through this was to consider it in the most abstract sense as the pursuit of justice. Harrison Gardner was a predator and a crook. Once she'd extracted Vanessa's cash, she could hand him over to the police and find some satisfaction in seeing him miss out on his well-padded retirement.

All the same, Carol hated that she was here at Vanessa's behest. She loathed the woman for the way she'd treated Tony over the years, from his brutal and neglected childhood onwards to her attempt to cheat him out of his inheritance. She despised herself for giving in to the woman's emotional blackmail. If Carol had been the only one facing the consequences, she'd have taken great pleasure in telling Vanessa to fuck right off and keep going. But the bitch had the power to do even more damage to Tony's future. And so she was here, on this chilly clifftop, watching and waiting.

To distract her from her destructive thoughts, she plugged earphones into her mobile and settled down to listen to one of the podcasts she downloaded regularly. The time drifted past without tedium and at last Balmouth started to stir. Dog walkers first. A couple with a pair of lurchers. An elderly man with a Border terrier. A young woman with a waxed jacket and a black lab. The dogs crossed paths with obvious familiarity, the lurchers frisky, the Border grumpy, the lab wagging its whole body in greeting.

A van drove into the village and parked beside the shop. A young man got out, took a bundle of newspapers from the passenger seat and rolled up the shutters that covered door and windows. The first podcast came to an end and Carol clicked on to the next.

She sat patiently through the morning life of the village. There was no sign of activity in Cove Cottage, however. Not a curtain twitched, not a light gleamed at the edge of a window. As the morning tailed off, she moved back out of sight to pee but when she took up her station again, it didn't look as if she'd missed a thing. Towards noon, three children came zigzagging up the slope at the back of the cliff with an over-excited springer spaniel running circles round them. They looked astonished to see Carol, muttered to each other and veered off back down towards the shore. Now she felt guilty for being a killjoy.

The sun burned off the last of the clouds by lunchtime and she had to remind herself she wasn't here for pleasure as she tucked in to her cheese and salami sandwiches. Carol was about to bite into an apple when her phone rang, loud in her earphones. Startled, she dropped the fruit and answered before she'd registered the name on the screen. 'Carol?' The voice was unmistakable.

'Vanessa,' she said wearily.

'How are you getting on? Have you tracked the bastard down yet?'

'I'm not sure. I've found the holiday cottage, but the curtains are closed and there's no sign of life.'

'Well, you have been busy.' Vanessa managed to make the praise sound like an insult. 'Where are you? Exactly?'

'I'm on a clifftop in Northumberland trying to look like a very assiduous bird watcher.'

'Yes, but where? Don't be coy, Carol. I need to know.'

'Why? I'm managing this.'

'And if something happens to you? If you have an accident? If Gardner turns on you? I'm sure you'll have told one of your old cronies what you're up to. I'm not carrying the can if you disappear. Tony wouldn't like that one little bit, would he?'

Did she never give up? Not water on stone so much as a hammer drill. 'I'm in a village called Balmouth. Watching a house called Cove Cottage. But I don't think there's anyone in it. I've been here since dawn.'

'Better give it till dusk, then. Maybe Gardner's turned into a creature of the night.'

'You'd know, Vanessa.'

A dry chuckle. 'Good to see there's still a bit of fight in you, Carol. Stick with it. Let me know as soon as you've dealt with him.'

The call ended abruptly. 'Fuck you,' she yelled, enjoying the feeling of letting rip. She pulled out her earphones and straightened her spine, then ran through a set of her exercises in a bid to loosen the tension Vanessa had provoked. Then she stood up and stretched, stiff from sitting for so long. Time to make a move. Do a circuit of the village and find another vantage point. Maybe in the dunes?

She took her time descending, careful of her footing, conscious that her knees were protesting at being wakened from their fixed position. A sign in the store window promised a coffee machine, so she went in and helped herself to an insipid-looking cappuccino. Exchanged a few words about the weather with the man she'd seen opening up earlier and who clearly couldn't be bothered developing conversation with someone he'd likely never see again.

Carol walked back along the front, sipping her coffee, and casually turned down the ginnel by Cove Cottage again. And felt as stupid as she'd ever done when she passed the gable end and saw a man sitting at the wrought-iron table with a glass of white wine and a book. It hadn't occurred to her that Harrison Gardner would go straight out to his sheltered back yard, invisible from her viewpoint on the cliff. Because who'd sit in a yard with no view when the sea was spread out before you? She hadn't bargained on the fact that the sun had moved round and turned the yard into a sun trap.

If indeed it was Harrison Gardner. On a quick pass, it was impossible to be certain. He looked the right sort of age. But he was wearing a baseball cap pulled low and wraparound sunglasses. Not to mention a rather distinguished beard that had featured in none of the photographs she'd managed to track down. She carried on without a backward glance and turned left so she was obscured by what turned out to be a low stone byre converted to a studio holiday home.

Carol pulled up the photos of Gardner she'd loaded on to her phone. Only one gave her what she needed. Ears were always the giveaway. Change the hair, stick in coloured contacts, alter the eyewear. But there was nothing you could do with the ears, short of mutilation. She hunkered down and finished her coffee, letting a few minutes pass. Then she set off back down the alley, unhurried, casual. Gardner didn't even look up. She gave him a quick glance as she passed, just enough to compare it with the photograph she'd committed to memory.

There was no doubt in her mind. She'd found Harrison Gardner.

45

When police officers have insufficient evidence, they tend to go on fishing expeditions. That's not generally an option open to profilers; we have to wait for the evidence to come to us.

From *Reading Crimes* by DR TONY HILL

'We need to bring in Mark Conway,' Rutherford said. 'Good work, Paula. It would have been great if you'd broken the wee shite, but how you read his reactions is good enough for me. Let's get Conway in and nail him to the wall. Eight murders, and nobody joined up the dots? What kind of coppering do they go in for in Bradfield?'

'All due respect, sir, we've got no evidence.' It was Sophie who spoke up. Paula couldn't disagree with her.

Rutherford scowled. 'We're not arresting him, just inviting him to come in and answer some questions.'

'Which he might not want to answer,' Paula said.

'Most people don't know they can just tell us to piss off,' Steve said. 'Chances are he'll come right along with you. He might be screaming for his brief all the way, but he'll come.'

'Steve's right,' Rutherford said. 'Set Paula on him with the psychological thumbscrews and we'll get something. Meanwhile, Stacey, pass all the contacts from Martinu's computer on to Karim. Karim, talk to them. See what they know about the set-up between Conway and his cousin. And Sophie – you worked for Conway. You must know people in the organisation you can talk to about him. Do some digging, use your contacts. Remember, we're the ones you owe your loyalty to now.'

Sophie looked, Paula thought, as if she'd swallowed some particularly unpleasant medicine. She was going to have to learn the hard way that when you were a cop, all the old allegiances counted for nothing. You drew on the bank of trust till you'd leached it dry. It never ceased to amaze her that she'd managed to hold fast to Elinor. But maybe it was simply that so far, she hadn't needed anything from Elinor that wasn't given freely. 'You want me to front up Conway?' she asked.

'It makes sense,' Rutherford confirmed. 'You're across it already. Alvin, link up with Paula on this. It won't hurt to show a bit of muscle on the doorstep.' He glanced at his watch. 'Sophie, does he work late?'

She shrugged. 'Depends what's going on. But he makes a big thing about working smart, not working long. When he's in the office, he's usually gone by six.' She scoffed. 'I always suspected he just carried on working at home. He didn't seem to have much of a social life. He definitely isn't a party animal.'

'Helpful. Do us a background brief when you've done your fishing.' He fixed his stare on Paula. 'You still here?'

*

Mark Conway lived less than a mile from his company headquarters on the outskirts of Bradfield. Although it was less than a mile from one of the main roads into the city, it was surprisingly secluded. There were a handful of sprawling modern houses on the road, all with triple garages and electronic gates, which Paula suspected belonged to footballers. Conway's home, by contrast, had probably started life as a substantial farmhouse. From the side, the roofline resembled an upside-down letter W; it made the place look like two houses glued together. It was a design Paula had seen all over the north of England. Conway's version was built of dressed local stone. The roof slates had the gleam of good repair and the paintwork round the windows and the porch looked smart and fresh. A horseshoe of mature trees protected it to the rear and a low drystone wall separated it from the road, with a traditional wooden five-bar gate closing off the pea gravel drive. The soft glow of indirect lighting shone warmly from two of the ground-floor windows.

Looking at the satnav map, Paula realised it was only about three miles from Bradesden via a network of country lanes. You could probably get there without troubling any ANPR cameras. Always convenient for nefarious doings.

The gate wasn't locked, so they drove up to the front door. Alvin tugged an impressive iron bell pull and an incongruous series of electronic chimes rang out from inside. It was always the details that betrayed people, she thought. Mark Conway had learned how things were supposed to look, but that doorbell was all wrong.

Mark Conway opened the door just wide enough to stand in the gap. Baggy white linen shirt over khaki cargo shorts, bare feet. He looked relaxed but curious, eyebrows raised in a question.

Paula and Alvin both flashed their IDs and the curiosity was replaced by resignation. 'I've got nothing to say to you people.'

'We'd appreciate your help in a major inquiry we're dealing with right now,' Paula said, amiable but firm. 'Can we come in? It's a bit chilly out here.'

'I don't care if it's freezing. Unless you've got a warrant, you're not crossing my threshold. And I've already told you, I've got nothing to say. So you may as well go back into the warmth of your car and leave.' He was equally amiable, and equally firm.

Paula shrugged. 'You're quite within your rights, of course. But I should warn you, we tend to draw inferences from refusals like yours. Because people with nothing to hide have no reason to fear talking to the police. So when someone tries to stonewall us, we are inclined to look at them a bit more closely.' She pulled a rueful face. 'Because we think they just might have something they're keeping hidden. Something that might have unpleasant consequences if it were to come out. Up to you, of course.'

Now his charm slipped from his face as if it had been wiped off with a damp rag. 'That sounds very like a threat to me. Are you threatening me, officer?'

'No, sir. Just making an observation.'

'I don't like your tone. You should know that your chief constable is a good friend of mine.'

The first recourse of the rich and powerful, Paula thought. Bludgeon me with your influential contacts. But she wasn't having any of that. 'I doubt it, sir.'

He looked affronted, his chin jutting forward. 'Are you calling me a liar?'

'No, sir, just ill-informed. Our unit is not answerable to

the chief constable of Bradfield Metropolitan Police. We come under the direct control of the Home Office. So, we don't actually have a chief constable for you to be a good friend of. Sir, can I ask you to reconsider your decision not to talk to us?'

'You can ask but you're wasting your breath. Why would I say anything to you? You've got my cousin locked up, I can't even speak to him. I don't know what trumped-up charges you're laying on him, but I'm not giving you the chance to do the same to me.' He made to close the door, but Alvin leaned his weight against it. 'Get off!' Conway sounded genuinely outraged to be thwarted on his own doorstep.

'Your cousin is singing like he's auditioning for the *X Factor,*' Alvin said. 'If I was you, I'd want to get my version on the record. First one out of the blocks always looks the most credible. You must know that, you'll have had to mediate in plenty of disputes over your business career.'

It was a good pitch, Paula thought. 'What have you got to lose, if your hands are clean?'

'I don't know what you're trying to frame my cousin for, so I don't know how to avoid something you could twist to his disadvantage. So I am refusing to answer any of your questions. If you want to talk to me, arrest me. If you want to come into my house, get a warrant. And in the meantime, fuck right off.' He pushed the door again, and this time Alvin stepped back. Nothing else he could have done, Paula thought.

They walked back to the car in silence. 'That went well,' Alvin said as he started the engine.

Paula twisted in her seat to look back at the lit windows. Mark Conway was outlined against the light, his face a dark blur. 'There's a kind of man who thinks money and power insulates you against the rules the rest of us live by. I don't care what Inspector Valente says about Mark Conway. In spite of his performance of being one of the good guys, I think he's one of the other kind and I think he's in this up to his perfectly shaped eyebrows.'

Alvin grinned as he pulled on to the road. 'I didn't like him either.'

'All we need is some shred of evidence. One loose thread we can pull on to unravel this whole case.'

'He's the kind of man who carries nail scissors to cut off all the loose threads,' Alvin grumbled.

'One way or another, we'll just have to blunt his blades.'

46

I've spent hours interviewing patients over the years. Some of them have committed terrible crimes, but many of them have been brought into our care before they have reached that pitch. But no matter how well prepared I am before those initial interviews there is always a bolt from the blue that takes me aback.

From *Reading Crimes* by DR TONY HILL

Getting his plan off the ground had gone better than he'd expected. Salty Davy Smart, the prisoner who effectively ran the library, had been delighted at Tony's suggestion. And so *Books to Share with Your Kids* had been booked in for the following afternoon. Four men had turned up at the appointed time and had been only mildly disgruntled that no actual books had arrived yet. Salty Davy had unearthed a battered copy of Hans Christian Andersen fairy tales that had found its way into a donated box of assorted books. It was a long way from what he had in mind, but Tony had skimmed it in his cell overnight and reckoned the language of the translation was simple enough to be a starting point.

They'd sat round a table in the furthest corner of the library, as far from casual encounters as possible. Tony had never felt this nervous facing a group of students. Two of them looked barely old enough to be in an adult prison, one still ravaged by teenage pimples, the other by the kind of tattoos that made potential employers blanch. The third was in his twenties. He had shaggy blond hair, a wispy beard and the fidgety twitches of someone who was barely managing to satisfy the drug habit that had put him behind bars in the first place.

'Thanks for coming,' Tony began.

'Makes a change,' Wispy Beard said. 'Anything to relieve the monotony.'

Before Tony could get started, they were joined by a man he recognised as one of the Lithuanians that Matis Kalvaitis hung out with. He nodded gravely and sat down. 'I join you,' he said. 'I can read but my English not good.'

There was another man lurking behind him. The Lithuanian half-turned and said, 'Gordo, get in here.'

Gordo glowered, chubby arms crossed tightly over his chest, shaven head cocked to one side as if daring Tony to make something of it. 'I don't need to waste my time on this.' His accent was local. Tony imagined he was the Lithuanian's muscle, paid in tobacco or drugs or phone cards.

'I'm here, you're here. Sit down.' There was no room for argument. The big man sat. He didn't look happy.

Tony managed a strained smile, trying to cover his unease. The drugs that swilled around in the prison made for unpredictable responses. If any of them were boosting their confidence with something extra, there was no knowing what might set them off.

None of the usual group ice-breakers Tony had used in the past were going to work with this lot. No point in splitting them into pairs to learn what they could about each other in five minutes, then introduce their partner to the group. Prisoners guarded themselves too carefully for that. No point either in asking them to introduce themselves; they would simply proffer what lies seemed most utilitarian. So he began with, 'I'm Tony. Some of you might have heard me on Razor Wireless.'

'You're the shrink,' Pimples said.

'I am. I've worked with a wide range of people over the years.'

'Nutters,' Gordo ground out.

'Not just nutters. But one of the things I have learned is that we can improve the life chances of our kids with one simple thing. And that's reading to them and with them.'

'You got kids, then?' Tattoo Boy spoke. It didn't sound like a challenge, more of a genuine question. But in prison, making assumptions could get your face rearranged.

'I don't. But I was one once. Here's what I know about kids and reading. If they have bedtime stories, if they discover the magic of books when they're tiny, they do better at school. They concentrate better, they're more interested in learning, and they find it easier to look at the world through someone else's eyes. But the best thing, from your point of view, is that it builds a bond between you and your kids. Reading stories with them is something they'll remember for the rest of their lives.'

Silence. Gordo looked bored, the others, blank. Tony persevered. 'I'm guessing none of your dads ever read you a bedtime story.'

'You've got to be joking,' Pimples confirmed. 'He was too busy getting off his face.'

'Never saw him,' Tattoo Boy said.

Gordo snorted. 'Only thing my old man read me was the riot act.'

'No father,' the Lithuanian said. 'And my mother not read.'

Nothing from Wispy Beard.

'We're going to get some kids' books delivered soon, so we can work with those. Right now, all we've got is this.' Tony picked up the Hans Christian Andersen. 'It's old-fashioned fairy tales. Some of them you might know from Disney movies. But I thought we could make a start on these today.'

'Make a start, how?' Wispy Beard was paying attention now, chewing at his bitten fingernails.

'I want to help you develop your reading skills.'

Gordo unfolded his arms and slammed his hands on the table. 'Are you saying you think we're thick? That we can't read?'

'No. There's a difference between being able to read on the page and being able to read aloud.' He gestured at the Lithuanian. 'Like your friend here who can read, but wants to improve his English reading aloud. You want to give your child the best possible experience when you share a story. Something to cherish. That's what we're aiming for. But even if some of you can't read very well, there's no shame in that. There are a lot of reasons why people can't read, and they're nothing to do with intelligence.'

A mutinous stare from Gordo. His presumed boss picked his teeth with a thumbnail. The other three stared at the table.

Tony ploughed on. 'So what I thought we'd do was each read a bit from the story, so I can get a sense of how comfortable each of you is with reading aloud?' Stony silence. 'I'll start, then. I thought we'd begin with a story called *The Ugly Duckling*.' He picked up the book and began at the page he'd bookmarked. '"It was spring in the farmyard. Mummy Duck had laid some eggs in her nest. She had been sitting on them to keep them warm. And one sunny morning, she felt the egg shells begin to crack. She was very happy to see six little duck chicks hatch from the eggs. But when she looked at the chicks, she got a surprise."' He stopped and offered the book to Pimples.

He took it reluctantly and began to read in a painfully slow monotone. '"One of the baby ducks looked diff . . . different from his bro . . . brothers and sisters. They were yellow and he was brown. They were little and cute and he was big and . . . clumsy. He did not fit in. All the other ducks called him names and picked on him."' The end of the paragraph was an evident relief. He thrust the book at Tattoo Boy who looked at it as if it might bite him.

'"He was . . . "' It was an obvious struggle. He had to sound out the words in his head, forming the shape in his mouth before he spoke it out loud. '"He was . . . very unhappy . . . in the farm . . . farmy . . . "'

'Farmy?' Gordo scoffed. 'What's a fucking farmy?'

'Farmyard,' Tony said. 'We're not here to have a go at each other. We're here to support each other. We're going to come across unfamiliar words here, and we'll help each other.' He smiled encouragement at Tattoo Boy, who had a thin sheen of perspiration on his top lip. 'Do you want to carry on?'

He nodded. '"In the farmyard. So he made up . . . his mind

to run awe . . . away."' He wiped the sweat off with the back of his hand and gave Tony a thumbs-up.

'Great start, both of you. Thank you.' He nodded towards Wispy Beard. 'Your turn.'

He took the book and frowned at the page. 'I'm dyslexic,' he said.

'Bollocks,' Gordo muttered. 'Nobody's thick any more, are they? It's dyslexic or what do they call it? ADHD? Total bollocks.'

Wispy Beard flushed. 'I've been tested. It's not bollocks. But I'll give this a try. I want to be able to share with my son. I never had the chance with my dad. He died before I was born. In Iraq.' He took a deep breath and ran his finger along the line. '"One . . . nith"? No, that doesn't make sense. One night?'

'That's right,' Tony said.

'"One night, when they weer . . . were all as . . . asleep"?' He was guessing, clearly, and it was an effort, but he was working at it. '"He rep . . . crep? Crept! Out of bran." No, that's not it. "Out of the barn!"' He grinned. '"Out of the barn. He went to the river and hid in the reds." Reds?'

'Reeds,' Tattoo Boy said, looking over his shoulder. 'Reeds, man. Is that them tall grass things you get beside rivers, like?'

'That's right,' Tony said. 'Well done, you're going to get the hang of this when we get proper books to work with. Because you're dyslexic, there's a little work-around we can use to begin with. I'll work on one particular book with you, and you can learn the story well enough to tell it to your lad. So when you get out, you can get a copy of that particular book and read it together. And it'll help you develop your reading skills.'

He fiddled with his beard and nodded acknowledgement at Tony. He went to pass the book to Gordo, but he slapped it away. 'Fuck this for a game of soldiers,' he said. 'We're not fucking babies.' Tony's scalp tightened with anxiety.

Gordo turned to the Lithuanian. 'It's a bloody insult, giving us kids' books like this to read. He comes in here, treating us like we're too fucking thick for proper books. Condescending cunt.' He was on his feet now, his face plum with rage. 'I'm not going to sit here and let him treat you like you're a fucking retard.'

'These are the books you'll be reading to your kids. That's why we're working with them.' Tony was also on his feet now, trying to keep eye contact with the furious man.

'You're supposed to be teaching us, not making fucking fools out of us.' He waved a hand at Wispy Beard. 'Farmy. Reds,' he mocked. 'Come on, boss, you've got more important things to do.'

The Lithuanian leaned back in his chair and laughed. 'Clever bastard doctor,' he said. 'Six months this cunt is my muscle and I never knew. You cannot read, Gordo. You are the retard, not me.'

The man roared in fury and tipped the table over, sending it crashing to the floor. He took a step forward and grabbed Tony by the throat. 'Don't come the cunt with me,' he yelled, slapping the side of Tony's head with his free hand. It felt like an explosion inside his brain. The hand on his throat was tightening, the other hand had become a fist heading for his face. A bedlam of noise filled his head.

Then nothing.

47

Everybody thinks their view of the world is civilised and appropriate. They cleave to their taboos, they know their limits. What's amazing is how quickly we find reasons to cross those red lines.

From *Reading Crimes* by DR TONY HILL

Carol had found a spot in the dunes where she could keep obs on Harrison Gardner's cottage. There was no exit from the back yard apart from climbing the wall, and she didn't anticipate him choosing that as a means of leaving his property. But just in case, she'd set herself up opposite the end of the alley so she had a view along most of its length. Now she knew he was in residence, there was nothing to stop her confronting him. But she wanted to wait until darkness fell.

There were practical reasons for that. If there was any kind of showdown on the doorstep, it would be less likely to be witnessed after nightfall. Fewer people would be around and it would be harder to see anything from a distance. But there were also psychological reasons. Daylight held few threats. But everyone knew that bad things happened after dark. And she needed all the help she could get.

There was no escaping that what she planned was fraught with risk. Gardner hadn't looked like a man used to physical confrontation, but people found unsuspected reserves when they were under threat. Nobody knew that better than her. And she had no backup. No team covering her, nobody who'd come running if she called.

She'd had to fly solo in the past, but she'd been younger then. More significantly, she'd had no direct experience of what violence and violation felt like. She'd never be that gung-ho again. Not after what she'd gone through over the years.

Carol understood intellectually that PTSD had turned her into a risk-taker. But knowing it and combatting it were two very different things. She'd come some distance thanks to Melissa, but she had no idea how fronting up Harrison Gardner would feel. The only way to find out was to do it.

And do it unarmed, just in case.

The afternoon wore into evening and she remained undisturbed except for the startled intervention of a labra-doodle bounding through the dunes. He leapt backwards with a bark of surprise then took off in a different direction. She moved on from podcasts to an audio book to keep bore-dom at bay. Lee Child was the perfect choice. Improbable but somehow plausible, lots of action and an interesting set-up. Carol thought that if his hero was real, after what he'd been through in twenty-odd books, he'd be in dire need of Melissa Rintoul's services. Which reminded her to run through a set of exercises.

Just before nine, she judged it was time. There was no sign of life on the main street. Even the dog walkers were home in front of the TV or their computer screens. A tell-tale thin line of light ran along the top of the left-hand window in Cove Cottage. Harrison Gardner was home. Settled in for the evening, doing whatever he did to pass the time in his self-imposed exile behind closed curtains.

Carol stood up and stretched, shaking sand out of the creases in her trousers. She walked calmly out of the dunes, across the grass and paused on the edge of the road. Time to put on her old self, the one who instinctively knew how to find the weak spots in a defensive wall and barge through them. She wasn't sure whether she could still inhabit that Carol Jordan, not now she'd come so far. But she was willing to try. For Tony's sake, she was willing to risk losing the ground she'd so agonisingly gained.

She opened the gate. Not a creak from the hinges. If she'd been hiding out, she'd have made damn sure her gate creaked like a Hammer Horror movie door. Four strides and she was at the door. No bell-push that she could see, just an iron knocker in the shape of an ammonite. She gave it a double tap and stood close to the door. No reply, but out of the corner of her eye, she saw a quick spill of light as the curtain eased open.

Breathing faster now, she knocked again and this time she was rewarded by the sound of a key scraping in a lock. The door inched open, the gap curtailed by a chain. Half a face appeared, anxious lines in the forehead. It was the man she'd seen earlier and without his sunhat and wraparound sunglasses, there was no doubt about the identification. 'Yes?' There was nothing welcoming in his tone.

Carol smiled. 'Mr Gardner?'

He shook his head but she saw a flicker of fear before he managed to hide it. 'You've got the wrong house, there's no Gardner here.' The door began to close but Carol was too fast for him. She rammed her shoulder against it, pushing it back to the full extent of the chain.

'I am your worst nightmare, Harrison,' she hissed. 'I am nemesis. I am the woman with nothing left to lose.'

His eyes widened and he took an involuntary step backwards. It was all the leeway she needed. Grateful for the solid muscle she'd built during the barn renovation, Carol steadied herself and threw her whole body at the door. The screws holding the chain to the jamb tore free and the door flew open, thudding into Gardner and throwing him off balance. Before he could recover, Carol was inside, slamming the door behind her.

'Get away from me,' he screeched, rearing up against the wall. Carol grabbed him by the shirt front and hauled him away from its support then pushed him through the doorway into the room whose light she'd spotted from outside. He stumbled, bumping into a low table and falling backwards over it. He cried out and curled into a ball against a bookcase crammed with paperbacks. 'Get out,' he whimpered.

'Or what? You'll call the police?' She marvelled at how easily she'd found her way back to intimidation. 'I don't think so, Harrison. Now get up. Don't make me come and get you.'

He scrambled to his feet. 'Who the fuck are you?'

'Never mind who I am. It's who you are that counts.' She pointed to an armchair. 'Sit down.' When he hesitated she raised her voice. 'I said, sit down. Do not make me hurt you.' This was too easy, she thought as he collapsed into the chair.

She despised herself for how few scruples she had when it came to threatening a pathetic white-collar criminal. She doubted whether he'd ever thrown a punch in anger or even in drink.

Still, she had a job to do. 'You think you've got away with it, don't you? All that money salted away, and all you have to do is lay low for a while then slip out of the country once the heat's died down. Well, Harrison, you didn't do your research very well. Because one of the people you thought was an easy mark is the opposite of that.'

'I don't know what you're talking about.' There was a stubborn cast to his mouth which Carol was unhappy about. She wasn't comfortable with how easy she was finding it to bully Gardner. She'd hoped he would be a complete pushover.

'Let's not play games, Harrison. I know you're a crook, you know you're a crook. Ponzi schemes always collapse. You just weren't smart enough to get out of the jurisdiction before you got caught out. I appreciate you don't want to go to jail, and that's where I can help you out. All I'm looking for is a repayment of the money you stole from the person I'm representing. She doesn't want to go to the police. She's got a grudging respect for what you did. All she wants is her money back.' Carol leaned against the mantelpiece and swept her hand along it, consigning a crystal candlestick and a rather splendid carriage clock to smithereens. Shameful, rather than satisfying. But effective, judging by the panic on Gardner's face.

'Who? Who sent you? How did you find me?' His voice was a stutter of syllables crashing into each other.

'You should not have messed with Vanessa Hill.'

A moment of stillness. His mouth became a thin bitter line.

'What we're going to do is very simple. You're going to access whatever bank account has enough in it to cover what you took from Vanessa. You're going to transfer that money to her. And then I'm going to walk out of your life. And you should consider yourself very lucky to have got off so lightly.'

'And what if I don't? What are you going to do? Beat me up?' He gave a little snort. 'I doubt you've got the stomach for it. You're all bluff, I can tell.'

She didn't know where he'd got his nerve from, but it had come creeping back. 'You could be right,' she said. 'But Vanessa's another matter. She's killed before. The only thing that's keeping you alive right now is the prospect of her getting her money back.'

From behind her, the chilling sound of a familiar voice. 'She's right, you know, Harrison.'

48

The strategies the predator uses to stake their claim, to preserve their territorial advantage, to fend off enemies and rivals, are constantly shifting. The faster and more effective the adaptation, the higher that predator climbs up the food chain . . .

From *Reading Crimes* by DR TONY HILL

The body language was textbook, Paula thought the minute she and Alvin walked back into the ReMIT squad room. Rutherford and Alex Fielding stood opposite each other, a metre apart, both leaning in, heads thrust forward. He towered at least half a metre over her tiny frame, but nobody would have classed her as the lesser combatant. The most extraordinary thing about the scene was that it was playing out in the middle of the room. When Carol had been leading the team, confrontations happened behind the closed door of her office.

'You told me to leave the interviews to you,' Fielding said, her posture an accusation in itself. 'And what have you done so far? All I've seen is' – she looked around and pointed at Alvin – '*his* completely inadequate interviews with a handful of the nuns in York. Including two with dementia. My team have been busting a gut to get to grips with what's coming out of the ground, and you're doing nothing. Oh no, you're not doing nothing. You're doing the sexy case. The one that's going to end up in court. Maybe. If your so-called crack team can actually find anybody to charge with anything more than illegally disposing of a body.' She shook her head and looked around, contempt written all over her. Sophie Valente looked astounded. Karim and Steve Nisbet stared at the whiteboards and Stacey slouched even lower behind her screens.

But Rutherford wasn't in the least abashed. 'We've had to chase your team for case materials. It's quite clear from our brief that we are the go-to guys for the exceptional cases. The clue is in the name. *Major* Incident Team. Your detectives? Their job is to do the second-tier work. And that's what the skeletons are. They don't even look remotely like homicides. If the second lot of bodies had turned up completely independent of the skeletons, you wouldn't be anywhere near this case, DCI Fielding.'

Paula feared Rutherford would live to regret this argument. Alex Fielding was not a woman you'd willingly go up against, as Paula knew only too well. And they'd need her goodwill for future investigations when they needed boots on the ground to boost their numbers.

'In that case, get your DI out of my incident room. You want the credit? You can do the grunt work that goes with it. I'm going to the ACC to insist that these cases are separated. You don't get to run my incident room and have my guys running around doing the stuff that's beneath your lot. Stay away from the nuns and I'll stay away from your headline-grabbing homicides.'

'That's just stupid. The nuns might have evidence relating to our cases.' Rutherford was getting riled now. His neck was bright red against his white shirt collar.

'And if they do, I'll make sure you get it. Just the same as you'll pass on to my team any product from your interviews that might have a bearing on ours. If you can manage to get any product without muddying the waters beyond recognition.'

'What's that supposed to mean?'

'Father Michael Keenan. A key witness in how things were run inside the convent. How the nuns treated the girls. But now? He won't talk to us. Not a cheep. Not after you hauled him out of his house at the crack of dawn, arrested him and interrogated him. Well, thanks very much, ReMIT.' She bit her lip. Paula could almost read the *should have been me* on her face. 'Just stay away from the nuns.'

Rutherford shook his head. 'I'm afraid that won't be possible. DI McIntyre is on the morning flight to Galway. We need to interview the Mother Superior. I'm sure DI McIntyre will give you a full brief when she gets back.'

Paula couldn't quite keep the surprise from her face. Fielding clocked it and looked as if she might be a candidate for spontaneous human combustion. 'You've absolutely not heard the last of this,' she stormed at Rutherford before she marched to the door and slammed it behind her.

Rutherford watched her go, shaking his head. 'Is she always like that?' he asked the room.

Nobody replied. Fielding might be intemperate but it didn't take much insight to figure out that provoking her might not be the best route to take. 'I'm going to Galway?' Paula asked.

Rutherford gave a rueful grin. 'Looks like it. Better get your flight booked before Fielding buys every ticket on the plane.'

'Is there even a flight to Galway?'

'Not any more. The airport closed a few years ago. You have to fly to Shannon and hire a car,' Steve said. 'I went for a weekend with a lass last year. Rained solid for the entire forty-seven hours we were there. Nothing for it but to shag and drink.'

Rutherford tutted. 'Never mind hiring a car. Talk to the local garda and get them to send you a liaison officer to drive you around. Then they can't complain about us treading on their jurisdiction.'

'Great.' Paula sat down and battered her keyboard.

'You haven't told me how your interview with Conway went.' Rutherford perched on her desk as if nothing untoward had happened.

When exactly was she supposed to have done that, Paula wondered. 'That's because there was no interview. Conway refused to talk to us unless we arrested him, which I decided was a bad idea in the absence of any evidence. He refuses to let us in the house without a search warrant.'

'So all we've achieved is showing our hand,' Rutherford said. 'Now he knows how little we've got and that we'll be looking for more.'

Which was your idea. Paula gave him a dead-eyed stare then turned back to her computer. *Manchester Shannon flights,* she typed. She'd barely begun looking when a group message from Stacey pinged on her screen.

DNA lab results: The lab have extracted DNA from all eight victims of the second tranche of bodies. I've been running them against the database, both for direct hits and for familial results. I've got four direct hits and two indirect. The four direct hits are all from Bradfield:

Connor Weston
D'urban Swayze
Lyle Tate
Jason Campo

I've attached records and details for all four. Three listed as mispers.

Paula had to read it twice to make sure she wasn't imagining it. Lyle Tate. The boy whose supposed murderer had been behind bars long before the latest victim of a serial killer had been taken. Lyle Tate, the boy whose supposed killer was the focus of Carol Jordan's innocence investigation.

She clicked on the attachment. Lyle had three convictions for soliciting, one for possession of cocaine. He was NFA – no fixed abode – for the first two, but there was an address for the last two. He'd been reported missing but by the time he'd appeared in the system and anyone had joined up the dots, he was old enough to make his own choices.

Those choices had put him in the path of a murderer. But not the man who was serving life for his murder. She knew she was breaking the rules, but there was a man behind bars who didn't deserve to spend another day there. Paula took out her phone and called Carol's number.

49

Control is an illusion we all need to keep the chaos at bay. Losing control is what the predator fears. Losing control is when we make the mistakes that cost us most dearly.

From *Reading Crimes* by DR TONY HILL

It took every ounce of composure she possessed to stop Carol whirling round to face Vanessa. 'I gave you your chance, Harrison,' she managed to squeeze out. The adrenaline surge made her feel faintly nauseous.

Vanessa stepped forward into the pool of light thrown by the lamps, her hair gleaming soft in their glow. 'Did you really think I'd send someone in alone to sort this out? She's just here to soften you up. That's why she didn't lock the door behind her when you invited her in.'

She was dressed like the villain in a Bond movie, Carol thought. Long black leather coat over a tailored suit in supple grey leather. Black leather gloves, obviously. 'It's showtime, Harrison. I'm offering you the deal of your life. You pay me what you owe me, and we walk out of here. I won't go to the police, I won't harm a hair on your devious little head and you can get on with this magnificent life you've made for yourself.' She waved a hand at the cosy living room, making no attempt to disguise the sneer.

'And if I say no?'

Vanessa gave a theatrical sigh. 'You didn't mount your grand scheme to die an ignominious death in a shitty two-up, two-down in the arse end of nowhere. You've got more than enough salted away. She was telling you the truth. I have killed a man before. Up close and personal. It was him or me. And right now, when I think of what you've done to me, it feels like the same equation. Your life, or mine. So get your bank account on the screen and let's get this bloody mess sorted out.'

His eyes moved between the two women. 'I don't believe you,' he said. 'You talk a good game, Vanessa, but that's all.'

She took another step forward. 'I found you, didn't I?'

Technically, Stacey did. 'What would you rather, Harrison? Death or jail? I'm happy to call the cops and wait till they get here. Because we've done nothing wrong. You invited us in, after all.' Carol smiled.

'Either way you wouldn't get your money.' He actually smirked.

'Neither would you,' Carol snarled.

Vanessa took off one glove and theatrically struck him across the face. Left cheek, right cheek. Just as he had when Carol had burst in, he folded in the face of violence, letting out a scream of pain. 'That's just the beginning, you little shit. You've got more than enough to go around.' She fumbled inside her jacket and pulled out a leather sheath.

Seconds later a slender silver stiletto jutted from her gloved fist. She loomed over him, the blade touching the tip of his chin, a geriatric Valkyrie as terrifying as Brunhilde in her prime.

Gardner held his hands up in surrender. 'Fuck it,' he said bitterly. 'My laptop's in the kitchen.'

'Don't kill him while I'm gone.' It was a relief to get out of the room. Carol's pulse was a jackhammer in her throat and cold sweat was trickling down her back and her sides. She'd been kidding herself when she thought she was learning to control her PTSD. She was as much in its grip as she'd ever been.

The laptop sat on the kitchen table, the *Telegraph* website open to a business page. She carried it back and handed it to Gardner. 'You'll need to move the knife,' he muttered.

Vanessa obliged and stood where she could see what he was doing. Carol joined her just as he opened the site of a bank in the Caribbean jurisdiction of Nevis. He had to pass through four levels of password security, his fingers flying over the keys more swiftly than Carol could follow. Then an eye-watering balance appeared on the screen. 'Bloody hell,' Vanessa said. 'Five and a quarter million's just a bloody flea bite. You greedy bastard.' There was almost a note of admiration in her voice.

'I'm very good at what I do. Your bank details?' Vanessa nodded to Carol, who took a piece of paper from her pocket and handed it over. Gardner worked his way through the transfer then sat back with a sigh. 'All done. That's the beauty of private offshore banks. No stupid daily limits on transfers. You'll want to check it's arrived?'

Vanessa turned away and huddled over her phone. 'Hello,

old friends,' she said after a couple of minutes. 'How lovely to see you again.'

Gardner stood up. 'Now you can both fuck off.'

As soon as the door of Cove Cottage closed behind them, Vanessa crossed to her car, parked on the verge opposite. Carol had to hurry to catch up, reaching her just as she released the locks and went to open the door.

'What the fuck was that about? A knife to the throat? Are you crazy? You could have made me an accessory to murder.'

Vanessa raised her eyebrows. 'It wouldn't be the first time, Carol.' Fingers on the handle, door opening. 'Just keeping it in the family.'

Carol grabbed Vanessa's arm, drawing her away from the car. 'You don't get it, do you? You sent me to do a job, then you waltzed in and turned it into— I don't know, some sort of Tarantino gameshow.'

Vanessa pulled herself free. She chuckled. 'I like that. A Tarantino gameshow. Listen, if you wanted me to stay out of it, you shouldn't have told me where you were. I got the job done, didn't I? You'd have been there all night, smashing ornaments and chatting away. I thought you were tougher than that, but you're as soft as my useless son.'

Something inside Carol's head seemed to shatter, filling it with white noise. She grabbed Vanessa by the shoulders and screamed at her, spittle flying. 'Stay away from us, you bitch. We're done with you. Come near me or Tony again and I'll be the one with the knife. You want to take a chance on how soft I am? Bring it on, bitch.' She pushed Vanessa away from her, hard, so she faltered, then tumbled to one knee.

Carol stepped back, breathing hard, hating herself, hating her rage.

Vanessa looked up at her, calculating. Then she relaxed and pushed herself upright. She brushed the dirt from her knee, tutting at the damage. 'Have you any idea how much this suit cost? I should bill you.'

Carol shifted on to the balls of her feet, teeth bared in a snarl.

Vanessa gave a little laugh. 'Well done, Carol. But we're through now. No more fun outings for us. There's no reason why I should ever bother you or that pitiful excuse for a man I have to call my son.'

Carol turned and jogged down into the dunes. The alternative would have been to descend even further into the hell that evening had become. She'd never had a particularly close relationship with her parents – that had been the role of her brother Michael, and since they held Carol responsible for his death, they'd become even more distant. But she couldn't imagine living with the knowledge that Vanessa was your mother. It was amazing that Tony had survived her, a miracle that he had become the man he was.

There was a storm raging inside her now, a turmoil of panic and grief and disgust. All the work she'd done, all the progress she'd thought she'd made, all stripped away. She was back where she'd started, a failure. She walked down the beach towards the sea, distant at low tide, the ruffled surface silvered under a three-quarter moon that pulled her onward just as it pulled the sea itself.

She knew what she had to do. The question was whether she had the courage to do it.

50

> **The more the neuroscientists tell us about the workings of the human brain, the more we psychologists have to factor into our assessments. For example, it's now well-documented that frontal lobe damage can lead to personality changes including lack of inhibition, aggressive behaviour and risk-taking.**
>
> From *Reading Crimes* by Dr Tony Hill

Dr Elinor Blessing shrugged into her white coat, slung her stethoscope round her neck and slipped from the locker room to the coffee station next door. She filled her water bottle at the cooler, tuning out the chatter around her as she considered the morning rounds ahead of her. She was roused from her thoughts by a lanky junior doctor saying her name.

'You know him, don't you, Elinor?'

She half-turned. 'Know who?'

'The murderer on ward fourteen.'

'What on earth are you talking about, Chisholm?' More irritated than interested by the exchange, she turned back to her bottle.

'The murderer on ward fourteen. You know him.'

She sighed, exasperated. She didn't like Chisholm. He was flippant, dismissive and prone to making so-called jokes at patients' expense. This sounded like one of his usual inappropriate comments. 'Saying the same nonsense twice doesn't make it any clearer. You're not going to have much of a career as a medic if you can't explain yourself lucidly.'

He rolled his eyes. 'There's a guy in the side room on ward fourteen. Neurosurgery. He was brought in last night with a depressed skull fracture. He's under guard because he's a prisoner at HMP Doniston—'

'Tony?' Shock clutched at Elinor's chest. 'Tony Hill?'

Chisholm grinned triumphantly. 'I knew you knew him. I said to the charge nurse, Dr Blessing's wife worked with him before he went on the rampage.'

She was already halfway to the door. She paused and turned back to face him, eyes dark with anger, voice icy. 'Shut up, Chisholm. You do not go around breaching patient confidentiality in this hospital. Especially not when you're as full of shit as you are.'

Elinor yanked the door closed behind her, his words floating after her. 'But he did kill someone, there's no getting away from that.'

Down the hallway, follow the line of blue tiles to the lift, press the button, press the button pointlessly again. Fifth floor, follow the red tiles to the wards, twelve, thirteen, through the double doors to the reception desk of ward fourteen. Neurosurgery. Elinor only realised how grim she was looking when she registered the startled look on the nurse's face. She found a smile and stuck it on. 'You've got a patient called Hill? Tony Hill?'

A quick flash of curiosity, hidden immediately. Nurses hated giving anything away, especially to doctors who weren't *their* doctors. 'Anthony Hill.'

'What's the score?'

Reluctantly, the nurse said, 'We got him from Doniston General last night. Depressed fracture of the skull. Subdural haematoma. He's down for a burr-hole trephination later this morning with Mr Senanayake.'

'Is he conscious?'

'We've got him under light sedation.'

'OK. He's an old friend of mine. Can you have somebody beep me when he's come round after his surgery.' She showed her pager number to the nurse, who pursed her lips but took a note of it. 'Thank you. I'd like to take a quick look. Is he on the ward?' She made to head for the corridor leading to the four-bed wards.

'No, he's in a side room. Other way, round the corner. There's a prison officer posted outside. I'm not sure if you should . . .'

But Elinor was already gone. Outside a door sat a man in uniform. She worked the magic of the white coat plus a sense of purpose and swept past him with a nod. And there he was, in the dim light, head bandaged, arms outside the covers, one wrist handcuffed to the bed rail. Automatically she reached for the clipboard at the foot of the bed, the validation of her presence if the officer checked in on her. She cast an eye over the notes and the scans. Nothing too worrying. If a bleed on the brain could ever be dismissed as 'nothing too worrying'.

Everyone was diminished by hospital beds. It wasn't as

if Tony was a big lad to start with. He looked pale and frail, hooked up to beeping machines, dark circles round his closed eyes, nose swollen and purple. On the other hand, he was breathing without a ventilator and his pulse looked stable. She spoke his name softly. No response. 'We're here for you, mate,' she said, replacing the clipboard and leaving the room.

'What happened?' she asked the officer casually as she closed the door behind her.

'The usual kind of thing,' the man said indifferently. 'Got into a ruck with the wrong person. You the one doing the operation, then?'

'No, but I have an interest in cases like these.' She was already on her way back to the front desk. 'Thanks,' she said to the nurse. 'I'll pop back later, but keep me posted if there's any change, please.'

She checked her watch as she headed back to the lift. She was going to be late for her rounds, but not by much. Time to make a phone call.

Paula liked airports. She liked the anonymity and the possibility of the junk food Elinor frowned on. She liked browsing the kind of shops she'd normally not bother with, taking a delicious pleasure in the knowledge that she'd never be stupid enough to spend £700 on a handbag or a pen. And she liked that she didn't bump into anyone she had to give orders to or take orders from.

She was sipping a mocha topped with a ridiculous swirl of whipped cream when her phone danced on the table top and Elinor's name lit up on the screen. Surprised, since there was seldom any reason for Elinor to call when she was at the hospital, Paula snatched up her phone and took the call.

'Thank goodness I caught you before you boarded,' Elinor said without preamble.

'What is it? Is it Torin?' Paula's first thought, even though she wasn't technically the boy's parent.

'No, it's Tony.'

'Tony?'

'He's been admitted to neurosurgery.'

'At Bradfield Cross? But that's miles from Doniston. Why is he there, what's happened?' Anxiety raised her voice and a woman at the next table stared unashamedly.

'He's here because we're the regional centre of excellence for neurosurgery. Doniston General shipped him across last night. He's got a fractured skull and a brain bleed.'

'Dear Christ, no! That's terrible. What happened?' Paula turned her head, lowered her voice.

'I don't know any details. The officer guarding him said he got into a ruck. But look, Paula, don't panic. It looks like a pretty straightforward injury. It's a small bleed and it's not in a critical area. They've scheduled him for a routine op this morning, it should be a straightforward job. They'll drill a little hole and drain the blood to relieve the pressure and that should be the end of it. Well, they'll maybe leave a drain in for a day or two. But he should be absolutely fine. I just wanted to let you know. Because it'll be all over social media in no time, you know how leaky hospitals are.'

'Poor Tony. This is awful, Elinor. And a fractured skull?'

'It's not too bad, truly. From the scans, it looks like he might have hit something with an edge. A shelf or a table or something. But I'm no expert.'

'I can be there in half an hour.' Action, always the panacea for fear.

'There is genuinely no need. I'm calling not because I think you need to be afraid but because I wanted you to hear it from me.'

'Trust me, I'm a doctor?' Affection rather than sarcasm.

'Something like that. Now go to Galway and I will call you as soon as I hear anything at all. I promise.'

A thought struck Paula. She couldn't believe it had taken so long. 'I'll have to tell Carol.'

'You will. It does need to come from you.'

Paula sighed. 'This is so not what she needs. Not when she's making progress.'

'You can't not tell her.'

Paula gave a soft laugh. 'Not if I don't want to join Tony in neurosurgery.' She glanced up at the departures board. 'They're not boarding us yet, I'll call her now.'

But there was no reply. Carol's phone went straight to voicemail. Just as it had the previous evening. After the beep, Paula said, 'Carol, give me a call when you get this. It's important. I'm about to get on a plane, I'll be on the ground just before noon. Talk to you later.'

She stood up abruptly and, appetite gone, she walked away from her unfinished drink. She wondered where Carol was and why she wasn't answering her phone. She couldn't help a frisson of fear for her friend. How much more could Tony and Carol go through before one of them broke for good?

51

Even psychopaths have their breaking points. The issue is finding the pressure point that takes them there.

From *Reading Crimes* by Dr Tony Hill

Melissa Rintoul liked to arrive at work at least half an hour before her first appointment. Her standard preparation was a ten-minute meditation then a swift look through the appointment schedule to make sure she was primed for what lay ahead. Over the years, she had trained herself not to be taken by surprise. It didn't help patients if you showed your shock or revulsion at the things they told you. But even she struggled not to indicate that it was far from normal to find a client sitting on her doorstep, head bowed and arms wrapped tight around her knees when she arrived at half past seven.

'Carol,' she said, her voice calm and quiet. 'Why don't you come inside and have a cup of tea with me?'

Carol looked up, her face haggard and her red-rimmed

eyes empty. 'I've failed,' she said, struggling to her feet, staggering as her legs cramped under her.

Melissa held out an arm to steady her but Carol grabbed at the door jamb instead. She led her straight to her consultation room and Carol followed meekly, taking the chair that she gestured towards. 'Tea,' she said, going back to the reception area. She boiled water and dropped a couple of green tea bags into cups, aiming for speed rather than delicacy. She was back with Carol in a couple of minutes, handing her the drink. Melissa sat down opposite. 'Why do you think you've failed?'

Carol stared into her cup. 'Last night, I bullied someone. He wasn't a good person. But that's no excuse. Then I stood by while someone else threatened him with a knife. I did nothing to stop it. I colluded in it. The worst part is that I . . .' She sighed heavily. 'I revelled in it. While it was happening, I enjoyed that sense of power, even when I knew it was wrong. I hated myself but it was like a drug. I couldn't stop it.'

'Did either of you physically hurt this person?'

Carol shook her head. 'Not really.'

'"Not really"? What does that mean?'

Shamed, Carol muttered, 'I pushed him. He fell over. But he wasn't hurt, just scared. And then he . . . he caved in. But if he hadn't . . .' Another sigh. 'I think the other person would have hurt him and maybe I wouldn't have stopped her. I was so hyped up.'

'How did you feel? Physically, I mean?'

'My heart was racing, my pulse was pounding. I felt almost sick with the surge of adrenaline.'

'But you didn't actually attack this man. You kept control of yourself, Carol.'

Carol shook her head. 'No. I was so close to tipping over the edge and losing it.'

'But you didn't.'

'I was willing to. All this work I've been doing, all these exercises. I thought I was getting somewhere but at the first crisis, I fell to bits again.' She put her tea down and grabbed her hair with both hands, covering her face, rocking in her chair.

Melissa waited till Carol dropped her hands to her lap again. 'What did you do afterwards?'

Carol sniffed. 'I was so disgusted with myself. I've always been someone who tried to do the right thing. Tried to behave decently, honestly. I despise bullies. I don't think I abused my power when I was a police officer. I exercised power, I know I did, but I didn't exploit it. But now? I'm a stranger to myself.'

'What did you do afterwards?'

Carol stood up abruptly and walked to the window. With her back to Melissa, she said, 'I was beside a beach. I ran through the sand dunes and walked towards the sea. It was a long way out, it must have been low tide. I felt drawn to the sea. I wanted to walk into the sea and just keep going till none of it mattered any more.'

'I'm so glad you didn't do that, Carol. Can you tell me what it was that stopped you?'

Carol gave a little snort. 'The thing that always stops me. Duty. Obligation.'

'Obligation to whom?'

'Not to whom, to what.' She turned back, her face twisted in a sardonic smile. 'Justice. Making things right. See, I'd made a commitment I couldn't keep if I was at the bottom of the sea. So I dragged myself back up the beach and drove here. To confess my failure to someone who would understand why I despise myself so completely right now.'

'Please, sit down, Carol. It's not good to move so restlessly when you need to find the calm space inside yourself.'

Carol threw herself into the chair like a sulky teenager. 'I thought I was managing my PTSD, but it all went to shit at the first test.'

'No, Carol. You're not a failure. The fact that you are here and not at the bottom of the sea, not in police custody for beating someone up, not drunk in a gutter somewhere – all this tells me that you are the opposite of a failure. You are not in the same place as you were when you first arrived here. You have made progress, Carol. I know it doesn't feel like it this morning, but you are getting better.'

'But I'm not fit to be out in the world.'

'That's not true. And you are shifting from genuine remorse to self-pity, even in this short space of time. That's not a healthy place for you to be, and I think you know that very well, Carol. What we're going to do now is a series of exercises to ground you. To bring you back to where you want to be. To remind you of how that feels.'

And so Melissa began to lead Carol back through the process she had already taught her once. They were less than five minutes into the arm exercises when Carol collapsed to her knees on the floor and began sobbing, the abandoned weeping of a deserted child. Melissa knelt next to her and took her into her arms, holding her close but not tight. If she could make Carol feel safe through this catharsis, there was every chance that she'd see this as brief backsliding – two steps forward and one back, perhaps – and not as the disaster she'd believed she'd brought to the door that morning.

At last Carol had no more tears. She slumped against Melissa, exhausted. 'I'm sorry,' she croaked.

'No need for that. I promise, you will not sink this low again. You're here, and that's because this process is working. You trust me, don't you?'

Carol thought for a moment, then nodded. 'I think so, yes.'

'Now you have to extend that trust to yourself.' Melissa gave her a last hug then helped her to her feet. 'I have another patient right now,' she said. 'Before you drive anywhere, I want you to rest and to do a full set of your exercises. We have a room upstairs where you can lie down and sleep for a while.'

Carol followed her out through reception, where a middle-aged man slouched in a chair, glowering. 'I'll be with you in a moment, Pete,' Melissa said, leading the way upstairs to a tiny room furnished with a day bed and a side table. 'Stay here as long as you need,' she said. 'But before you leave, promise me you'll do your exercises.'

Meek as a child now, Carol nodded. 'Thank you.' She sat down as suddenly as if her legs had given way. 'I thought I'd never find sleep again when I came here in the middle of the night. I think I was mistaken.'

Melissa gave her most reassuring smile. 'Be kind to yourself, Carol. You deserve kindness.' And she left Carol, refusing to allow herself a moment's doubt that her patient would indeed find her way back to a version of herself with much less pain.

52

Most of the earliest texts on offender profiling insisted on dividing serial offenders into 'organised' and 'disorganised'. It was a binary that failed to stand up to any degree of close scrutiny. Serial offenders generally exhibit behaviour that falls into both of these areas of distinction.

From *Reading Crimes* by DR TONY HILL

Paula navigated Shannon Airport on automatic pilot, following the same signs as everyone else, clearing passport control effortlessly. 'Make the most of it before Brexit fucks everything up,' the young woman beside her in the line muttered. Paula emerged in the arrivals hall to be confronted by a man in a bottle green suit with shoulders like a prop forward and a shock of bright ginger hair waving a sign that read DI MCINTYRE, as if Diana were her first name.

'I'm McIntyre,' she said. 'Thanks for coming to pick me up.'

He beamed at her and extended a hand that completely enveloped hers. 'Detective Sergeant Fintan McInerny,' he announced in a voice that needed no PA system. 'I'm a regional detective based in Galway. At your service, ma'am.'

Paula winced. Like Carol Jordan, she hated the formal address. It made her feel like an irrelevant old lady. 'Skip the ma'am,' she said. 'Paula will do.'

He looked pained. 'My boss is a bit of a stickler. He wouldn't like that.'

Paula cracked a smile. 'Just go with "inspector" then, Sergeant.'

He grinned back at her. 'I've got the car right outside.' He reached for her overnight backpack. 'Can I take that?'

She let him. Feminism was all very well, but there was no need to suffer for it. Sergeants were called 'bagmen' for good reason. And McInerny looked as if he could tote her bag with his pinkie.

He was true to his word. Immediately outside the terminal a shiny four-by-four, elegant as a rhino, sat on double yellow lines with a uniformed garda standing next to it. He nodded to McInerny and walked away. They were out of the airport and on to the M18 motorway in a matter of minutes. There was no dawdling in McInerny's driving; he overtook like a fly half dodging a full back, coming right up on the car in front before swerving dramatically into the outside lane. Paula, who hadn't been in the West of Ireland since a very damp camping trip in her early twenties, was pleasantly surprised not to be dawdling along one of the country roads she'd travelled then.

As if reading her mind, he said, 'Have you visited here before?'

'So long ago it feels like a past life experience. A lot of

Guinness, a lot of live music and a lot of rain is what I mostly remember.'

'Nothing much has changed except the roads have got better and so's our economy. It's a shame it's raining now, this is a grand drive when you can see it.'

'Maybe it'll clear up.'

'I think it's set in for the day. But you're not here to see the view, are ye? Nuns, is it?'

'Just the one. She used to be the Mother Superior of a convent in Bradesden, just outside Bradfield.'

'I went to Bradfield once. My cousin married a lad from there. To be honest, I don't remember much about it. The reception was in an Irish club and it was more Irish than anywhere I've ever been in my life, if you take my meaning? So this nun, you think she'd been abusing the children in her care?'

'It looks that way. It's hard to track down the former residents. They were in care for the kind of reasons that don't tend to lead to stable regular lives. But what we have so far is one key witness statement about girls being beaten and psychologically tortured.' Paula stared out of the window. 'And around forty skeletons buried under the front lawn.'

McInerny whistled. 'That's not something that happens by accident.'

'The trouble is it's hard to prove abuse. There's no physical evidence of cause of death. And we've got the convent priest basically shrugging and saying, "children die".'

'And despite all the terrible things that have been coming out about what nuns and priests have been doing with the children and young people in their care over the years, there are still plenty of people who absolutely refuse to believe it. My nana, she's one. She thinks it's all a pack of lies from people who want to get money out of the Church. Everybody knows the Church is loaded and she thinks it's an easy touch for blackmailers and liars.' He shook his head. 'She's deluded, of course. But her generation, they've given their lives to the Church. How in the name of God are they expected to cope with the disgusting stories coming out all the time?'

'I take your point. But you don't think like that, right?'

'Me? God, no. I always thought the nuns were evil. Have you ever noticed, the word "convent" contains the word "coven"? We had one old bitch, she loved taking the ruler to the backs of our hands. We'd have to put them palms down on her table then she'd flex the ruler high as she could then wham! She'd let it go and I tell you, it would bring tears to the eyes of Superman himself. Jaysus.' He shivered theatrically. 'I can still remember the sting of it.'

'And nobody made a fuss?'

He roared with laughter. 'If you went home and complained, you'd get a bang on the ear. "You must have done something terrible to drive Sister Augustine to such a pitch," my mother would say. No, when it comes to nuns, I'd believe just about anything. You ask me, Hitler could have got them to run his concentration camps, no bother.'

'I'd have thought that was an outrageous statement until we found those buried children at the Blessed Pearl convent.'

There was silence for a couple of miles, then McInerny spoke. 'I was maybe a wee bit over the top there. My boss tells me I speak before I think. But we're not actually going to the convent of the Order of the Blessed Pearl itself, are we?'

'No, Sister Mary Patrick isn't living in the convent. I don't know why that would be? I'm not exactly au fait with the finer distinctions of life inside Catholic religious orders.'

'My guess would be that they know she's crossed a line and they don't want her contaminating the other sisters. They don't like exposing the postulants and novices to bad influences.' He snorted. 'Mind you, most of the old nuns are such a right bunch of old sadists, one more wouldn't make any difference.' He yanked the wheel sharply to the side as they shot past a lorry full of sheep with inches to spare. Paula was convinced the sheep looked as terrified as she felt.

'So she'd be in disgrace?'

'Right enough, but she's still living in a church property. I think it used to be one of the priests' houses. It's about a mile away from the convent proper. They're not taking their eye off of her.'

'Why don't they . . . I don't know, sack her?'

He laughed. 'You can't sack nuns. It's the very last job for life. You could be excommunicated, I suppose, but I never heard of that happening to anybody in these parts. I think they only do it for full-on heresy. Battering kids? Well, apparently that's not heretical.'

Before she could respond, Paula's phone rang. She pulled it out of her pocket and, seeing it was Carol, she killed the call. 'I need to return that call,' she said. 'Is there somewhere you can pull off? I'm sorry, it's confidential.'

'Sure, no worries. There's an exit slip a couple of miles up the road, I'll take that.'

Paula barely noticed the next few miles as she tried to work out what to say to Carol. She could hardly go, 'Do you want the good news first or the really really bad news?' Before she'd formulated her strategy, McInerny had parked up on the grass verge and was climbing out.

'I'll wait outside,' he said. 'Rain doesn't bother me, I've lived in it all my life. Besides, I can have a wee smoke.'

Left alone without excuses, Paula rang Carol's number.
'What's so urgent?' Carol said as soon as the line opened.

'You're not driving or anything, are you?'

'No, I'm alone. What is it?' A sharp intake of breath. 'It's Tony, isn't it? Something's happened to Tony?'

It was, Paula thought, exactly how she would instantly imagine any catastrophe call being about Elinor. 'He's in Bradfield Cross,' she said. 'But the prognosis is good.'

'What happened? Has he been attacked? I told them, he'll be vulnerable to attack, he's helped put a lot of people away.'

'I don't know the details of what happened. All I know at this point is that he was involved in some sort of a ruck. He either hit his head on something or somebody hit him, I don't know which. Elinor called me to tell me and she's got no access to information beyond the medical. She told me he's got a skull fracture and a brain bleed.'

'Oh God, no,' Carol moaned. 'So how bad is it? What did she say?'

'They're doing that procedure where they drill into the skull to drain the haematoma and reduce the swelling. Elinor says it looks pretty straightforward. Obviously she's not a neurosurgeon, but she can read a chart.'

'Is he conscious?'

'He's under sedation. I think they do it to keep the patient from moving around and doing more damage.'

'You think I should go?'

'Yes. I do. He's under guard, because ... well, because that's how it works. But once he's conscious, I'm sure Elinor can wangle you in.'

'I don't know if he'll want to ...'

They both knew what she couldn't say. 'This kind of thing resets the zeros, Carol. Recalibrates what's important.'

'I don't know . . .' Uncomfortable, she alighted on something to shift the conversation sideways. 'So when did this happen?'

'I'm not clear. He was moved to Bradfield Cross last night because that's where the regional neurosurgical unit is based. Elinor found out this morning when she went into work.'

'This morning? That can't be right?' Carol's voice was sharp. 'You left me two voicemails asking me to call you. The other one was yesterday evening. I didn't notice it till this morning, I was . . . I was busy, sorting something out. And then my phone died. But you left it yesterday.'

As if she'd needed a reminder that Carol was the sharpest detective she'd ever worked with. 'Yeah, that wasn't about Tony,' Paula said. 'I was going to leave that for another time, Tony's much more important than anything else.'

'I can't argue with that. But you might as well tell me now I'm here. Something to distract me.' She caught her breath. 'I need something else to think about till I can get back to Bradfield.'

'Where are you? You're not at home?'

'No. I'm— Never mind, it's not relevant. What's this other thing you have to tell me?'

'It's about the Saul Neilson case. You said it was purely circumstantial, yes?'

'That's right. And no body.'

'Well, now we've got a body,' Paula said.

'You've got to be kidding,' Carol scoffed.

'It's true. We got the DNA confirmation that it's Lyle Tate yesterday afternoon.'

'So where's he been all this time? How did he turn up?'

'Remember I told you about the second group of bodies in the convent grounds?'

'Yes. He's not one of those, is he?' Carol sounded as if there was a bubble of incredulous laughter just below the surface.

'He is. He's one of eight young men buried in a different area from the child skeletons.'

'A serial offender,' Carol breathed. 'Oh, my God.'

'One we didn't know existed. His victims all seem to have been young men, either homeless or living on the outside edge. But here's the thing, Carol. Some of those bodies are more recent than Lyle Tate. Saul Neilson couldn't have killed at least two of them because he was inside. Once we get all the forensics nailed down, you've got your boy off the hook.'

Now Carol laughed. 'Bronwen Scott's going to think I'm some kind of a witch.'

'That may not come as a surprise to her. Look, I've got to go, there's a poor Garda standing in the rain waiting for me to finish this call. I hear anything about Tony, I'll keep you posted. And if you want the DNA details, have a quiet word with Stacey.'

'Will do. Wish me luck,' Carol said. 'No, scrap that. Wish Tony luck. He needs it more than me.'

'You both deserve it,' Paula said, ending the call and tapping on the window to beckon McInerny back behind the wheel. And if there was any luck left over, she'd happily claim it. If Sister Mary Patrick still had God on her side, Paula would take all the help she could get.

53

One of the benefits a profiler can bring to the investigation is to suggest possible directions for inquiries. It's our job to help the investigators to keep an open mind.

From *Reading Crimes* by DR TONY HILL

It was hard enough keeping up with the forensics when he was face to face with Dr Chrissie O'Farrelly in the lab. But talking through results on the phone was almost impossible for Alvin. 'Hold on a moment, Doc, you're going to have to take me through that again.'

Thankfully, she chuckled rather than sighed. 'I'm going to email you the results, Sergeant, but I hoped it would be helpful to run through the headline points.'

It would be if I wasn't so far out of my comfort zone. 'I get that. I'm just not very familiar with this stuff.'

'Let me try again. On first pass, there are no indications of cause of death because we've got no soft tissue and no obvious damage to the bones. When I say "no obvious damage", I'm talking the kind of cuts and nicks we get from knife wounds, or fresh blunt trauma. No bullet holes in the skulls.' Her voice grew more serious. 'But there are a significant number of healed fractures. Arms, ribs mostly, but a few leg breaks and even a couple of old skull fractures. None of these is sinister in itself. Children have accidents. They fall out of trees, off swings, off walls. What is striking here is the proportion of injuries we're seeing. Forty skulls, indicating at least forty sets of remains. And so far we've recorded over seventy broken bones. That's a lot, Sergeant. I've got three pretty lively sons and between them they've racked up one broken collarbone.'

'That doesn't look good,' Alvin said. 'Would you say we're looking at evidence of abuse?'

'I don't make those judgements. That's for the likes of Tony Hill to work out.' A pause. 'You must miss him.'

'We do. But surely—'

'My job is to report the facts, to give factual conclusions, not tell you guys what to think. So I will say that there is a much higher level of skeletal damage among these remains than I would expect to find in a general population.'

'OK. I take your point.'

'The other news I have for you is that we have made some progress on the labels. The nuns may have taken a vow of poverty but that didn't extend to pants. Almost all of the underwear labels we've been able to identify came from Marks and Spencer. And of course there is a man in a cupboard somewhere who knows everything there is to know about M&S labels since the dawn of time. I'll send you his report, but the key points are these. Nothing more recent than six years ago. We've got fourteen underpants labels that originated between six and fifteen years ago. In the ten years before that, seven. Four from the early 1990s. Six from the 1980s. And that's where we're up to right now. The chemists are persisting for more results, but we're not hopeful.' She sighed. 'Poor wee buggers.'

'We see a lot of bad things in this job, but this is one of the worst. What kind of lives did these kids have? All these broken bones.' He shook his head. 'Because we're not looking for personal data, we've been able to get some information from Bradfield Cross hospital. One single case of a girl from St Margaret Clitherow's with a compound fracture of the arm in the last ten years. And yet you tell me there were dozens.' He could feel the rage bubbling up inside like heartburn.

'They would probably have had nuns who were trained nurses,' Chrissie pointed out. 'You should check that out. I'm not expressing a professional opinion here, because I'm as outraged as you are about all this. But it may not have been quite as grim as you fear.'

It was small reassurance. After the call, he turned to the reports Chrissie had sent over. The stark facts on the screen hit even harder than her words had. He thought about the way his own kids drove him to distraction sometimes. But he'd have cut his hand off before he'd have struck one of them. The idea of breaking a child's bones filled him with rage. He wished he hadn't given up his boxing training. There was nothing he'd have liked more right then than half an hour with the heavy bag.

54

A lot of people have a low opinion of the police. And over the years, I've met my fair share of officers you wouldn't want to break bread with, for all sorts of reasons. But most of the cops I've ever worked with aren't just dedicated to doing the job. They're committed to going the extra mile to get the right answers.

From *Reading Crimes* by DR TONY HILL

Stacey Chen had already decided that she didn't like DCI Rutherford's way of doing business. So while she understood that the way to a quiet life was to provide him with the information he required, she had no intention of letting that interfere with her personal work habits. There were two kinds of detectives, she'd realised over her years of quiet observation. The ones who listened to instructions and fulfilled them, often very efficiently. Full stop. Then there were the ones who paid attention to what they were told to do and then went about it in their own sweet ways. Stacey liked to think of herself in that second group. It gave her scope to do what the hell she wanted, as long as she ticked the boxes of what the investigation needed.

Carol Jordan had had a knack for picking detectives with a well-developed maverick streak whose effective result rate ran well above the average. So Stacey had always felt validated and vindicated by what she saw around her. The remnants of her old squad all had that same tendency of coming at things from an unexpected angle. She knew where she was with Paula and Alvin and, to a lesser degree, Karim. But Sophie Valente and Steve Nisbet were a different matter.

She'd checked them out online, of course. Her trawl had been disappointing; there was nothing there to suggest either of them was anything other than a rather dull straight line.

So, it was up to her and the old crew to prove ReMIT was worth its budget. Stacey had been trawling the databases for days, some of them via legitimate access, some via a variety of back doors she'd developed or invested in over the years, a couple thanks to favours exchanged with friends with more than a toe in the Stygian waters of the Dark Net.

She'd drip-fed details of the locations and official names of the Bradesden nuns to Sophie's incident room, and she'd filleted all she could lay hands on about missing young men in the right age range. The numbers filled her with dismay at the waste of potential they represented, even after she'd whittled the total down by cross-referencing them with criminal records, registered deaths and those who had resurfaced in their old lives years later.

And now the DNA results were coming in from the labs, she'd set her systems crawling through the databases again, trying for formal identifications of eight young men whose families and friends would finally find answers to the questions they'd been asking for years. Or, as Stacey suspected in some cases, not been asking. Because they didn't notice, didn't care or preferred an absence to the problems a presence brought.

The forensics teams had swept Martinu's vehicle for anything evidential but so far they'd drawn a blank. There appeared to be no DNA from any of the identified victims, and it wasn't because Martinu was a clean freak. His car contained the usual detritus of food wrappers, soft drink cans and parking receipts. Just nothing to indicate any of the victims had ever been there.

That made sense if he'd just been the gravedigger. But they only had his word for that. Stacey hadn't interviewed him, so her overview wasn't contaminated by having directly heard his version of events. It was easier for her to come at the case laterally. What if there wasn't anybody else? What if Martinu was himself the killer, putting on a performance that would protect him from the worst consequences of his actions? What would he need to have put in place to cover his back? He wouldn't be the first serial offender who had led investigators up the garden path. Literally, in his case.

Stacey had let the idea tick over in the back of her mind while she worked on what she'd been officially tasked with. And now she had cleared some space for herself to put her conclusions to the test.

If Martinu was the killer, how did he get his victims to their graves? Those young men didn't walk from the centre of Bradfield to the convent. They probably didn't come by bus, because the nearest bus stop to the village was a mile away on the main road and, frankly, Bradesden was the kind of place where lads like these walking through would provoke a call to the local community bobby. They didn't drive there, because none of them owned a car. She'd checked with DVLA. That was a matter of record.

The obvious answer – the only answer – was that Martinu had access to another vehicle. If it belonged to a friend or a family member, she'd be out of luck. But using a borrowed car to ferry round strange young men or their corpses was taking a lot of chances. He'd want to be in control of that environment.

Maybe he'd bought another car, a car he kept well away from where he lived. A garage somewhere else. A quiet side street where nobody would pay attention to a car parked for days at a time. It wasn't hard to hide a car in plain sight. You just had to choose an area where the local residents didn't have a parking problem that made every unfamiliar set of wheels a hate object.

It would have to be reliable. The last thing you wanted was a breakdown with a body in the boot. So that ruled out the truly dodgy end of the motor trade. Most people had no idea how to buy a legitimate car without their name and address ending up on the registration document. There was no indication that Martinu hung out with criminals, so there was a slim chance he'd done things the straight way.

Humming softly under her breath, Stacey made her way inside the labyrinth of DVLA. She'd been there before; it held no terrors for her. Their search engine was surprisingly competent for a government agency. And within seconds, she was presented with what she'd hoped for.

Jerome Martinu of Garden Cottage, Fellside Road, Bradesden, was the registered keeper of the Toyota SUV that the forensic scientists had been crawling over like human hoovers. And also a three-year-old black Skoda Octavia estate.

The corners of her mouth twitched in an almost-smile. Step one had produced what she'd hoped for. Now for the second step. Thanks to the ever-vigilant civil liberties organisations who made her job harder, the records for the number plate recognition system that covered almost every major road – and many minor ones – were only held for two years. But that might be enough to prove Martinu was in the habit of driving round the parts of town where victims had last been seen.

Stacey entered the details into the ANPR system. *Showtime, Jezza,* she thought.

55

The practical ways we deal with love and with anger are formed at a very early age. As Richard Dawkins says, 'The Jesuit boast, "Give me the child for his first seven years, and I'll give you the man," is no less accurate (or sinister) for being hackneyed.'

From *Reading Crimes* by Dr Tony Hill

'Used to belong to one of those Anglo-Irish families that lost all their money in the Great Depression,' McInerny said, gesturing with his thumb towards an ugly but imposing grey mansion on the outskirts of Galway. 'So the Blessed Pearl snapped it up and installed a bunch of nuns.'

'Nice view of the sea,' Paula pointed out, turning her head to look out of the other window.

'Doesn't really make up for the draughts and the damp.' McInerny suddenly wrenched the wheel and threw the car into a narrow side road. 'Whoa! Nearly missed the turning there.'

The road climbed steadily through high hedges and banks of gorse, not a house in sight till they rounded a bend and came upon a squat Victorian villa. 'Here we are.' He pulled into a gravel drive with weeds sprouting unchecked. For some reason, the house had been built at right angles to the sea view, so that only a couple of windows in the gable end benefited from it.

The door was opened by a woman in what Paula thought of as nun civvies. Grey skirt, white blouse buttoned to the neck, grey cardigan and a minimalist head-covering that barely skimmed her shoulders. She seemed to be at some indeterminate point of middle age and greeted them with a sweet smile. 'Good afternoon, how may I help you?'

'We're here to see Sister Mary Patrick,' McInerny said. 'Garda Sergeant McInerny. And Detective Inspector McIntyre.'

'Guards?' She looked astonished rather than afraid, and quickly crossed herself. 'Is it bad news?'

It was an odd question, Paula thought. Because when the cops came to call, it was never good news. Even when they came to report an arrest to victims and their families, it was a reminder of the bad thing that had preceded it. 'Sister Mary Patrick?' Paula asked.

'Why don't you come in and I'll see what's what?' The nun led them to a small parlour close to the entrance vestibule. 'I'll just go and . . .' she added vaguely as she disappeared.

The room was plainly furnished with generic modern chairs around a table that looked like it had escaped from a coffee shop. A print of the Virgin Mary cradling her dead son hung above a fireplace with a dust-covered grate. 'Cheery,' Paula muttered.

McInerny grunted. 'You wouldn't call the Catholic Church happy-clappy.'

The door opened to reveal a tall woman in a black nun's habit, crucifix on her breast, amber rosary beads gleaming at her waist. 'I am Sister Mary Patrick of the Order of the Blessed Pearl,' she said, her voice firm and clear, her Northern accent faint but definite.

She swept across to the table and sat with her eyes fixed on Paula. McInerny might have been invisible. He rattled through the introductions again, explaining that Paula was from Bradfield, but the nun remained unmoved. She must have been handsome in her youth, Paula thought. High cheekbones, a slender nose, a chiselled jaw that was barely beginning to sag. Paula knew from the files that she was fifty-nine, but she'd have guessed at least five years younger, in spite of the violet shadows under her dark blue eyes.

'You know why we're here,' Paula said.

'Do I?'

'The remains of forty children have been found in the grounds of the convent where you were Mother Superior. I can't believe nobody mentioned that to you.'

'I have nothing to say about this.' She folded her hands loosely on top of the table.

'You were responsible for the girls in your care.'

'The convent has been there since the 1930s. There were several reverend mothers before me.'

Paula took out her phone and consulted the email Alvin had sent her. 'How long were you in charge at St Margaret Clitherow?'

'I'm not entirely clear what right you think you have to question me, Detective. This is not your jurisdiction.'

'Detective Inspector McIntyre is here with the full support of the Garda Síochána,' McInerny interjected. *Good man.* 'It will save everyone a lot of time if I don't have to repeat all of her questions over a jurisdictional quibble.' He pulled out his phone. 'And I will be recording this interview so that we all know where we stand.'

Sister Mary Patrick was momentarily disconcerted but she recovered herself quickly. 'Very well. To answer your question, I was Mother Superior for twelve years. Until the convent closed five years ago. I spend a brief period in the Mother House at York and then I was sent here.'

'Why were you sent here? What's your role here?' Paula's tone was casual but her interest was not. Was this punishment? Or warehousing?

'Prayer and contemplation.'

'All by yourself?'

'You have already met Sister Dorothy. She is housekeeper here. Sister Mary Francis and Sister Margaret also live here.'

'Praying and contemplating?'

'You'd have to ask them. I am not responsible for them.'

'It seems an odd place for a mother superior to end up.'

'Running a convent, a girls' home and a school is a very demanding occupation. I did it for twelve years. A time of renewal is a needful thing.'

'And are you renewed yet?'

Sister Mary Patrick simply stared at her, blank of expression.

'I'd like to go back to those years when you were at Bradesden. Our forensic experts tell us that at least fourteen of those bodies date from that period. It's hard for me to get my head round this. But fourteen dead girls were illegally disposed of while you were in charge.'

Sister Mary Patrick sighed and shook her head. 'There's nothing sinister in that. Children die. These children had nobody to claim them. We gave them the dignity of a Christian burial.'

'Under cover of darkness? To me, that looks like you had something to hide.'

'We had a duty not to upset the living. Little girls are easily upset.'

'And without bothering with the inconvenience of death certificates?' Paula couldn't keep the ice from her voice.

'I know nothing of that.'

'How can you know nothing? You had legal responsibility for those girls.'

She gave the ghost of a smile. 'I delegated it. Sadly, Sister Gerardine who was in charge of the girls' health needs is now afflicted with dementia. She's living in the Mother House in York but these days she doesn't even know her own name. So I doubt she will be of much assistance to you.'

Paula understood she was facing a formidable opponent. It would take all her skills to garner any substantive evidence against Sister Mary Patrick, a woman who had clearly planned for this eventuality. She took a short moment to tamp down her incredulous anger. 'We have witness statements alleging brutality and psychological torture at St Margaret Clitherow. There are specific accusations against you.'

'I'm sure there are. Some of the girls we dealt with at the Blessed Pearl were quick on the uptake as well as utterly amoral. As soon as this story hit the news, I knew there would be opportunistic liars quick to make unsubstantiated allegations. The church's failures to deal with abusive priests over the years has made us a cheap target for charlatans. I could probably give you a list of the names of these accusers. In their eyes, we're an easy payday.' She pushed her chair back. 'Now, I have been very generous with my time and my answers but I have reached the limit of that generosity. So, if you have nothing more?'

'I do, as it happens. I wanted to ask you about your groundsman, Jerome Martinu.'

Now something crossed her face that might almost have been surprise. 'What about him?'

'He dug the graves, right?'

She inclined her head in acknowledgement. 'He did.'

'Without question?'

'He understood his duty to the convent.'

'Were you aware of any other graves he dug within the convent grounds?'

She gave a little shrug of indifference. 'Only the one.'

56

The cases that always took the most out of me were the ones that awoke echoes from my own past. Sometimes I learned as much about myself from the process of drawing up a profile as I did about the offender.

From *Reading Crimes* by DR TONY HILL

Another day would make little difference to Saul Neilson, Carol told herself as she hurried down the stairs of Melissa Rintoul's consulting rooms. She'd talk to Bronwen Scott when her mind was clear. No time to thank Melissa or even to say goodbye. Right now, there was only one place she wanted to be.

She ran down the lane to where she'd left the Land Rover, tearing off the parking ticket stuck to its windscreen and throwing it on to the passenger seat. She started the engine then forced herself to pause for breath. Melissa's words bubbled up in her head. 'Before you leave, promise me you'll do your exercises.'

Carol knew it made sense. Not just for her own sake but in the best interests of everyone else on the road between Edinburgh and Bradfield. And so she sat behind the wheel and worked her way through the now-familiar exercises, trying to banish her impatience and instil a sense of calm.

By the time she'd finished, her breathing was steady, her palms no longer sweating. She plugged her phone into the sound system and chose the playlist mix of Jocelyn Pook, Lisa Gerrard, Jóhann Jóhannsson and Ólafur Arnalds that she'd put together to help her stay chilled and in balance. Only then did she ease out of the parking space and into the traffic.

In spite of her best efforts, her imagination was working overtime. What if the injury was worse than Paula had admitted? What if Tony had sustained more profound damage? She'd worked cases where people's personalities had been permanently affected by brain injury. What if that happened to him? What if he wasn't the same man when he recovered? How would he cope if he'd lost his ability to empathise? Or his capacity to analyse the manifestations of human behaviour and draw unexpected conclusions?

Would he even *be* Tony any more? The last time they'd spoken to each other, he'd told her he loved her. True, he'd then broken all contact with her until she'd taken steps to recover from the PTSD she was still in denial about. But she'd done that now, she was on the road to rehabilitation. What if he couldn't recognise that in her? What if he didn't feel the same about her? If he no longer loved her?

And what if she didn't feel the same about him?

'This is ridiculous,' she shouted. She reminded herself that she'd been trained to deal in facts. Speculation was only valuable if it led to answers. And there could be no answers till she had seen him for herself.

The journey seemed endless, even though she knew she was making good time. Carol tried to think about other things. About the difference the DNA evidence could make to Saul Neilson's case. It certainly led to a strong supposition that Lyle Tate was one of a string of victims who couldn't all have been killed by Neilson, since at least two of them had died after he'd been incarcerated. But she had to acknowledge it didn't completely exonerate him. To do that, Paula and her team needed to find a killer and tie him to Lyle Tate's death. That would take them over the line.

But there were other avenues she could explore. Tate had had a flatmate. There must have been other people who knew him. As far as Carol could tell from the original defence material, the effort to find anyone who might have spoken to him after he left Neilson's flat had been desultory. She'd wondered why that had been. His defence solicitor wasn't a name she was familiar with.

To take her mind off Tony, she decided to call Bronwen. This late in the afternoon, she'd be back from court. 'Carol,' Bronwen said. 'Have you got news for me?'

'I'm working on it,' Carol said, not ready yet to pass on what she had. It was hard to break the habit of building a complete case before she let an outsider anywhere near it. 'I've had a chance to look more closely at the defence files and it doesn't look like his solicitor was very diligent when it came to looking for witnesses to Lyle's movements after he left Saul. I've never heard of this lawyer. Was there an issue there?'

Bronwen snorted. 'Just a bit. Saul had too much money for Legal Aid so he hired an old school friend who hadn't defended a murder before. Or anything like that serious.

And because Saul didn't have any experience with the criminal justice system he didn't realise his mate wasn't out of the top drawer.'

'Obviously he should have gone for you,' Carol said drily.

'Obviously. You think there's any mileage in it after all this time?'

'I won't know until I try. Do you know where I can find Lyle Tate's flatmate?'

'I thought you were the investigator?'

'I am, that's why I asked the question. So, do you have any idea?'

'No, sorry. You'll have to dig that up yourself. You could start with the flat they shared.'

Carol rolled her eyes. 'No, seriously? You think?'

Bronwen laughed. 'Let me know when you've got somewhere.' She cut the call. Really, Carol thought, being on the same side as Bronwen wasn't so different to being up against her. Maybe later tonight she'd try Tate's old flat. After she'd seen Tony for herself.

The miles passed slowly but they passed. When she saw the motorway mileage sign that read BRADFIELD 15, she called Elinor. 'I'm sorry to bother you, Elinor,' she said.

'I've been expecting to hear from you. Paula said she'd managed to get hold of you.'

'How is he?'

'They operated this afternoon and the signs are good. They've reduced the haematoma and when I checked in about an hour ago, the last of the seepage had stopped. He's sedated, but the prognosis is looking good. I spoke to the neurosurgeon and he thinks there's probably no need to operate on the fracture as it's not actively pressing on Tony's brain.' Elinor was brisk but reassuring.

'Can I see him?' Carol knew she sounded desperate but she didn't care.

'If it was up to me, I'd say yes, absolutely. But it's not quite that straightforward. Because technically, he's a prisoner. There's an officer on guard outside the ward, checking people in and out.'

'You managed to get in, though.'

'Yeah, but I'm a consultant on the staff here, nobody's going to question my right to be there.'

'Please, Elinor. Can't you think of something?'

A pause. Elinor sighed. 'Where are you?'

'About twenty minutes away.'

'I shouldn't even be contemplating this . . . you know the Starbucks opposite the main hospital entrance? Meet me there in half an hour.' And she was gone.

Elinor used her pass to open the locked door to Ward 12. 'It's visiting hours in here, nobody will look twice at you,' she'd said on the way in. She walked past the nurses' station to the end of the corridor then led Carol into a walk-in cupboard. The shelves that lined it were stacked with laundered bed linen and surgical scrubs. 'Green or navy blue?' Elinor asked.

'Does it make a difference?'

'Not really. Whatever you're wearing you'll be found out as soon as anyone asks you a question.'

'Navy blue, then. It goes better with my hair.'

Elinor grinned. 'Your hair's mostly going to be covered.' She rummaged through the pile and handed Carol a set of scrubs then moved along the shelves to find a hat and mask. 'Let's go full-on,' she said.

Carol stripped to her underwear and pulled on her disguise. 'How's that?'

'Pretty good. Let the mask hang round your neck till we get out of this ward.' She slung her stethoscope round Carol's neck. 'OK, let's do it.'

Carol stuffed her clothes at the back of the bottom shelf and followed Elinor. Heads together in muttered consultation, they made it out into the main corridor and to the Ward 14 entrance. Carol tugged the mask over her nose and mouth. The nurse on station barely glanced at Carol. 'Back again, Dr Blessing?'

'Last check for tonight,' Elinor said.

They headed down the hall. The prison officer paid more attention than the nurse had. 'Another visit, Doc? I wish I got as much attention from you ladies as he does.'

Elinor chuckled. Hand on the door. 'Don't wish too hard for what you want, officer. Next time it might be you lying in there. I just need to check his vitals and my colleague here has to make sure the tube's clear.' She pushed the door open and they slipped inside.

In the dim light, Tony looked like a statue on a tomb. Carol took a moment to collect herself then approached the bed. A bandage circled his head, a thin plastic tube snaking out from under it and into a plastic bag held on a drip stand. The bag was empty, the tube almost completely clean apart from a single thread of blood about an inch long. She stared down at the face she loved, its familiar planes and curves more still than she'd ever seen him. His was a mobile face, constantly changing in response to what he saw and heard and felt. Even in repose, the sharp intelligence in his eyes was discernible. But now there was nothing. Just the marks of injury. His chest barely moved with his shallow breaths. Carol stretched out a hand and touched the arm that was cuffed to the bed, the warmth of his skin a reassurance.

She glanced at Elinor. 'Is he really all right? He looks ... he looks absent.'

'He's sedated, Carol. If he's stable tomorrow, they'll let him come round. If he was in danger, he'd be on the High Dependency ward. I know this seems like a catastrophe to you, but honestly, to these guys, this is a routine case.'

Carol felt tears pricking her eyes. 'Will you get me back in to see him after he's conscious? I need to speak to him, Elinor.'

She saw the sympathy in her friend's eyes. 'Of course. But I think we should go now, before the guard starts wondering what's taking so long.'

Carol bent impulsively and kissed Tony's cheek. 'I'll be back,' she said. 'Sleep well.' Then she followed Elinor from the room and back into a world of sound and movement, knowing she would not be happy till Tony was back there too.

But for now, at least she had something to distract herself with.

57

The art of diverting an interview is one that psychopaths excel in.

From *Reading Crimes* by Dr Tony Hill

The nun's words hit Paula like a shock of static electricity. Then she caught sight of the faint smirk of satisfaction Sister Mary Patrick hadn't quite managed to hide. 'And what one would that have been?' Paula demanded, a low threat edging into her voice.

'I am not a good sleeper,' she said. *Bad conscience,* Paula thought. 'I often wake up in the night and struggle to get back to sleep. And so I get up and spend some time in prayer. Or I read devotional literature. There was a little attic room at Bradesden that we used as a kind of library and I would often go there in the night when sleep had failed me. It has a single window which overlooks Jerome's vegetable garden.' She paused, considering how to proceed.

'And you saw something?'

She nodded. 'Usually, I paid no attention to the view,

because there was no view to speak of. It was too dark to see anything. But on one night in particular, there was a clear sky and a full moon and the garden was lit up like a Paul Delvaux painting. And then movement caught my eye. At first, I couldn't really make out what was going on so I turned out my reading light. When my eyes grew accustomed to the dark, I could see it was Jerome and another man carrying a bundle across the garden to one of the raised beds. They were made out of old railway sleepers, so they were quite sturdy.'

Paula realised she was holding her breath and forced herself to breathe naturally. 'Go on,' she said.

'They lifted the bundle over the lip of the raised bed. It looked quite heavy. There was a spade on the ground and Jerome climbed up on to the edge of the bed with it. He shovelled soil for a short time. I presumed he was covering whatever they'd put in there. Then they walked back towards Jerome's cottage.' Sister Mary Patrick started working the fingers of one hand over the amber beads of her rosary. She seemed to think she'd reached the conclusion of what she had to say.

'Did you get a good view of the other man?' Paula asked.

'I did. Even though it was some distance away, the moonlight was bright enough to see clearly. I knew Jerome as soon as I saw him.'

Now for the crucial question. 'And did you recognise the other man?'

Sister Mary Patrick fixed her with a level gaze. *She knows how to work the room. She must have run the convent like her personal empire. No wonder none of the sisters was giving her up.* 'I would not say this if I were not certain,' she said at length. 'To bear false witness is, as you doubtless know, against the

Eighth Commandment. In our church, we regard those as moral imperatives. The man with Jerome that night was his cousin. Mark Conway.'

Paula did not let her face betray her excitement. 'And you're absolutely certain of this?'

'Oh yes. It wasn't simply that I recognised his face, although that is the case. But that was confirmed by what he was wearing.' She paused again. She clearly revelled in the power that tantalising them gave her.

'And what was he wearing?' For now, Paula would play the game.

'The only thing I ever saw him wearing. He would visit Jerome regularly, which is how I came to meet him. Conway would come round to watch football on TV with his cousin. And he invariably wore a Bradfield Victoria top. They are very distinctive, Inspector. Bright canary yellow.'

'So, let me get this straight. In the middle of the night—'

'Not the middle of the night, Inspector. It would have been around one in the morning,' the nun corrected her as if she were a particularly slow student.

Paula acknowledged the correction with a wry smile. 'In the early hours of the morning, Jerome Martinu and his cousin Mark Conway buried something in a raised bed in the vegetable garden?'

'That's right.'

'What was this bundle wrapped in?'

'I couldn't tell. Something light-coloured is all I could make out. There was some sort of tape or rope holding it together.'

'And the shape?'

'It wasn't any particular shape. Quite long, quite bulky.'

'Like a dead person?'

'I don't know what a dead person taped up in a bundle looks like,' she said disdainfully.

Paula gave herself a moment to get a grip on her temper. 'Can you remember which of the raised beds this was?'

She frowned. 'It's a long time ago. It must have been six, maybe seven years. I don't know if the beds are still configured in the same arrangement. As far as I can recall, it was the second ... or possibly the third from the left as I was looking at them from the window.'

'Did you ask Martinu about it?'

She raised her eyebrows. 'Why would I? The garden was his concern.'

'It didn't strike you as suspicious?'

The tip of her tongue ran swiftly along the underside of her top lip. 'I really didn't give the matter much thought. It was a curious incident, but why would I leap to suspecting a man who had worked for us for years, who was trustworthy and reliable and discreet, of any wrongdoing?'

'You didn't think they might be burying a body?' Paula asked. She was struggling to keep her composure through these ridiculous responses.

'I am not a police officer,' the nun said with an air of contempt. 'I do not view the world through the lens of suspicion. I assumed it was some sort of fertiliser.'

'Fertiliser? Wrapped in black bin bags? What kind of fertiliser would that be?'

'Animal carcases make good fertiliser, don't they? Inasmuch as I gave it any thought, I imagined it might be a dead dog.'

'A dead dog.' Paula let the words hang in the air.

'A passing thought, Inspector.'

'You're telling me you thought it was normal behaviour

for your groundsman and his cousin to be burying a wrapped-up dead dog in a vegetable bed under cover of darkness?'

Sister Mary Patrick lifted her chin slightly. 'I had more important considerations than that.'

'Really. Here's the thing, Sister. I do have a suspicious mind. And what I'm wondering is whether you kept quiet about what you saw that night because you knew that if you reported Jerome Martinu and his cousin to the police, he'd shop you in a heartbeat. And you had too much to hide to risk that, didn't you?'

58

Over the years, I've met people who are seduced by what they see as the glamour of serial murder. I'm pretty good at walking in other people's shoes, but I've never managed to wrap my head round that. There's nothing glamorous about serial homicide . . .

From *Reading Crimes* by DR TONY HILL

Campion Boulevard carved a line through the centre of Bradfield that demarcated communities as effectively as the Berlin Wall. On one side, the thriving city centre with its various money-making machines, from shops and bars to insurance headquarters and art galleries. On the other, the former Victorian mill landscape. Some of the old industrial brick buildings had been renovated and transformed into so-called luxury flats that everybody knew were really a different kind of machine for making money. Others stood semi-derelict like rotten teeth in a Victorian smile. In the gap sites between were squat buildings that had been thrown up between the wars to house workers displaced by slum clearance. The flat Lyle Tate had lived in was in one of those jerry-built blocks. A scabby concrete stairwell whose ground-level reek of urine morphed into the funk of stale cooking and rotting rubbish led to an open third-floor gallery that ran the length of the building.

Carol picked her way along the dimly lit landing, accompanied by the sounds that leaked from badly fitting doors and windows. *EastEnders* theme tune; a man and woman having a shouting match about a pizza; a raucous burst of Amy Winehouse; a throbbing bass line from something Carol was delighted she didn't recognise.

Lyle Tate's former home was the last door she came to. Someone had painted it purple, drips and smears making it almost a statement rather than a demonstration of incompetence. A dirty plastic doorbell had a smudge of purple paint down one side. It produced a long deep buzz when she pressed it.

She didn't have to wait long before the door was opened by a skinny boy in a mohair sweater and fashionably ripped jeans. He had a pair of flip-flops on his feet, revealing toenails painted the colour of black cherries. Sculpted black hair and a goatee emphasised a face like a satyr on a Greek vase, an impression only slightly marred by a scatter of pimple scars around his sharp nose. He looked her up and down with an air of faint amusement. 'I think you're in the wrong place, love,' he said.

'Are you Gary Bryant?' Carol asked.

Eyebrows elegantly raised. 'Oh no, you've missed him by about six months. He got sent down for dealing, love. What did you want him for? I don't mean to be a bitch but you're very much not his type.'

'I wanted to talk to him about Lyle Tate.'

Now the affectations fell away. 'Poor Lyle, that was terrible,' he said.

'Did you know Lyle, then?'

'Know him?' He perked up. 'I think I was the last person to talk to him the night he died.'

This was far more than Carol could have hoped for. 'That's interesting. Sorry, I don't know your name?'

He frowned. 'Are you police? Only, you haven't identified yourself.'

'My name's Carol Jordan. I used to be a police officer. A detective. But I'm ... retired.' It was a hard moment. The first time she'd admitted that as her status.

'So why are you looking to talk to Gary about Sugar Lyle?'

'There's some question over the validity of Saul Neilson's guilt.'

He gave a harsh bark of laughter. 'You're kidding me. You telling me you fucked it up? And now you're, what? Trying to get out from under?'

'Not me, no. It wasn't my team who investigated Lyle's murder. I wasn't even a BMP officer at the time. And I'm freelance now.'

'So who you working for? Who cares what happens to the bastard who offed Lyle?'

'An organisation called After Proved Guilty. Look, can I come in and talk to you? It's freezing out here.' She gave him her best smile. These days, she didn't think there was much wattage, but it was better than nothing.

He stuck his head out of the door and looked past Carol, checking nobody was watching. 'I suppose,' he said, leading her down a narrow hall. Someone had painted a mural along one wall. Carol recognised a stylised version of a corner of Temple Fields, the rainbow flag flying above the frontages of bars, fast food joints and a tattoo parlour. There was even a corner of the Indian restaurant where she and Tony had often sneaked off for a curry in mid-investigation.

'Nice work,' she said.

'Cheers. I did it when I moved in last year to stop the place looking like a complete shithole.'

She followed him into the living room. Another mural, this time of the park in Temple Fields with its riotously decorated bandstand. 'Is this what you do, then? Murals?'

He shrugged. 'These ones are for me. Mostly I do shit for rich bastards who want a Caravaggio on their dining room wall.'

Apart from the mural, it was a typical young man's flat. Bean bags, futon sofa with a grubby cover, ratty carpet with more stains than original colour. Dirty mugs on a cardboard side table made to resemble a stack of pizza boxes. The room smelled of stale takeaways overlaid with coffee. 'You live here alone?' Carol asked.

'Yeah, for as long as I can afford to.'

'You didn't tell me your name.'

'Not just a pretty face, then?' The archness was back.

'It'll take me about seven minutes to find out, so do yourself a favour and save me the bother.' She smiled to take the sting out of it.

He snorted. 'Sit down, Carol Jordan. I'm Captain Scarlett. No, really,' he added, seeing her frown. 'I changed it by deed poll as soon as I was eighteen. I'll show you my passport if you don't believe me. People call me Cap.'

She eyed the futon. She'd sat on a lot worse. She grinned at him and perched on the edge. 'So, Cap, how come you didn't come forward to say you'd seen Lyle that night?'

'Simple, love. I didn't know anything about it. The next morning I was off at the crack of sparrowfart to Australia.'

'Australia?'

'Yeah. Big island in the Pacific. Where Kylie comes from.'

Carol rolled her eyes. 'What were you doing in Australia?'

'Following my boyfriend. He was a DJ. He'd scored a long-term gig in a club in Sydney so off I went like a good little camp follower.' He gave a flounce and fell back into one of the bean bags. 'We weren't exactly keeping up with events in the Old Country. So the first I knew about Sugar Lyle was when I came back last year. Gary knew he was going down and he wanted somebody to sublet the flat to. I asked what had happened to Sugar Lyle and he told me the poor boy had been murdered. And nobody had seen him since the night before I'd left.' He caught her eye. 'And don't go looking at me like that, I could no more murder a sweet boy like Sugar Lyle than fly back to Australia without a plane. Where I would not be welcome since the DJ and I did not part on the best of terms.'

'So when exactly did you see Lyle?'

'I'd been for a farewell burger with a couple of pals. Graphic artists, they've got a studio in Manchester, in the Northern Quarter. They'd gone off to get a train around ten so it must have been about half past.'

After Saul Neilson claimed Lyle had departed. 'Where did you see him?'

'There's an alley just off the main drag in Temple Fields. It opens out about halfway down into a courtyard. There's an old reading room or something there with a little porch, three steps up. It's a bit of a hang-out for boys looking for custom. Lyle was the only one there, he was all huddled up on one of the steps. I stopped to say hello but he wasn't up for a chat. He said he was on his way home, but he'd come over all faint. He'd had a nosebleed, he said. He was really fucked off. Said it had totally wrecked his evening. I left him to it and carried on my merry way.' He lolled back and pulled a shiny scarlet vape from his pocket. He pressed the button and took a couple of quick primer puffs before delivering a cloud of coffee-scented vapour into the room.

Carol kept a straight face, not revealing what this information meant to her. 'I don't get it,' she said. 'It was my understanding that Lyle didn't show up on the CCTV around Temple Fields that night.'

A shout of laughter. 'Oh, such beautiful innocence. Dear Carol Jordan, all of us lost boys know exactly where all the CCTV cameras are. We know every twisty route through the labyrinth so you can't see where we've been and where we're going and what we're doing and who we're doing it with. If Lyle didn't want to show up on screen, he'd have worked his way across Temple Fields and out the other side and your lot would have been none the wiser.'

This was news to Carol. But it didn't surprise her. 'And if there's an inconvenient camera, you just black out the lens,' she said wearily.

His tricorn smile was wicked. 'That's for amateurs.'

'And you didn't see anyone with Lyle?'

A puff of vapour enveloped his head. 'No. Lyle was on his own, feeling sorry for himself. And I was on my way home to finish packing. And I didn't notice anyone else hanging around apart from the usual wastrels. And none of them could make Lyle disappear.'

'I'm going to need you to give us a sworn affidavit about your encounter with Lyle.'

'What? You want me to help get his killer off the hook? You've got to be joking.'

'No, I want you to help me nail the real killer. Saul Neilson didn't kill Lyle Tate. There's new evidence that proves that.' *Well, almost.* 'And I think we can replace Saul Neilson behind bars with the bastard who actually did kill Lyle. Are you up for that?'

He cocked his head to one side, considering. 'It goes against the grain to help the police, Carol Jordan. But I suppose you're not really police.' He leapt up and crossed to the mural. 'You see that one there?' He pointed to a capering figure in a canary yellow shirt. 'That's Sugar Lyle in his Bradfield Vics top. He never wore it when he was working. He kept it for Lyle time. I so don't get football. Too much mud and violence. But Lyle loved the Vics. And I did like Sugar Lyle. So, OK. I'll help you.' That tricorn smile again. 'And if it gets my name in the papers, it's bound to drum up some work. Which, frankly, I could use right now.'

59

When we enter somebody's home, we immediately make judgements about them based on their level of cleanliness, their taste, the contents of their kitchen cupboards (if we get that far). So when we gain access to the home of someone suspected of serial offences, we tend to look at that environment as if it's a kind of primer that will elucidate them to us. But sometimes, we are dealing with a highly sophisticated mind; a mind that creates a stage set that its creator believes will hide rather than reveal. It's up to us to look behind that veil to what lies out of sight.

From *Reading Crimes* by DR TONY HILL

Everyone in the ReMIT squad room had stopped what they were doing. Even Stacey had come out from behind her screen to join the huddle round Alvin's desk. Rutherford had already ejected him from his chair so he could be front and centre in front of Alvin's computer. The sound quality from its speakers was tinny but the audio file that Sergeant McInerny had pinged across the Irish Sea to Alvin was as crisp as a radio broadcast.

When they reached the revelations about Mark Conway, Sophie gasped and Steve muttered, 'Fuck me. Nailed by a nun.' Rutherford shushed them and leaned in closer to make sure he missed nothing.

At the end, Karim muttered, 'That Paula, she is pure class,' to Alvin, who grunted in agreement.

Rutherford pushed back in the chair, almost running over Karim's foot. He stood up, chest out and shoulders back. 'This is what we've been waiting for. Sophie, assign some bodies from Fielding's crew to make up the numbers. Alvin, Steve, Karim – get over to Mark Conway's house and bring him in. Arrest him if need be. Chen – get a warrant in place for a search of his house and vehicles.'

'What about his office?'

'Yes, that too, if you can manage it.'

The look Stacey gave him could have sliced granite. 'I'll see what I can do, sir.'

'Shouldn't we wait for Paula? She cracked this, it should be her collar,' Alvin rumbled.

'We haven't got time to sit on our hands. Besides, this a team. We don't chase individual glory here, Alvin. I'll speak to the Crime Scene Manager, make sure we've got a full forensics team on board. Alvin, arrange transport to the scene. Chen, why are you still standing here?'

Stacey didn't react. She simply leaned across Alvin's keyboard and copied the interview across to her system then walked calmly to her chair and started typing. Target of warrant, reasons justifying the issuing of a warrant, locations to be covered by the warrant. She checked the list of duty magistrates and chose one she knew they'd worked with in the past. If she'd done a good job of pitching their reasons, he'd issue the warrant electronically. If not, he'd come back to her on Skype and she'd have to be persuasive. It wasn't a skill that came naturally to her face to face.

Meanwhile, Alvin lined up his search team. He'd use the officers from Fielding's team to secure the property and the outbuildings. The house search he'd leave to the three of them because they knew best what they were looking for. Once he'd arranged for transport and confirmed the forensics team was on standby, he ambled over to Stacey's desk, hands stuffed in his trouser pockets. 'How's it looking?'

She shrugged. 'This mag usually comes back pretty quickly if he's happy. My guess is he's running it past somebody else. We just have to wait and see. When's Paula due back, do you know?'

'Her flight gets in around six. I'll try and stall the start of the interview till she gets back. But I don't think the boss will go for that.'

'Me neither.' Stacey sounded glum. 'It's not just that this is Paula's work product . . .' She tailed off, not wanting Alvin to think she didn't rate him.

'It's that she's better at the head-to-head than any of us.' He glanced at his watch. 'I'm going to get a pie from the canteen, do you want anything?'

'Chips,' Stacey said.

Alvin gave her a puzzled look. 'You never eat chips.'

'I want to feel bad about myself because all my digital wizardry got knocked out of the park by a nun. Which is about as medieval as it gets.'

He patted her shoulder and headed out of the room. But

before he could satisfy their cravings for junk food, his phone rang. 'Get back now,' Stacey said. 'The warrant's through.'

There was nothing subtle about ReMIT's arrival at Mark Conway's house. But it soon became obvious there was nobody there to be alarmed about the arrival of a cavalcade of police and scene-of-crimes vehicles. Alvin directed the BMP officers to check out the garage and the other outbuildings and to secure the house once they'd taken the battering ram to the back door. 'Makes it less obvious if Conway comes back in the middle of our fun and games,' Alvin said. From the well-equipped utility room, he called Sophie in the incident room to report Conway's absence.

'Can you get someone to check whether he's in his office?' Alvin asked.

'Have we not got a team at his office?'

'We didn't get the warrant for his office. Just his home. The magistrate didn't think there was sufficient cause for us to raid his company HQ. At least, not yet.'

'Why did nobody tell me that?'

Alvin decided to treat that as a rhetorical question. 'So, we're going to crack on with searching the house. The forensics crew are on site.'

'We're going to end up with egg on our faces,' Sophie said. 'I'm as keen as anyone to catch this killer but I simply can't believe Mark Conway is a serial killer. Full stop. And young boys? That makes no sense. I got no gay vibe off him, ever.'

Alvin shrugged. 'Doesn't mean he wasn't perving over teenage boys. If we've learned anything from the whole #MeToo thing, it's that powerful men are very good at using their power to hide the bad stuff they do.' He wanted her to stop defending Conway so he could get on with his job but she was the ranking officer so he had to put up and shut up. He stared unseeingly at a shelf of laundry products and let it wash over him.

'Yeah, but a lot of the time their behaviour was an open secret among the poor sods who had to keep their mouths shut to save their jobs and their own reputations. I never heard anything like that about Mark. Sure, he was supportive of young men coming up in the business. He often talked about how he'd had to overcome so many obstacles when he was starting out. But he held out a hand to young women too, there was nothing inappropriate in any of it.' There was a defensive note in her voice, as if she was waiting to be shot down in flames unreasonably.

'Well, maybe you're right and we're all going to look like bunch of fuckwits. But I wouldn't like to try to pull the wool over Paula's eyes.'

Sophie harrumphed. 'Nobody's infallible, Alvin.'

'I need to get on, guv,' he said, closing down the call. He knew who his money would be on if this were a race. 'Right. Steve, you take the home office. Karim, living room. I'll do the master bedroom.'

Gloved and suited up, he moved upstairs, checking each room on the first floor as he went. The master bedroom was unmistakable. Not only was it the largest, with a luxurious en suite bathroom and a separate bedroom, it was the only one that showed any sign of being inhabited. The laundry basket contained underwear, socks, a T-shirt and a dress shirt, the pillows were randomly depressed and the duvet on the superking bed was rumpled. Clearly Conway didn't have live-in staff, or even a daily housekeeper, even though he could have readily afforded it. Alvin wondered whether that was because he was anxious about prying eyes.

A massive TV filled most of the wall opposite the bed. Alvin picked up the remote and flicked it on. The default was a sports channel showing a repeat of Liverpool's remarkable European Championship semi-final victory over Barcelona. Not a glory likely to crown Bradfield Vics' season any time soon, Alvin reckoned. Next to the remote on the bedside table, a thin hardback called *Black Boots and Football Pinks*. Alvin picked it up and thumbed through it. Some sort of nostalgic tribute to the beautiful game.

There was little else of interest in the room. No drugs stash in the bedside table drawers, unless you counted a box of vitamin C and zinc supplements. No porn tucked under the mattress. No sex toys in the ottoman at the foot of the bed, unless a fake fur winter-weight throw was what turned you on. Even the decorations on the walls – three framed, signed Bradfield Vics shirts – gave nothing away about who Mark Conway was beneath his carefully confected public image.

The bathroom offered no surprises. An array of expensive toiletries lined the glass shelves. A box of condoms, a blister pack of ibuprofen, a half-squeezed tube of haemorrhoid cream, a jar of CBD muscle rub, a tub of cotton wool buds and an electric razor were the entire contents of the mirrored bathroom cabinet. In the shower, a large sponge sat in a chrome caddy alongside shampoo and shower gel. Conway didn't even have gold taps, which Alvin had thought was compulsory for any self-respecting self-made man who was also a football fanatic.

The dressing room revealed that his suits were all made-to-measure by the same Bradfield tailor. Alvin, a relatively recent immigrant to the city, didn't recognise the name of a craftsman who had made his reputation in the 1990s providing sharply styled suits for a slew of famous actors and musicians. He did recognise that the quality of the clothes made his own off-the-peg M&S sale suit look shabby.

Opposite the twenty or so suits were about three dozen dazzlingly white shirts, sheathed in dry cleaner's plastic. Next to them, a tie hanger with an array of silk ties that would have left Alvin scratching his head over the choice every morning. Who had the time for stuff like this? Well, obviously a man who didn't have kids and had control over his own working life.

The end wall was divided into open cubicles above three shelves of shoes. Dress shoes arranged from tan through to black. A dozen pairs of trainers. Deck shoes. Chelsea boots. An old, creased pair of Docs that were the only nod to the kind of world Alvin inhabited. The cubicles were just as neatly organised. Jeans and joggers. T-shirts and sweatshirts folded, grouped by colour. Shorts, likewise.

And right in the middle, if Sister Mary Patrick was to be believed, the body disposal outfit of choice for Mark Conway. Four cubes filled with an array of Bradfield Victoria replica shirts, home and away.

Alvin pulled out the top cube. Eight neatly folded tops, the current season's home kit on top. He flipped through the pile, realising they were arranged in chronological order. There was no way of knowing which shirt the nun had spotted, except that it would have had to have been more than five seasons ago, given when the convent had closed its doors. To be on the safe side, he bagged and tagged all of the canary yellow home shirts. There was nothing more for him to do; it was time to leave the bedroom to the forensics team for what he expected to be a fruitless search for traces of young men who might or might not have been here over a long span of years.

He headed downstairs, hoping Steve or Karim might have had more luck. But before he had the chance to seek them out, another figure emerged from the utility room, barely recognisable in her white suit and hood.

'Boss!' Alvin exclaimed. 'I wasn't expecting you for another—' he glanced at his watch. 'Hour and a half at least. How did you manage to get back so soon?'

'On my broomstick,' Paula said. 'There was an earlier flight to Liverpool, I don't know how I made it. Then I got the local traffic boys to whizz me over here. So where's Conway?'

'All I know is, he's not here.'

'Bugger. What have you got there?'

'A pile of Conway's Bradfield Vics' replica shirts. Not that I imagine there'll be anything there for forensics to find. And I don't suppose there's any chance of your nun picking out the particular shirt in question.'

'More chance of the Pope joining a boy band.' But she frowned, as if something was tugging at her memory. 'Lyle Tate,' she said slowly.

'One of the victims, right?'

'Yes.' She drew the word out over a few syllables. 'Somebody went down for his murder. He couldn't have done the most recent bodies because he was banged up. So unless he was working with Conway on the earlier murders, it's got to be a miscarriage of justice.'

'That takes us where, exactly? You think the perp on the Lyle Tate murder can maybe give us Conway?'

'That's not what I was thinking, but I suppose it's an outside possibility. No, what I'm getting at is that I took a look at the Lyle Tate case. And according to the accused, the reason for the blood in his flat was that Tate had a nosebleed earlier in the evening. If that's true – and it's looking likely now that we got the wrong guy, since he couldn't have done the later victims – if he'd got into a struggle later, his nose might have bled again. What do you think? Maybe one of Mark Conway's football shirts has traces of blood?'

Without them noticing, Karim had approached. 'These Conway's shirts?'

Alvin nodded. 'Chronological order, looks like.'

'Surely he'd have washed them if he'd got any blood on them?' Karim said.

'Fuck,' Alvin breathed. He pushed past Paula and hustled into the utility room. She followed and found him gazing at a shelf of laundry detergents.

'What is it?'

'They're all non-bio. Non-allergenic.'

'Still takes stains out,' Paula said.

A wide grin spread across Alvin's face. 'I've got one word for you, boss. Chromophores.'

60

Some killers know they're smart. They believe they can outsmart the system, and they often succeed to a depressing extent. But sometimes their very cleverness can start to work against them as they come up with more and more elaborate ways to outwit the forces pitted against them.

From *Reading Crimes* by Dr Tony Hill

Incredulous, Chrissie O'Farrelly stared at Paula and Alvin. 'You're not serious? Look, I mentioned something in passing to Sergeant Ambrose. It's right out there on the edge of what's possible. It's science that's not been tested in the courtroom. Hell, it's barely made it into the peer-reviewed literature.'

'It's all we've got at this point,' Paula said.

'You don't even know you've got it, if I understand you correctly.'

'But there's a good chance,' Alvin chipped in. 'I thought you scientists liked a challenge?'

Chrissie shook her head. 'Oh no, you don't catch me out like that. I've been flattered by experts. I don't even know how we'd go about something like this. We'd certainly end up destroying the garment because we'd have to test so many pieces. And your DCI would be screaming about his budget.'

'Murder always trumps budget in my book,' Paula said.

'If there's a point to it, yes.'

It felt like stalemate. Paula had been convinced by Alvin's sketchy explanation: 'There are these chemicals called chromophores that make blood look red. Washing them gets rid of the visible stain. But the bit of the blood with the DNA in? It stays in the material if you've washed it in non-biological detergent,' he'd said. It sounded unlikely to Paula but Alvin was positive he'd got it right. And now Chrissie O'Farrelly was snatching away the one corroboration they had of Sister Mary Patrick's evidence. But Paula wasn't going to give up without a fight. 'What about your students? You must have some keen young researchers who'd love to make their mark by helping to solve a high-profile series of murders? Science doesn't move forward because people are scared of busting their budgets, Chrissie. Give us a break here.'

Chrissie fiddled with her pen. 'I can't make that call on their behalf. It'd have to be done after hours, when the equipment isn't being used for cases that are logged and listed.'

'But it could be done?'

'You just don't know when to back off, do you, Paula?'

'Not when it comes to serial murder. This man has killed eight people that we know of. We don't know why he's doing it, but the chances are his eighth victim isn't going to be his last. Unless he's Chinese and he's got some warped idea about lucky numbers. God, listen to me, I sound like Tony on a mad day. Chrissie, he's going to keep doing this until we stop him.' She meant what she said, and it shone through. What was the point of them if they couldn't go the extra mile when it truly was a matter of life and death?

Chrissie looked away, refusing to meet the judgement in Paula's eyes. 'I'm on your side,' she said. 'But I don't know whether I can deliver what you're asking.'

Thanks to the club website, they'd narrowed down the likely shirts that would have been current at the time of Lyle Tate's murder and placed them in separate evidence bags. Paula dumped the bags on the table and pushed them towards Chrissie.

'Try. That's all we're asking. You'd be examining these shirts anyway on the off chance of trace evidence. Just push it the extra mile. Please.'

Chrissie gave a tired smile of concession. 'No promises. I'll talk to the person who raised it in the conference I was at. See if I can figure out how to proceed. Don't put any probative weight on this yet, Paula. Don't be saying, "We've got you bang to rights, your shirt's going to put you away."' She caught Paula's look of surprise and chuckled. 'Yes, I know what you lot are like.'

'We'll be as silent as the graves where those young men were buried,' Alvin said. 'Do what you can for us.'

'Don't raise your hopes too high. It might come to nothing. Don't stop looking for other ways to make your case.'

'As if,' Paula said.

They both longed to go home, to make a brief escape into the normality of family life where the confrontations were never as grim or as dangerous as the ones they faced at work, the place where they could close the door on the horrors for a short time. Paula and Alvin both had their own justifications for what they did. For Paula, it was a kind of bargain – 'If I face down the darkness and the pain and the rage out there, in return, my family will be safe.' For Alvin, it was a simple equation – 'Every villain I take off the streets is one less potential threat to my family.' Both understood the strength they derived from their home lives. Even when the battle lines were drawn – and every family had its battles – they knew this was what mattered.

But tonight, they needed to draw on another kind of family. Every case had its own momentum. And there came a tipping point in every case where it might be won or lost. That was when the team had to come together and share. When Carol had been running ReMIT, there had been no question of her not being part of that brainstorming. This time round, nobody even suggested Rutherford should be included. It saddened Paula that there seemed to be a divide between the DCI and the rest of them. It wasn't good for morale and that wasn't good for creativity.

They met in a corner of the Skenfrith Street police canteen, Alvin and Steve equipped with loaded burgers to accompany their mugs of tea. Paula brought them up to speed on their visit to the lab and Chrissie O'Farrelly's promise to look at the possibility of invisible blood. 'The science just gets weirder and weirder,' Karim observed.

'Talking about weird – that house of Mark Conway's is well weird,' Steve said through a half-chewed mouthful. He swallowed. 'It's completely impersonal. Even the pictures he's got framed in his office are like a parody of what you see on the telly – Conway shaking hands with famous people, Conway with some footballer's arm draped over his shoulders, Conway posed with the rest of the directors of Bradfield Vic. But you look beyond that and there's nothing. No family photographs, no personal letters, no stash of greetings cards from anybody special.'

'He's right,' Alvin said. 'Bedroom's like a stage set. Nothing that gives anything away beyond the superficial. Well-groomed rich man who loves football. I don't have any sense of who he is or what he's like.'

'I've told you what he's like,' Sophie sighed. 'He's a decent guy who's built up a successful business from nothing. He encourages his workforce, he doesn't exploit his position in a sleazy way. I still can't get my head round the idea of you all thinking he's some kind of monster.'

'We don't talk about monsters here,' Paula said. 'Just people who do monstrous things. When we had the benefit of Tony Hill working with us, we learned to stop demonising people who perpetrate atrocities. It makes them bigger and stronger in our imagination. And it makes them invisible because we're all subconsciously looking for somebody monstrous. I've come across quite a few serial offenders now, and not one of them was larger than life.'

Sophie glared at her but said nothing. Paula wished they'd got off on a better footing, but she wasn't going to ignore the evidence slowly building up against Mark Conway just because he'd once promoted Sophie, or given her a pay rise. Or, God help them, been a referee on her police application form. 'So, Karim, any clues in the living room?'

'Bland, neat, tidy. My mum would love him. He's got a cupboard full of DVDs and not a single porno that I could see. A lot of football, a lot of blockbuster action movies. Nothing that would make you go, "Hmm, that's a bit shonky."' Karim swigged from his can of Coke. 'There was one thing, though. One of the BMP guys told me about it.'

'Don't keep us in suspense, then,' Steve cut in. 'We're not coming up to the ad break in a cop show, for fuck's sake.'

Karim flushed. 'There's another car in the garage. Conway's got a Porsche four-by-four, which he's presumably driving around in. But there's this other one—'

'Is it a black Skoda Octavia estate?' Stacey interrupted.

Karim was thunderstruck. 'How did you know that?'

'I didn't. But I've been ANPR-tracking a black Skoda Octavia that's registered to Jerome Martinu. What's the index number?'

While Karim consulted his notebook, Paula said, 'Why?'

Stacey shrugged. 'I wondered whether Martinu might actually be the killer after all. And if so, he'd likely need another vehicle. So I checked the DVLA records and found the Skoda registered to him.'

'More Martinu's kind of wheels than Conway's,' Alvin said thoughtfully. 'Maybe another attempt to throw sand in our eyes.'

Karim showed the number in his notebook to Stacey. 'That it?'

She nodded. 'The same.'

'You said you'd been ANPR-tracking it. Has it done anything interesting?' Paula asked.

Stacey nodded again. 'Every few weeks, it shows up coming into the centre of Bradfield. It's not coming in directly from the Bradesden direction. It's the way you'd come in from Conway's house, over the Harriestown bridge. It crosses town towards Temple Fields then parks in the Pay and Display behind Uniqlo. Then a couple of hours later, it heads back out of town the way it came.'

'Any visuals?'

'I've pulled some images but I've not had a chance to look at them yet. I could use another pair of eyes, there's a lot of stuff.'

'Karim, get stuck in as soon as we're done here. Well done, picking up on the strange car. And brilliant work, Stacey.' Paula grinned. 'Next time, maybe give me a hint? Have forensics had a look at it yet, Karim? Can you chase that? We need to establish who's been driving it. And if there's any trace DNA that matches our victims.'

'I'm on it, guv.'

'This is all starting to look a lot stronger,' Paula said. 'But we've got a way to go before we can be confident about a result. The most important thing is to find Mark Conway. We got lucky with the relatively isolated nature of the house and the fact that we were able to tuck the vehicles out of sight round the back during the search. Amazingly there seems to be nothing so far on social media. And the one advantage in us not getting the warrant for the office is that they've not been alerted to our interest. Sophie, can you make some discreet inquiries? I presume you know people inside the organisation?'

'I'll see what I can do.' It was a less than convincing response, but they were of equal rank, so Paula felt obliged not to call her on the lack of enthusiasm in front of the team.

She stood up, signalling they were done. 'I'm heading back out to Conway's place now. In case he comes back tonight, I want one of us there alongside the BMP team. Karim, Stacey – don't stay too late working the ANPR images. Alvin, Steve – go home and get some sleep. I want you with me at Conway's house by seven tomorrow.' She raised an inquiring eyebrow at Sophie. 'You'll let us know if there's anything we should know from the Incident Room? And Conway's people?'

'Of course.' Sophie stood too, meeting Paula's eyes. 'I know where my loyalties lie.'

And that's what makes me uneasy. Paula smiled and walked away. She was almost beginning to like Sophie. She really hoped that wasn't going to prove a mistake.

61

We never work with certainties. It's always 'on the balance of probabilities' with us ...

From *Reading Crimes* by Dr Tony Hill

The news of Carol's discoveries would have kept till morning, but she wanted to keep herself clear next day in case Tony recovered consciousness and she could see him. So she texted Bronwen Scott from outside Cap Scarlett's flat. Need to meet tonight. Have new info. Where and when?

The reply came when she was only a hundred metres further down the street. Mine. Soon as you like. Followed by an address less than ten minutes' walk away. Bronwen Scott lived on the sixth floor of a converted Georgian mill that had once housed hundreds of looms producing miles of cotton and linen cloth. It had been converted to flats a dozen years before, establishing itself from the start as prime real estate in the city centre.

Carol stepped out of the faux-industrial lift into a hallway with brick walls and lustrous wide floorboards. Halfway down, Bronwen stood leaning casually in the doorway, dressed for an evening at home – bare feet, denim jeggings, a baggy pin-striped granddad shirt. 'Thanks for coming over,' she said as Carol approached. She moved in for a formal half-hug and air kiss. Taken aback, Carol stiffened momentarily then forced herself to respond.

'I knew you'd want to hear what I've found out as soon as possible.'

Bronwen led the way into a living room like a feminine take on a gentlemen's club. Leather and wood, but soft leather upholstery instead of the buttoned and stuffed kind. The wood was pale oak, rich grain buffed to a warm glow. Bookshelves lined one wall, their spines brightly coloured and modern rather than ancient leather-bound volumes. There were a couple of sculptures in bronze of women apparently in conversation on a bench. A low table in front of a long sofa was strewn with papers, a pad and pencil carelessly tossed down on top of them.

'Nice place,' Carol said.

'I was at school with the developer. She asked me to invest in the project at the start, and this was my payday.'

'Good move.' Carol stood awkwardly, waiting for an invitation to sit.

'Drink?'

'I'm fine, thanks. I don't want to keep you from your work.' She gestured towards the table.

'It looks worse than it is, I'm nearly done. But sit down, you don't have to stand on ceremony here.'

Easy for her to say, Carol thought, uncertain how much she trusted her new best friend. She settled into an enveloping armchair that was almost too much. *Talk about being softened up.* 'I've met Saul and, like you, I'm inclined to think he's not a killer. Since then, I've made a couple of important breakthroughs. Well, one of them is more serendipity than down to my investigative genius,' she admitted.

'Sounds intriguing.' Bronwen curled up in a corner of the sofa, legs tucked neatly under her.

'I had dinner with Paula McIntyre the other night. And I told her what I was working on.'

'It's so important to keep those lines of communication open in this work.'

'She's my friend, Bronwen. That's the line of communication I have with her.'

'Of course. But DI McIntyre is such a good operator. So, did she have some startling information from the files that nobody got round to telling Saul's lawyer about?'

'You have a very suspicious mind.'

'So would you if you'd been on this side of the fence as long as I have.'

A pause. 'This is not going to work if you see me as someone to beat my former colleagues with.'

Bronwen spread her hands and looked repentant. 'I'm sorry, Carol. Lazy force of habit. But if they were all like you and Paula . . .'

'I assume you've been following the Bradesden convent story on the news?'

Bronwen frowned. 'Yes, but—'

'There's a second group of remains.'

'As well as the skeletons?'

'Eight bodies. Young men. And they've been murdered. The assumption is a serial offender.'

'Bloody hell. How on earth have they kept the lid on that?'

'Hiding in plain sight. Everybody's over-excited about nuns and skeletons. It's amazing that there hasn't been a leak from the other side of the investigation. But it's early days, it'll break sooner rather than later, I suspect. Anyway, they're starting to get DNA through from these victims. And Paula called to tell me one of them is Sugar Lyle Tate.'

'You're saying Saul Neilson is a serial killer?'

'No, no. Quite the opposite. There are at least two victims killed more recently than Lyle Tate. Saul was already serving his sentence by then. So it's very unlikely he had anything to do with Lyle's death. He was telling the truth, Bronwen.'

Her grin was completely spontaneous. 'Bloody hell! Carol, that's extraordinary.' She laughed. 'I knew I was right to get you on board.' She jumped up. 'Champagne!'

Carol shook her head and steeled herself for the admission. 'I don't do alcohol any more.'

Bronwen sat back down abruptly. 'Of course. How stupid of me. I'm sorry.'

'Don't apologise. If you want to celebrate, we'll go out for a curry one of these nights. Also, don't get over-excited yet. There's always the outside possibility that the police will try to claim Saul was involved with another person in killing young men, and that his partner in crime just carried on.'

'That would be a hard case to make.'

'Even harder, given what I found out tonight. I've found the missing witness.'

Bronwen frowned. 'What missing witness?'

'The one who's been in Australia since the day after Lyle disappeared. The one who knew nothing about the murder or the trial till he came back to the UK. The one who talked to Lyle in Temple Fields *after* he'd left Saul's place.'

'You're kidding?'

'I don't joke about murder. Lyle told him about the nosebleed. He's willing to give us an affidavit. That plus the serial nature of the offence should be enough to get Saul in front of the Criminal Cases Review Commission, no?'

'Yes. Yes and yes again. Where did you find this guy?'

'He's living in Lyle's old flat. He took over the tenancy when Lyle's former flatmate went down. I couldn't believe it myself. But sometimes the luck turns our way.'

'Not luck,' Bronwen said. 'You did what any decent detective would do. Victimology. Isn't that what your pal Tony used to push so hard?'

The use of the past tense made Carol flinch. 'Pushes. He still pushes it. He's not dead, he's just . . .'

'Temporarily out of the game, I get it. Sorry, I seem to be massively putting my foot in it every time I open my mouth tonight.'

Carol stood up. 'I'll give you a full report as soon as I can.'

'Make a note of your expenses. We've built up a bit of a war chest, one way and another. It's important none of us feels exploited. And obviously we'd want you to become one of us.'

'I'm not making any snap decisions right now,' Carol said. 'There's things I need to sort out.'

'Anything I can help with?'

Carol gave a regretful smile. 'Got to slay those dragons all by myself.' *And yours is not the help I'm looking for.*

62

Somewhere deep inside, even the most arrogant and organised killer believes they will be caught. Some even come to crave it. But they all think they have an escape route planned.

From *Reading Crimes* by Dr Tony Hill

Paula was insistent that there be no visible presence at Conway's house. If he did come back, she wanted him to be unaware that his house was stuffed with police officers. Well, not quite stuffed. Three uniforms, two AFOs and her. She hadn't asked for the AFOs but Fielding had insisted that if her officers were being sent to apprehend a killer, she wanted armed officers on site.

She took up station in the window of the master bedroom with a thermos jug of coffee, thanks to Conway's kitchen. It gave her an uninterrupted view of the drive and beyond to the road. The other officers were scattered around the ground floor, the two armed men on constant patrol among them. A fourth uniform was in an unmarked car parked nose out in a side lane a couple of hundred metres further down the road.

There was nothing more trying than a stakeout in the dark. Staying alert was a bitch. You couldn't show a light, obviously. Paula had taken to listening to audio books, her phone thrust deep in a trouser pocket to hide any tell-tale glow. But she could only put one earphone in at a time, because she had to listen out for any suspicious noises. It made John le Carré's tenterhooks a little less gripping.

It had been worse when she still smoked. The agony of going without a cigarette for hours *and* having to stay awake without a nicotine hit was probably a breach of the human rights regulations relating to torture. At least with a vape, she could risk the occasional pop. And Mark Conway's bedroom had the additional advantage of an en suite loo, thus overcoming the biggest problem for women officers on stake-out.

Just after one, a set of headlights came up the road and swung in at the gate. 'Base to all units,' Paula said into her radio. 'Be aware. Vehicle approaching.' Assorted responses came over the air.

It wasn't a Porsche. It wasn't even a four-by-four. It was a dark BMW saloon, the details difficult to establish because the headlights were blazing. A figure emerged from the passenger's side and crossed in front of the headlights.

Paula used up all of her swear words before Rutherford even arrived at the front door. She was reprising them under her breath as she ran down the stairs and elbowed aside the PC who was dithering behind the front door. She yanked the door open and hissed, 'Move the car, sir. We're running dark here. We don't want to put the frighteners on Conway. Please. Tell your driver, round the back.'

Rutherford shifted his weight forward as if to argue the point but as he moved, the spill of light from the car headlights illuminated her face and whatever he saw there changed his mind. He looked over his shoulder and shouted, 'Maxwell, take it round the back and kill the lights.' He glared at Paula. 'Do I get to come in now?'

She stepped back to let him enter. 'We've moved our vehicles into the garage. We've done everything we can to make the place look clean.'

They squared up in the hallway, Rutherford standing over her, right on the edge of too close. 'What makes you think he'll come back?'

'Because he hasn't done a runner yet. He's confident he's in the clear. If he thought there was any possibility of him being charged with these murders, he's got the resources to get away. Even though we've got his passport tagged. We've kept his name out of the investigation. So far, social media's clean. Stacey's got all sorts of alerts out to warn us if the word gets out.'

'And that's good enough for you?'

'Always has been in the past. Stacey is amazing.'

'And a law unto herself, if what I hear is true.'

Paula shrugged. 'I'm not interested in the gossip of envious inferiors. As far as I'm concerned, whenever we've relied on Stacey's evidence in court, there's been no suggestion of her crossing a line.'

He harrumphed. 'Builders call it back-filling. Believe me, I'm going to be taking a close look at DC Chen's work product going forward. But right now we need to be sure what we're doing here. Mark Conway is a successful businessman, a public figure in this community. He's also on the board of Bradfield Victoria FC. How certain are you that he's your man? Could it not be the cousin? The cousin and the priest together? I've been looking at the file and I think you're being precipitate here.'

'We've got the eye-witness testimony of Sister Mary Patrick.'

'Who will almost certainly be facing serious charges herself. Had it occurred to you she might be trying to finagle a deal for herself because of her "cooperation"?' He made the quotation-mark sign in the air which always provoked feelings of violence in Paula.

'I didn't prompt her. She was the one who brought Conway into the conversation. She knew him well enough to recognise him. She said he always wore his football shirts when he was visiting his cousin. She's impressive, sir. Even if her reputation is trashed by then, she'll be a striking figure in the box. We're waiting for forensics on the Skoda and also on Conway's football shirts. If it turns out Conway's DNA is all over the car, it'll be hard to argue it was driven by Martinu on those visits to Temple Fields.'

'And that's another thing,' he continued, almost as if she hadn't spoken. 'These DNA tests on invisible stains? What in the name of the wee man is that all about? Have you been reading science fiction? Or the *Beano*?'

Paula swallowed her anger at being treated with so little respect. 'Dr O'Farrelly mentioned to Sergeant Ambrose a new technique for finding DNA from bloodstains after the visible stain has been washed out. She told him it only worked if non-biological detergent had been used. Because he's a good detective, Sergeant Ambrose noticed the suspect's laundry detergent was non-bio. He put that together with the knowledge that Lyle Tate had a nosebleed on the night he died and thought it was worth a punt to see whether there was any DNA left on one of Conway's shirts. It's what we're meant to do, sir. Form hypotheses based on what we *do* know and test them.' Her voice was tight, her words clipped.

'Nosebleed? Where are you getting that from? I didn't see anything about a nosebleed in the post mortem report.'

Paula took a deep breath. 'That's because it's not in the post mortem report. It formed part of the defence in the trial of the man who is serving time for the killing of Lyle Tate. A man who is almost certainly innocent if this is the work of a serial killer.'

'And you knew this how?'

Paula glared at him. 'Because I remember the case. Sir.'

He turned his back on her and paced the hallway. 'I came here with the intention of calling off this stake-out. I still think you're a long way from a case we can take to court. But we're all here now. You've got until ten this morning. Then we'll review the situation.' He grabbed the front door handle and made to leave.

'Your car's round the back, sir. It'd be easier and more secure if you left that way.' She watched him blunder down the hall in the dark. Then the murmured exchange with one of the other officers. Then the back door opening and closing. She waited till she could see the BMW headlights disappearing down the road before she went back upstairs to her vigil. She radioed, 'Base to all units. As you were.'

The gradual lightening of the sky brought no change. The occasional car passed the end of the drive but none of them was a Porsche four-by-four. Paula's mouth was dry and bitter from too much coffee, her eyes sore and gritty from too much staring into the dark. The uniformed officers had been relieved at six, the AFOs two hours earlier. By eight, the daylight was so bright she had no compunction about using her phone.

'Morning, gorgeous,' she said when Elinor answered. 'Sleep well?'

'I missed you. Are you still on stake-out?'

'We are. It's been a long n— Oh fuck, I have to go.' Paula ended the call just as the Porsche came into sight on the road. She hit the radio button. 'Base to all units. Eye contact with suspect vehicle. Turning into driveway now.'

The big SUV slowed to a halt as it approached the front door. The engine stilled and Mark Conway climbed out of the driver's seat. He shook his legs and rolled his shoulders as if he'd been sitting too long.

'Base to Mobile One. Move into position across the drive. Repeat. Move into position across the drive.' Paula spoke softly, as if Mark Conway might hear her through his double-glazed windows. His retreat would be cut off inside a minute.

As she had this thought, something caught Conway's attention. He was staring at the ground, turning his head this way and that, angling his line of sight to give him different perspectives. Abruptly, he straightened up and stared intently at the house.

'The fucking gravel,' Paula said. Churned up by half a dozen vehicles, and none of them had thought to rake it over.

Conway was already back behind the wheel, the engine roaring into life.

'Base to all units. Mobilise. Mobilise now,' Paula yelled, running down the stairs and heading for the front door. She pulled it open just in time to see the police car hadn't quite completed its manoeuvre to close off the drive. Conway must have stamped on the accelerator for the Porsche surged towards the gap. He almost made it. But the Porsche smashed into the wing of the police car so hard it rocked on its suspension then, almost in slow motion, turned on its side.

'Fuck, fuck, fuck,' Paula shouted as the four-by-four rocketed down the road. A marked police car slid to a halt beside her and she jumped into the passenger seat. 'Go,' she cried, dragging the seat belt across her body as the car raced down the drive in a scatter of gravel. 'Blue lights,' she commanded. 'And two tones.'

The AFOs were right behind them in their Range Rover, washing them in blue light and deafening sound. The Porsche was already out of sight but Paula knew there was nowhere to go for the best part of a mile. Then they'd hit morning traffic and the bottleneck of the bridge over the River Brade.

As they approached the junction, Conway came into view, snarled up in traffic waiting to turn right. 'Got him,' Paula breathed.

Too soon. With barely a pause, the Porsche mounted the footpath and careered onwards. Because it was a country lane, there were no lampposts to impede him. His wing mirror clipped a Give Way sign, but it didn't stop him.

Paula's driver looked terrified, but he followed in the wake of the four-by-four. As they hurtled on, Paula saw the white face of a terrified teenager in school uniform who'd thrown himself into the hedgerow. They lurched round the corner. 'I think we're catching him,' the PC in the back seat said, excited as if he was playing Grand Theft Auto.

They weren't. A voice yelled from the radio. 'Lay-by ahead, pull in and let us past, we're faster than you.'

Paula swivelled in her seat to see the passenger in the Range Rover gesticulating wildly. 'Pull over, like he said.'

They tore into the lay-by, tyres screaming and let the Range Rover thunder past. Paula's driver set off after it, gears crunching as he tried to keep up. 'The bridge,' Paula moaned. 'It'll be solid.'

She'd barely uttered the words when they heard a deafening bang, a scream of metal, the sound of collapsing masonry and a series of whooshing splashes.

Whatever had just happened, it sounded like Mark Conway's bid for freedom had ended spectacularly badly.

63

> The German philosopher Friedrich Nietzsche gave a stern warning to those of us who confront the worst that we do to each other. 'Whoever fights monsters should see to it that in the process he does not become a monster. And if you gaze long enough into an abyss, the abyss will gaze back into you.' It's a warning we would do well to heed. Empathy is a necessary tool but we have to guard against the horrors we see becoming our new normal.
>
> From *Reading Crimes* by DR TONY HILL

There was no mood of triumph in the ReMIT squad room. A job well done was a righteous arrest that ended with a successful conviction. Now the murder of Lyle Tate and seven other young men would never be a job well done. In his feverish rush to escape, Mark Conway hadn't secured his seat belt. When he misjudged the gap and careered into the bridge abutment, his Porsche had stopped but he hadn't.

Arriving at the scene moments later, Paula had been gripped with shock and revulsion. She'd seen plenty of blood over the years, but that didn't mean she'd lost sight of its significance. One life lost, other lives changed utterly. And now answers would forever be denied to those whose lives had been altered forever by Mark Conway's crimes.

'At least now we know he did it,' Steve said when Paula walked through the door. 'Innocent people don't run.'

'Well, that's bollocks,' Alvin said. 'All sorts of reasons why innocent people run. I'm not saying Mark Conway was innocent, but we're no closer to proving him guilty than we were last night.'

Paula crossed to her desk and sat down. Karim gave her a sympathetic look. 'Should you even be here, boss? I mean, you've had a shock. You probably need a bit of space.'

'I'm fine,' Paula said. 'I need to write my report while it's fresh in my mind.'

Before she could start, Rutherford and Sophie walked in together. The DCI took a few steps into the room then stopped. 'Well, that wasn't the result we were looking for. We've got a dead body and a worryingly thin file of evidence.'

'There'll be forensic evidence in due course,' Alvin said.

'You hope.' He shook his head in disgust. 'Looks like DCI Fielding will be the one to get a clean result, even though it'll only be assault, preventing the lawful and decent disposal of all those bodies, failure to register death. Small beer compared with serial murder.'

Paula and Stacey exchanged a look. They both knew policing wasn't a competitive sport. Even the best results were always tainted with the crime that had preceded them.

Sophie, ever eager, chipped in. 'Theoretically, you can get a life sentence for preventing the legal disposal of bodies.'

'If it ever gets to court,' Rutherford said cheerily. 'From what we know, those nuns aren't the kind of witnesses the CPS rejoices in.' He frowned as the sound of Alvin's phone ringing cut across his words.

'It's the lab,' Alvin said, taking the call. Instantly he had everyone's attention. 'Hello, Doc.' Then he frowned as he listened. 'Just hold on, would you? I want to put you on speaker, we're in the middle of a ReMIT briefing and the whole team needs to hear this.' He fumbled with his phone then held it up. 'Could you just say again what you told me?'

They all leaned in and strained to hear Chrissie O'Farrelly. The tinny voice said, 'What I told you is that your idea of looking for invisible DNA that's been stripped of its chromophores is looking very promising. One of our researchers is very keen to make it work and he thinks he's worked out how to do it.'

'That's good news, Doc,' Alvin said.

'It's interesting news, Sergeant. But it might prove to be unnecessary. We found a fingerprint on the end of one of the pieces of tape used to bind the body wrappings. Whoever did the taping clearly wore gloves. All we've got apart from this are smudges. But I think he had already used the roll of tape for innocent purposes. He wouldn't have thought to cut off the first couple of inches before he put it to more nefarious use. So we do have a single clear print.'

'Is it on the database?' Rutherford butted in. 'DCI Rutherford here, sorry we've not met yet, doctor.'

'It's not on the database.'

There was a collective sigh. Karim actually groaned.

'But don't worry,' she continued. 'I spoke to the path lab

this morning and even though they're up to their back teeth in human remains from the convent, a very helpful technician printed Mark Conway's body when they brought it in.'

Paula realised she was holding her breath.

'And?' Rutherford obligingly asked.

'It's a match. We can definitely say that Mark Conway had handled the adhesive tape that bound one of the murder victims. I hope that helps.'

'It takes us a long way down the road,' Rutherford said. 'You'll keep on with the DNA though?'

'It's running as we speak. You know the chromophore theory is untried in the courtroom, yes?'

'It's not going to a courtroom, though, is it?' Rutherford said. 'But it's going to cover our backs.'

'Not for me to say. I'll be in touch as soon as I hear anything.' And the line went dead.

Before anyone could react, the door to the squad room opened and a uniformed PC hurried in, pink and flustered. 'DCI Rutherford?' He looked around, uncertain.

'What is it, Constable?' Rutherford asked impatiently. 'I'm in the middle of something here.'

'The custody sergeant sent me up. Martinu's been with his solicitor. Now his cousin is dead, he's insisting he needs to make a statement.'

Amid the exclamations, Rutherford said, 'Sophie, take Karim and see what Martinu has to say for himself. Before the day's out, I want him charged with illegal disposal on all the bodies, the girls and the young men. And accessory to murder. And no deals on the table.' Everyone, including Sophie, looked surprised. Alvin muttered something under his breath as they made for the door.

'DI McIntyre?' Rutherford continued.

'Sir?'

'There will be an inquiry into this morning's fiasco. Best thing all round is if you go on gardening leave till that's done and dusted.'

Paula was taken aback. 'That could be weeks. Months. And I've got my report to write.'

'You can do that from home and email it in to me. You have to look at it from my point of view. It's easy to interpret what happened out there as recklessness on our part. It'll be all over the media, and social media. I can't have you doing frontline police work until that's laid to rest.' He folded his arms across his chest and set his mouth in a firm line.

'Doesn't that make it look like you think Paula was out of order? Surely we should have her back?' Alvin protested.

'It's OK, Alvin,' Paula sighed, getting to her feet. 'The DCI is right. ReMIT's too new to have a proper track record. You need to look squeaky clean.' She picked up her bag. 'I'm not worried about an inquiry. I'll be back.'

'Though possibly not in this unit,' Rutherford said.

That was an insult Paula couldn't stomach. 'You're the boss. Much better to stick with the DI who thought the suspect was the good guy.' And she walked right past him, head high, refusing to allow him the satisfaction of seeing how upset she was. She'd save that for Elinor.

They met in the Starbucks opposite the hospital where they'd had their first coffee together years before. Paula's flat white lasted longer than her flat recitation of the morning's events.

'He sounds like a fuckwit, Rutherford,' Elinor said.

'Not so much a fuckwit as a careerist. He's all about how it makes him look.'

'Couldn't be more different from Carol.' She sighed.

'Speaking of Carol ... after you rang, I called down to neurosurgery. Tony's conscious. And apparently coherent.'

For the first time in days, Paula felt a lightening of spirit. She grinned like a happy drunk. 'That'll be a first.' She leaned across the table and gave Elinor a smacking kiss on the lips. 'That's wonderful news. Have you called Carol?'

'I thought you'd like to tell her yourself.'

Sober now, Paula said, 'I think it's time for her and Tony to talk to each other again. You got Carol in to see him when he was unconscious. How hard could it be to get her in now he's awake?'

'It's a completely different situation. He was unconscious, that's the point. She couldn't upset him by being there. But now? What if he's still determined not to see her?'

'There won't be a better time for ages, Elinor. Once he's discharged back to prison, the only way they'll see each other is at visiting time. And that's no place to start a reconciliation. They're our friends. Surely we owe it to them to help them rebuild their relationship?'

Carol had kept the scrubs she'd worn on her previous visit to Tony's hospital room. As Elinor had instructed her, she was wearing them when they met in the hospital café. Elinor handed over her stethoscope again and also a clipboard with a printed form that said COGNITIVE EXAMINATION at the top. 'That'll buy you some time,' she said.

Carol looked uncertain. 'What if he doesn't want to see me?'

'He can say so. I'll go in with you. If he wants to you leave ... well, you're no worse off than you are now.'

Carol gave a twisted smile. 'At least that way we'll know he's making a good recovery. That he's not lost his memory.'

Paula put a hand on her shoulder. 'It's time, Carol. He needs to see how courageous you've been.'

'If you'd seen me the other night, that's not how you'd describe me.' Carol visibly pulled herself together and stood up. 'Let's do it,' she said.

'See you later,' Elinor said to Paula, stooping to kiss the top of her head. 'Don't fret.'

The two women walked in silence to the lifts and down the corridor to where a different prison officer sat reading a cycling magazine. He didn't look up till they were right beside him, Elinor's hand on the door handle. 'We need to do some tests,' she said.

'Be my guest,' the guard said, already engrossed in his magazine again.

Carol's heart was thudding in her chest as she followed Elinor into the room. She felt nauseous, on the edge of tears. She looked past Elinor to where Tony lay, eyes closed, face pale apart from the bruising around his eyes and the still-swollen nose, one wrist handcuffed to the bed.

'Hello, Tony,' Elinor said softly.

He grunted and opened his eyes, focusing on the white coat then looking up at her face. He smiled. 'Elinor.'

'I've brought someone to see you.' She stepped to one side.

Carol opened her mouth to speak but no sound emerged.

'Carol?' A moment's confusion. 'Why are you wearing a hat?'

'Because she's pretending to be a nurse,' Elinor said.

He struggled momentarily and Carol was gripped by the conviction that he'd tell her to go. 'I can't see you properly,' he complained.

'I'll go if you want.'

'No. Come closer.'

She took a couple of steps forward and he visibly relaxed into the pillow. They gazed hungrily at each other, taking in every detail of the other's changes.

'I'll leave you to it,' Elinor said.

Neither of them paid any attention as she left. 'You look . . . terrible, actually,' Carol said.

'I feel surprisingly good. Must be the drugs. But I was always rubbish in a fight. You look good. Strong.' He managed a faint smile. 'A bit short on sleep, maybe.'

'I've had a busy week.'

He groaned. 'Oh God. Vanessa. I am so sorry.'

'She's the exception that proves your rule about there being no such things as monsters. It's amazing you turned out as well as you did.'

'What? Serving time for manslaughter, stripped of my professional credentials?'

'When you put it like that . . .' She smiled without tension for the first time in as long as she could remember. How could it be that after so long an estrangement they could simply slip back into this easy an exchange?

'Paula tells me you've been seeing someone for the PTSD?'

'Several successive somebodies. None of the conventional therapies worked for me.'

'Of course they didn't. You're too private and you're too good at figuring out what they want to hear. So what did work?'

'Don't laugh. Bodywork. I do these exercises—'

'I've read about it – EMDR. And it's helped?'

'I have a long way to go but yes, it's given me back some control. Now when I panic, I know what it is. I can recognise when it starts and I can head it off.'

'I'm pleased for you.'

She laid a hand on his. 'And I'm not drinking. You got me over the worst and I've been solid.' She heard a tremble in her voice and stopped.

'I've missed you,' he said.

'I missed you too. I know you pushed me away for my own good, but it's been the hardest thing I've ever had to deal with.' Carol swallowed hard. 'All that kept me together was the last things we said to each other after you were sentenced. You remember?'

He closed his eyes momentarily. 'Of course I remember. Three words apiece, three words we'd been running away from forever. I love you.'

She felt a tremble in her chest. Could you really feel your heart contract? 'I love you too. I want us to find a way to make that work.'

He coughed, something in his throat like the lump in hers. 'I've been doing a lot of thinking. I've had plenty of time—'

'I thought you were supposed to be writing your book?' Forcing herself to keep it light.

'You can only write so many hours a day.' He sighed. 'Carol, we've spent years together, you and me, dealing with the worst things that human beings can do to each other. We've seen things nobody should have to see. We've confronted people who strain our belief in the possibility of redemption.'

'We've saved lives, though. We've made some things better.'

'No question. But since I've been in prison, I've started to find positive ways to make things better. I've been teaching meditation on the prison radio. Don't laugh.' He chuckled. 'OK, my first class in helping dads to read to their kids didn't go so well. But it's starting from a positive place. And what about you? I hear you're using your skills not to put criminals behind bars but to free people who shouldn't be there in the first place. How's that going?'

She smiled. 'Beginner's luck. Looks like my first attempt might be working out.'

'Feels good, doesn't it?'

'I've not had much time to enjoy the experience.' She resisted the impulse to stroke his face. 'I was too busy worrying about you.'

'I'm tougher than I look. You should know that. But here's the thing.' He was speaking more slowly now. Tiring, she thought. But he wasn't giving up. 'I've been forced to figure out a new future for myself. Nobody is going to let me anywhere near a patient or an offender profile again. My past is done with and to be honest, I'm not altogether sorry. But that set me thinking about my future. And what I realised was we both spent so long staring into the darkness we forgot about the light. I'm tired of the darkness, Carol. I want to come out into daylight. And I think you've got to the same point as me at the same time as me.'

As his words sank in, she recognised herself in them. He was right. She was so, so tired of pushing back against a tide that never seemed to turn. Tony had put into words what she'd known subconsciously for some time. 'Hope,' she said. 'At the risk of sounding like some politician's cheesy soundbite, I think we both need hope.'

'You're right. And in our own different ways, we're starting to find it. Carol, I know it's the best part of a year till they let me out, but when they do, do you think we might do this together? The hopeful thing? The positive thing?'

'We should try, Tony. We really should try.'

ACKNOWLEDGEMENTS

Like the song says, there are more questions than answers. And the more books I write, the more gaps in my knowledge I discover. Thankfully, there are people out there who willingly put their expertise at my disposal. Sometimes I ignore what they tell me for dramatic effect, but mostly I absorb it gratefully and play it back to my readers.

This time, I'd like to thank the following: Ann Cheshire, whose insight and practice in working with people with PTSD gave me a way forward for Carol Jordan; Triona Adams, whose personal experience fleshed out my limited knowledge of convent life; Professor Lorna Dawson of the James Hutton Institute, whose knowledge of the earth beneath my feet means I'm always on solid ground; Mari Hannah for her insider knowledge of prison practicalities; Professor Niamh Nic Daied for the chromophores; James and Marilyn Runcie for the ice cream; Dame Professor Sue Black for the hairy soup; and Jackie Johnston, whose name I have taken in vain thanks to her generous support of the Punjabi Junction Social Enterprise.

And then there are the people who always have my back; Jane Gregory and her team at David Higham Associates; Lucy Malagoni at Little Brown, Amy Hundley at Grove

Atlantic and David Shelley at Hachette UK, whose editorial advice and support makes everything better; Anne O'Brien and Thalia Proctor for keeping everything in order; and Laura Sherlock who could, given half a chance, make the trains run on time.

Last but definitely not least: Jo Sharp, for putting up beds, putting up blinds and putting up with me, always with a smile.